Robert G. Barrett was raised in Bondi where he has worked mainly as a butcher. After thirty years he moved to Terrigal on the Central Coast of New South Wales. Robert has appeared in a number of films and TV commercials but prefers to concentrate on a career as a writer.

Also by Robert G. Barrett in Pan

YOU WOULDN'T BE DEAD FOR QUIDS
THE REAL THING
THE GODSON
BETWEEN THE DEVLIN AND THE DEEP BLUE SEAS
DAVO'S LITTLE SOMETHING
WHITE SHOES, WHITE LINES AND BLACKIE
AND DE FUN DON'T DONE
MELE KALIKIMAKA MR WALKER
THE DAY OF THE GECKO
RIDER ON THE STORM AND OTHER BITS AND BARRETT
GUNS 'N' ROSÉ

ROBERT G. BARRETT

The *Boys* from *Binjiwunyawunya*

PAN
Pan Macmillan Australia

First published 1987 in Pan by Pan Books (Australia) Pty Ltd
This edition published by Pan Macmillan Australia Pty Limited
1 Market St, Sydney

Reprinted 1990, 1991, 1992 (twice), 1993, 1994, 1995, 1996, 1998, 1999,
2000, 2001, 2003, 2005, 2007, 2008, 2009

National Library of Australia
cataloguing-in-publication data:

Barrett, Robert G.

The boys from Binjiwunyawunya

ISBN 978 0 330 27165 3.

I. Title

A823.3

Printed by IVE

MIX
Paper from
responsible sources
FSC® C018183
FSC
www.fsc.org

DEDICATION

Ex painters and dockers and old SP bookies aren't bad blokes — and neither is my Uncle Artie in South Melbourne.

This book is dedicated to him.

ACKNOWLEDGEMENTS

The author is donating 10% of his royalties to be divided between Greenpeace and The Aboriginal Inland Children's Mission.

CONTENTS

The Boys from Binjiwunyawunya

Price Galese rarely if ever got a full-on case of the shits. He might get a bit stroppy when he was tired now and again and again. But the shits. Hardly ever. There wasn't really a great deal for the suave, silvery haired casino owner to get the shits about. He was a millionaire several times over. He owned a mansion in Vaucluse, had a charming, attractive wife and three fine sons. His string of thoroughbred racehorses kept winning like it was going out of style, much to the grief of every rails and SP bookmaker in Sydney. And his gambling casino — the Kelly Club — staffed with employees who literally loved him, was almost a licence to print money. Apart from that, he was a doyen of Sydney society, idolised by the church, charities and just about every other citizen of that rather large, bustling city between Newcastle and Wollongong known affectionately as 'The Old Steak and Kidney'. So what reasons would Price Galese have to get the shits?

Naturally, in his line of work he'd have to get rather serious now and again when different things were on his mind... like having to order a hit, chase up a defaulting punter or sort out a dicey cop or politician. But these little 'business matters' were generally sorted out pretty smartly, with a minimum of fuss, and Price would soon be back to his ever-smiling, urbane, likeable self. However, this particular Saturday night in the Kelly Club office after closing time, it was obvious to the small group of trusted employees gathered around him for an after-work drink, that Price had a dose of the shits something good and proper. His jaw was clenched tight and his dark brown eyes were glowering as he spun the dial on the safe after closing it. And when he flopped down in the padded leather seat behind his desk and took a sip of his Scotch and soda as he scowled at nothing in particular across the highly polished oak top, his normally happy face looked about six feet longer than the Great Wall of China.

There was silence for a few moments after Price sat down. George Brennan glanced across at Eddie Salita, sitting in the corner absently picking at his nails, then over to Billy Dunne sipping on an Old Grandad and Coke next to Les Norton, who was seated comfortably with his eyes closed as he savoured the delights of his second chilled stubbie of Fourex. Actually George had noticed over the last couple of nights that something seemed to be eating at Price, but they'd been busy and he was a bit toey about asking him. But it was quiet in the office now, the week was over, and with only Price's closest employees grouped around him George decided to put it on him.

'Price. Is everything all right old mate?' he asked quietly.

Price Galese glanced over at his manager, then just as quickly looked away again. 'Yeah, everything's sweet George.'

'You sure?'

'Yes George. I'm sure.'

Billy Dunne decided to put his head in as well. 'Yeah, bullshit Price. Something's on your mind. What is it?'

'I just bloody well told you. Nothing. Jesus, what's up with you blokes?'

Finally Price caught Norton's eyes, which were now half open and giving him one of those 'Come on. Don't piss in our pockets. We know you better than that' kind of looks. Staring back at the big, red-headed doorman for a moment, he raised his hands, palms up, before slapping them down on the edge of his desk as he shifted his gaze across to Eddie Salita.

'Yeah. Righto,' he sighed loudly. 'I suppose I might as well tell you what's going on. Eddie knows, so you boys may as well know, too.'

'That's a bit more like it,' smiled Les. 'Now what's up?'

Price glanced around the room before taking in a deep breath and exhaling it angrily through his nose.

'I'm being shafted boys. Blackmailed. Getting it well and truly shoved right up my arse and taken to the cleaners. And when I say blackmailed — I mean just that. Fuckin' blackmailed.'

There was an astonished silence for a few moments before Les spoke. 'Who the bloody hell's doing this?' he asked in disbelief as he sat upright in his chair.

'Who?' replied Price. 'A dirty, rotten bloody Aborigine in Redfern — that's who.' Price glared around the room at the three speechless faces in front of him. 'Yeah that's right,' he continued. 'An Abo. I'm being shafted by a rotten fuckin' boong. And I don't like it one little bit.'

The silence in the already hushed office seemed to double in intensity, if that was at all possible. Not only was it unusual for Price to let go with such an outburst, but to think that someone — an Australian Aborigine of all people — was blackmailing one of the most powerful men in Sydney was almost too astonishing to contemplate. Norton was about to speak when Price cut him off abruptly with a wave of his hand.

'Yeah all right Les, I know,' he said tiredly. 'You've got a soft spot in your heart for the Aborigines because you grew up with them in Dirranbandi or wherever that joint is you come from. And I've got nothing against them either. They're an unfortunate people. But believe me. This guy is just an out-and-out cunt. He's shoving the pineapple right up my date. And getting away with it.'

Eddie Salita could only shake his head and shrug his shoulders helplessly in agreement. Price took another deep breath before slumping back in his seat.

'Anyway,' he sighed again, rubbing his hand almost despairingly across his face. 'Seeing as we're all here, I suppose I may as well give you boys the whole bloody story.'

It appeared Price owned a huge block of industrial land — about a hectare — in Lawson Street, Redfern, just across from the railway station. He'd picked it up years ago in a gambling debt. The previous owner, an old SP bookie, had got into Price for a fair bit of money and gave him the deeds as security till he could come up with the readies. Unfortunately for the old bookie, but fortunately for Price, he died of a heart attack at City Tattersalls Club about a week later, so Price finished up with the land. After the funeral he and his lawyer, Sheldon Drewe, checked it out and there wasn't much on it. An unoccupied smallgoods factory and an old clothing factory that was also abandoned. A couple of dusty, run-down offices were paying a minimal rent along with an old Greek who had an equally dusty, run-down fish'n' chip cum hamburger shop. Price intended getting rid of the lot and left the deeds with his lawyer and the rent-collecting in the hands of a local estate agency; but with more important things on his mind he ended up letting the matter slip. This was almost fifteen years ago, but G. J. Coles had recently approached Drewe with an offer, wanting to put a New World Supermarket and community centre on the site. Their offer was $1.5 million and Price couldn't believe his luck. It was money for old rope as far as he was concerned, so, absolutely jubilant, he issued instructions to sell immediately. There was, however, a snag. The land had to be untenanted and the contract signed no more than a month after Coles made their offer or the deal would fall through as the company was also negotiating for another site in Newtown.

At first this didn't seem like any problem. There were only two tenants in what was left of the building, and the old Greek couldn't believe it when Sheldon Drewe landed on his doorstep with an offer of $25,000 to get out. He was gone that quick he left three pieces of flathead and a battered sav still bubbling in the oil as he and his wife and six kids ran out the door. But the other tenant turned out to be a different kettle of fish altogether.

A half-caste Aborigine, Percy Kilby, had taken a ten-year lease on the remaining office calling it the Aboriginal Welfare and Entitlement Council or AWEC. In reality it was nothing more than a rort to get money and grants from the State and Federal governments and give Percy a legitimate cover for his illegal activities; which were mainly hot gear, bogus charities, and ripping the government off for whatever he could. Percy had the welfare of his people at heart about as much as Idi Amin cared for the citizens of Uganda. But he was cunning. A good talker and ex-organiser for the militant Builders' Labourers Federation, he knew just how to manipulate people and blend racism with his people's drinking and employment problems to suit his own needs. It hadn't taken Percy long to trace who the owner of his office was, and when he did he just smiled to himself and sat back biding his time. So when Drewe came along with his offer to leave the premises it was like finding that elusive pot of gold at the end of the rainbow. Not that Percy was a completely unreasonable man. As soon as he found out about the Coles deal, and knowing that the party making him the offer to get out was rather on the shady side and owner of one of the biggest casino in Sydney, Percy couldn't get out fast enough either. Except that Percy wasn't going to take the offer of new premises for AWEC and $25,000 like the Greek bloke. Percy's travelling price? Half a million dollars — in cash.

14

'So that's about it in a nutshell, boys,' said Price, making an open-handed gesture. 'This Kilby's got me by the bloody short and curlies. And there's fuck-all I can do about it.'

There was another silence while the boys mulled over what they'd just been told. Then George Brennan spoke.

'What do you mean there's nothing you can do, Price?' he said, turning to Les and Billy. 'What's wrong with sending our two nice doormen here over to jump up and down on his ribcage a few times. Percy'd soon get the message to piss off.'

Price just made another despairing gesture. 'No way in the world, George. Can you imagine the headlines in the papers if I did that: "Casino Operator Sends Thugs in to Bash Aboriginal Welfare Officer". Right next to a photo of him in hospital, covered in bandages with a couple of drips sticking out of his arms. It'd look terrific wouldn't it.'

George nodded his head and gave Price a look of glum approval. 'Yeah. I see what you mean. But what about Eddie?'

'Hah!' Price gave a short, scornful laugh. 'Don't think I haven't thought of that. If there was half a chance I could use Eddie, Kilby'd be with his ancestors in the dreamtime right now. About five miles off Sydney heads. No, the bastard told Sheldon that if anything nasty happens to him or he disappears there's a letter left in his safe and another with his lawyer.' Price shook his head again. 'The black bludger's done his homework all right.'

'Shit! I see what you mean,' said George, walking over to the bar. 'Anybody else want a drink while I'm here?' There was a general shaking of heads, then continued silence as George made himself a tequila and grapefruit juice and sat down again. 'Well, what do you intend doing Price? . . . What can *we* do?'

'Ohh I'm buggered if I know,' Price replied wearily. 'I'm buggered if I do. He's got me by the nuts.'

'Why don't you just give him the half a million and be done with it?' said Billy. 'You're still gonna finish another million in front. It's not a bad result.'

'*What!*' roared Price. 'Give that dirty black shithouse 500 grand. You're kidding. I'd rather miss out altogether.'

'Yeah but . . . aren't you just cutting your nose off to spite your face?'

'Billy. It's not the money, mate. It's the principle.' Price paused to take in the looks he got from his last statement. 'Well . . . maybe it is the money to a certain extent,' he added offhandedly. 'But that's still not the point. I absolutely refuse to let some bloody smarty shove it up me for half a million bucks. And I don't give a stuff whether he's black, white or purple with pink spots.'

'So what do you intend to do?'

'What do I intend to do? Billy — your guess is as good as mine.' Price looked up for a second, then buried his face in his hands in annoyance and frustration. 'Ahh I'm buggered if I know.'

All eyes focused on Price, his head resting on his hands, his face a picture of abject misery. For all his millions and his occasional villainy, you couldn't help but feel sorry for him. He was too good a bloke to be turned over like that by someone who was nothing more than an out-and-out arsehole at the best of times. And like he said, there was quite a bit of principle involved. If the word ever got out that one of the most powerful men in Sydney had got shafted by an Aboriginal ex-builders' labourer from Redfern, Price'd be the laughing stock of the Sydney underworld.

The gloomy silence in the office continued, broken only by the faint ticking of an old cuckoo clock Price had put up on the wall as a novelty. It was almost ten to four. Then the silence was broken by another odd sound and all eyes switched to Les Norton, sitting on his seat with his eyes closed and his head tilted back slightly. From deep down in his throat was coming this low, rumbling chuckle. Every now and again his shoulders would quiver and his body would shake from the pit of his stomach up to his chin as tiny sniggers came from his nose. Billy, Eddie and George continued to stare at Les for a few moments as the rumbling seemed to get louder. Price took his hands away from his face and stared at Norton in open-mouthed amazement before turning to the others.

'Is he laughing?' he asked, incredulous. The chuckles suddenly got louder as Norton's chest began to shake like a jelly. 'Are you laughing, Les? He is. The idiot's laughing. Can you believe it? He thinks it's funny. Here I am being rolled for half a million bucks by some cunt and he thinks it's hilarious. You bloody big imbecile. I always knew you were a wombat — I'm bloody well convinced of it now.' Price waved his hands in the air and looked up as if he was pleading to a higher authority. 'Jesus Christ! I don't believe it.'

Norton continued chuckling to himself for a while, then opened his eyes and gave a tight smile all around the room.

'So,' said the big, red-haired doorman, nodding at each

of them including Price. 'The big, bad Sydney heavies, eh? Some heavies. One poor, skinny spook from Redfern's put the bustle on you and you've all shit yourselves. Fair dinkum, you don't blame me for laughing do you? One lousy Abo — and he's got you buggered.' Norton got up out of his seat and all eyes followed him as he went to the fridge and collected himself a fresh stubbie of Fourex. 'And you, Eddie.' Les turned to the wiry, dark-haired figure sitting in the corner. 'You call yourself a hit man. Hah! You couldn't hit a bull in the arse with a shovel full of wheat.'

'Oh yeah,' replied Sydney's deadliest killer, allowing a flicker of a smile to crease the corners of his ice-green eyes. 'And are you going to tell me you know a better way of getting rid of this Kilby cunt?'

Norton removed the top from his Fourex and took a swallow. 'As a matter of fact Eddie,' he said, belching lightly before dropping the twist-top in the rubbish basket with a rattle, 'I do.'

There was silence once again in the plush office, and if anything it seemed to deepen at Norton's last remark. All eyes followed him back to his seat. Even Price's anger, especially after Les's erratic behaviour and the verbal he'd just given all of them, particularly Eddie, gave way to profound curiosity. Price stared intently at the big, red-headed Queenslander sitting, sipping smugly on his fresh drink.

'What do you mean, Les?' said Eddie, after a few seconds. 'You do?'

'Just what I said Eddie. I reckon I know a sneak way of getting rid of this Kilby rooster.'

'Are you fair dinkum, Les?' said Price, now sitting up in his seat with his arms folded across his chest. 'You're not just talking through your arse are you? You dead-set reckon you know a way of getting this Kilby prick off my back?'

'Yes, Price,' nodded Norton slowly. 'I'm pretty certain I do.'

'How?'

'There's an old saying,' started Les.

'Ohh here we go,' chuckled Brennan. 'He's off with the Queensland bush philosophies again.'

'Like I was saying,' continued Norton, doing his best to ignore the overweight casino manager, 'there's an old saying. There's more ways of killing a cat than choking it with cheese. And there's another one. It takes a thief to catch a thief. Is that right?'

'Yeah all right,' said Price. 'That's okay if you're William

17

Shakespeare or something. But what's it got to do with this fuckin' boong over in Redfern?'

'How long have you got before this Coles deal has to be signed and all that?' asked Les.

'Three weeks from today. I might be able to squeeze another couple of days out of them — but no more.'

'Righto. That should be enough. I'm gonna have to ring my brother back in Dirranbandi.'

'Not Murray?' said Price, a smile forming on his face for the first time that evening. 'Jesus you're not bringing him down again, are you? He's even madder than you.'

'No. Murray won't be coming down. But he'll be organising it from up there. Or at least what needs to be organised up there.'

'What do you mean — organising it from up there?' asked Eddie.

Norton smiled across at the wiry little hit man and took another swallow from his stubbie. 'Remember when we necked that bloke from Melbourne, Rossiter, and you said you might show me a little trick or two you learnt in Vietnam?'

'Yeah.'

'Well this time, I might show you a little trick or two. And you can only learn these ones in outback Australia.'

'Yeah?'

'Yep. And this one's a ripper, Eddie.' Norton smiled cheekily around the room. 'As you city slickers like to say, it'll really blow your mind.'

'Well come on,' said Price. 'Give us the drum. What's going on? What are you going to do?'

'I can't explain it to you right now. But I'll ring Murray first thing Monday morning. He should have things sorted out up there by Tuesday, and I'll let you know if it's on on Wednesday. Okay? But I'd better warn you, Price. It's going to cost you.'

'Oh hello. I knew it.' Price smiled derisively. 'There's an ask attached. And how much is the bloody ask?'

Norton closed one eye and looked up at the ceiling for a moment or two. 'Somewhere between fifty and a hundred grand. Closer to fifty. And I'm gonna need two or three weeks off from work to set it all up.'

'What?' roared Price. 'Give you a hundred grand and three weeks off from work.' Price turned to the others, then back to Les. 'Can you believe this cunt? How are you off for socks and undies. Would you like the Rolls to run around in, too?

Bad luck I haven't got a nice seventeen-year-old daughter. You could have her as well. Go to the shithouse will you.'

'Please yourself, then,' said Les, and shrugged. 'Let this mug rip you off for half a million dollars — and make a complete dill of you at the same time. And then wait till the word gets out about it. They'll be running tour buses up here full of people wanting to laugh at you.' Norton drained his stubbie. 'Makes no difference to me,' he added.

Price was stung by his last remark and he also knew that Norton had him in a corner. But he trusted Les completely and there was something in the doorman's confident attitude that suggested he just could have something up his sleeve that might be worth a shot. And Price, above all, was a gambler.

'All right,' he nodded slowly. 'A hundred grand it is. When do you want it? Now?'

'No. We'll do this strictly by the book. Straight up and down. Just open a bank account in my name with a hundred grand in it because I'll have to make quite a few cash withdrawals over the next two or three weeks — of which I'll see that you get an itemised account for each one. And if there's some money left over and this all goes to plan there might even be a little drink in it for me. What do you reckon?' Norton added with a smile.

'There'll be a hundred grand in your name in the ANZ bank at Bondi Junction first thing Monday morning,' nodded Price. 'Sheldon can take you up there and you can sort out the signatures and all that. Okay?'

'Leave it till Wednesday. 'Cause I won't know for sure whether it'll be on till then.'

'Okay.'

'And if I have to take the time off, Billy, can you get Danny McCormack or someone up here?'

'Sure. No problems at all.'

'Right then,' said Norton, tossing his stubbie in the bin as he moved to the bar to get a fresh one. 'That's about all I need for the time being.'

'Hey hold on a minute,' protested Eddie Salita. 'Don't leave us all up in suspenders, Les. This is all very blood mysterious. Strange phone calls to Dirranbandi. Secret bank accounts. Time off from work. Just what are you up to?'

'I'll let you know a bit more about it on Wednesday. But Eddie. If this works out like it should — mate, you'll dead-set shit yourself. Now,' Norton added, glancing around the room. 'Anybody else want a drink while I'm up?'

19

They ended up leaving the club around four-thirty. Norton refused to elaborate any more on what he'd already told them, despite persistent and sometimes exasperated questioning from Eddie and Billy. He just kept the smug smile on his face and told them to be patient, they'd know what was going on on Wednesday — all going well.

Sunday Les didn't do a great deal. As was his normal procedure at the end of his working week, he was up around lunchtime. And as it wasn't a bad late spring day he went down to North Bondi for a hang in the sun and a mag to some of his old football mates from Easts. He went for a paddle on a surf-ski he borrowed from the surf club, had a few beers at the Icebergs in the late afternoon, then it was a huge stack of takeaway Chinese food and home to watch the Sunday night movie on TV. Warren, who shared with him, invited Les down the Sheaf at Double Bay for a bit of a rage and maybe bring a couple of girls back home for a drink later, but Norton declined, saying he wanted to have an early night as there were a few things on his mind and he intended getting up early in the morning.

Norton glanced at the phone a couple of times while he was watching the movie, but didn't bother to ring his brother. He knew Murray and Elaine used to like to get on the drink on Sunday night, kick up their heels on the dance floor at the Dirranbandi RSL, then come home, lock the bedroom door securely so the kids couldn't hear what was going on, and get stuck into it like a couple of teenagers at a drive-in. Norton couldn't help but chuckle as he glanced at the phone once more during a commercial break and checked his watch again while he finished his sixth can of Fourex for the evening.

Les hit the sack at eleven and was up just before six the following morning. He had a quick run and a swim, got the papers, and with a steaming mug of coffee in his hand rang his brother around seven-thirty.

Murray was out the front of the old house, fiddling around under the bonnet of the new Land Rover he'd bought from the proceeds of the opal sale with Price, when he heard the phone ring. Elaine had only just left in the Holden panel van to take the kids to school and he squinted at the huge, red-dust cloud the car left behind as it disappeared into the gum-tree scattered distance. While he clumped towards the house he wiped his grease-stained hands on his old moleskins.

Grungle followed him as far as the verandah where he flopped on a dusty woollen rug next to the flyscreen front door.

'Hello,' said Murray, sitting on the edge of one of the lounge chairs, a little curious at hearing the STD pips.

'G'day Muzz,' said Norton. 'It's your even-lovin' brother Les.'

'Meggsie. Holy bloody shit. How're you goin' son?'

'All right, Muzz. Yourself?'

'Good as gold. How's life in the big city treatin' you?'

'Ohh you know. All right, sort of.'

Les chatted away about different things for a minute or two, asking his brother how the family was, and things in Dirranbandi and Queensland in general. Then he got down to business.

'Listen Muzz. You got much on at the moment?'

'Ohh, not really ... why?'

'You interested in earning a lazy five grand?'

'Five grand.' Murray's ears pricked up. Hustling for a dollar ran in the Norton family and when it came to diving on a quick earn Murray wasn't far behind his brother. 'I reckon I just might. Who do I have to kill?'

'You don't have to kill anybody. I just want you to go out and put a proposal to three old mates of ours that might.'

'Where?'

'Out Binjiwunyawunya.'

Murray burst out laughing and so did Les. 'So,' guffawed the leathery faced dingo trapper, 'it's like that is it?'

'Yeah,' chuckled Les. 'It's like that. Listen, I'll tell you exactly what's goin' on. And don't make me have to repeat myself because this bloody call's costin' me a fortune.'

Les explained to his brother what was happening between Percy Kilby and Price, and told him the plan he had in mind. When he was finished Murray was laughing like a drain and raring to go.

'Price is giving me a pretty good bank to get this together, Muzz, so whatever the boys want tell them it's sweet. And I reckon with a bit of luck I just might be able to squeeze another five grand out of the wreck for you. That's ten grand. Not bad just for going for a drive out in the bush.'

'Yeah? I wouldn't exactly call a trip out to Binjiwunyawunya just a drive in the bush eh?'

'Fair enough. But you're gettin' a bit more than just wages — and you're doing nothing else.'

'Yeah, okay.'

21

'Ohh yeah. One more thing, Muzz. You know that old landing strip the Yanks built out near there during the War.'

'Yeah.'

'Is that still all right? Could you land a small plane there?'

'It was all right the last time I was out there. That was about eight months ago. I reckon it'll still be okay.'

'Good. Cause that's how I'm gonna bring 'em down to Sydney.'

'Shit! You're not muckin' around are you.'

'Ohh mate. This is all very Frederick Forsyth, this one.'

'Who?'

'Don't worry about it. But listen don't forget, Muzz, we've only got a couple of weeks to do this. So tell the boys if they're interested to be ready to roll Thursday morning. Okay?'

'No worries mate.'

'Right.'

Les chatted on for another minute or two, shared another laugh with his brother, then hung up saying he'd hear from him first thing Wednesday morning.

Mmhh, thought Les, looking at the phone after he'd hung up. A charter plane to Queensland and back, twice, and ten grand for Murray. That's sure going to cut into that hundred thousand. Oh well he laughed, who gives a stuff? It'll be a bit of fun doing this and be good to see the boys again. Just then the door to Warren's bedroom creaked open and out staggered the young, fair-haired advertising executive in his black Japanese dressing-gown. He walked unsteadily into the lounge room, yawned and blinked groggily at Les a couple of times.

'Hello Shintaro,' said Norton cheerfully, noting his flat-mate's hungover state. 'And how was the Sheaf last night?'

'Iwuzzgood,' mumbled Warren. 'I finished up in Archie's after it closed.'

'Jesus, you're a glutton for punishment, aren't you.'

'Yeah I know. Shit, what time is it?'

'Gettin' on for eight.'

'Shit, is it? I'd better get my finger out. I gotta be at bloody Cremorne by nine. Fuckin' hell. I don't feel like it.'

Warren shook his head tiredly and staggered into the bathroom, leaving Les staring thoughtfully at the phone while he finished his mug of coffee.

On the other end of the line, just outside of Dirranbandi,

Murray was doing pretty much the same as his brother, only without the mug of coffee. With a craggy smile on his face he climbed across the lounge room in his riding boots, stepped out onto the verandah and looked at Grungle.

'Well, Grungle old mate,' he smiled. 'Looks like we've got a bit of a drive on tomorrow, son.' As he spoke he dug the toe of his boot into the dog's scar-covered stomach and gave it a bit of a rub. 'I suppose I'd better go and fill a few tins with petrol and water.' Murray wandered into the junk-strewn yard to find some empty drums. Grungle stayed where he was in the shade, rolled clumsily over on his side and farted.

That evening, during dinner, Murray told his wife he'd be going bush for a couple of days and would probably be back either Wednesday night or lunchtime Thursday. This didn't come as any surprise to the tall, lean bushwoman. Murray would often disappear off into the outback, pig shooting, chasing dingos and wild dogs for the government, or any number of things he might get up to with no-one around. The only thing that mildly surprised her was that he was going away for just a couple of days this time.

Feeding time, especially the evening meal, was always a bit of a hoot in the Norton household. Although it was constantly almost heatwave conditions outside, Elaine would always serve up stacks of hot roast meat with baked and boiled vegetables, all swimming in gravy, followed by sweets smothered in steaming custard and cream. This would all be washed down with mugs of strong, heavily sugared, almost boiling tea from a huge china teapot in the middle of the old wooden table that filled most of the dining room. None of the family had a clue about etiquette or table manners, and if Leo Schofield ever happened to put his head in the Norton dining room at teatime he would have passed out on the spot. Murray's family ate with their knives, forks, hands and any other blunt instruments or utensils that happened to be hanging around the room; if they could have eaten with their feet they would have used them as well. Grungle would push his way in through the flyscreen door and wait at the edge of the table for a handout. And so would Murray's pet wedge-tailed eagle, Ernie.

Where most people, especially city folk, would keep a budgerigar or a lovebird as a pet, Murray — being a Queenslander, where they always like to try and do things a little bigger — had Ernie. He found the poor little bugger when he was barely a chick, dehydrated and almost dead at the base of the tree underneath his nest. Some so-called 'sports shooter' had shot his mother just for fun, so Murray picked up the poor little fellow, wrapped him in a piece of wet cloth and nursed him back to life. And the eagle had stayed with him ever since. Murray also caught up with the 'sports shooter' a couple of days later in a pub in Dirranbandi, bragging about how clever and what a great shot he was. Murray took him out of the pub, flogged him unmercifully against his car, then broke the butt of the scoped 32/40 Marlin against his arm — and also the 'sports shooter's' arm in the process. In his job for the government eliminating pests, Murray had probably shot and killed more wild dogs and feral pigs than any man in Australia. But the idea of seeing imbeciles shooting defenceless animals just to satisfy their egos and sexual inadequacies got right up Murray's nose. 'Sports shooters,' he used to say. 'I wonder how long the pricks would last if they ever gave the animals a gun.'

Ernie was a pretty good bird and a lot of fun, but he did have one mean, vindictive streak in him. If Murray didn't give him what he thought was his fair share of scraps from the table, he would hop up on Murray's favourite lounge chair and shit on it. And Ernie didn't shit like your average seagull or park pigeon: Ernie would leave enough whitish-grey crap behind him to fill an ice-cream carton. Elaine was convinced that Ernie had had more than his fair share of scraps this night so she told him to piss off and get his feathered arse out of her kitchen. Not liking this, Ernie gave her a dirty look as he got to the flyscreen and was just about to raise his wedge-tail up in the air and leave a little going-away card on the dusty dining-room carpet when Elaine sprung him out of the corner of her eye. The next thing the toe of her riding boot, accompanied by a 'You rotten bastard,' caught Ernie right up the backside, to propell him through the door and land in a flurry of squawking, cursing feathers a couple of metres in front of the wooden steps.

'Now. What were you saying love?' she said, returning to the table and hacking off another great slab of beef which she unceremoniously dumped in the pool of gravy on Murray's place. 'You're pissin' off somewhere tomorrow morning?'

'Yeah,' replied Murray. 'Only for a couple of days though.'

Seated either side of him, Wayne and Mitchell, their two sons, stopped stuffing themselves for a moment to look at their father in anticipation. The sinewy curly-haired lads were the image of their father, except for their mother's soft hazelgreen eyes, their slightly bucked teeth and cheeky young freckles. And like all kids they hated school and loved the bush.

'Ohh Dad. Can we come too?' they chorused.

'No. You can't come this time fellas.'

'Ohh Dad.'

'Shut up and eat your tucker.'

'Where are you goin' anyway, love?'

'Out to the channel country.'

'That far, eh?'

'Yeah, I'm going out to see the boys from Binjiwunyawunya.'

'Ohh shit!' Elaine let go a shriek of laughter. 'Jesus I love those blokes. Say hello to Chalky, Mumbles and Yarra for me. In fact I'll give you one of my chocolate and strawberry cakes to take out to them.'

'Righto. They'll be rapt in that.'

'When are you leaving?'

'About four. So I'll be goin' to bed early.'

Elaine nodded her head. 'I'll get some tucker ready for you to take with you. And seein' as you're going to bed early...' Elaine smiled as her hand snaked out underneath the table and grabbed her husband on the knee. 'I might get to bed a bit early myself.'

Wayne and Mitchell continued eating noisily, completely mystified at the funny looks their parents were giving each other.

Around four the following morning Grungle was sitting waiting patiently in the darkness on the front seat of the Land Rover, next to the thermos of hot tea and the lunch his master's wife had prepared. She'd also filled Murray full of bacon and eggs and was now standing on the verandah having a hug and a kiss before he left.

'Well, I'll see you in a couple of days or so mate,' said Murray, giving her one last hug before he turned and walked down the front steps.

'All right Love. Take care,' she replied with a wave and a smile.

Murray was about halfway to the car when a couple of sleepy voices made him stop abruptly and spin around.

'Why didn't you say goodbye to us, Dad?'

His two sons had come out on to the verandah and were standing in the light from the kitchen, either side of and leaning half asleep against their mother.

'Well,' grinned Murray a little sheepishly as he started walking back up to them, 'it's pretty early and I didn't want to wake up my two best mates in all the world.' He hugged his sons to him and planted an affectionate kiss on both their foreheads.

'Doesn't matter,' mumbled Mitchell. 'You should've said goodbye, Dad.'

'Yeah you're right mate,' replied Murray, smiling at the wonderfully cranky look on his son's face. 'I did the wrong thing. I'm sorry. Anyway, I'm only gonna be gone a couple of days. But I want you both to look after the place and do what your mother tells you. Okay?'

'You needn't worry about that, Dad,' said Wayne. 'She hits almost as hard as you.'

Murray started the car and with a toot of the horn headed off down the driveway towards the faintest flicker of pink and mauve staining the cobalt of the dawn sky. Grungle gave a throaty bark out the window as Ernie zoomed down out of the darkness to land at the side of the driveway and watch as the Land Rover rumbled past. There was another toot on the horn and the next thing they'd left the drive and were on the red-dirt road heading in to Dirranbandi.

Murray picked up the main road out of town and then, with one foot on the accelerator and the other banging on the floor in time to some country radio station playing Gary Young and The Rockin' Emus twanging their way through 'I'm Runnin' Late For Gwandong', he headed for the small town of St George. There he picked up the Balone Highway, straight to Cunnamulla, where he took the Mitchell Highway to Charleville. Taking advantage of the even bitumen he hoofed it a bit because after that it was all red dust and loose gravel for a while, and then worse... practically nothing after the tough cattle town on the Warrego River. Murray was there just as the shops were opening a little after nine. He then turned west on the dirt road past Lake Dartmouth, and drove on over the Blackwater River.

More country music, from some other radio station, twanged away on the radio while outside the blinding sun climbed higher into the sky and the Land Rover sped further into western Queensland, spewing choking bulldust out behind it in a billowing red cloud. Homesteads or any signs of civilisation soon began to disappear except for the odd refrigerator cum mailbox standing by a gate at the side of the road, generally with the bleached skull of a steer perched on top as a grim decoration. On either side of the road stretched the shimmering flat plains, their monotony broken only by countless grey termite mounds, more bleached bones of various animals, and pepperings of brittle-looking shrubs and trees that were almost as red and dry as the soil they clung to so precariously. Beyond the plains loomed a horizon of low, uneven mountain ranges, blue in the distance. These always gave Murray the feeling that eons ago, during the dreamtime, some giant had come along and decided that these ranges were too high; so he scooped the tops off and turned them all into plateaus. Now and again small flocks of startled emus or bustards would gallop off into the spinifex and stinging trees, joined occasionally by equally small mobs of scraggy red or grey kangaroos. Wedge-tailed eagles, hawks and crows would sometimes appear drifting languidly in the hot air currents like scraps of burnt paper, then dive and disappear into a landscape as drab and gaunt as the people and creatures that inhabited it. The great master painter never bothered with too much on his palette when he made this part of Australia. Any colour schemes he left to be chosen by the relentless hot winds and the burning outback sun.

Murray checked his watch about an hour later as a change in the terrain — from semi-desert to huge outcrops of granite and ashen boulders, interspersed with orangy brown carpets of wild hops — told him he was getting into the McGregor and Coleman Ranges. At the edge of the trickle that presently passed for the Kyabra Creek, thirty or so kilometres this side of Windorah, he decided to stop so he and Grungle could have a piss and stretch their legs.

After he'd had a leak, Murray got the canvas water bag from the front of the Land Rover and took a good long swallow. Normally he would have poured some in his hat for Grungle but the dog found a small pond in the creek bed and happily slurped up all he needed. He trundled back up to his master and they stood in the still, hot silence by the side of the car idly watching a huge antlion buried in the sand, its jaws just below the surface, snap onto another ant almost as big and drag it beneath the surface to suck it dry. A monstrous greeny black goanna, almost two metres long, lumbered up over a boulder and looked intently at them for a few moments, possibly wondering if the weird-looking dog was going to give chase; but Grungle wasn't the slightest bit interested in this heat. Its body swaying rhythmically from side to side, the goanna finally lumbered off disturbing a pair of fat, white, speckled geckos sitting on a rock. They appeared to have heavily-membrane-lidded eyes only for each other. Murray always liked the ubiquitous little geckos with their flattened spade shaped tails and funny little hands. He walked over to them for a closer look. It wasn't long before the two lizards brought their heads up and started their awful, high-pitched hissing scream that was supposed to terrify him but was nothing more than a bluff from the delightful, harmless little creatures. Murray chuckled to himself and watched them continue with their hissing for a few moments before he turned to Grungle.

'Come on mate,' he smiled. 'It's not hard to see we're not wanted round here. Let's piss off.' Murray looked at his watch once more. 'We might stop again for a bit of lunch in a while, eh. What do you reckon?'

It's hard to imagine, but as he jumped up on the front seat of the Land Rover it looked like Grungle nodded his head in agreement.

An hour or so later they'd passed Windorah — where the Barcoo and Thompson Rivers join to form a creek, the Cooper — and were on the banks of the Whitulah River.

It was almost noon, Murray's stomach was rumbling constantly and Grungle also looked like he was getting ready to gnaw the butt off his master's AR-15 sitting on the back seat, so they pulled up for some lunch. Murray opened up the overnight bag and found a thermos full of sweet white tea, strong enough to stand a pinch-bar up in, and two roast beef and home-made chutney sandwiches about the same size as a *Webster's Dictionary*. There was also a bag of roughly chopped meat for Grungle and the bones from Sunday night's sirloins. Murray fed the dog first and then, with the car doors open, got stuck into his sandwiches while he gazed fondly at the still rugged, yet increasingly beautiful countryside around him.

The Whitulah was nowhere near full but a fairly steady stream of clear water, trickling languidly over the smooth white stones that formed its bed, showed there had been a little more rain than usual during this year's dry. Patches of huge golden king orchids moved gently in the warm breeze at the edge of the river and took advantage of the extra moisture, along with a few small beds of Sturt's beautiful white desert roses — their bright crimson centres looking almost like drops of blood. Silver wattle and giant silver elkhorns vied for space on the river bank, among great smooth rocks whose shiny whiteness was stained by spreading patches of brown and green moss. Murray's attention, however, was directed mainly to a pair of beautiful olive-backed orioles singing melodiously in a magnificent golden wattle tree. There were plenty of other birds around but the orioles' shrill clear sound seemed to rise easily above the others' before they were abruptly interrupted and driven from their tree by a flock of noisy white corellas who started fighting as soon as they landed, squawking and jostling each other for a better position. Murray smiled and shook his head, and even Grungle seemed to wince and wish they'd shut up.

A movement in the bushes a few metres behind the wattle made Murray freeze and tentatively move towards the loaded submachine gun on the back seat. It was a wild dog. At this distance Murray couldn't miss; he'd nail the savage carnivorous pest and besides doing the bush a favour get the bounty on its scalp. But when the animal nosed its way a little further out of the bushes Murray could see it was a rare black dingo, probably attracted by the smell of the food and the noise. Grungle sensed the dingo's presence, spotted it, and immediately began to bristle.

'Hold on mate,' said Murray, taking Grungle firmly by the collar. 'We'll let him go. There's not too many of them left — and he ain't gonna do too much harm out here.'

The black dingo heard Murray's voice and vanished as quietly and mysteriously as it had appeared.

Murray finished his sandwiches, gave his stomach a rub, and the dog's too. 'Well. What do you reckon mate? We get crackin'? With a bit of luck we should be there in another four hours or so.'

Grungle seemed to nod his head in agreement and hopped back up on the front seat. Murray rinsed the thermos in the creek and they were soon on their way again.

The road on the other side of the Whitulah was now nothing more than a dusty, uneven, rock-strewn trail, across which crawled numerous thick growths of orange desert pea. The plains were way behind them now and by the time they had pushed through the metre or so of water that formed Farrars Creek and past a dot on the map called Currawilla, they headed into an even worse stretch of road leading towards another dot, Pulparara.

The landscape around them changed dramatically once more. Precipices and mountains, thrown up by volcanoes and hewn by water rushing through them millions of years ago, formed ragged ridges along either side of the narrow dirt road. Massive orange, ochre and mauve cliffs would often tower over the Land Rover. Some were smooth, as if cut by a hot knife through butter, while others were weathered into frighteningly weird patterns and shapes by man's greatest enemy and the leveller of all things on earth — time. Pools of crystal-clear water and equally clear streams and billabongs teeming with fat white-necked herons would appear at the bases of these ochre ridges and redstone cliffs. White-barked cedars, flooded gums and monstrous green tree ferns were everywhere. Stinging trees and squat cabbage palms, their delicate fronds spread out like a Spanish senorita's fan, were also in abundance.

Murray spun the wheel violently to avoid two huge and plump stumpy-tailed lizards asleep on the dirt track. 'It's been a while since we've been out here mate, eh?' he grinned at Grungle, bouncing madly all over the front seat. 'Still the grouse though, ain't it?' The bushman's dog appeared to nod once more in agreement as if he too loved and appreciated the rugged, remote beauty of these parts.

Vine-tangled trees full of birds overhung the narrow track, and banks of colourful wild flowers grew everywhere. Blue, wild tomatoes edged alongside pink and mauve hollyhocks. Golden spur valleias, looking almost like orchids, intertwined with orange quandong, or native peach. Purple fan flowers grew neck and neck with coral and yellow drumstick shrubs while more bursts of orange desert pea kept scrambling across the track, looking like tongues of flame.

The laughter of kookaburras echoed off the cliff faces along with the screeching of galahs, cockatoos and parrots and the screaming and arguing of the channel-billed cuckoos that have a rotten habit of laying their eggs in other birds' nests. Murray had turned the radio off ages ago; the screeching and squawking of the dozens of varieties of birds, although at times unbelievably raucous, was all the music he needed.

Just across the small but beautiful Diamantina Lakes, where the Mayne and Diamantina Rivers meet, Murray stopped again to check his map, the odometer and the compass on the dashboard.

'Not much further now, Grungle old son,' he smiled, running his finger across the map. He gave the dog a rough pat on the head and they lurched on their way again.

Another ten kilometres or so past another dot on the map,

Springvale, Murray found what he was looking for — a row of a dozen cycad trees lined up along the side of the road like a column of tin soldiers. Even through the dust-covered windscreen Murray could clearly make out the hundreds of tiny red-backed wrens hopping nimbly amongst the protection of the trees' bayonet-sharp leaves.

'There it is mate.' Murray grinned at the dog and swung the Land Rover off the track at the last cycad. He drove back to where the cycads hid the start of another trail and followed it for about five kilometres till the bumpy trail suddenly opened up into a landscaped clearing of approximately one acre with a huge old rambling homestead. At just on four-thirty Murray switched off the motor and smiled happily at Grungle. They were there. Roughly 250 kilometres in from the Northern Territory border and right on the Tropic of Capricorn. Binjiwunyawunya. Place of plenty of water and a full stomach.

No matter when it was, every time Murray pulled up at Binjiwunyawunya and the old house built out in the middle of nowhere he never ceased to be amazed at the strange beauty of the place and the sheer incongruity of it all. The white wooden homestead, with a wide verandah running around the front and the two sides, was built right into the red-ochre table-topped mountain that loomed over it. Part of the verandah was shaded by white, wooden lattice work with vines, fruit and different coloured bougainvilleas growing through and around it in a haphazard display of magnificent colours. Pink, gold, blue, crimson, white. More vines and flowers spread across the green, galvanised-iron roof in the middle of which was a large disc-antenna for picking up satellite TV signals. Flower beds, shrubs and small native trees dotted the landscaped clearing in front and to the sides of the house, where a set of sprinklers played jets of water across them and the neat green lawns. There were numerous pebble-edged ponds filled with huge white lilies and hibiscus over which dozens of spindly-legged waterbirds skipped and danced as they pecked at the insects and tiny fish in the crystal-clear shallows.

The gum tree-dotted mountain behind the homestead swarmed with more birds and held a natural mineral spring that bubbled into the chain of ponds to one side of the house before it disappeared into an underground stream. This spring ensured a steady supply of water for the house and gardens even in the severest drought and the owners often used to joke about how people in the cities paid a dollar for small bottles of Perrier and other spa waters while they used to throw it all over their gardens nonchalantly. Murray smiled and shook his head once more in wonder at the sheer magic of it all before he and Grungle got out of the Land Rover. Just as they did so, a huge swarm of exquisitely coloured butterflies drifted over them and flew on towards the mountain.

Two absolutely gorgeous young Aboriginal girls, no more than twenty and wearing nothing but a pair of brief Spank running shorts that emphasised their ripe full-breasted bodies, stopped what they were doing amongst the ponds and squinted over towards the car, their hands above their eyes. One was holding a hose, the other a small pitchfork. As soon as they recognised Murray and Grungle their lovely dark faces broke into beautiful, shy, pearly grins that only Australian Aborigines seem to manage; huge grins that are totally infectious and look as though they can light up a room or a cloudy day all on their own.

'Murray,' they chorused excitedly. Both girls dropped what they were doing and giggling happily to each other came running over. 'How are you, darling? You too, Grungle.'

'Hello Numidi. Hello Nantjinin. Shit it's good to see you again.' Murray threw his arms around them and hugged them to him and kissed them warmly as they giggled and squealed affectionately. 'How are you girls?'

'Terrific, Murray,' replied Numidi happily. 'Especially now that we've seen you.'

They squeezed and held each other for a few moments more, then Nantjinin looked up into Murray's eyes.

'What brings you out here anyway?' she asked cheekily. 'Was it to see one of us, oh great white hunter?'

'Don't bloody great white hunter me you cheeky little bludger, or you might get a boot right in the bum. I came out to see the boys. Where are they?'

'In the house,' said Numidi.

Just then a voice sounding like it was trying desperately hard not to laugh called out from the homestead.

'By the livin' bloody Jesus. Here's trouble.'

Murray turned to see three Aboriginal men, wearing black cotton headbands and running shorts, grinning at him from the top of the stairs running up to the house.

'Hello fellas,' he chuckled. 'How're you goin' there?'

With his arms still around the girls' waists and Grungle trotting happily behind, Murray returned the grins and walked over towards the house.

The happy faces on the verandah belonged to the men Murray had travelled over a thousand kilometres to see, through semi-desert, mountain ranges and hidden trails. The owners of the unique homestead at Binjiwunyawunya: Tjalkalieri, Mumbi and Yarrawulla. These were their true native names, but ever since childhood Murray and the rest of the family had called them Chalky, Mumbles and Yarra. And as Aborigines the boys from Binjiwunyawunya were something else. Walking slowly towards them, Murray never ceased to be amazed at the way they never seemed to change in appearance — even in the thirty-odd years he had known them.

Each man had to be at least seventy, but none looked a day over thirty. It was uncanny. Their teeth were all white and perfect, set in faces scarcely lined except for a few wrinkles around the eyes and sides of the mouth, probably caused from laughing too much. Not a grey hair amongst the short, curly crops on their domed heads and not an ounce of fat on their smooth, wiry bodies. Bent slightly over the railing, the folds in their stomach muscles looked like squashed-up piano accordions. Chalky, the shortest, had the makings of a small, straggly beard. But the one oustanding feature of all three men was their bright, almost electric-blue eyes. While nearly all Aboriginal people have brown eyes, these were a piercing blue and even though their faces were creased with laughter Murray could sense the energy behind those eyes and almost feel them boring into him as he ambled towards the homestead.

Even though he had known them all his life, and his father even longer, there was still a bit of mystery about Tjalkalieri, Mumbi and Yarrawulla. Evidently they were the last of a small lost tribe that originally lived in Central Australia, somewhere between Lake Eyre and a remote part of the Flinders Ranges. Whatever happened to this mysterious tribe no one was ever quite sure; the three never discussed it much. But it probably suffered from hostility from the other tribes or was more than likely wiped out by the sheer, stupid brutality of the early white settlers in the area. The three men moved up the channel country sometime in the late 1920s or early 1930s, buying the property at Binjiwunyawunya with money they'd made from the sale of a number of sapphires they'd brought with them from the Flinders Ranges. Old Joe Norton, Murray's father, had got to know them during the Second World War when he was in the AIF, and they had remained firm friends ever since.

When the money from the sapphires eventually ran out the boys, who were all excellent artists, made a fairly reasonable living selling paintings. It was mainly through the paintings that they managed to maintain the property in an amazing, almost oppulent style. But there was a bit more to Tjalkalieri, Mumbi and Yarrawulla than being three simple Aboriginal bush artists.

You would think having a nice big property way out in the middle of nowhere, it wouldn't take long before the boys would be inundated with hangers on, which is often the case with the Aboriginal people; as soon as one of them kicks on he suddenly finds himself swamped with relatives. Cousins he or she has never heard of seem to turn up unexpectedly from all over Australia for a ride on the gravy train. But any natives who knew of Tjalkalieri, Mumbi and Yarrawulla — especially the ones in that area, except for a few good-looking young lubras the boys often liked to take under their wings — were terrified of the blue-eyed tribesmen from Central Australia and gave the entire area a wide berth. For the boys from Binjiwunyawunya were also Nungari. Powerful black medicine men, possessors of secret knowledge and masters of black mysteries that go back thousands of years. Kurdaitcha men. Assassins. Aboriginal hit men. This was another way the boys from Binjiwunyawunya made quite a few dollars in their spare time; and there were none better throughout the length and breadth of Australia at doing what they did.

The boys were genuinely glad to see Murray. He was the son of an old and valued friend, they'd known him and his brothers and sisters since childhood, so there was plenty of laughing and warm, firm handshakes all round, with quite a bit of pushing and shoving thrown in. The girls stayed in the background giggling musically while they patted Grungle, who sat on his backside panting happily at what was going on around him.

'Well, Murray old fella,' said Tjalkalieri, who generally did most of the talking. 'It sure is good to see you.'

'Yeah,' replied Murray. 'And it sure is good to see you blokes again too.' Murray let his gaze drift softly across the verandah over the beautiful gardens where a red-kneed dotterel had just speared a tiny green frog in the shallows of one of the ponds. 'I'll tell you what,' he said shaking his head in admiration. 'You've sure got the place lookin' a treat.'

'Yeah. That's the girls,' agreed Yarrawulla, smiling over at Numidi and Nantjinin. 'They sure do a good job. We might even have to give 'em a rise.'

'You can afford it,' said Murray. 'You blokes have got heaps.'

'Ah I don't know so much,' said Tjalkalieri, shaking his head. 'The painting caper's not as good as it used to be. Every Abo that can hold a brush seems to be getting in on the act lately. The buyers in the cities'll take just about anything, too. Half the time they can't tell the difference between good stuff and shit. And it doesn't make it any easier to get your price.'

'Well then,' drawled Murray slowly. 'It seems like I might've just come along at the right time.'

'Yeah?' Tjalkalieri smiled knowingly at the two others, then back at Murray. 'And just what exactly did you have in mind Murray ... old mate.'

'I might have a nice little earn for you Chalky. That's if you and the boys are interested. It's one of your specialities, too.'

'A little earn eh?' said Yarrawulla. 'That sounds all right.'

'Yeah. And it's an easy one. I reckon you'll like it.'

'Well, why don't we go inside and talk about it over a couple of drinks,' said Tjalkalieri.

Murray took off his hat and banged the dust out against the leg of his moleskins. 'Now you're talkin' my language. After twelve hours in that bloody Land Rover I'm fangin' for a cold beer.'

'I don't know about a cold beer.' Mumbi winked at his two mates. 'But we might have a flagon of brown muscat we can pass around.'

Murray threw back his head and roared laughing. 'That'd be the bloody day,' he chortled. He swatted Mumbi across the head with his hat and followed the laughing Aborigines into the house.

The place had hardly changed since the last time Murray was out there, except for a few more paintings hung in the teak-lined corridor that ran past the bedrooms into the lounge. The three owners moved into the lounge towards a monstrous black leather ottoman which faced a colonial brick fireplace. A beaten-copper funnel was built into the fireplace and above the hearth a gun rack, holding a number of military and sporting rifles and several pistols, was built into the wall. More paintings and indoor plants were spread around the lounge room while a remote-control stereo TV with a VCR on top and an almost state-of-the-art Marantz stereo system took up nearly an entire wall.

'Oh Murray,' said Tjalkalieri, as he motioned him towards one of matching padded-leather lounge chairs, 'that's Mammanduru and Koodja.'

Murray turned to the spacious kitchen across from the lounge, where another two beautiful Aboriginal girls, about twenty, wearing tight T-shirts and skimpy running shorts were fussing around the sink and some copper pots of food cooking on the large porta-gas range. Zephyrs billowed the curtains in the bay window above the sink while behind the girls the huge cedar table was set with correctly placed plates and cutlery and crisp red table napkins in shiny silver napkin rings. An exquisite flower arrangement was positioned in the middle of the table and it was obvious the table had been set for some time.

'Hello girls,' smiled Murray. 'Pleased to meet you.'

The girls smiled shyly back, then giggled at each other and continued with what they were doing where they were soon joined by the other two girls.

Murray noticed the table had already been set for eight people. 'Hey?' he said curiously. 'You've... ah... already set the table for eight.'

Tjalkalieri smiled and the Aboriginal men had a bit of a chuckle amongst themselves. 'We knew you were coming about four hours ago. Good thing you didn't shoot that old black dingo, he's a mate of ours.' Tjalkalieri ignored the look on Murray's face. 'Come on,' he said. 'Grab a seat.'

Murray sat down opposite the others and next thing Numidi placed a tray of icy cold beers down on the coffee table. Fourex for Murray and three bottles of Stag Lager for the others.

'Cheers anyway, fellas,' said Murray, raising his bottle.

'Yeah. Cheers Murray. Good to see you again.'

They all took a healthy pull on their bottles and started talking amicably amongst themselves while the girls fussed around in the kitchen to a Warumpi Band tape playing softly on a large ghetto blaster.

About a dozen or so beers between them later, the light, fairly breezy conversation began to drift off and there was a noticeable silence; within a few seconds Murray could feel three pairs of electric-blue eyes studying him closely. Tjalkalieri shifted his gaze to the kitchen and the girls turned the cassette off and disappeared into another room, leaving the food simmering. Murray looked down the neck of his beer bottle, and as the eyes continued to stare at him intently he sucked in a deep breath and stared back at them for a moment before speaking.

'Well,' he said, easing back a little further into his chair. 'These beers are okay, but I suppose it's about time we got down to business.'

'Yeah,' replied Yarrawulla. 'Why don't we?'

'Yes Murray. Tell us why you've travelled all this way out here — almost surprising us. And what this little earn is you may have for us.' Tjalkalieri settled back a little further on the lounge next to Mumbi who still didn't say anything.

'I was nearly gonna ring you up before I left,' chuckled Murray, 'but I half-pie tipped you'd know I was coming.' He paused and studied his bottle of beer absently once more. 'Anyway, I'll try and get straight to the point. It's Les's idea. He rang me about it yesterday morning.'

'Ahh bloody Les,' laughed Mumbi. 'And how's he going, down in Sydney?'

'He's goin' all right.'

'That's good. Give him our regards next time you hear from him.'

Murray shrugged and smiled. 'You might be seeing him yourselves before long — with a bit of luck.'

Murray began to tell the boys what Les had told him over the phone about Percy Kilby and the trouble he was causing Price Galese. He stressed that Kilby was a bit of a no-good egg and getting rid of him would be absolutely no skin off anybody's nose. He then explained Les's plan and emphasised that if they were interested they would have to be prepared to leave early Thursday as there was a time factor involved. He didn't say how much Les was offering them through his boss, wanting to see if they were interested first. When he'd finished the boys were still staring at him but the intense, probing looks had now turned to one of gradually increasing amusement . . . almost laughter.

'So,' said Tjalkalieri, a chuckle rippling through his body. 'You want us to go down to Sydney and sing this Kilby fella a bit of a song, eh?'

'Yep, that's right. Les wants you to go down and sing

37

him to death. Point the old bone at him. You've done it plenty of times up here. Do you reckon you could do it in a big city?'

'Can a duck quack?' asked Yarrawulla.

'Fair enough.'

'I hate to sound mercenary,' said Tjalkalieri. 'But we do have to eat. How much is Les prepared to pay us to do this? If we should all agree.'

'Yeah,' agreed Yarrawulla. 'Your brother's a good bloke and all that. But when it comes to parting with a bit of gilt, Les wouldn't give you frostbite if he owned Antarctica.'

'I've got to agree with you there,' laughed Murray, 'but he said whatever you want. Thirty, forty grand.' Murray gave his shoulders a bit of a shrug. 'Whatever.'

'Forty grand. Shit!' Tjalkalieri smiled at the others. 'This Price Galese must want this Kilby bloke out of the way badly.'

'He does. But like I said, if you're interested you've got to be ready to go on Thursday.' Murray drained his bottle of Fourex. 'Anyway, why don't you talk it over amongst yourselves. I'll go and get another beer.'

Murray went to the double fridge in the kitchen, got himself a Fourex and sat back down while Tjalkalieri, Mumbi and Yarrawulla rattled away between them in their native tongue. Murray could speak quite a few native dialects but he knew absolutely nothing about this one. So he sat there sipping his beer in silence while the others earnestly discussed his offer. After a few minutes the discussion ceased and once more the three pairs of piercing blue eyes were studying him closely.

'Well. What do you reckon?' asked Murray, returning their stares.

Tjalkalieri nodded his head slowly for a moment before answering. 'Yeah, we've thought it over. We'll do it. Mind you, it sounds like this one could be quite a bit of mucking around — and we're not real keen on having to go all the way down to Sydney. But we'll do it. Fifty grand though, Murray. We feel this Price Galese fellow can afford it.'

'Fair enough. Fifty grand it is.'

Tjalkalieri raised his bottle and the others did the same. 'Well. Here's to Sydney,' he said.

'Yeah. And Percy Kilby,' said Murray, raising his Fourex also.

'It'll be the late Percy Kilby around this time next week,' added Mumbi, with a bit of a sinister smile. Murray smiled back and they finished their beers.

As if on cue, the girls reappeared and resumed whatever they were doing amongst the pots and pans. Koodja took away the empties on the coffee table and replaced them with four fresh beers, giving Murray an odd but sweet smile as she put his Fourex down in front of him.

'Brascoe still in the same place?' asked Murray, getting to his feet a couple of seconds after she went back into the kitchen.

'Yeah. Down the corridor, second on your left,' replied Yarrawulla.

Murray clomped down the corridor, used the toilet, then sat back down in the lounge room and continued drinking.

'So what's Les got in mind about us getting down to Sydney?' asked Tjalkalieri. 'I suppose we'll have to drive up to Mt Isa and catch a plane.'

'No. He mentioned something about that old airstrip the Yanks built out near Boulia. I think he's going to charter a plane and fly out there and pick you up.'

'Jesus. This is very Frederick Forsyth, isn't it?' said Mumbi.

'Who?'

'Don't worry about it, Muzz.'

'Do you want to ring Les now and tell him we've agreed?' Tjalkalieri nodded towards the phone on an old desk out in the corridor.

Murray took a quick glance at his watch. 'No, it's a bit early yet. He's probably down having a few beers. I'll wait till after tea.'

'Yeah. It should be ready soon. Hey Numidi. How long before tea's ready?'

'About fifteen minutes,' came a voice from the kitchen.

'Lovely,' smiled Tjalkalieri. 'Time for another one.'

They finished another beer and Numidi called them into the kitchen where they spread themselves around the old cedar table, with Murray in the guest spot at the end facing Tjalkalieri.

'What're we havin' anyway?' asked Murray, undoing his napkin.

'Ohh, I shot a few fruit bats the other night,' said Mumbi. 'We've stewed them up with some witchetty grubs and yams and a few wild berries. Got a big jar of sugar ants there for dessert too.'

'Sounds nice.'

'Yeah Murray,' smiled Yarrawulla. 'Like the bloke said in that movie. You can live on it — but it tastes like shit. Try some of this instead.'

Yarrawulla had no sooner spoken when one of the girls placed a steaming bowl of potato, leek and smoked-salmon chowder down in front of him. Another girl brought in a huge wooden bowl brimming with crisp caesar salad which went in the middle of the table, and another brought in two chilled bottles of Clarendon Estate 1979 Beeren Auslese which went on one side of the salad, and a bottle of Wolf Blass 1974 Shiraz which went on the other.

'Hey this soup isn't half bad,' said Murray, taking a liberal slurp from his bowl.

'Yeah, it's tasty,' smiled Mumbi, reaching over and filling Murray's glass with the Beeren Auslese.

Murray took another couple of slurps of soup and a large mouthful of wine. 'Shit this wine's sweet. Bloody nice though.'

'Yeah,' said Tjalkalieri. 'Generally Victorian wines aren't that sweet. Actually, it'd be better as a dessert wine. But you know what us ignorant dumb savages are like. We go for all that sweet sticky shit.'

'Yeah,' said Murray, taking another mouthful. 'Still, I suppose this stuff'll do when you run out of sweet sherry.'

Murray finished his soup just in time for Mammanduru to place his entree in front of him. Tiny freshwater lobsters, barbecued to perfection in chilli and garlic, on a bed of fluffy rice and chopped, fresh coriander. The meat literally fell off the shells and melted in your mouth.

'Jesus, these bloody yabbies are all right,' said Murray, chewing away with delight. 'I'll have to get the recipe off you and give it to Elaine.'

'How is Elaine these days?' asked Yarrawulla. 'Still cooking up those ferocious meals like she does?'

'Yeah, that's her all right. You'd think we had a team of sumo wrestlers livin' in the house. My two young blokes'll end up lookin' like Arnold Schwarzenegger by the time they leave school.'

Next came the main course. Fresh barramundi cutlets, stuffed with caviar and anchovies, in a saffron, cream and pernod sauce accompanied by more rice and crispy stir-fried vegetables. Once again, cooked to perfection. The girls had joined them at the table now with Koodja sitting next to Murray where she didn't say much but just smiled and made sure he had enough on his plate.

'Jesus, where did you girls learn to cook like this?' asked Murray, smiling back at her as he wolfed down some more barramundi.

40

Nantjinin answered for Koodja who was smiling shyly into her food. 'Tjalkalieri taught us,' she said.

'Ah, I might have known. Well keep up th good work Chalky.'

'Glad to see you're enjoying it, Murray. Though I suppose I should apologise offering you red wine with seafood.'

'Yeah. Well I wasn't going to say anything. But seeing you've brought the subject up. It is a little galling having to drive over a thousand Ks through the wilderness then get served red wine with seafood. Still...' Murray took a mouthful of the Wolf Blass, 'it's not a bad drop of the old claret all the same.'

'Yes. It's not a bad... claret. Is it?' Tjalkalieri shook his head and smiled at the others.

It didn't take them all that long to polish off the fish — with Murray eating almost the equivalent of a whole barramundi on his own — and then the girls brought out dessert, which wasn't anything special. Wine trifle with homemade rockmelon ice-cream and banana, raspberry and paw-paw custard.

'Hello,' said Murray, 'I've got you this time. There's definitely sweet sherry in the bloody trifle.'

Tjalkalieri tilted his head and held up his hands apologetically. 'Sorry about that, Muzz. But you know how it is. Old habits die hard.'

'That's all right mate. I understand.'

After they'd finished eating, the girls cleared the table and Numidi brought out four freshly made mugs of Vienna coffee. The men sat there sipping and talking for a while till Murray glanced at his watch and eased his chair back from the table.

'Well, it's getting on for half past seven,' he said, getting to his feet and licking some whipped cream off his top lip.

'I might ring Les and tell him what's going on.'

'You know where the phone is,' said Mumbi.

'Yeah. I might give Elaine a ring too.'

Murray clomped down the corridor and did just that, talking to the kids as well and telling them he should be home some time tomorrow. Then he rang his brother in Sydney.

'That you Murray?' said Les when he heard the STD pips.

'Yeah. I'm out at Binjiwunyawunya now. How's things?'

'Good. So you got there. How was the trip?'

'Piece of piss.'

'That's good. Anyway, what'd the boys say? Are they interested?'

41

'Yeah, they're keen.'

'Ahh. Bloody ripper.'

'But they want fifty grand. They reckon your boss can afford it.'

'Fifty! Shit. Oh well, don't matter. Tell them that's sweet.'

'Okay. So what do you want to do?'

'When are you heading back to Dirranbandi? Are you in any hurry to leave?'

Murray glanced towards the kitchen where he knew the huge fridge was jammed with Fourex and four beautiful young girls were cleaning up and probably not doing anything in particular after that. 'Well... you know I don't like to be away from the family for too long. But I suppose I can hang around here a bit longer for you. Why, what's up?'

'Well, I've got to sort out a few things down here tomorrow morning. Can you ring me from there say... two-thirty tomorrow?'

'Sure. No worries. Do you want to speak to the boys yourself?'

'No. I'll more than likely see them out at Boulia on Thursday. And you said they're keen to do it.'

'Yeah. Chafing at the bit.'

'Good. Well I'll let you go Muzz, and I'll hear from you tomorrow.'

'Okay. See you then Les.'

'See you, Muzz. Say hello to the boys for me. Hey! Have they got any sheilas staying there with them?'

'Yeah reckon. Four top little sorts... I mean three.'

'Ahh you lying prick. There's four there. No wonder you don't mind staying there — you cunt.'

'I'll ring you tomorrow Les. See you then mate.'

'Yeah, you bastard. And don't you forget.'

Murray was still laughing when he clomped back into the lounge room where the others were sipping Drambuies.

'And how was your brother?' asked Tjalkalieri after Murray had sat down and picked up the liqueur glass full of Drambuie one of the girls had left for him.

'He's good, Chalky. Said to say hello and all that. He was going to have a yarn to you but he reckons he'll be up here himself on Thursday. I've got to ring him at half past two tomorrow to make sure.'

'Anything else?'

Murray glanced towards the four girls cleaning up in the kitchen and chuckled to himself. 'No. That was about it.'

They sat there comfortably, the four of them, sipping their liqueurs and chatting about the coming events. Suddenly Murray got to his feet saying he'd better go out and feed Grungle, but Nantjinin called that they'd alredy given him a forequarter of lamb from the fridge and a litre of milk. Murray finished his Drambuie, got another Fourex, then sat back down in the lounge while the boys tried to figure out what they were going to do that evening. Get stoned and listen to some music, watch TV or throw a video on. Murray said it didn't worry him what they did as he'd been up since four, and after the long drive, the drinks and all that grouse food he was just about buggered. The boys, not really used to drinking and eating so much early in the week themselves, said that if he was going to have an early night they couldn't see themselves being too far behind him.

The girls had joined them by now, drinking Bacardis and Coke. Someone dropped a movie in the VCR and they all sat there talking and half watching the film. It was a real lemon. Some Australian show called *Bullamakanka*. The only thing remotely amusing in it was some boofheaded-looking bloke running around in a beret chasing after a pig called Matilda.

'Fair dinkum,' said Tajlkalieri, disgust all over his face. 'There ought to be law in this country to stop them from making movies like that. It's lower than the Pakistani basic wage.'

The girls had paired themselves off with the owners of the homestead by now, with Koodja sitting on a cushion on the floor near Murray's feet and looking him up and down every now and again with what seemed a bit more on her mind than whether he'd enjoyed tonight's meal and how his car went on the trip out. Eventually Murray stretched his arms out and let go with a cavernous yawn.

'Well,' he said, rubbing his hands across his face. 'You can stick this movie in your arse. I think I might hit the sack. I'm buggered.'

'Yeah, I don't blame you,' said Yarrawulla. 'This movie'd turn you off a baked dinner.'

'I put your overnight bag in the guest room,' said Numidi. 'Do you want to have a shower or anything first?'

'Yeah. I wouldn't mind to tell you the truth. I've got red bulldust in my hair, my ears, up my bum. And my armpits smell like grandpa's socks.'

'I'll show you how to work the shower,' smiled Koodja.

'Thanks.'

She led him down the corridor to the well-appointed guest room, with its neatly made double bed, brown Aboriginal motif decor and large curtained window overlooking the gardens. She waited while he got a clean T-shirt and a pair of Stubbies out of his overnight bag, then led him back down the corridor to the spacious, tiled bathroom.

'Do you want to have a bath or a shower?' she asked.

'I'll settle for a shower thanks Koodja,' replied Murray. And I wouldn't mind you running the loofah over my back, he thought as he watched her in her almost non-existent shorts reach through the sliding smoked-glass windows of the cubicle and turn the taps on.

'There you go,' she said, running her hands through the steaming jets of water. 'If you need anything — just give me a call,' she added with a sly smile.

'I think I'll be all right thanks,' replied Murray, returning her smile. He watched her as she closed the bathroom door quietly behind her, then dropped his clothes and got under the shower.

There was something about showering in hot mineral water that Murray couldn't quite explain. Even though the water was a little hard it seemed to bubble as it left the nozzle and caress his body like velvet, vitalising his skin and soothing away any aches or bruises from the long, dusty drive. Maybe this is why the boys always look so young, he mused, remembering his wife telling him something about women in the city paying a fortune for tiny atomizers of perfumed spa-water to spray on their faces. He dried off with one of the fluffy white towels folded in a rack, wrapped another one around him and had a shave in the large vanity mirror built around the marble basin. There were several bottles of skin conditioner, deodorant and after-shave sitting neatly to the side. He sprayed some Mennen under his arms and settled for a bit of Monsieur Rochas to splash over his face.

'Well, I certainly feel a lot better after that.' He smiled at the others as he stood in the entranceway to the lounge in his T-shirt and stubbies.

'You look a lot better, too,' laughed Mumbi.

'You don't smell half bad either,' giggled Numidi. 'I can smell you from over here.'

Murray smiled back a little self-consciously. 'Anyway gang, I'm gonna hit the sack. Thanks for the grouse meal girls — and you too fellas. I'll see you in the morning.'

'Goodnight Murray. Sleep tight,' came the chorus from the loungeroom.

Back in the guestroom, Murray felt tired but he also felt a strange kind of freshness from the shower. He switched off the main light and turned on the small fluorescent one behind the bed. There were several copies of *Hooves and Horns* on a small table so he decided to read for a little while before he went to sleep.

He was standing there flicking through a couple with his back to the door when he heard it click open then close again. He turned around slowly to see Koodja standing there in the soft light wearing nothing but a pair of skimpy, pink knickers and a brief, white nightie held up by two tiny bows across her shoulders. The nightie barely covered her bum and appeared to be so delicate that if you looked at it hard it would disintegrate.

'Koodja?' said Murray, blinking up from the magazine. 'What's . . . what'd you want?'

'Oh nothing,' she replied coyly. 'Tjalkalieri told me to look in and make sure our special guest was all right.'

'Oh he did, did he?' Murray had to smile at her little white lie.

'Yes.'

'And did Tjalkalieri tell you I was a happily married man?'

'Yeah. He mentioned something about it.' She shrugged, making the two little bows dance. 'But that's okay. I only came to make sure you were all right.'

'Mmhh.'

Koodja moved to the other side of the bed and climbed in under the covers.

'I thought you said you were tired?' she smiled up at him, patting the space next to her.

Murray put the magazine down and looked at the exquisitely beautiful young girl for a moment. In twelve years of marriage to Elaine, Murray had very rarely strayed from the straight and narrow. He loved his wife and two sons fiercely and would kill anyone who happened to so much as lay a finger on any of them. But here he was, quite weary, a long long way from home, and his senses clouded somewhat from all the wine, beer and liqueur. And after all, he was only human.

Koodja smiled up at him devilishly and ran her tongue slowly across her top lip. Murray drew back the covers and climbed into bed next to her. She immediately slid across to him and wrapped her arms around his neck. Murray ran

45

his hand up over her ribcage and cupped her almost unbelievably firm breast in his hand. He squeezed it gently and the delicate, pink nipple straight away firmed up under the soft massage of his thumb. The next thing he was kissing her and her hot, sweet tongue was darting hungrily, enticingly into his mouth.

'Koodja,' he whispered quietly. 'You're right. I am tired. Real tired.' He kissed her again. 'But I'm not that tired. I don't think I could ever get that bloody tired.'

The following Wednesday morning in Sydney, Les was up at six a.m. He had a run on Bondi, got cleaned up, had breakfast and was in the lounge room on the phone to Price when Warren got out of bed about eight. Price was having breakfast next to his swimming pool when Les told him it was on and he'd be needing that $100,000. Price replied that Sheldon Drewe would need a little bit of time to organise things, but to meet him at Bondi Junction at twelve-thirty. Price sounded a little sceptical over the phone, but he was no doubt still interested to see what Norton's strange plan was all about. They chatted on for a few more minutes with Les hanging up saying he'd fill him in a bit more as things started to progress. The next call was to Eddie Salita, with Norton jotting down a name and address on a pad next to the phone before he hung up.

'You're up and about early this morning,' said Warren, sipping coffee and noticing Norton in a clean pair of jeans and a freshly ironed, button-down collar blue shirt.

'Yeah,' replied Les, stroking his chin as he looked up from the piece of paper in his hand. 'I've got a fair bit on today . . . and the next few days. I might even be away for a few days.'

'Yeah. Where you going?'

'Not far. I just mightn't be here for a few days, that's all.'

Warren stared at Les for a moment while he sipped his coffee. 'Something to do with work?'

'Something like that. But don't worry, I'll be here to cook tea for you tonight.'

Norton winked Warren a goodbye, grabbed his wallet and headed out the front door. As he started the car he checked once more the name and address Eddie had given him over the phone. His first stop would be Kingsford Smith airport.

He had no trouble finding a parking space when he pulled up opposite the flight facilities area twenty-five minutes later.

He crossed the road and walked across to the small parking area outside the main terminal that services Lord Howe and Norfolk Islands. However, instead of going in there he headed for a small doorway a few metres in front and to the left. He stepped through it into a huge hangar with a number of small aircraft parked there, most of them getting some sort of maintenance. Several mechanics in overalls were walking around, others had there heads stuck in the cowlings of the machines they were working on. Through the open end of the hangar Les could see more private aircraft taxiing along the tarmac while dozens of others were parked neatly around the perimeters of that part of the airfield. Rows of office doorways with the names of the various air charter companies faced the end of the hangar, and above them was another row of offices flanked by a narrow walkway with a ricketty-looking wire mesh guardrail. A set of steep wooden stairs led up to these offices and Norton took two at a time. He found what he was looking for at the end of the walkway. A chipped white door with Boomerang Aviation written in faded red letters on the front. Underneath, in smaller letters but just as faded, read Kingsley Sheehan, Proprietor. Norton gave the door a rap with his knuckles and a cheery voice called him in.

Les stepped into a small, bright, if a little untidy office. Manuals, logbooks and various other aviation magazines and books were stacked on shelves around the walls, above which were hung maps of Australia and a few dog-eared posters. A tiny kitchen with a coffee machine ran off to Norton's left and at the far end of the room was a large, glass-topped table next to a tan corduroy lounge and a couple of lounge chairs. Sitting on the lounge, underneath a curtained window with his legs crossed and reading the paper was a round, almost boyish faced man with a neat brown moustache that curled slightly at the end. He was wearing a short, black leather jacket and scarf and perched jauntily on his head was, of all things, a World War Two pilot's peaked leather cap. For a moment Norton thought he was watching a rerun of Gregory Peck in *Twelve O'Clock High*.

'Are you Kingsley Sheehan?'

'That's me boss,' grinned the pilot, getting up from his seat.

Even without the grin Norton could see the pilot was one of those waggish people with a permanent twinkle in their eye. The type that rarely get the shits and love a practical

47

joke. Norton also knew he was a mate of Eddie's from Vietnam, so he had to be close to forty, yet Kingsley Sheehan didn't look much over twenty. Norton returned the pilot's warm handshake and introduced himself as George.

'So what can I do for you, George?' asked Kingsley, offering him a seat. 'You want a coffee?'

Norton shook his head. 'Eddie Salita told me to see you. I need to charter you and your plane for a couple of trips. He recommended you.'

'Eddie sent you, did he?' At the mention of the name Sheehan's grin intensified and his eyes lit up noticeably. 'How is he these days?'

'Good. He said to say g'day to you.'

Kingsley paused for a moment and looked Les up and down. It was obvious from Norton's appearance, and his being sent to him by Eddie Salita, that the job he had in mind wasn't going to be an ice-cream run or a joy trip over the Blue Mountains.

'So. What did you ... have in mind George?'

From the even way the pilot spoke Norton surmised that he didn't give a stuff much what he did; just as long as the price was right.

'All I want you to do, is fly me out to a place near Mt Isa, pick three blokes up and fly them back to Sydney. Then fly them back about four or five days later.'

Sheehan blinked for couple of seconds. 'Is that all?'

'Yeah,' shrugged Norton. 'What'd you expect.'

'Well. Being a mate of Eddie's, I wouldn't have been surprised if you'd have wanted me to napalm a couple of suburbs of Brisbane or something.'

Norton shook his head. 'No, that's all it is. Just pick up three blokes and bring them back to Sydney.'

'Have these blokes broken out of gaol or something. Not that I give a fuck.'

'Turn it up. They're just three old blokes living on a property out there — that's all.'

'Okay.' The pilot still sounded a little surprised and possibly a little sceptical. 'Anyway, where exactly are we going?'

'You know where Boulia is?'

'Yeah. Know it well. Got a big bitumen airstrip there. Piece of piss.'

'Good. Well we're not going there. We're going about a hundred kilometres west of there, where the Yanks built an

48

airstrip during the war, between Lucknow and Chiltern Hills. You know it?'

The pilot nodded his head. 'I've flown over it a few times.'

'Can you land a plane on it?'

'If it's not too rooted I can.'

'It's all right. A mate of mine was out there a few months ago. Said it's okay.'

'Fair enough. I'll take your word for it.'

'All right then, Kingsley.' Norton folded his arms and looked at the boyish pilot for a second. 'How much do you want?'

'Two trips. Four blokes the first time. Three the second.' Sheehan drummed his fingers on the table for a moment as he looked at Norton with one eye closed. 'Nine thousand dollars, all up.'

'Righto,' replied Les without so much as a blink.

It was Kingsley's turn to blink. He'd obviously asked Norton top dollar, but the emotionless way Les accepted the fee made the pilot wish he'd asked for more.

'I want to leave here by about seven tomorrow morning. Is that okay?'

'Sure. No worries.'

'And how long'll the trip take?'

'About seven or eight hours — there and back.'

'Right.' Norton rose from his seat and shook hands with Sheehan once more. 'I'll see you about seven.'

'Okay George. I'll see you then.'

Kingsley walked Les to the door and watched him walk back along the walkway. This is a funny one he thought as he closed the door and went back to his coffee and the paper. Seems almost too good to be true. Then again, knowing bloody Eddie Salita, it probably bloody well is.

That was easy enough thought Les as he drove back towards the city. And he doesn't seem like a bad sort of bloke either. Don't know about the flying cap and scarf, though. And the nine grand. Then I've gotta give Murray ten and they want fifty. Price isn't going to get much change from his hundred grand. Twenty or so minutes later, Les pulled up and parked his car in Regent Street, Redfern, not far from the main shopping centre and the railway station.

He strolled up to Redfern station and sat down beneath a few young gum trees doing their best to add some green to a small, concrete park in Lawson Street. Almost directly opposite was a long brick wall covered in colourful Aboriginal murals — ships from the first fleet, kangaroos, natives holding spears and boomerangs etc. — and behind this, covered in rubble, was Price's block of land. On the Regent Street corner stood the old brick building.

It was dirty, run-down and covered in old posters, mainly for rock bands and venues. Most of the windows were broken and the main one, where the smallgoods factory used to be, was boarded up with palings and sheets of rusty, galvanised iron. The abandoned fish shop looked all sad and forlorn, and across the dust-caked window there was still a crude sign in white poster paint: 'Fresh Mulett Fillets — $4 a kilo'. Les noticed the word 'Mullet' was spelt with only one 'l' and two 't's. Next door along was Percy Kilby's office. The main window was painted over in the Aboriginal flag colours of red, yellow and black and the letters AWEC were written across it in white. Underneath in small letters, also in white, was what it stood for. A solid olive-green door was on the right and even from across the road Les could make out a Bob Marley poster and one for a land rights march either pinned or pasted to it. So this is Kilby's little bolthole is it, he mused.

Norton sat there for a while in the spring sunshine, studying the building and the area in general. Cars cruised along Lawson Street and trains rumbled in and out of the station while a steady stream of commuters and other pedestrians filed past. Before long more pieces of his plan began to fall into place.

Facing the traffic lights at the other end of Lawson Street was an old hotel, the Thames Tavern. It was by no means the Chevron Hilton. Flanked by some second-hand and other ancient clothes shops, the front doors were patterned with dull brown and green tiles built into the old bricks that the owners had obviously tried to tart up with cheap, grey paint. Above the two bars facing the street was an awning daubed with beer company slogans, while above this were two small, brick-balconied verandahs which Norton guessed would be part of the accommodation area. He stared at the old pub for a few more moments, smiled, grunted something to himself, then got up and started walking towards it.

If the Thames Tavern looked grotty outside, the interior was even worse. It was badly lit, with a few black plastic chairs and tables covered in cigarette burns scattered around a pair of badly abused pool-tables. A worn-out looking jukebox was up against one wall and around this were several unkempt patrons, who, although it was nowhere near lunchtime, looked as if they were all well on the way to getting drunk. A tired-looking, horribly made-up blonde barmaid in an old blue cardigan was hovering in front of the beer taps. Norton approached her, a half smile on his craggy face.

'Yeah, what'll you have love?' she whined in a reedy voice that seemed to be piped straight down her nostrils.

'Is the owner or the manager in please?'

'He's down in the cellar. Who'll I say wants him?'

'I wanted to see about some accommodation.'

The barmaid gave Norton a double blink. Clean-shaven, in a freshly ironed shirt, and not smelling of stale booze, he definitely wasn't one of the usual clientele.

'Hold on,' she said politely. 'I'll just go and get him.' She moved to the end of the bar, bent over and screeched down to the cellar. 'Hey Ross. There's someone here wants to see you about a room.' A muffled voice called out something from the cellar. 'Righto,' replied the barmaid. 'He'll be up in a few minutes. He's just changing a keg.'

'Thanks.'

'Do you want a drink while you're waiting?'

Norton screwed his face up slightly at the thought of what it would probably be like. 'Yeah, righto. Give us a middy of lemon squash.'

Oddly enough the squash was beautiful. Not from a machine, plenty of ice and two fresh slices of lemon. Norton downed it in about four swallows and ordered another. He was halfway through it and leaning against the bar when a man came up from the cellar.

'Hello mate,' he said, wiping his hands on the seat of his jeans. 'I'm Ross Bailey, the owner. What can I do for you?'

He was a fairly solid bloke, a little overweight, not a bad style, possibly around thirty, with neat brown hair and a trimmed moustache. From his broken nose and bustling kind of manner, Norton tipped he was either an ex-footballer or policeman.

'My name's, ah... George Dunne,' said Les. 'I need one room for four people, for five days. Maybe a week.'

'One room for four people?'

'Yeah. Myself and three Aborigines.'

The owner narrowed one eye and looked at Les a little sceptically.

'It's all right. They're dancers. I'm with an advertising

agency and we're bringing them down from Queensland to do a TV commercial. We were going to put them up in a motel at Double Bay, but they insisted on staying in Redfern for some reason.'

'Ohh it's lovely round here,' chuckled Ross Bailey. 'I don't blame them. What sort of ad is it?'

Norton looked across the bar to a blown-up photo of Dennis Lillee pinned on the wall. 'Ahh ... World Series Cricket.'

'Australian Aborigines doing a cricket ad?' The owner looked at Les quizzically.

'Yeah. It's a new concept one of our writers thought up. Instead of using West Indians we're using Aborigines. It's just a gimmick.'

'Fair enough,' smiled the owner. 'Sort of, come on Abo come on eh?'

'Hey, you've got it,' grinned Norton. 'Yeah.'

'Well come on up and I'll show you the rooms.'

The owner picked up a set of keys and came round from behind the bar. He led Les past the bottle shop, down a corridor and up a dusty, thinly carpeted set of stairs to the first floor.

'Actually, the room I wanted was one of those with the balconies facing the street,' said Norton, following behind. 'The boys like to see the sun first thing in the morning.'

'Those rooms are double rooms all right,' said the owner. 'But they're already gone mate.'

'Gone?'

'Yeah. Me and my girl have got one. And two old blokes have got the other.'

The owner went to unlock the door to one of the rooms facing the landing.

'How much do you want for a room for the week?' asked Les.

'Well, four of you. Even in the one room I'm still going to have to charge almost the full amount.' The owner thought for a moment, 'Say $200.'

'I'll give you 500 if we can have one of those front rooms.'

'Five hundred dollars?'

'I'll tell you what. I'll make it 750. And don't worry about a receipt.'

The owner quickly shut the door he'd just opened. 'Fuck Barney and Tom,' he said. 'I'll thrown them in 15 for the week. Come on. I'll show you your room.'

Bailey led Les into room number 9. Actually it was three

rooms in one; two bedrooms with two single beds in each, a bathroom and a larger room which led onto the small verandah overlooking Regent Street. The carpet was a bit chatty, like the curtains, but it was fairly bright, there was a laminex table in the middle of the main room and an old, yellow vinyl lounge and two matching chairs. A small colour TV faced this and a mantle radio sat on a shelf on one of the walls. Apart from that it didn't look as if anyone lived there.

'They must travel light, whoever's staying here,' said Norton, opening the frosted glass doors that led onto the verandah.

'Yeah. They're just a couple of old pensioners,' replied the owner. 'They spend most of their money on piss.'

Norton grinned to himself as he stepped out onto the tiny red-tiled balcony. The AWEC offices were barely 200 metres away and if the front window hadn't been painted over you'd have been able to see Kilby in person. What a stroke of luck, thought Norton. The boys'll be able to point the bone at him easy enough from here. Any closer and they'd be able to stick the thing fair up his arse.

'Yeah. This'll be perfect, Ross,' said Norton, stepping back inside and closing the doors behind him. 'Now, what do I owe you? Seven hundred and fifty bucks, right?' The owner shrugged a reply. 'Well here's 250 in advance.' Les fished his wallet out of the back pocket of his jeans. 'I'll give you the rest next week. And like I said. Don't worry about a receipt if you don't want to.'

'Sweet as a nut,' replied Bailey, putting the money in his pocket without bothering to count it. 'When did you want to move in?'

'About lunchtime tomorrow.'

'No worries. I'll have the girl clean it out and run the vacuum cleaner over it for you.' Bailey gave Les the key and they filed back down the stairs, Les telling the owner he'd see him tomorrow.

Well how good's this, thought Norton, giving the old hotel one last look as he strolled back to his car. This is all falling into place easier than pissin' the bed when you're drunk. Whistling happily to himself he got in his car and headed for Bondi Junction.

Norton had paid his phone account, had a coffee, and was sitting in the Oxford Street Mall sipping a carrot and apple juice when he saw Price's Sheldon Drewe approaching, accompanied by Price's accountant, Russell Ticehurst. With their neat short hair, inquisitive clean-shaven faces and steel-rimmed glasses the men could have been brothers. Both were wearing sober but expensively tailored, charcoal-grey suits, the only difference being the stripes in Ticehurst's suit were thicker than Drewe's. They spotted Les, smiled briefly and walked over.

'Hello Les. How are you?' said Sheldon.

'G'day Shell,' replied Norton, getting to his feet.

'You know Russell?'

'Yeah. I met you up the game. How are you Russ?'

'Good thanks Les.'

'Well. Will we go and get this thing sorted out?'

'Yeah, why not? Did you bring the dough with you?'

The lawyer held up a black briefcase he was holding and they proceeded to the bank.

Sheldon made a quick inquiry at the counter and in no time they were ushered into the office of the manager, Mr Bill Sturgess. A tall broad-shouldered man in his early forties, Sturgess used to play Rugby League for Easts too, but a bit before Norton's time. Les recognised him from playing touch football up at Waverley Oval and sometimes down Centennial Park. There were quick handshakes all around and then they got down to business.

Although Norton knew how to get a dollar together quicker than the next bloke, the actual working in dollars and cents bored him absolutely shitless; even having to fill out a tax return once a year nearly drove him round the bend. So he just sat there in the manager's air-conditioned office like a stale bottle of piss while they sorted it all out between them. Terms like negative gearing, short-term interest rates and diversification of liquid assets were bandied about — which Norton let go right over his head — and the next thing he'd signed some papers and had an access account with his name and a whole lot of numbers on it. He took out $25,000 of those numbers in fifties and hundreds and placed them in a thick, black plastic bag he'd brought with him. A few minutes later he was out the front of the bank walking with the others towards the car park behind McDonalds. After a brief goodbye Les got in his old Ford, the others got into Sheldon's new Mercedes, and they went their separate ways.

Les still had about an hour left before Murray would ring, so he fiddled around the house and got a Greek-style lamb stew ready for tea while he was waiting. At bang on two-thirty Murray rang.

'Hello Les?'

'Yeah. How are you Murray?'

'Good mate. You got everything sorted out down there?'

'Yeah. Smooth as silk. I'll tell you what's going on.'

Les explained briefly how he'd chartered the plane and arranged the accommodation for himself and the three others in Redfern. The money was taken care of and all Murray had to do was be out at the old airstrip at ten-thirty the following morning.

'You know how to get out there all right, don't you, Muzz?'

'Yeah, no worries. It's only about two hours from here.'

'You don't mind having to stay out there another night?'

Murray glanced towards the kitchen where Koodja and the other girls had just finished cleaning up after lunch and were now preparing Bavarian chocolate cake for tea plus duck á l'orange from a brace of six Yarrawulla had caught and prepared the day before.

'Ohh no,' he grinned. 'I suppose I can force myself to stay here another night. I just hope Chalky doesn't serve red wine with the poultry this evening — that's all. It's definitely not a go.'

'What was that?' queried Les.

'Nothing. Nothing at all.'

'Yeah? Arseholes. You're up to something out there. Generally I need an elephant to drag you away from Dirranbandi for more than five minutes.'

'Turn it up, you're my brother. Jesus, if I couldn't put myself out for a couple of nights for my family what sort of a bloke would I be?'

'Mmhh.'

'Anyway, everything sounds like it's sweet. So I'll see you tomorrow morning.'

'Yeah, righto.'

Les said to give his regards to the others, then hung up saying he'd see them all on Thursday morning. Murray's definitely up to something up there he thought, smiling at the phone for a moment. He's my brother. I can tell. Oh well, good luck to him, whatever it is.

It wasn't a bad spring afternoon — sunny, quite warm, with a nice light breeze coming from the north-west — so Norton put his banana-chair out in the backyard to lie down and have a bit of a think. There wasn't really all that much to think about and he ended up dozing off. He woke up about five, had a shower, put on a tracksuit and got tea ready.

Warren arrived home and by seven he and Les had finished the stew and were sipping coffee, watching the news on Channel 2 and ripping into a cherry cheesecake Warren had brought home from some exclusive little Swiss cake shop in Woollahra.

'So you're going to have another early night tonight, eh?' said Warren.

'Yeah. I've got to be up by six again tomorrow.'

'Jesus I'd love to know what's going on. You're taking a few days off from work — to do what, you won't say. You're going away somewhere — you won't say where, but it's not far. And you've had this smirk on your dial since Sunday.' Warren shook his head. 'I'd love to know what you're up to you big drop kick.'

Norton laughed at the look on Warren's face. 'Jesus you're a nosy little prick. I'm not up to anything. I'm just showing some old blokes around Sydney. That's all.'

'Yeah, I'll bet.'

'That's all it is. Anyway, I might tell you about it next week — if you're lucky. Now,' Norton smiled and winked at his flatmate, 'anything worth watching on TV tonight?'

There was a Jack Lemmon and Walter Matthau movie on Channel 7. They watched that, plus a bit of Clive Robertson's news, then both hit the sack around eleven. Les was asleep almost the minute his head hit the pillow. He was really looking forward to seeing his brother again, and the three old friends.

For some reason, possibly watching a little too much TV, Les woke up feeling like he could have done with a bit more sleep. But he felt a bit better after he got cleaned up and had a mug of tea, and was out the front door and in his car heading for Mascot by six-thirty. Kingsley Sheehan, pilot extraordinaire, on the other hand was all bright-eyed and bushy tailed when Les walked into his office just before seven a.m. His eyes were sparkling, the old leather flying cap was set at its jaunty angle, even his moustache seemed to bristle like a porcupine on a cold winter's day. He was whistling softly to himself and seated once more beneath the window. He looked up from his cup of coffee and morning paper when Les walked in.

'G'day George,' he smiled. 'How are you mate?'

'Pretty good Kingsley,' replied Les, stifling a yawn. 'It's not a bad day outside.'

'Yeah, it's a beauty. You looking forward to the trip?'

Norton nodded and threw a small overnight bag up on the table, unzipping it almost in the same movement.

'Here you are,' he said, pulling out a wad of money. 'There's $2,500 there. I'll give you some more when we get back and the rest when you fly the boys back. Okay?'

'Sure,' replied Kingsley, catching the money as Les tossed it to him. He gave it a quick count and stuffed it in the inside pocket of his flying jacket. 'Thanks George.'

'No sweat.'

'Well,' Kingsley folded his paper and drained his cup of coffee. 'I suppose we may as well get going eh.'

'Suits me.'

Kingsley stood up, picked up a small leather briefcase, opened the door for Les and closed it behind them without bothering to lock it. Then he followed Les down the steps into the hangar.

'What sort of plane have you got?' asked Les.

'A Beechcraft Super King Air 200.'

With nobody else around their voices seemed to echo slightly in the tinny atmosphere of the hangar.

'Yeah. They any good?'

'Perfect for this type of job. There it is over there. The white one with the green and gold markings.'

As they stepped out of the hangar the noise increased noticeably from the prop and jet wash of the various planes taxiing around and taking off. Gusts of wind sweeping across the tarmac blew dirt and dust in their faces and swirled around their ears, making Kingsley take a firm grip on the peak of his cap. Les followed him across to a sleak aeroplane with twin propellers and a row of seven round windows along the fuselage. The door, with a set of steps built into it, was open. Norton followed Kingsley into the aeroplane and the pilot closed the door behind them and spun the seal.

If the plane was sleek and narrow on the outside, the interior was even more so. There was nowhere near enough room to stand up properly and not enough for you to stretch your arms out on either side. Eight single seats, complete with adjustable lights and little fan nozzles above your head, were squashed up against the windows on the sides. Jesus, a man wouldn't want to be suffering from claustrophobia, thought Les. But it was fairly clean with freshly vacuumed brown carpet stretching from the cabin to a small roped off luggage compartment at the rear.

'Doesn't seem like a bad sort of a bus,' said Les, having a bit of a look around. 'You own it, do you?'

'Yep,' smiled Kingsley. 'This is the pride of the fleet, this one.'

'You got others have you?'

'No, just this one. But it's the pride of the fleet.'

The pilot sat down in the cockpit and placed a set of headphones over the top of his flying cap.

'You want to sit up here?' he said, motioning to the empty seat next to him.

'No, this'll do,' replied Norton, sitting down in the one just behind and across from the pilot. 'There's a bit more room to stretch my legs.'

'Suit yourself.'

Kingsley placed his briefcase on the empty seat next to him, adjusted his headphones and began to fiddle around amongst the myriad of dials, switches, handles and pressure and oil gauges, etc. in front of him. The next thing, the propellor on the left whined then sputtered and hummed into action; the one on the right did the same thing a second or two later. They throbbed and hummed in unison for a few minutes while he let them warm up, then very slowly the aircraft began to move forward. Expecting it to be quite noisy, Norton was somewhat surprised at the quietness inside the cabin and imagined it would be even quieter once they were airborne.

'Sydney Control. This is India-Bravo-Charlie for Mt Isa. Request taxi. Over.' Norton heard a faint crackle beneath the pilot's headphones. 'Five minutes. Roger Sydney Control. Will wait.'

'What was that all about?' asked Norton, starting to take a bit of an interest in proceedings now that they were moving.

'I have to get a clearance for take off. You know — which runway to use and all that.'

'Yeah. And what'd they say?'

'Wait five minutes.'

'Oh.'

The minutes ticked by with the engines throbbing away steadily not far from Norton's window. Kingsley had brought the aircraft to a halt in front of some others on the edge of the tarmac well away from the domestic and international terminals. There was another faint crackle beneath Kingsley's headphones. 'Roger, tower,' replied the pilot and they began to move forward again.

'We off this time are we?' asked Les.

'Like a bride's nightie,' replied Kingsley.

They taxied around the perimeter of the airfield then stopped at the start of a long, empty airstrip. The headphones crackled again, Kingsley muttered 'Roger' or something into the microphone, and moved a lever something like the automatic gearstick on a car. Les was forced back in his seat and they began to gather speed along the runway. The roar from the engines increased dramatically, Les was forced further back into his seat, there was a slight, almost noiseless bump, the sound in the cabin changed and they were off. Kingsley muttered something else into his microphone as he banked the plane in a semi-circle and from out his window Norton could see the ocean disappearing behind them as they winged their way inland.

While they were taking off Norton couldn't help but notice the excited, happy look on the pilot's face and the almost dramatic flourishes of his hands as they moved across the dials and switches and eased the joystick backwards and forwards. It was obvious Kingsley really dug his flying and the leather cap and scarf even seemed to add more effect to the show; plus a pair of copper rimmed, aviator dip-style sunglasses he'd casually slipped on. If Kingsley had screamed 'Messcherschmitts eleven o'clock high' into the mike and let go a burst of machine-gun fire it would not have surprised Les in the least.

'You don't mind this piloting rort, do you, Kingsley old chap,' chuckled Norton.

'Mate, there's nothing like it,' replied the grinning pilot with a quick shake of his head. 'You're up here on your own. No cunt to annoy you. It's the grouse, George.'

'Is that how you met Eddie? When you were flying in Vietnam?'

'Yeah. Actually I met him the second time he was over there.'

'Yeah. Eddie backed up a second time didn't he? With the Yanks or something?'

'That's right.'

'What was the shifty little bludger doing the second time round when he was over there?'

'Didn't Eddie ever tell you?'

'No. Not really.'

'Well if Eddie didn't — I don't suppose I should.'

'Fair enough,' smiled Les.

They continued in silence for a few minutes with Norton gazing out the window at the ground below, watching it change from smoky brown to olive green. Every now and again it would be interspersed with mountain ranges and tiny ribbons and mirrors of silver that were rivers and lakes. Eventually the incessant humming and the rise and fall of the propellers had Norton yawning and feeling quite drowsy.

'Well, if it's all the same to you, Kingsley,' he said, stretching his arms out by his sides. 'I might just close my eyes for five minutes.'

'Go for your life. I'll wake you when we get there.'

Norton eased his head back a little further into the seat behind him, stretched his legs out in front of him as far as he could and yawned once. In no time he was dead to the world.

'Righto George, wake up mate. We're almost there.'

'Huh. What was that?' Norton blinked his eyes open groggily to find the pilot shaking his leg.

'We'll be there in about twenty minutes. Jesus you can sleep George.'

Norton looked blankly at the grinning pilot and checked his watch. He'd been asleep almost three hours. He looked out the window and noticed the landscape had changed sharply from a pleasant brown and green to a harsh, reddish amber, broken now and again by low, cerulean mountain ranges and the flash of the odd bore-water tank or earthen dam. Even from high up you could see the heat shimmering off the plains in the clear blue distance.

'Shit, it sure looks dry down there,' he said.

'Yeah,' agreed Kingsley. 'It's hard to imagine it flooding every year, eh?'

'You got a shithouse in this thing?'

'Just down the back.'

Norton had a leak in the cramped toilet and returned to his seat.

'Listen,' said Kingsley. 'I won't be able to stick around too long when I touch down. There's a storm front moving across between Townsville and Mackay and I want to make sure I beat it back to Sydney. So we'll just have time to pick up your friends and zap straight out again. Okay?'

'Yeah righto,' replied Les, a little disappointed. He was hoping to be able to talk to his brother for a while.

'Anyway, there it is. Just as the Yanks left it.'

Norton glanced out the window at the deserted airstrip

as the Beechcraft began to bank and descend. Murray's Land Rover and the group of people clustered around it waving up at them brought a huge grin to his face.

'Here they are now,' said Murray, his hand over his eyes as he squinted up into the clear blue sky.

'Just on a quarter to eleven,' nodded Tjalkalieri. 'Your brother wasn't far out.'

They got their bags out of the car and watched intently as the plane circled the airstrip a couple of times before it landed in a great cloud of dust, twirling leaves and twigs. It taxied towards them, turned, then stopped with the propellers still ticking over about 100 metres away. The door swung down and a grinning Les came jogging over through the swirling red dust and noise from the prop wash. Kingsley appeared at the bottom of the steps where he waited, watching them while he stretched his legs.

'Hey Muzz. What's doing mate,' yelled Les, grabbing his brother and pumping his hand vigorously.

'G'day bloodnut. How are you goin?' Jesus it's good to see you again.'

Grungle recognised Les and jumped up all over him. Les grabbed him, rolled him over and gave the happily panting dog a couple of hefty whacks in the ribs. 'Hello Grungle. You ugly little bludger. Chalky, Mumbles, Yarra. How are you goin' fellas?' With the grin still plastered across his face, Les shook hands and hugged the three black men in their dark-blue tracksuits who acknowledged his greeting and quickly introduced him to the four young girls smiling fit to burst as they clustered round the Land Rover.

'You're not gonna bloody believe this, Muzz,' said Les, 'but we gotta piss straight off again. Evidently there's a storm front coming and we can't stick around. That's why he's left the propellers still going.'

'Ah, what a bastard,' cursed Murray. 'I wanted to have a bit of a yarn to you.'

'Yeah. Me too.'

'Anyway,' Les turned to the three men. 'If you blokes want to toss your gear on the plane and say goodbye to the girls we'll get going.'

'Righto Les,' said Tjalkalieri.

Tjalkalieri, Mumbi and Yarrawulla took the three girls in a tender embrace, and from underneath the plane Kingsley watched as the girls kissed their men goodbye so passionately you would have thought they were all leaving to go and join the French Foreign Legion for twenty years.

'Pity I'm not going too,' grinned Murray at Koodja, who was wearing a pair of pink Spank running shorts even briefer than the other girls'. 'Then you could kiss me goodbye as well.'

'How about I just kiss you for staying.' Koodja grinned back, threw her arms around Murray's neck and planted a huge, moist kiss fair on his mouth.

'No wonder you didn't mind staying the last couple of nights — you rotten low bastard,' Les glared at his brother.

'Turn it up mate. And not a word to you know who,' Murray added with a wag of his index finger.

Les couldn't help but laugh. 'Anyway, here's a present for you.' He pulled a small plastic bag out from under his shirt and tossed it to his brother. 'Easiest ten grand you ever earned.'

Murray half closed his eyes and shook his head over the sexy young Koodja's. 'Ohh I don't know about that,' he said.

'Anyway, come over and meet the pilot. He's not a bad bloke. He's a mate of Eddie's.'

The boys said a last goodbye to their women, then picked up their overnight bags, plus a larger, black canvas one which Mumbi and Yarrawulla carried between them, and walked across to the aircraft. They gave the pilot a friendly smile and climbed on board.

'Kingsley. This is my brother Murray.'

'G'day Kingsley,' smiled Murray, almost pulverising the pilot's hand. 'Pleased to meet you.'

'Yeah,' winced Kingsley. 'You too Murray.'

'Anyway mate,' said Les. 'I suppose we'd better get cracking.'

'Okay Les.' Murray shook hands with his brother once more. 'Bad luck we couldn't have had a bit of a yarn, eh?'

'Yeah. It sure is. But I'll give you a ring over the weekend and tell you how everything's going.'

'Okay Les. See you then mate.'

'See you Muzz. Don't forget to say hello to Elaine and the kids for me.' Norton climbed the steps and disappeared into the aircraft.

The pilot looked up at the doorway for a moment, then back at Murray, 'Les eh? That's funny. I thought his name was George.' He shook his head at the blank look on Murray's face. 'This is all very Frederick bloody Forsyth isn't it?' He

shook his head again before he too climbed up the steps.
'I'll see you again Murray.'

'Yeah righto Kingsley. See you mate.'

Murray jogged back to the four girls and they all stood
there waving as the Beechcraft taxied back to the other end
of the runway, turned and idled for a moment before it sped
back along the tarmac and roared off into the shimmering
outback sky. The girls kept waving till it disappeared from
sight, then they all bundled into the Land Rover and drove
off.

About two or three minutes later, as they were bouncing
along the almost non existent dirt road back to Binjiwunyawunya, Murray turned to Koodja sitting alongside him.

'Hey, Koodja.'

'Yes,' she smiled.

'Who's bloody Frederick Forsyth?'

Koodja looked at him blankly and shrugged her shoulders.

'Isn't that the bloke that owns the hardware store out at
Winton,' chimed in Mammanduru from the back seat.

'No. You're thinking of old Fred Foster the butcher,' said
Numidi.

'Oh well. Buggered if I know,' said Mammanduru.

They continued on in silence.

Inside the plane, Les gave the pilot a quick introduction to
the boys, telling them briefly his name was Kingsley. He
didn't bother to introduce them individually, figuring he'd
never remember their proper Aboriginal names and their
nicknames were just a personal thing between them and the
Nortons; to introduce them to an outsider as Chalky, Mumbles
and Yarra would only be demeaning. Although he was smiling
and acting quite blasé about it all, Kingsley was none the
less quite mystified as to what was going on around him.
It wasn't every day he flew out to the middle of nowhere
to pick up three of the strangest looking Aborigines he'd ever
seen in his life, especially with those almost hypnotic electric-
blue eyes. Even now he could still feel the way they seemed
to bore into him as he walked past them to get to the cockpit.
And what about those four young spunks standing next to
that Murray bloke's car? They were gorgeous. They looked
like their daughters, but the way they kissed them goodbye
there was no way they could have been. Then George, or
Les, or whatever the big red-headed bloke's name was, was
recommended to him by Eddie Salita. That was enough to

set the alarm bells ringing in itself. But nothing illegal seemed to be going on and the money was there all right, in cash. It was just a bit odd, that was all. But they could have anything in that big, black canvas bag. Kingsley smiled to himself, kept his thoughts the same way, and flew on.

'What's in the bag anyway?' asked Les, motioning towards the compartment at the rear with his thumb.

'We'll show you in Sydney,' replied Tjalkalieri, shifting his bright blue eyes towards the pilot.

'Fair enough,' nodded Norton.

'Anyway bloodnut,' grinned Yarrawulla, giving Les a slap on the thigh. 'How have you been the last few years? You're certainly looking well. How's Sydney been treating you? We've heard a few stories.'

'Ohh shit!' Norton tossed back his head and laughed. 'Where do I bloody-well start?'

The rest of the return journey was spent swapping yarns and reminiscing, going right back to when Les was just a snotty-nosed schoolboy going to Dirranbandi Public School... and beyond that to when they first met Les's father before he got married. They were so engrossed in laughter and conversation, with that and a Northwest tailwind they were circling Mascot aerodrome before they knew it. Less than four hours after they'd taken off they were on the ground walking towards the hangar and Kingsley's office.

'Just wait here for a sec,' said Les, when they were in the hangar. 'I'm just going to duck up and settle with the pilot.'

Kingsley smiled a goodbye to the boys, adding he was pleased to have met them, and Les followed him up to his office.

'There you are Biggles. There's another two grand.' Norton handed Kingsley another wad of money. 'The boys'll give you the rest when they get off the plane next week. All right?'

'No worries mate,' smiled Kingsley, 'You're welcome to do business with me again any time you want. When do you reckon they'll be wanting to go back?'

'Probably next Thursday. Maybe Wednesday.'

'Good as gold. I'll be here.'

'Okay. Well I'll probably see you then Kingsley.'

'Righto. See you then... George. Or whatever it is.'

Norton paused by the door and smiled evenly at the pilot. 'George'll do. I like it. It's a good honest-sounding name, don't you think?'

'Call me what you like but don't call me late for breakfast eh?'

'Yeah. Something like that.'

'Righto boys,' said Norton, back down in the hangar. 'Let's hit the toe for Redfern?'

He carefully picked up the black canvas bag and they strolled out to where he'd left his old Ford. The next thing they'd joined the afternoon traffic along South Dowling Street and were heading for the Thames Tavern.

Ross Bailey wasn't around when Les and the boys walked into the foyer, so they went straight up the stairs. Les opened the door to number 9 and showed it to the boys who were already starting to exchange very disdainful looks amongst themselves.

'Jesus, what a fuckin' dump,' said Tjalkalieri, gazing scornfully around the main room after Les had closed the door behind them. 'Is this where we're staying? It looks more like the shithouse in a Turkish prison.'

'I don't reckon it's that bad,' replied Les, walking towards the verandah. 'You've got a top view.'

'Yeah. On a clear day you can see right across the room.'

'Hey, you seen the size of these bedrooms,' called out Mumbi. 'There's two mice in here and they're both hunchbacks.'

'You are kidding, Les?' added Yarrawulla. 'If this place was any smaller you'd have to go out in the hallway to change your mind.'

'All right,' said Les, opening the door to the balcony. 'I agree, it ain't the Waldorf Astoria. But for fifty grand for five days work I'm entitled to throw you all in a Valiant station wagon underneath a bridge with a couple of flagons of plonk.'

'That could be worse than this?' said Mumbi.

'Anyway come out here. I want to show you something.'

They followed Les out onto the balcony for their first glimpse of the view across Redfern, which after the peaceful beauty of Binjiwunyawunya looked like hell on earth with its smog, pollution, fumes and noise from the trains and traffic thundering and roaring past.

'Yeah, it's real nice, Les,' said Tjalkalieri. 'Has that pilot bloke refueled yet. If we hurry we might be able to get the four-fifteen back to Boulia.'

'Hold on a second, Chalky,' said Norton. 'Before you go

getting your bowels in a knot, just let me show you something.'

Les pointed out the block of land in question and the old building with the AWEC office. He told them exactly what was going on between Price and Kilby and explained why he'd chosen that particular hotel, even if it was a bit on the grotty side.

'A bit on the grotty side,' said Yarrawulla, his blue eyes flashing. 'That's like describing the Battle of Stalingrad as being a bit noisy.'

'Yeah okay, Yarra. But remember, you're only going to be here a few days, and Kilby's only just across the road. Mate, it's perfect. You'll be able to knock him off like shit from here.'

'Fair enough I suppose,' muttered Tjalkalieri, a little reluctantly. 'Jesus, the things a man has to put up with just to try and earn a quid. Come on, let's go back inside. The air out here's that thick you don't breathe it, you eat it with a knife and fork.'

They trooped back inside and Norton closed the door behind them.

'Well when do you want to start work?' he asked.

'Ah we'll probably start getting things organised now,' said Tjalkalieri. 'Then start chanting first thing tomorrow. Maybe tonight. The sooner we get this over and get out of this shithouse the better.'

'What are you going to do?' asked Mumbi. 'You sticking around or are you gonna piss off?'

'No, I'm here for as long as you are Mumbles,' replied Les. 'Anything you want, just tell me. Food, drink, whatever. Just tell me and I'll go and get it. I'm also hanging about to make sure nothing happens to any of you.'

'Thanks Les,' said Yarrawulla. 'You're a regular bloody Mother Theresa.'

The boys had a quick discussion amongst themselves as to their sleeping arrangements. Yarrawulla and Mumbles would go in one room, Les and Tjalkalieri in the other. They'd start getting things together straight away and more than likely start the chant that night, taking it in four hour shifts. They left the black canvas bag in the middle of the room and started unpacking the few clothes they'd brought with them, hanging them up on some wire coat-hangers in the cheap plywood wardrobes. Les said his stuff was still in the boot of his car, which he'd parked at the rear of the hotel. He trotted down and got it and was back in a few minutes. When he returned the three others were sitting on the old vinyl lounge, in front of the blank TV set, not saying anything but with odd half smiles on their faces. Les twigged something was going on so he tossed his overnight bag through the open door of the bedroom and returned their stares.

'What's . . . going on?' he asked, a little suspiciously.

'Les. We just remembered. There was something we forgot to tell you,' said Tjalkalieri.

'Yeah. What's that?'

'Well. To make this thing work we've got to have something belonging to Percy Kilby.'

'You mean, like an article of clothing or something?'

'No. Something from him. Of him. Like a few drops of sweat or some saliva.'

'A few drops of his blood is what we really need,' said Yarrawulla.

'Blood? How the hell am I gonna get some of Kilby's blood?'

'We don't know,' said Tjalkalieri quietly. 'But if you want this thing to work properly — you'll have to get some.'

'Now you tell me. Shit! This is going to be nice.'

Norton jammed his thumbs in the pockets of his jeans and began to pace moodily around the room, while the others continued to study him intently from the lounge, looks of slight amusement on their faces. Norton knew there had to be a snag sooner or later. And now here it was. Go up and get some blood from this bloke, just like you're asking him for a light or what time it is. But Norton was half expecting problems. Things were all falling into place too smoothly, almost too good to be true. Jaws clenched firmly he paced around a minute or two longer, then turned to face the others, angrily snorting a burst of air out through his nostrils.

'Fair dinkum, you're making it hard. The only way I can see of doing it, is to go up and belt him in the nose and mop it up with a hanky or something. The only trouble is, it could fall back on Price. And if he gives a description of who hit him and he kicks the bucket not long after, it could all fall back on me.' Les looked at the others and shrugged his shoulders. 'But what else am I going to do? I can't just walk over there and cut his throat.'

'That method's no good anyway,' said Tjalkalieri, slowly shaking his head.

'No good. Why not?'

'It has to be done unsuspectingly. It works better if the victim doesn't know he's being pointed. That bit of violence could break the spell and Kilby could realise something is going on. It might not stop us getting to him, but it would certainly make it a lot harder.'

'Shit!' cursed Norton again. 'Shit! The next thing you'll be telling me not to come back unless his blood's RH negative or something.'

'We don't really give a stuff if it's strawberry malted,' chuckled Mumbi. 'Just as long as you get us a few drops.'

Norton let out an exasperated sigh. 'I guess I'm just going to have to work some bloody thing out I suppose.' He stared despondently at the three others for a few seconds as he picked at his chin. 'There's a phone down in the foyer. I'm just going to duck down and ring someone up. I'll be back in a few minutes.'

Groping around in his pockets for some twenty and ten cent coins, Les jogged down the thinly carpeted stairs and found a phone not far from the front door.

'Hello Lyndy. It's Les. Is Eddie there?'

'Oh hello Les,' came the pleasant voice at the other end. 'He's out in the garden mucking around with his roses. I'll go and get him. How are you Les, anyway?'

'Good thanks Lyndy.'

A minute or so later Eddie's happy, and at the same time excited, voice came on the phone. It was obvious he was more than interested in how things were going.

'G'day Les. How are you mate? I heard you got your mates down from Bindi ... where ever it is. How's it all going? Everything sweet?'

'That's what I'm ringing about Eddie. I need some advice.'

Les still didn't explain fully what was going on for the time being, but he told Eddie how he needed to get a sample of Percy Kilby's blood. He didn't say why; Eddie could try and guess a reason if he wanted to. But he promised he'd fill him in on everything before much longer. The wiry little hit man thought for a few seconds before answering.

'I was just thinking. We had a situation like this once back in Nui-Dat. We had to get a positive ID on an ARVN colonel who we suspected was a VC regular. And we had to do a blood test without him knowing it. I'll tell you what to do. What sort of watchband have you got?'

Norton absently hooked his index finger under his watchband and gave it a flick. 'One of those stretch, stainless-steel ones. You know, metal-flex or whatever you call them.'

'Perfect. Can you get hold of a small file?'

68

'Yeah. I've got one of those three-cornered ones in the boot of the car.'

'Right. Well I'll tell you what you've got to do.'

With the phone glued to his ear, Norton listened intently to Eddie while a smile formed on his face which didn't take long to turn into a huge grin. Eventually he knew everything he needed and hung up, thanking Eddie and promising once more he'd keep him informed of developments. Five minutes later Norton was sitting in a chair in front of the others, his watch in one hand, and filing away at the edges of the watchband with the other. He wasn't saying anything, just sitting there filing away, a look of amused determination on his face.

'Just what the hell are you up to?' asked Yarrawulla.

'Mind your own bloody business,' replied Norton. 'You've got your ancient secrets. I've got mine.'

'Fair enough,' chuckled Tjalkalieri, who with the others kept staring at Les with fascinated amusement.

After a while Norton stopped his filing, ran his finger along the edge of the watchband and gave a grunt of satisfaction. 'That ought to do,' he said with a nod of his head. Then he slipped his watch back on; only instead of slipping it back on to his left hand, as was customary, he slid it onto his right. With the others still silently watching him, he unzipped his overnight bag and pulled out one of the bundles of money, peeling off $250 which he stuffed into the front pocket of his jeans.

'There's about ten grand in that bag,' said Norton, zipping it back up. 'If you guys want any just help yourselves. And your fifty's there any time you want it.'

'That's okay Les,' smiled Tjalkalieri. 'We've got some money. You can pay us when we finish the job.'

'Okay, suit yourself. Anyway,' Norton started to tidy himself up as he stood there facing the others, 'I'm off to see your mate Kilby and try and get your blood for you.'

'You're going over now?' said Mumbi.

'Like Chalky said, Mumbles. The sooner you get this done the sooner we can all get out of this shithouse. See you when I get back.' Norton closed the door behind him and once more jogged down the dusty stairs to the foyer and out the front door.

The big Queenslander was expecting the interior of the AWEC office to be pretty much like the dilapidated building it was housed in. But inside it wasn't all that bad. Bright and reasonably tidy, the front door faced a solid wooden desk with a covered electric typewriter sitting on it in front of a swivel chair and a number of metal filing cabinets. These in turn faced an inexpensive brown cotton ottoman with a small magazine-strewn coffee table in front of it. Several leafy pot plants were propped up in the corners and several posters — land rights, anti-apartheid, plus a framed one of Malcom X — adorned the walls. To the right of the desk was another door with PRIVATE KEEP OUT written on it, and sitting on the edge of the desk was a tall, rangy Aboriginal man sporting a fresh crewcut, grey tracksuit pants and a matching sweatshirt. Going by the scar tissue around his eyes and a nose even more flattened than usual, Norton couldn't picture him as being Percy Kilby and tipped him to be either an ex-boxer or a footballer. And probably one of AWEC's thugs. The man on the desk glanced up from the *Greyhound Recorder* he was reading and gave Norton a quick once up and down.

'Yeah?' he said expressionlessly.

'Oh hello,' said Les, politely and clearly. 'I was hoping to see Mr Kilby. Is he in by any chance?'

'Mr Kilby's busy at the moment,' was the dull reply. 'You want to leave a message?'

'Oh! Oh, well yes, all right' said Norton hesitantly and with exaggerated politeness. 'My name is ... Vernon Stroud. I'm with the ah ... Chartered Accountants Against Apartheid. I was hoping to give Mr Kilby a donation on behalf of myself and my colleagues.'

'Ohh yeahhh.' The tallish Aboriginal swung his legs off the desk and switched on half an oily smile. He'd seen all this before. As far as he was concerned Les was just another trendy white do-gooder wanting to hop on the anti-apartheid bandwagon. So they'd slip some poor dumb Abo a few bucks, then tell all the other trendies back at the office or wherever that even though they were white they were dead-set against apartheid and weren't they wonderful, caring people and not at all racist. Until a family of Aborigines bought or rented a house in their street, then they'd raise hell with the local council to try and get them kicked out. But a hypocrite's money was no different from anyone else's as far as the thug from AWEC was concerned.

'Well like I said,' purred the man on the desk. 'Mr Kilby's a little busy at the moment. But if you ah ... want to leave the money with me that's okay. I can give you a ... ah, receipt for it.'

'Oh dear,' replied Norton quietly. 'That's a shame. I'll have to come back, because I wanted to give it to him personally. I've heard so much about him. Oh well, it doesn't matter.' He began to make a slow but nervous gesture for the door.

'Hey hold on a minute. He might've finished what's he doing. I'll give him a call.' He reached across the desk and hit a button on the intercom. 'Hey Perce.'

'Yeah?' was the scratchy reply.

'There's a bloke here wants to make a donation — in our fight against the regime in South Africa.'

Norton couldn't help but notice the cynicism in his voice at the last statement.

'How much,' scratched back over the intercom.

'How much did you want to donate boss?' smiled the man on the desk.

'Two hundred and fifty dollars. Is that all right?' replied Norton.

'Two-fifty Perce.'

There was a pause for a second. 'Send him straight in.'

'You can go straight in mate.'

The tall Aborigine clicked off the intercom, opened the door behind him, and ushered Les into the other office.

Kilby's office was roughly the same size as the first one, and with roughly the same furnishings. An almost identical ottoman with a coffee table about the same size as the other, the same kind of desk, only minus a typewriter, and the same number of metal filing cabinets. More pot plants filled the corners and a similar number and style of posters hung on the walls — the framed one this time being of Martin Luther King. An Aboriginal land rights flag, red and black with the yellow sun in the middle, almost covered one wall and a stack of cartons with a canvas tarpaulin draped over them almost took up another. Seated behind the desk, on a rather plush looking leather chair, was Percy Kilby.

In his early forties, with neat dark hair going grey around the temples, he was fairly stocky but nowhere near as tall as the other man. Like his mate, he too had a broken nose and scar tissue over his eyes, but not to the same extent. His one outstanding feature, however, was his eyes. Sinister and piercing, they seemed to dart everywhere at once and there was a noticeable hardness glowing from within. Relaxed in his chair, his hands across his chest, fingertips pushed together, Kilby was wearing a pair of brown trousers and a matching collarless beige shirt. He smiled thinly when Les walked in but didn't bother to get up and didn't bother to offer his hand.

'So,' he said evenly. 'You wish to make a donation to our movement, Mr...?'

'Stroud,' replied Norton, still acting nervously. 'Vernon Stroud. I represent the Chartered Accountants Against Apartheid.'

'That's... real nice of you Mr Stroud. Frank, will you get me the donations receipt book.'

'Sure,' replied the taller man. As he moved towards the door he pushed a swivel chair on castors across to Norton with his foot. Norton thanked him quietly and sat down. Frank was back in a few seconds with a dog-eared receipt book which he placed on the desk in front of Kilby.

'Now,' said Kilby, picking up a biro. 'How much did you wish to donate Mr Stroud?'

'Two hundred and fifty dollars for the time being,' replied Norton, pulling the money out of his jeans and placing it on the desk. 'We should be able to give your people some more at a later date.'

'Extremely decent of you Mr Stroud. I'll just make this out to the CAAA. That should be all right eh?'

'That'll be fine,' smiled Les.

Kilby scribbled something almost unintelligible in the receipt book, ripped off the docket which he handed to Les and dropped the $250 into a draw of the desk at the same time. 'There you are Mr Stroud.' He winked. 'If only there were more people in the world like you — what a wonderful world it would be.'

'Why thank you Mr Kilby,' beamed Les. 'That's one of the nicest compliments I've ever had. I can't wait to tell them back at the office.' Norton was all sweetness and light, but underneath he felt like throwing up all over Kilby's polished wooden desk.

Now that they'd got Norton's, alias Stroud's, money, there was a sudden silence in the room that thick you could have cut it with a knife. Kilby and his stooge Frank exchanged surreptitious looks and may as well have had a sign above them saying 'Okay Stroud, we've got your money. Now how about doing us a favour and pissing off.' After a second or two Les could just about read their minds and figured it was time for him to make his final move.

'Well Mr Kilby,' he said, getting to his feet and throwing in a bit of a staged cough. 'Your assistant said you were quite busy so I guess I'd better get going.' Kilby half smiled an acknowledgement: it was the least he could do for $250. 'Anyway I must say it's been an absolute pleasure meeting you.'

Norton smiled and offered Kilby his hand. As the AWEC leader begrudgingly extended his across the desk, Norton clumsily knocked the swivel chair with his foot and made an awkward shuffle forward, spearing the underside of his right wrist over Kilby's right hand. The sharpened edges of Norton's watchband scraped across the bony top of Kilby's right hand just behind the knuckles. Not enough to do any real damage but enough to break the skin and make it bleed.

'Ow, shit!' cursed Kilby, holding his hand in front of him and staring at the thin trickle of blood.

'Oh dear me. What have I done?' cried Norton in mock horror. 'Here, let me have a look at that.'

'No it's all right. It's only a scratch.'

Before Kilby could say another word Norton had taken hold of his hand, whipped a white handkerchief out of the back of his jeans, and was mopping furiously at the slight bleeding. 'Oh God I am sorry,' said Norton, continuing to dab away with his hanky. 'My watchband must have done it. Dear or dear I feel such a fool. I am sorry.'

Les managed to wipe off a bit more blood before Kilby snatched his hand away.

'Don't worry about it,' he said thinly. 'It's only a scratch.'

Norton stood there looking all stupid and apologetic as Kilby and Frank both scowled at him. 'I think I'd better get going,' he flustered. 'I've made a complete fool of myself.'

Nobody said anything but Frank opened the door and stared blankly at Norton. Les muttered a quick goodbye and shuffled out. Then, trying not to burst out laughing, he started strolling briskly back up Lawson Street.

'Christ, what a fuckin' goose,' said Kilby, licking at his hand as Frank closed the office door. 'Where did you bloody well find him?'

'He just walked in off the street,' shrugged Frank. 'I never seen the dill before in my life.'

'What'd the flip call himself? The Chartered Bumsuckers Against Apartheid or something,' sneered Kilby contemptuously. He took Norton's $250 back out of the draw and dropped it on the desk. 'At least his money's all right. Cash too.' Kilby looked at the money and gave a chuckle. 'What do you reckon we ought to do with it?'

Frank reached underneath his sweatshirt and pulled out his copy of the *Greyhound Recorder*. 'Ronnie Sprod's got that dog going down at Dapto tonight. Rocket Johnny. Reckons it's a moral, and he owes us a favour. It'll be 6–1, too.'

'Righto.' Kilby slid some of the money across the desk. 'There's $200. Duck over the TAB and throw it on. We'll have a feed and a drink with the rest.'

'Beauty,' said Frank picking up the money.

'Hey, you got a Band-Aid out in the office?' said Kilby, giving the back of his hand another lick.

'Yeah, there's a packet in the draw. How is it?'

'It's only a scratch. More annoying than anything else.' Kilby looked up at Frank and chuckled. 'I don't think it'll kill me.'

Les Norton had a look on his face like a cat that had just drunk a gallon of King Island double cream when he walked back into room number 9 at the Thames Tavern. He'd only been gone around half an hour, and Tjalkalieri, Mumbi and Yarrawulla were still sitting on the lounge just as he'd left them.

'Well, well, well,' he smiled smugly. 'If it isn't Huey, Dewey and Louie, waiting for Unca' Donald to come back from the lolly shop. What's doing nephews?'

With the hint of a smile flickering round their electric-blue eyes, the three men continued to stare at Les for a few moments. They didn't say anything, but from the smug grin on Les's face they guessed he'd pulled something off. Finally Tjalkalieri spoke.

'Not much is doing at all Les. What about you? I'd say from the look on your big boofhead you've been up to something and you're breaking your neck to tell us.'

'Yeah, what have you done in the last half-hour?' asked Mumbi. 'Did someone show you how to add up to twenty-one without having to take your pants off?'

Norton nodded his head and continued to smile complacently. 'Cheeky little bunch of cunts, aren't you? Well have a go at this.' He pulled the hanky out of the front pocket of his jeans, opened it up to show the drops and smears of blood, then dropped it in Tjalkalieri's lap. 'What do you think of that?' he said, folding his arms across his chest.

Tjalkalieri snatched it up and the expression on his and the other men's faces changed immediately. They said something quickly to each other in their native tongue, then turned to Les.

'This is a blackman's blood,' said Tjalkalieri seriously, still holding the hanky.

'That's right,' winked Norton.

'Kilby's?'

'Right again.'

'How did you manage it so quickly?' Now it was their turn to be somewhat admonished.

'I don't think I ought to tell you,' said Norton cheekily.

'Suit yourself. Don't tell us,' shrugged Yarrawulla. 'And we won't tell you what we've got in the bag.' He nodded to the black canvas carryall still sitting in the centre of the room.

Norton grinned and dragged a chair over in front of the others. 'Wait till you hear this,' he said as he sat himself down. 'It'll crack you up.'

Les told them everything he'd said and done from the moment he rang Eddie to when he walked out of the AWEC office. When he'd finished the others were openly laughing amongst themselves — but they were also visibly impressed.

'Well I've got to hand it to you,' said Yarrawulla. 'That was terrific. And this.' He ran his fingers lightly along one edge of the blood-smeared hanky. 'With the fresh blood on it. You've got no idea what this means. It's perfect.'

'I wouldn't mind meeting this Eddie Salita fellow too,' said Mumbi.

'I'm certain Eddie'd like to meet you blokes as well,' chuckled Norton.

The three men suddenly went into a spirited conversation between themselves, in their native tongue again, grabbing at the hanky and pointing and looking towards the balcony every now and again as they spoke. Then just as suddenly as they started, they stopped and once again all three stared at Norton. This time their mood had changed into deadly seriousness.

'Les,' said Tjalkalieri. 'What time will Kilby be in his office till tonight. Did he say?'

'I don't know,' shrugged Norton. 'I didn't ask. It's nearly half past four. I suppose they'd be getting ready to go home now.'

'Do you think you could use that phone in the foyer again and find out.'

'Sure,' shrugged Norton again. 'Why?'

'We're thinking of getting a beam going right now. While we've got this fresh blood and he's so close. It's too good a chance to miss. We could make the spell that strong, nothing could break it.'

'Righto. I'll duck straight down and ring up.'

Fishing around in his pockets for more change, Norton trotted down to the yellow phone in the foyer.

I suppose they'd be in the Yellow Pages thought Norton as he picked up the heavy phone book. But what would it be under? I'll try the White Pages first. He put the first book down and was about to try the other when he had to smile. Tucked into a corner of the small glass-framed list of advertisers above the phone was a white business card. Superimposed on the red, yellow and black Aboriginal flag was Aboriginal Welfare and Entitlement Council. Percy Kilby, Secretary, was in one corner and the phone number was in the other. Well that figures, thought Les. It's only a hop, step and a jump across the road. They'd have to come in here for a drink now and again. Still smiling, he dropped the coins in the slot and pressed the buttons. It wasn't long before a gruff voice came on the other end which he recognised as Frank's.

'Hello. Aboriginal Welfare Council.'

'Yes, it's Mid-City courier service here. We have a parcel to go out to your office. Could you tell us what time you close tonight please?'

'Hold on.'

Frank put the phone down in the front room and walked into Kilby's office.

'Perce. There's a courier service on the phone wants to know what time we're leaving here tonight.'

Kilby's shifty brown eyes darted across to the tarpaulin-covered cartons stacked up against the wall.

'Knobby Jones's coming over to have a look at some of those hot VCRs at five-thirty. I suppose we'll be here till six.'

'Righto.' Frank went back into the front room and picked up the phone. 'We'll be here till six.'

'Thank you.'

Norton hung up, then took the stairs two at a time.

'They'll be there till six o'clock.'

Tjalkalieri took a quick glance at his watch. 'That gives us just on an hour and a half.' He clapped his hands together quickly and looked at the others. 'Right. Let's go.'

As one the boys jumped up off the lounge, Mumbi and Yarrawulla went into their bedroom while Tjalkalieri began to unzip the canvas carryall.

'What happens now?' asked Norton.

'Now? Now we start to earn our fifty grand. We start taking away Percy Kilby's Kurinata.'

'His what?'

'His Kurinata. His life essence. You wanted to know what was in the bag. Well grab a seat, keep out of the road and I'll show you.'

Norton moved a seat closer to the wall and eased himself down to watch as Tjalkalieri began to unpack the bag.

The first things he pulled out looked like three wooden shields, painted in a criss-cross diamond pattern in red, brown, yellow and white ochre. Some of the diamonds were coloured in, others were outlined with lines of dots, giving it an almost glowing effect. He positioned the shields around the room, but at an angle so they all faced the balcony.

'What are they?' asked Norton.

'Tjuringa boards,' replied Tjalkalieri, returning to the bag. 'Sort of shields. They help to protect us from the power of the bone.'

Next to come out of the bag were two small animal-skin sacks full of fine red sand and tied at the top like a schoolkid's marble bag. Tjalkalieri measured out a dozen handfuls which he placed around the room in the shape of a half diamond, the point facing away from the balcony.

'What's that? Just plain sand?'

'It's desert sand from right out in Central Australia, where the Pitjanjatjara tribe used to live. Sacred ground.' Tjalkalieri turned to Norton with a calm but sinister smile as he took the last fistful of sand and let it run slowly through his hand onto the floor. 'A man's life goes like the sand, Les. Sometimes fast. Sometimes slow. But when a man is pointed — that's the end of him.' Tjalkalieri opened his hand and let the sand run through.

A slight shiver ran up Norton's spine at the odd look on the blue-eyed Aborigine's face and the quiet yet deadly serious tone of his voice. It then occurred to him just what he was dealing with, and what he'd so far taken so lightly. These three men were going to kill another man by mental telepathy. Percy Kilby was going to be slowly murdered and not even know what was happening. Murder over a distance by thought transference. No weapon, no evidence, no motive. And no trace of the killers. The perfect crime. Norton stared at Tjalkalieri in awe as he bent back over the bag. And white people demeaned and patronised the full-blooded Australian desert Aborigine. Looking on them as nothing more than ignorant, dirty savages. Almost encouraging them to drink cheap booze and sniff petrol, then stand back and laugh as they died and their culture going back hundreds of thousands of years — a culture so breathtakingly beautiful, yet so simple it's almost an enigma — is plundered and destroyed. What an unbelievable paradox. On the one hand they were simple, aimless natives, running around in the desert not far removed from the Stone Age. On the other hand their minds were thousands of years, light years, in front of the white man's. To have the ability to kill someone by mental telepathy. Another chill ran up Norton's spine and he felt as if the room had suddenly turned several degrees cooler.

Tjalkalieri dipped into the bag again and brought out two shapeless objects wrapped in a sheet of white cloth. When he opened it up they looked like a pair of fluffy housewife's slippers, only in a dusty discoloured beige.

'I know what they are,' said Norton. 'I've seen photos. They're Kurdaitcha bouts.'

'That's right Les.'

'They're funny looking things. What do you make them out of?'

Tjalkalieri carefully ran his hands over the boots as he slowly and easily placed them on the floor. 'Emu and cockatoo feathers. The real downy and fluffy ones, held together by human blood. The rest is made from kangaroo and euroglider fur.'

'Human blood?'

'That's right Les.'

Tjalkalieri then went back to the bag and just as carefully brought out another object, also wrapped in white cloth, which he tenderly placed on the floor next to the boots. 'This is it, Les,' he smiled. 'This is the big one. This is the bone.'

Painstakingly he unwrapped it and laid it out on the sheet of cotton. It was slender and white, about twenty centimetres long and made from the forearm of a dead woman. It was ground to a point at one end and at the other was a blob of a black resinous substance something like pitch. Attached to the bone with more of the tarry substance was a length of firmly plaited, light brown chord, about half as long again as the bone. The fragile little object, if somewhat macabre,

appeared innocent enough, but there was a definite and eso-
teric aura radiating from it — an aura that defied description
and explanation.

'So that's it eh?' said Norton, more than a little awestruck.
'The dreaded bone.'

'Yeah,' replied Tjalkalieri, crouched on his haunches looking down on it. 'That's it all right.'

Norton couldn't help himself. He had to get up and walk
over for a closer look. 'What's all that black stuff?' he said,
pointing to the end. 'It looks like tar.'

'It's a sort of glue. You make it out of spinifex bushes.
You beat them with a stick, burn them, then blow away the
ashes and collect the residue. When it cools off it goes as
hard as pitch.'

'Yeah,' said Norton slowly, now more curious than ever.
'And what's that bit of rope, or whatever it is, made out
of?'

'Human hair.'

'Human hair?' Norton had to think for a moment as he
studied it. 'But it's a sort of brown colour. All you people
have got black hair. C'ept for the kids. They've got sort of
tawny hair.'

Tjalkalieri smiled and gave Norton a wink. 'Let's just say
it's a bit of sneak go. Mother-in-law's hair.'

'Oh.' Norton shrugged and continued to stare, fascinated,
at the weird object.

A movement to his left caught Norton's eye. He turned
around to see Mumbi and Yarrawulla had come back out
of the bedroom. But it was a different looking Mumbi and
Yarrwulla from the two natives that had got on Kingsley
Sheehan's plane earlier in the day.

The tracksuits were gone and both men were stripped down
to black-cotton G-strings. Their black string headbands, the
sign of a circumcised man, were still wrapped around their
heads, only they were now adorned with grey and white falcon
feathers. A small piece of bone, about five centimetres long,
was pushed through the fleshy part beneath their noses and
red, white and black ochre paint had been liberally applied
to the upper parts of their bodies. Mumbi had three black
circles — one over each breast and another painted over his
navel — which were joined by parallel black lines and outlined
with white dots. Yarrawulla had two rows of red circles, which
were also outlined with white ones, running across his col-
larbones down to his groin. Standing together they looked

like they'd just stepped out of the pages of a book on ancient Aboriginal mythology.

Norton stood back and blinked as they walked across the room to Tjalkalieri. 'Jesus, that was a quick paint job,' he said.

'We don't muck around when we get going,' replied Mumbi.

'You got the stone?' said Yarrawulla to Tjalkalieri.

'Yeah. Right here.'

Tjalkalieri produced what looked like a small piece of sharpened quartz, and while the others held their arms out he made a small incision in the vein near the fleshy parts of their elbow. Then he did the same to himself. Once the blood started to run all three let it drip over the bone, making it look even more sinister.

'Righto,' said Tjalkalieri. 'Who wants to wear the boots?'

'I suppose I may as well go first,' said Yarrawulla, sitting down on the lounge and pushing his feet out in front of him.

As he did so Tjalkalieri took hold of the long skinny toe on each foot, next to the big one, and reefed it back with an audible crunch. Yarrawulla closed his eyes and winced but didn't make a sound.

'Jesus, what are you doing?' asked Les.

'Dislocating his toes' replied Tjalkalieri. 'You have to before you're allowed to wear the Kurdaitcha boots. It's okay, I'll set them back later.'

Norton gave his big red head a shake. 'Shit! What next?'

Yarrawulla slipped the feathered Kurdaitcha boots on and stood up as Tjalkalieri carefully handed him the bone and opened the door to the balcony. With Mumbi next to him, Yarrawulla took the bone in his left hand, the length of chord in his right, and moved over to the open door where he pointed it out across the balcony towards the AWEC office and started moving it around almost like he was playing a fish on a rod. Then with Tjalkalieri standing just behind them like he was giving them some sort of encouragement, he and Mumbi began to chant in their native tongue, at the same time performing an odd little dance, shuffling quickly from one foot to the other.

Norton watched them from a discreet distance for about five minutes before going over and sitting down on one of the chairs. After another ten minutes or so, while the chanting continued, Tjalkalieri came over and squatted down next to him.

80

'How's it going?' asked Les.

'Good. We've got him.'

'What? You mean he's dead already?'

'No.' Tjalkalieri shook his head. 'It doesn't work like that. We've only just made the point. The contact. It won't hit him for a while yet. We'll go for a little longer, then we'll knock off and start again tomorrow. But Jesus, we've got a good point going. One of the best ever.'

'That's good,' nodded Les. 'So how long do you reckon it'll take?'

Tjalkalieri closed one eye and picked at his chin for a moment. 'Monday maybe. Probably Tuesday. Wednesday at the most.'

Norton was visibly impressed. 'Tuesday eh? Shit that's all right.'

'We got off to a good start. It makes all the difference.' Tjalkalieri winked up at Norton and gave him a pat on the leg. 'Even though we were bagging you before, you did the right thing moving us into this dump.'

They sat there for a few more minutes in silence as Mumbi and Yarrawulla continued to chant and perform their odd little dance. Finally Les spoke.

'What're they singing anyway, Chalky?'

'The chant? Oh the words go something like this:

'Percy Kilby. May your heart be rent asunder.

May your backbone be split open and your ribs torn asunder.

May your head and throat be split open.

May your liver bleed and be drowned in its own blood.

May your bones become like sand.

May you be sick and still hungry when you eat.

May you howl like a dingo.

May you groan like a bullfrog.'

Tjalkalieri shrugged. 'You know, Les, the usual thing. You've heard one chant you've heard the lot.'

Norton smiled but shook off a chill running through his body at the same time. 'Shit that is a nice song, isn't it? Who wrote the words. Paul McCartney?'

'Rodgers and Hammerstein,' winked Tjalkalieri. 'I can't see it getting in the top forty though.'

They continued watching in silence for what must have been almost half an hour. Then, as abruptly as they started, Mumbi and Yarrawulla stopped.

'Well if that don't get him, nothing will,' said Yarrawulla, closing the balcony door before he turned around.

'Yeah, it was a good point,' said Tjalkalieri, rising to his feet. 'A very good contact. I could sense it from over here.'

Norton stood up also. 'Hey how come you didn't join in the sing-along anyway?'

'My turn tomorrow,' smiled Tjalkalieri. 'I get to dress up in all different gear and make-up.'

'Yeah?'

'Too right. I come out dressed up like Boy George. White smock with all numbers on it. Funny little black hat. Paper ribbons. Everything.' Tjalkalieri gave Norton a cheeky wink. 'You wait till you see it Les. It's a gas.'

Norton had to chuckle at Tjalkalieri's sarcasm.

'Tell you what,' said Mumbi, running a hand over his face. 'I could go a cup of tea. That chanting knocks the shit out of you.'

'Yeah, I don't suppose they'd have a kettle in this brothel would they Les?' asked Yarrawulla. 'I'm fangin' for a cuppa.'

'I wouldn't mind one myself, to tell you the truth,' added Tjalkalieri. 'Can you do something there Les?'

Norton stared at the three of them, shaking his head almost in disbelief; especially at Mumbi and Yarrawulla. For the last half an hour or so they'd been totally absorbed in singing some bloke to a cruel, diabolical death and now they'd knocked off for a cup of tea. Just like that. Like they were working on the roads or something and suddenly noticed it was time for smoko. Knock off and put the Billy on. Les shook his head again.

'So now you want a cup of bloody tea, eh?'

'Yeah,' intoned Tjalkalieri. 'Why. What's wrong with that?'

'Nothing I don't suppose,' shrugged Norton. 'It just seems a bit odd, that's all.'

'A bit odd?' queried Mumbi. 'What do you mean — a bit odd? We've just been chanting our guts out for the last half a bloody hour, covered in paint and feathers and shit. Christ, surely we're entitled to a cup of tea aren't we?'

'Yeah my oath,' said Yarrawulla, plonking himself down on the lounge. 'We work strictly to union rules here son. Half an hour on. Half an hour off. Don't start trying to break down conditions on us Les.'

'Union rules. Break down conditions,' nodded Les sourly. 'I suppose the next thing you'll be wanting a 17.5 per cent loading on that fifty bloody grand.'

'Well,' smiled Tjalkalieri. 'We weren't going to mention

that part of our award at this stage, Les. But seeing as you've brought it up.'

Norton threw his hands up in the air. 'Ohh get stuffed will you.' He took a glance at his watch, now back on his left wrist. 'Look, it's nearly six o'clock. And I don't like your chances of getting a cup of tea in this joint.'

'What about room service?' chuckled Mumbi.

'Room service. In here?' said Yarrawulla. 'You'd get better room service on death row.'

Norton ignored both of them. 'Why don't I duck out and get us some food and we'll have dinner? Some Chinese or something. And I'll get some cartons of tea while I'm at it.'

Tjalkalieri turned to the others, extremely po-faced. 'What do you reckon, comrades? Are we going to accept this blatant breakdown in our award and conditions? No tea supplied.'

'It's a lot to have to accept from the management,' agreed Mumbi, sitting down on the lounge next to Yarrawulla. 'What do you reckon brother?'

'I don't know mate. I don't like it. I reckon we'd only be scabbing on ourselves if we accept it. But,' Yarrawulla winked over at the others, 'jobs are hard to get these days I suppose, so I guess we'll just have to put up with these sweatshop conditions.'

'Thanks,' said Norton, going to his bag and getting out a notepad and biro. 'Now if you workers would just like to tell the management what you want to eat, I'll go out and get it. Plus your cups of fuckin' tea of course.'

Les wrote down what they wanted — fried rice, soups, sweet and sour, etc., plus his own — then put the list in his shirt pocket.

'Don't be too long either, will you Les,' said Tjalkalieri, watching Norton move towards the door. 'As work delegate, I can tell you the members aren't very happy about what's going on.'

Les paused as he opened the door and glared back at the three of them. 'You know the unions are fucking this country don't you,' he said, then closed the door and disappeared down the stairs.

As Norton was heading up Regent Street in search of a Chinese takeaway, Knobby Jones had pulled up in his Ford station wagon outside the AWEC office to view the hot VCRs. A very tall, powerfully built man in his early forties, Jones too had a broken nose and a bit of scar tissue around his eyes; a legacy from his football days but mostly from his dealings in the Sydney underworld. However, unlike his two dubious business acquaintances, Jones had thinning dark hair, going grey, and he was white.

'G'day Knobby. How's things mate?' smiled Kilby as the tall figure strode into his office.

'Pretty good, Perce. How are you? G'day Frank.'

'Knobby.'

'So this is them, eh?' asked Jones. He moved towards the VCRs stacked against the wall, raised the tarpaulin and gave them a quick once-over. 'Yeah they look all right. How many did you say was here again?'

'Thirty,' replied Kilby. 'Twenty Nationals and ten Sanyos. All the grouse Knobby, and straight out of the container.'

'And what'd you want for them did you say?'

'Well. They're worth 900 each in the shops. A third of the ticket's nine grand. Say eight and a half the lot. What do you reckon?'

Jones nodded his head at the cartons in a look of grudging approval. 'Yeah, fair enough.'

'In fact the Sanyos have got infra-red remote control. Here, I'll show you.'

Kilby rose from his desk, walked over to the VCRs and bent down to point to the writing on the side of one of the cartons.

'There you are, you see that? Remote control. Only the very best for you, Knobby old mate.'

Kilby straightened up to smile at Jones, but the smile unexpectedly vanished to be replaced by a look of pure eye-bulging shock. He sucked in a choking gasp of air and fell against the cartons clutching at the small of his back.

'Ohh, Jesus Christ!' he screamed, his eyes jammed shut with pain and disbelief.

Astonished at the suddenness of it all, Frank stood and watched his stricken boss for a moment or two. 'Shit! Are you all right Perce?' he finally said, worry written all over his face.

Even Jones, who was a hard man, was concerned at the agonised look on Kilby's face. Like Frank he too could see that Kilby was in a great deal of pain. 'What's the matter Perce?' he asked.

'Ohh, my fuckin' back,' Kilby managed to gasp out.

Kilby had no sooner said that when he doubled up and

began clutching at his stomach. He let out another shriek of agony and fell down on his knees against the wall. Frank and Jones exchanged worried, puzzled looks for a few seconds as they stared at Kilby. Then Frank bent down to help his suffering boss.

'No, don't touch me,' cried Kilby quickly. 'Don't touch me.'

With the others watching apprehensively, Kilby crouched for a few moments, eyes clenched tight with agony. Then as suddenly as the pain came on, it disappeared. Kilby blinked his eyes open in astonishment for a few seconds and slowly got to his feet. The pain had gone but his mouth felt dry and bitter and a lot of the colour had drained from his face.

'Are you all right Perce?' asked Frank.

'Yeah, what was that all about?' asked Jones.

'I don't know,' replied Kilby, still running his hands gingerly over his stomach and back. 'I've never felt anything like it. It was as if someone had just hit me in the back with an axe — then stabbed me in the guts with a red-hot poker. Christ, talk about pain. You've got no idea.'

'You might've slipped a disc or something for a second when you bent down,' suggested Jones. 'I've done that. It's a bastard.'

'Yeah. But what about the pain in my stomach?' Kilby walked over and slumped down behind his desk.

Jones shook his head and shrugged a reply. 'I dunno. Anyway, Perce. I've got to piss off. I've got a million other things to do. I'll send Jolly around to pick this stuff up in the morning. He'll give you the dough then. Okay?'

'Yeah, righto.' Kilby made a gesture with his hand from behind the desk, scarcely looking up. He was still visibly shaken. 'I'll see you later, Knobby. Frank'll see you to the door. I'm still not feeling the best.'

'That's okay,' replied Jones. 'I'll give you a call through the week. Take care. See you Perce.'

'Yeah. See you Knobby.'

After he'd seen Jones to the door, Frank returned and gave his boss another worried look. 'You feelin' all right now Perce?'

'Yeah, I don't feel too bad. But Jesus, I'm fucked if I know what hit me just then. Fair dinkum, I've never felt pain like it.'

Frank nodded sympathetically. 'I don't suppose you'll feel like having that feed now.'

Kilby slowly brought his gaze up to his heavy. 'That's

the funny part about it, Frank. I'm hungrier now than I ever was.'

Norton didn't have too much trouble finding a half-decent Chinese restaurant just around the corner from the hotel. He ordered the food and while it was being prepared went to a hamburger shop opposite and ordered three polystyrene cups of tea, taking a punt before the owner put the lids on that the boys all took milk and sugar. The girl in the restaurant gave him a cardboard carton for the food so he stopped at the bottle shop in the hotel and bought a dozen stubbies of Fourex; not taking a punt on the boy's beer tastes this time... if they didn't like Fourex they could go without. As it happened, the boys weren't real keen on the Queensland fighting foam, though they managed to force down two bottles each. They gave the tea the thumbs up however, and on a rating of one to ten gave the Chinese food a begrudging four and a half, not that they left too much in the containers when they'd finished.

Then the workers sent the management down to get another dozen bottles of beer — Stag Lager this time — which they demolished pretty smartly while they sat around watching TV. The boys told Les they were tired not only from the chanting and the plane trip, but they honestly couldn't handle the polluted air and city tap-water after Binjiwunyawunya so they were all in bed before ten. Les joined them not long after, making two phonecalls before he did.

The first was to Warren, to ask sarcastically if he could manage without him and were there any messages. Warren said he could, and there weren't. The next was to Price at the club to make sure Danny had turned up and to tell him everything appeared to be going to plan. Price said everything was shipshape at the club but he still sounded sceptical about Les's strange scheme and would liked to have known a bit more about what he was doing with that $100,000. Eddie was sitting in the office opposite Price and he too was dying to know a bit more, but Norton just laughed saying not to worry he'd tell them some more on Saturday night and it would all be over one way or the other by Wednesday.

'Eddie. What do you reckon the big red-headed prick's up to?' said Price, drumming his fingers on the desk as he stared at the phone after Les had hung up.

'I'm buggered if I know Price,' replied the little hit man, giving his head a shake as he too glanced absently at the phone. 'It's something bloody weird though. He rang me earlier wanting to know how to get a blood sample from that Kilby without him knowing it.'

'Blood?' Price screwed up his face and switched his gaze from the phone to Eddie. 'What in the hell would he want Kilby's blood for? What the hell are they up to over there in Redfern? Black magic or some fuckin' thing?'

Eddie let out a bit of a snigger. 'I don't know to be sure, Price,' he said slowly, 'but it just might be, you know. It just might be.'

The two of them continued to stare at the phone in silence for a few moments while outside the office the sounds of the Kelly Club coming to life echoed softly through the frosted glass door and the polished red-cedar panelling.

While Les and the boys had been getting into their mundane Chinese takeaway earlier, Percy Kilby and Frank were seated comfortably in the Tai-Ping restaurant, spending what was left of Norton's, alias Vernon Stroud's, donation to AWEC, and enjoying the very best the renowned Chinese restaurant had to offer. Kilby's earlier discomfort had not been completely forgotten, it had been pushed aside as they both ordered up plenty with money being no object. They'd finished the triple-decker prawns and lobster medallions in chilli and garlic, accompanied by a chilled bottle of '73 Taylor's white burgundy, and the waiter had just deposited their fingerbowls on the table and two cracked mudcrabs with black-bean sauce, steamed to perfection and smelling good enough to turn the heads of the diners at the surrounding tables.

'Jesus, how good are these,' said Frank after he'd finished his first delicious mouthful.

'Yeah I know,' replied Kilby, his eyes rolling with delight as he tore into his. 'They're the grouse aren't they?'

Frank raised his glass of wine and grinned disparagingly at his boss. 'Here's to the Chartered Accountants Against Apartheid.'

Kilby raised his glass and grinned back. 'Here's to apartheid in general. It and those white do-gooders all full of shit. They're the best thing that's ever happened. Let's hope to Christ South Africa stays flavour of the month for the next ten years. We'll be eating here every night.'

They both threw back their heads and roared laughing, then continued enjoying their cracked crab in almost silent ecstasy.

Frank and Kilby were just about finished and ready to order something else to drink when Kilby unexpectedly dropped his last piece of crab back onto his plate. His sauce-spattered mouth gaped open, his eyes widened with apprehension, and he began to stare into space. He gripped the edge of the table tightly and fearfully as his stomach began to heave violently as though he was attempting to hold back a series of uncontrollable hiccups. Next thing, his breath started coming out in short, choking gasps and his mouth opened and closed noisily like he was trying to belch and swallow at the same time.

Frank stopped eating and stared at his boss's convulsions in disbelief. This was the second strange attack in less than four hours. 'Hey Perce,' he asked nervously. 'Are you all right mate?'

Kilby had let go of the table and was now clutching fearfully at his stomach. 'Frank. Help me out to the toilet will you? For Christ's sake!' he gasped between bouts of heaving.

'Sure mate.'

Frank quickly got up from his seat and slipped his arm around his boss's waist. With Kilby almost doubled over in agony as he clutched at his stomach, Frank helped and guided him to the toilet as swiftly as he could, through the tables, past the astonished looks of the other diners and almost knocking over a waiter coming from the kitchen as they stumbled past.

Once he was in the toilet, Kilby burst into the nearest cubicle and began vomiting. Terrible, searing retches that sounded almost as if he was going to bring up his intestines. This gasping, horrendous sound was broken now and again when Kilby violently broke wind. He was in an appalling state. All Frank could do was stand there helplessly and watch his ashen-faced boss slumped against the wall of the cubicle bringing his heart up.

After about five minutes Kilby stopped. He let out a deep moan of relief and turned to Frank, who could scarcely believe the gaunt face staring at him from the cubicle. His boss's eyes were puffed and bloodshot; his dark brown face had turned a dirty slate grey; his hair was damp and sweat was running down his cheeks and dripping off his chin. He staggered across to the wash basins, turned on a tap and began slopping cold water across his face while he gulped the odd mouthful down.

Worry all over his face, Frank watched Kilby in silence

for a few minutes. 'How are you feeling now mate?' he finally asked. 'You any better?' He had never seen his usually fit and tough boss in such a state.

Kilby didn't answer at first. He leant face down in the basin, still gasping and spluttering water as he tried to get his breath back. After a while he tilted his head back and drew in a deep breath of relief. 'Yeah. I think so.' He blinked groggily.

'Must've been that bloody crab, eh?'

Kilby shook his head lightly. 'No it wasn't that,' he sighed. 'They were only fresh in this morning. I don't know what it is. But Jesus, I've never spewed like that in my life.'

'You don't have to tell me. I could see it. It was terrible.'

'In my back pocket, Frank. Get my wallet and go out and pay the bill. Then come back and get me will you. I'll wait here. I'm still too fucked to move.'

'Yeah, righto mate.'

Frank took the money, walked out to the front desk and paid the bill. The head waiter, having seen Frank helping his boss to the toilets and knowing Kilby was a regular, came over and asked if everything was all right; he was as surprised as he was worried because he knew the quality and freshness of the food was second to none — especially the mud crabs. Frank assured him there had been nothing wrong with the food, his boss was just sick from the flu, that's all, and he'd be fine once he was outside and got some fresh air.

Kilby was still propped in front of the wash basins, slopping water over his face, when Frank returned. Oddly enough, considering the horrendous bilious attack he'd just been through, Kilby had almost regained his composure. The colour was back in his face and his stomach didn't feel too bad even though only minutes before he'd almost turned it inside out. Frank had his arm around his waist but Kilby was almost able to walk through the restaurant and out to the car under his own steam.

'Yeah, it's a funny one, Perce' said Frank, once they were inside the AWEC Toyota panel van and he was driving his boss home to Stanmore. 'You looked half dead only a little while ago. Now you don't look too bad.'

'Yeah. It's got me fucked. And you're not going to believe this, Frank.' Kilby shook his head and gazed out the window for a few moments before he spoke. 'You know how crook I was back there at the Tai-Ping, and I brought everything in me up.'

'Yeah.'

'Well now I'm starvin' fuckin' hungry again. In fact you can pull over at that hamburger shop up ahead. I'm going to get half a chicken.'

Frank switched on the indicator and now it was his turn to shake his head. 'I think you'd better see a doctor tomorrow Perce.'

Norton was up around seven-thirty the following morning. Considering the narrowness of the bed, the one lousy pillow and the lumpy mattress, he had slept quite soundly. Tjalkalieri was already in the bathroom when Les climbed into the tracksuit he'd brought with him. Mumbi and Yarrawulla were seated on the lounge in their tracksuits also, listening to the radio when Les walked into the main room. They looked like two men who had just lost their entire life's savings at the races and picked up a purse with two dollars in it as they left the track.

'Fair dinkum. This is a nice how-do-you-bloody-well-do, this is,' Mumbi grumbled as soon as he spotted Les.

'Oh hello. What the bloody hell's up now?' yawned Norton.

'No cup of bloody tea in the morning. That's what's up,' replied Yarrawulla.

'Cup of tea. Cup of tea. Fair dinkum, you're like a lot of old sheilas.'

'Hey don't worry about the old sheilas,' said Tjalkalieri, who had just walked into the room. 'No cup of tea. No chant.'

'My oath,' nodded Yarrawulla. 'We are not amused.'

'Oh for Christ's sake,' said Norton. 'Just give me five minutes to have a crap and clean my teeth and I'll go out and get you a gallon of the shit. Anything to keep you happy.'

'Get some fruit while you're down there,' said Mumbi. 'Some apples and oranges and that.'

'And a packet of those muesli bars, too, Les,' said Yarrawulla. 'I don't mind them. They're all right.'

'Are you sure there's nothing else you want?'

'No. Not for the moment,' shrugged Tjalkalieri, who had now joined the others on the lounge. 'But don't be too far away at lunchtime.'

'Oh I'll be here, don't worry. You won't be able to miss me. I'll have my butler's uniform on.' Norton laughed as he shook his head in disgust and went to the bathroom.

When Jolly pulled Knobby Jones's panel van up onto the

footpath outside the AWEC office around eight a.m., exhaust fumes, dust and other pollutants were just starting to thicken the air around Redfern, drifting off up into the windless sunny sky to form the yellow blanket of smog that generally settles over Sydney by mid-morning. Jolly, a medium-built, dark-haired guy who always liked to dress well, was oblivious to all this. All he had on his mind was getting a packet of cigarettes before he started loading up all those hot VCRs. He sprinted across to the shops just around the corner from the Thames Tavern.

Jolly, whose real name was Mick Rodgers, got his nickname because he was a pretty happy sort of a bloke. Someone once referred to him as Jolly Rodgers and somehow the name stuck. Jolly wasn't real keen about work, especially the nine-to-five caper, so he generally did a bit of SP or whatever else he could get his hands on, hanging around with various shifties in the Eastern suburbs. Which was how he got to know Les Norton and how he got to be moving hot VCRs for Knobby Jones. But Jolly — happy, mildly dishonest or whatever he was — was more than a little surprised when he almost bumped into a familiar red-headed figure ambling around the corner into Regent Street. A tall red-headed figure carrying a cardboard carton full of fruit, biscuits and takeaway cups of tea under his massive right arm.

'Hello Les,' he said happily. 'Fancy bumping into you here. How're you going?'

Norton too was taken a little by surprise, and not all that overjoyed, at someone seeing him lurking around the streets of Redfern. 'Oh... g'day Mick,' he half smiled. 'How's things?'

'Pretty good. What're you up to?' Jolly couldn't help but notice the extra stubble on Norton's jaw and couldn't help but think it a little odd him being up so early in the morning... especially seeing as he worked so late on Thursday night. But Jolly always minded his own business and only asked more or less out of polite conversation.

'Nothing really,' replied Norton cautiously. 'I was just driving through so I thought I'd stop and get some fruit. An old mate of mine's got a shop just round the corner.'

'Oh.' Jolly noticed the four paper cups of tea in the carton, plus the packets of biscuits, but decided not to say anything.

'What about yourself Mick?'

'I'm just delivering a bit of stuff for a bloke. That's all.'

'Oh.' Norton knew of Jolly's somewhat shifty demeanour but declined to elaborate on that either.

They had a brief conversation while the cars whizzed past and the pedestrians scurried across Regent Street to the station. Then Les said he'd better make a move as he was illegally parked down the road.

'You going down the Sheaf on the weekend, Mick?'

'Yeah. I'll be there Sunday for sure.'

'Well I'll have a beer with you then, eh?'

Fancy someone spotting me in Redfern of all bloody places thought Les as he turned into the hotel once he made sure Jolly was out of sight. And this hour of the bloody morning too. Oh well. Can't see him making any difference. Norton walked to the stairs only to find someone else he knew coming down. Ross Bailey, the owner.

'Hello George,' Ross said cheerfully, rattling a great ring of keys in his hand. 'How are you this morning?'

'Oh g'day Ross,' Norton replied, wondering who he was going to bump into next. 'I'm good thanks.'

'Everything all right? Room okay?'

'Yeah, good as gold thanks Ross.'

'I'll have the girl change the sheets and vacuum the place out for you later.'

Norton's brow knitted for a moment as he thought over Bailey's last statement. If a cleaning lady came into the room and saw the boys running around covered in blood, paint and bird feathers and chanting away like demons with bones shoved through their noses she'd be likely to flip out. And if she vacuumed up all the little piles of sacred sand it could stuff up the proceedings as well. Yes, they could certainly do without a cleaning lady in room 9 at the moment.

Norton took the hotel owner gently by the elbow. 'Ah, look Ross,' he said easily. 'I was going to mention this to you earlier. Those three blokes in that room up there come from this really primitive tribe from right out in the middle of nowhere. They're almost still in the Stone Age.'

'So?'

'Well. One of their tribal customs — and a very strict one — is no women in their living quarters.'

Bailey looked at Les blankly. 'Is that right?'

'My oath. In fact I'm glad I bumped into you, because if a woman had of happened to have walked into that room, there'd be the biggest blow-up ever.'

'Go on.'

'You better believe it. If they ever catch any sheilas in their living quarters back in the desert they cut their bloody throats.'

'Christ!' Bailey looked at Les incredulously for a moment, then a bit of a twinkle began to form in his eye. 'Listen George,' he said, moving a little closer. 'This mightn't be any of my business. But how do they get on when they want to have a root?'

'Mate. They only fornicate on special, ceremonial occasions. Two or three times a year at the most.'

'Fair dinkum?' Bailey, the sort of bloke who loved nothing better than a bit of business and would screw just about anything he could get his hands on, was somewhat taken aback by this. He continued to stare at Les and then a deep, lecherous chuckle began to rumble out of his throat. 'I'll tell you what,' he laughed. 'I'd like to be around when they go off. I reckon it'd be like a twenty-one gun salute.'

'You're not wrong there,' laughed Norton, giving Bailey a slap on the shoulder. 'When they're finished it looks like a Mr Whippy van's just been overturned in the tent.'

Bailey threw back his head and roared laughing. 'Anyway George,' he said, returning Les's friendly slap on the shoulder, 'I'd better get going too. I'll get the girl to leave the sheets and that outside the door. Okay?'

'That'll be great thanks Ross.'

Bailey paused for a moment. 'Listen George. If you ah . . . want a couple of flagons of plonk for 'em or something. Just go down and see the girl in the bottle shop. On the house,' he added with a wink.

'No, that's all right' smiled Les. 'Hey, there is something you could get us though.'

'Sure. What is it?'

'Could you get us an electric kettle and a teapot?'

'Sure, no worries. I'll leave it outside the room with the sheets. I'll get some cups and all that too.'

'Good on you. Well, I'll see you later Ross.'

'Yeah. See you after, George.' Hoping to Christ the boys' tea hadn't turned too cold by now, Les took the stairs up to room 9 three at a time.

Across the road in the AWEC office, Percy Kilby could have been a lot happier than he was, considering Rocket Johnny had got up at Dapto and paid almost 8–1 on the TAB. However, winning $1,600 didn't quite seem to compensate for the rotten night's sleep he'd just had. Fortunately his stomach felt a lot better but he was headachy and weak and his eyes were puffed and grainy from lack of sleep. Unable to sleep, he'd been in the office since just after seven, hoping to catch up on some bookwork. But all he'd done since he got there was sip on a mug of coffee and stare moodily at his desk. Frank, on the other hand, had not long walked in with the morning paper under his arm and was quite jubilant.

'Three dollars seventy-five for the win Perce,' he grinned. 'I told you that pot licker of Ronnie's was a goer.'

'Yeah. Terrific Frank,' muttered his boss irritably.

Frank smiled across from where he was seated on his boss's desk, reading the sports section. 'Bad luck you're still crook Perce. I wouldn't mind backin' up at the Tai-Ping for another lash at those muddies.'

'I'm not all that crook, Frank. I'm just bloody tired. I had a cunt of a night's sleep.'

'Yeah?'

'Yeah.' Kilby sighed and ran a hand across his eyes. 'All I did all night was dream.'

'Nightmares eh?'

'Ohh just bloody weird. I kept dreaming these three old black blokes were after me.'

'Black blokes?'

'Yeah. Real full-bloods. All done up in feathers and bones through their noses. Like something out of a thousand years ago. They kept chasing me with spears — all over some desert somewhere.' Kilby buried his face in his hands. 'Buggered if I could get to sleep. Every time I'd doze off I'd keep seeing these old blokes with these weird blue eyes.' Kilby shook his head tiredly. 'Fair dinkum, Frank, it was that real at times it scared the shit out of me.'

Frank moved his gaze from the paper across to his boss. 'I reckon you ought to see a doctor Perce.'

Kilby was about to say something when an abrupt 'shave and a haircut — two bits' rapped on the door and in walked Mick Rodgers.

'Hello boys,' he grinned, cheerfully rubbing his hands together. 'What's doing?'

'Ah, Mr Rodgers,' smiled Frank, looking up from his newspaper.

'What's doing?' said Kilby morosely. 'Eight and a half grand's what's doing. You got it with you?'

'Right here in my kick,' replied Jolly, the grin still plastered across his face. He pulled a fairly bulky envelope wrapped in a plastic bag out of his back pocket and dropped it on the desk. 'There you are. You want to count it?'

Kilby stared at it for a moment. 'Count it will you Frank. I'm too bloody tired.'

Luckily the money was in neat bundles of hundreds and fifties so Frank was able to count it fairly quickly without breaking into a sweat or giving himself a migraine in the process.

'Yeah. It's all there Perce,' he said, pushing the money across the desk.

'Good.' Even though it was quite an amount of cash, Kilby dropped it in the top drawer uninterestedly. 'Okay. You may as well give him a hand to load them up. I'd help you but I'm too rooted to move.'

'Yeah. I was just going to say you don't look too good on it Perce,' said Jolly. 'What's up?'

'I think I'm getting the flu,' replied Kilby shortly. He let out a sigh and dropped his face back into his hands.

'It's a proper bastard, isn't it,' nodded Jolly. 'There's a lot of it going around too.'

Frank produced two small wooden wedges, jammed them under the office doors, and they started loading up the panel van. Between them — even taking their time and stopping for a bit of a perv on any girls walking to the station — they had them all loaded up in less than half an hour. Jolly slammed the rear doors of the van and then lit a cigarette, offering one to Frank which he declined.

'You want to come inside for a cup of coffee before you go?'

'No. I'll piss off thanks Frank. The sooner I get these unloaded back at Bondi, the sooner I can get down the beach.'

'Fair enough.' Frank watched Jolly puff away at his cigarette for a few seconds. 'I don't suppose you'd get over Redfern way very often?'

'Not very often,' replied Jolly. He took another huge drag on his cigarette and leant back against the side of the van. 'It's funny though. I just bumped into a bloke I know from down the beach.'

'Yeah?'

'Yeah. One of Price Galese's bouncers from up the Kelly Club.'

At the mention of Galese's name, Frank's ears pricked up and some of the tiny wooden cogs in his bony head started ticking over.

'Did you say one of Price Galese's boys?'

'Yeah. Les Norton. Big red-headed bloke.'

At that brief description Frank's ears pricked up a little more. 'What's he look like again ... this Les Norton?'

Jolly described Norton again, only this time throwing in Les's bushy eyebrows and his Queensland drawl. Now the cogs in Frank's half punch-drunk brain were whirring into overdrive. Les Norton began to sound very suspiciously like a certain chartered accountant who had called into the AWEC office the day before.

'What'd this mate of yours say he was doing in Redfern?' he asked evenly.

'Nothing,' shrugged Jolly. He flicked the cigarette butt out into Lawson Street. 'Just said he stopped by to get some fruit. That's all. Seemed a bit funny though, seeing him here at eight in the morning.'

'Mmhh.'

'Anyway Frank,' said Jolly, jangling the car keys out of his pocket. 'I'm gonna get crackin'. I'll see you later.'

'Yeah,' replied Frank slowly. 'I'll see you later Mick.'

Once he was back inside and had removed the wedges from under the doors, Frank couldn't tell his boss fast enough what Jolly had just said to him out the front. Kilby listened, but his tiredness and illness still had him uninterested.

'Yeah, there might be something in what you say, Frank,' he muttered, his head still resting on his hands. 'It's more than likely just a coincidence though.'

'Fair enough,' replied Frank, 'but if I happen to spot that big red-headed prick still hanging around I'm going to front him.'

'Yeah, do that Frank.' Suddenly Kilby winced and clutched at his stomach again.

'What's up?' asked Frank.

'Ohh shit. I'm starting to get those pains in the gut again.'

Back in room 9 at the Thames Tavern, Tjalkalieri and the boys had resumed chanting. Earlier, they'd complained about the tea being half cold — naturally — and Mumbi had bitten into a partly-rotten apple. The muesli bars were okay, though. Norton assured them they could stop complaining about the tea from now on as he was getting a kettle and a teapot, and he'd buy a dozen packets of Kinkara as soon as it arrived. Yarrawulla told him he could shove his Kinkara up his big red arse; they wanted Twinings English Breakfast or Prince of Wales. Norton told them that he'd hire a Sherpa guide and bring the tea down from Tibet if that would make them happy. The boys said they'd think on it. Tjalkalieri had got into the chanting now; after putting a bone through his nose and painting a design on his chest and back, something like a pair of black braces and waistband surrounded by tiny red and white circles. A number of red and white circles were painted across his forehead also. Mumbi was seated on the lounge next to Norton, casually peeling an orange as they watched the other two do their stuff.

'How come you're not doing any chanting Mumbles?' asked Norton, watching avidly as Tjalkalieri skillfully manipulated the bone and chord.

'Flexitime,' replied Mumbi, spitting several pips into his hand.

'What?'

'I'm on flexitime. I don't start till about ten-thirty.'

'You're kidding aren't you? What do you think this is? The public bloody service?'

Mumbi shrugged his shoulders. 'That's the way we work, bloodnut. If you don't like it — stiff shit.' He took another bite of his orange and spat some more pips into his hand. Norton shifted his gaze from the balcony to the floor and shook his head.

The boys chanted and danced non-stop till twelve-thirty sharp; then they abruptly knocked off for lunch. They'd taken it in turns to have an hour off at a time, but always making certain there were two men constantly chanting. Les was there to watch them most of the time, except when he had to go out and get the sandwiches, and ended up spending almost an hour scouring Redfern in an effort to find a place that sold Twinings Prince of Wales tea. Consequently he wasn't in all that good a mood when he got back to room 9 and made a brew, using the kettle and teapot that had been left outside the door with the sheets. But the boys were quite happy for a change, giving the tea a resounding thumbs up. They even said the chicken and salad sandwiches were okay too, though they would have preferred wholemeal bread to plain brown. Les prostrated himself on the floor and begged forgiveness, swearing on his mother's dying oath that it would never happen again.

'Okay,' Les said, slapping his hands together and checking his watch after they'd all finished eating. 'One o'clock, back to work. Come on.'

'Hey, don't go putting the bustle on Les,' said Mumbi, draining his cup.

'I'm not putting the bustle on Mumbles. But you're being paid to work you know. Not to sit around drinking tea all day.' He gave them all a thin smile as they stared up at him impassively from the lounge. 'Of course I wouldn't dream of trying to break down any of your conditions. I'm even going to make afternoon tea for you later on. In fact what time would you chaps care to have your afternoon tea?' he added sweetly.

'Three o'clock on the dot,' replied Tjalkalieri quickly. 'And we knock off at quarter to five sharp.'

'Quarter to five? You're supposed to work till bloody five.'

'Fifteen minutes washing up time,' said Yarrawulla.

'Fifteen minutes to have a bloody wash? You're kidding.'

'How long do you think it takes to wash all this blood and shit off?' said Mumbi.

'Shouldn't take you quarter of a bloody hour.'

'Hey,' said Tjalkalieri. 'You just make sure you've got the soap and towels waiting in the amenities room at quarter to five, mate. Or the management might find it's got a rather large industrial dispute on its hands — and we haven't even discussed site allowance yet!'

Norton shook his head once more and started picking up the cups and saucers and tidying the mess. 'The unions are fucking this country,' he said. 'You know that don't you.'

Meanwhile, over at the AWEC office Percy Kilby was getting sicker and sicker as the day grew longer.

His headache, bad enough as it was to begin with, got worse. He felt weak as a kitten, his eyes were watering, his temperature was up, and his nose was running like a tap. He would have gone home to bed but he felt that crook he was too tired to move. At ten he told Frank that if anybody called he wasn't in. At eleven he got Frank to put a sign on the door saying the office was closed for the day. Frank suggested he drive him home, but apart from being too tired to move Kilby said he'd had a gigantic argument with his wife on Wednesday and had belted her one. The thought of being in the house all afternoon, in his condition and with her nagging at him, was just too ghastly even to contemplate. He'd end up choking her. The odd part about it all, though, was despite his illness he was still hungry. At twelve he sent Frank over to get him three meat pies and half of litre of chocolate milk. Sitting in the office, Frank couldn't believe it as he watched his sick and suffering boss sneezing his head off and trying to blow the sinuses clean out of his nose while he wolfed down the pies with sauce.

'Perce. You're going to have to see a doctor, mate. This is getting ridiculous.'

'Yeah I know,' mumbled Kilby between gulps of pie and gravy. 'But I just got to get something into my stomach. I'm bloody starving.'

Frank shook his head. 'It just doesn't seem right mate. You're as sick as a dog and you're still stuffing all that rubbish into yourself. What do you reckon?'

'What do I reckon?' Kilby finished the last pie and wiped the sauce from his mouth. 'I reckon you can go over and get me some chips. Plenty of 'em. With vinegar too. And a large bar of fruit-and-nut chocolate. And hurry Frank — cause I'm still bloody hungry.'

Frank shook his head, then walked over and got his boss what he wanted. By the time he'd got back Kilby had brought up the three pies and chocolate milk and was ready to go again, hungrier than ever.

In the Thames Tavern the boys kept up the chanting till they stopped for smoko at three, then continued till they finished for the day at four forty-five sharp. For the last hour and three-quarters all three men had joined in the chant, giving Kilby a solid blast of non-stop bone pointing till they called it quits. Norton was a little curious about this last burst of enthusiasm because so far they'd stuck strictly to their so-called union rules — with their flexitime, tea breaks, washing-up time and whatever else they could think up just to annoy him. He inquired about this while he watched them getting cleaned up.

'We don't do any more chanting now till Monday,' answered Tjalkalieri, wiping the last of the paint and blood from him with a small face cloth.

'No more till Monday?' said Norton. 'That seems a bit strange. You've only been going for what? . . . barely two days. Won't the spell or whatever it is wear off?'

'That's where you're wrong, Les,' said Mumbi. 'Don't worry. We've given him heaps the last couple of days. Now we let him off the hook for a day or two and he starts to think he's getting better.'

'That's right,' chipped in Yarrawulla. 'We sort of lull him into a false sense of security. He thinks he's over it and bingo! On Monday we all get into the act and hit him with the old double whammy. And by Tuesday, it's adios señor Kilby.'

Norton nodded his head and continued to watch as they finished cleaning up and changed back into their tracksuits.

'So what do you intend to do all weekend?' he asked.

'Nothing,' replied Tjalkalieri. 'Sleep, read, just take it easy. We won't even leave these rooms.'

'Yeah?' Norton was a little surprised. 'Don't any of you want to go for a bit of a walk or something. Take in a movie?'

Tjalkalieri shook his head. 'That chanting takes a lot out of us you know. We're pretty buggered. Besides, we've built up a kind of an aura in this room with the spirits. For any of us to leave could damage the aura.' He smiled at the look on Norton's face. 'I know it's a bit hard for a wombat like you to fathom, Les. But that's the way it goes.'

'Fair enough,' replied Norton with a shrug of his shoulders. 'But what about your girls back at Binji. Do you want me to give them a ring and tell them you're all right.'

Yarrawulla shook his head and sat down on the lounge. 'No need to Les. We sent them a telegram before we went to bed last night.'

Norton screwed up his face. 'A telegram? I don't remember any of you going to the post office.'

Tjalkalieri winked at Les as he and Mumbi joined Yarrawulla on the lounge. He didn't say anything, just tapped his middle finger against his forehead; then all three of them smiled up at the look on Les's face.

'Bloody hell,' muttered Norton. 'What next?'

'What next?' smiled Mumbi, rubbing his hands together. 'A nice cup of tea'd go down well Les.'

'Yeah. Then you can get us something to eat,' added Yarrawulla. 'How about some pizzas tonight boys,' he said, turning to the others. 'I don't think I could handle another gutful of that so-called Chinese food.'

'Not a bad idea,' nodded Tajlkalieri. 'I'll have a large pepperoni.'

'Pizza it is then,' said Norton quietly, still shaking his head.

By this time Kilby's condition back at the AWEC office had deteriorated further. Just before five he closed the office and got Frank to drive him home, promising him he'd definitely be seeing a doctor first thing tomorrow. Kilby continued to sneeze, cough, blow his nose and groan the entire journey. Then about five minutes from his house he stopped sneezing, turned to Frank and stared at him in amazement.

100

Frank caught his boss's eye and looked back at him curiously. 'What's up now Perce?' he asked, starting to get more than a little worried again.

Kilby continued to stare at Frank for a few moments before answering. 'Frank' he said incredulously. 'You're not going to believe this.'

'Believe what Frank?'

'You know how crook I've been all day.'

'Yeah.'

'Well mate, I feel as good as gold now.' Kilby took in a deep breath through his suddenly cleared nose, held it for a moment, then let it out. 'I feel terrific, look at that, clear as a bell. That stinkin', rotten flu must've worn off.'

'Yeah?' Frank kept looking curiously at his boss. 'I dunno Perce. Fifteen minutes ago you looked like you were ready to kick the bucket.'

'I know. But I'm telling you I feel fine now. Better than I've felt for ages.'

Frank pulled the car up outside Kilby's house but didn't turn the motor off. 'I still don't know, Perce,' he said, more mystified than ever. 'I still reckon you ought to be in bed. And see a doctor first thing tomorrow.'

'Ohh bullshit.'

'All right, suit yourself. Anyway, do you want me to call around in the morning?'

Kilby blinked at his employee. 'Why, where are you going now?'

'Home. I'm gonna have a few beers first, then I'm going home.'

'Well I'm coming too.'

Frank continued to stare at his boss. 'Yeah . . . but.'

'What do you mean, yeah, but. Aren't I allowed to have a beer with me old mate after work?'

'Yeah sure. But.'

'Well. Come on, let's go. I don't want to go inside, I'll only end up hitting her on the chin again.'

Frank put the car into gear and did a U-turn. 'You're the boss,' he shrugged, shaking his head at the same time.

'And stop at the TAB on the way. I still haven't picked up our winnings yet.' Kilby threw back his head, roared laughing and gave Frank a friendly punch on the shoulder. 'We'll give that a nice nudge before the night's out Frankie boy, I can tell you.' Kilby laughed again. 'You reckon I don't feel good.'

101

Frank continued to shake his head as he weaved into the traffic. 'You're the boss,' he repeated.

Kilby managed to get good and drunk all right that night. They hit the Redfern RSL about six and left just after eleven in separate taxis. Kilby was that happy and relieved at his sudden and unexpected recovery from the flu or whatever it was that had laid him so low the last couple of days he gave Frank $250 from the winnings at the TAB and then made sure he never put his hand in his pocket the rest of the night. Consequently both men had hangovers the following morning big enough to sell advertising on. But Kilby was so glad it was only a hangover he almost enjoyed it — the headache, the furry tongue, and the feeling that his head was a length of guttering and several people were banging on it with tyre levers. Compared to what he'd just been through it was almost enjoyable, so he didn't bother to take Frank's advice and ring a doctor. A glass of Eno's, two digesics and a feed of bacon and eggs and coffee had the AWEC boss feeling almost on top of the world.

Les Norton, on the other hand, never went out. After getting the boys their pizzas, orange juice, Stag Lager and whatever else they wanted, they ate and settled down to a boring night watching TV. When the old John Wayne movie finished at ten-thirty they were all yawning their heads off and so tired all they wanted to do was go to bed anyway.

Norton figured the boys would be tired from all that chanting and would be hot candidates for an early night; maybe there was an aura in the room like Tjalkalieri said and it was making him tired as well. Though by now — although he didn't like to admit it to himself — Les was beginning to get just a little sceptical about this bone pointing. He trusted Tjalkalieri and he knew the boys had done it in the bush, but in the big city it could be a different kettle of fish altogether. Especially with what struck Les as their rather flippant attitude towards it now that they'd started. Going like mad one minute, then turning it off for the weekend, then hitting Kilby with their so-called 'double whammy' or whatever it was on Monday. He hoped to Christ they knew what they were doing and he hoped to Christ it worked or he'd end up making a nice dill out of himself and Price would be more than entitled to take the $100,000 back out of his thick Queensland hide. A few doubts and misgivings were swirling around in Norton's mind when his head hit the pillow that night, but he slept soundly enough. Even Tjalkalieri's snoring, coming from barely a metre away, didn't bother him.

So, unlike his two adversaries, Norton woke up around seven-thirty feeling rested, refreshed and without the slightest trace of a hangover. He was first up, so after finishing in the bathroom he decided to go up and get the boys some steak sandwiches for breakfast before they had a chance to start whingeing.

It wasn't much of a day when Les stepped out of the Thames Tavern — cloudy with a cool southerly in the air and the thick band of black clouds gathering across the city skyline promising rain before lunchtime or early afternoon at the latest. There were quite a few people about for early on a Saturday morning. Mostly heading for work, thought Les, and not looking too happy about it either as they pulled their collars up against the wind and walked briskly towards the station.

The Greek in the hamburger shop whipped up the stack of steak sandwiches pretty smartly, throwing on plenty of extra onions as Norton ordered. The shop also sold the morning papers so he got two of each plus some bottles of fruit-flavoured spa water and dropped them in the carton as well. On the way back Norton ducked out to the hotel carpark to make sure his car was all right. He was quite pleased to see that apart from a few pigeon deposits across the roof and bonnet the old Ford was resting quite comfortably next to a couple of cars equally as battered and dirty as his. Well for Redfern that's a plus he thought. Though I might pull the coil lead out before I go to bed tonight. Not that anyone would want to steal it. But there just might be someone around here who needs my old Ford more than I do. Les was whistling softly to himself as he jogged up the stairs to room 9.

'Jesus, don't tell me you've managed to make yourselves a cup of tea while I was away.' He stepped into the room and kicked the door shut behind him with his foot. 'Must've been quite an effort for one of you. That teapot can get pretty heavy when it's full of water.'

Yarrawulla looked up expressionlessly from where he was sitting. 'We had to, Les,' he said taking a sip from his cup. 'You make it that weak it needs a pair of crutches to get out of the pot.'

'Fair dinkum.' Norton chuckled and shook his head as he placed the carton on the table in the middle of the room.

103

'It wouldn't matter what I done. One of you drop kicks'd have a go at me over it.'

Tjalkalieri got up and smiled at Norton as he walked over and had a look in the carton. 'You know what, Les,' he said, 'you're right.' He gave the big red-headed Queenslander a wink and a friendly slap on the back. 'These steak sangers don't look too bad though.'

They mustn't have been because in less than twenty minutes there wasn't a crust, a skerrick of meat or a shred of onion left, and Mumbi had made a fresh pot of tea. They sat around reading and half listening to the radio while they sipped their tea. It was all very relaxed with no one saying much and the next thing it was well after eleven.

Flicking through the sports section, Les noticed that one of Price's horses was in a welter at Canterbury that afternoon. A couple of the tipsters had it down for a place and according to the papers it was 8-1. Norton wouldn't have minded having something on it but he wasn't too sure of its form and there were some other things on his mind as well. Although he could have, he didn't want to get into the habit of running backwards and forwards to the TAB all day and leaving the boys in the room alone. Running out to get the food for a few minutes at a time was all right, but he would have preferred to be with them the whole time. Especially in that old pub on a Saturday afternoon in Redfern; anything could happen. He was probably overreacting a little, but you never knew. Someone could start banging on the door while he wasn't there and upset the boys. A drunk could wander up from downstairs and cause trouble. The two old pisspots who originally had the rooms could come back and start something. Even a drainpipe merchant could unsuspectingly climb up over the balcony intent on robbing the joint. Yes, he was no doubt overdramatising things, but knowing his luck he'd only be out of the room a few minutes and something would go wrong. He'd stay with the boys and keep an eye on them. He'd appointed himself minder and that's exactly what he would do. There was too much at stake. And besides, it would be all over in three or four days, one way or the other. But he wanted to back that horse and he'd have to get in touch with Price to get the drum on it.

That was another thing. Les wasn't all that keen to ring Price just yet because Price would want to know what was going on, and what could he tell him? Yeah Price, it's all sweet. The boys chanted for a day and a half; now they've knocked off for the weekend. Chanted? Price would say. What's with this chanting? How was he going to explain that to him? How was he going to explain anything to him? Unless you knew just what was going on the whole idea was preposterous. Even *if* you knew what was going on, the whole idea was still preposterous. But he wanted to back that horse and he had to know if it was going first. He stroked his chin thoughtfully for a moment then glanced at his watch. It would be no good ringing Price now anyway. He'd either be out at the track or over at his trainer's stables at Randwick. What about George? No, he'd be out playing handball somewhere. Billy? Billy'd be either helping his wife with the shopping or watching his kids play soccer. Norton glanced over to the open balcony door where the southerly was sending a thin mist of rain across the tiled deck from a sky that was beginning to reflect Norton's mood. Wait a minute. What about Eddie? He folded his paper, got up and closed the balcony door.

'I'm just going to duck down and make a quick phone call fellas.' There was an almost imperceptible nodding of heads as the boys continued reading. 'I'll only be a couple of minutes.' This time there was complete silence. 'Yeah righto Les,' said Norton out loud to himself. He checked his pockets for change and went out the door.

Eddie answered the phone immediately.

'Hello, is that you Eddie? It's Les.'

'G'day Les. How's it goin' mate?' Eddie sounded quite pleased to hear Norton's voice.

'Ohh, not too bad.'

'So what's happening over there in beautiful downtown Redfern? Is Kilby still alive, or have you knocked him or what?'

'No. He's still alive,' replied Les a little hesitantly.

'Still hanging in is he? How did you go with that watchband caper? Did it work?'

'Yeah. Like a charm. Thanks for that Eddie.'

'That's okay. Anytime you want any more dirty tricks just give me a call.'

'Yeah, I will,' laughed Les.

'So,' said Eddie. He paused for a moment but the chuckle was still in his voice. 'What can I do for you this time? You wouldn't be ringing me up on a shitty day like this unless you wanted something.'

'Ohh no ... not really.' Norton wasn't actually lying, but

he wasn't quite telling the truth either. 'It's just that I mightn't get a chance to ring Price tonight and I wanted you to give him a message. That's all.'

'Yeah?'

'Just tell him everything's sweet and we still should have a result Tuesday. Wednesday at the most.'

'Good as gold. I'll be seeing him at the game tonight, so I'll tell him then.'

There was another short pause before Eddie spoke. 'You sure there's nothing else?'

'Well,' drawled Norton. 'I did happen to notice in this morning's paper, Dealer's Choice is running in the seventh at Canterbury.'

'And you want to know if it's going?'

'Yeah.'

'Price was talking about it last night. It's coming back from a spell. But they reckon each way it's a fairly good thing.'

'All right. Well look. I haven't got the Brute's phone number with me. Can you get something on "the Murray" for me?'

'Sure. How much?'

Norton hesitated for a second or two and screwed his face up as if he was in some sort of pain. 'Two-fifty each way.'

'Sweet as a nut. I'll ring him as soon as you hang up.'

'Good on you Eddie.'

'Listen, before you go. You sure there's nothing else you want to tell me? How about filling me in a bit on what you're up to over there.'

'Monday for sure, Eddie. Tell Price I'll ring him Monday night and I'll dead-set give you the drum then. Okay?'

'All right Les. I'll tell him you're going to ring him Monday evening. And I'll make sure I'm there when you do.'

'Good on you Eddie. Thanks mate.'

'Well I'll hear from you Monday.'

Yeah thought Norton after he'd hung up. I just hope to Christ I got something to tell you that makes sense by then. Oh well. He stared absently at the phone for a few moments, then returned to room 9.

The maid, or whoever, had left fresh sheets and pillowcases outside the door and Norton bundled them up under his arm and took them in with him. A fresh pot of tea was sitting on the table so he poured himself a cup then stood in the middle of the room slowly sipping it while he looked at the others, who continued to read their papers in silence, treating him almost as if he wasn't there.

'So what's doing anyway?' said Norton after a minute or two.

There was continuing silence till Tjalkalieri finally looked up from his newspaper. 'Did you... say something Les?' he asked, raising his eyebrows slightly.

'Yeah. As a matter of fact I did Chalky. I asked what's doing. I didn't really mean anything by it. I was just... you know. Trying to make conversation.'

There was silence again for a few moments. Then Mumbi spoke. 'What's doing, did you say Les?' he said slowly. 'Nothing's doing Les. It's a prick of a day outside and seeing as we've been working like dogs the last couple of days we're going to take it easy. Sit around. Read. Listen to the radio. And in a few minutes I might even turn the TV on. Okay?'

'I told you that yesterday Les,' said Tjalkalieri. 'Fair dinkum. What do we have to do to get something through to you, Norton? Write it on a message stick and shove it in your arse?'

'All right you team of cunts,' said Norton. 'I was only bloody asking. Christ, you've got to be the greatest lot of narks I ever come across in my life.' He moved over to the balcony and peered sourly out through the glass door at the thin sheets of rain the southerly was wafting in from the street.

'If you're looking for something to do,' said Yarrawulla, 'instead of standing around like a stale bottle of piss, why don't you go out and get us some lunch.'

'Yeah, my oath,' chimed in Yarrawulla. 'It's after bloody twelve and I'm starving. In fact we shouldn't even have to bloody ask you. It should be here on the table.'

Norton turned from the balcony and gave them a smile that had about as much warmth in it as a mile under the polar ice-cap. 'And anything in particular you'd like for lunch...boys?'

'Yeah,' replied Tjalkalieri brightly. 'Some more of those steak sandwiches, Les. Those last ones were spot on.'

'Spot on were they? Oh I'm so pleased.' Norton went into the bedroom, put his tracksuit top on and got some more money. 'And anything else you might like while I'm out?' he asked with exaggerated politeness.

'Yeah. A bit more fruit,' said Yarrawulla.

'And another carton of milk,' added Mumbi. 'For the tea.'

'Oh yes of course. We mustn't forget our bloody tea, must we?' Norton glared at each of them as they ignored him and continued to read their papers. He zipped up his track-suit top and left the room, trying his best not to rip the door off its hinges as he went.

Fair dinkum, he thought, those three skinny little pricks are going to drive me round the bend before this is all over. Get us this. Get us that. Cups of tea. Fruit. Muesli bloody bars. Pizzas. But inside he couldn't help but chuckle a little. He knew the boys' nature, and that most of the time they were just trying to goad him and if he blew his stack he'd only be playing into their hands. Then they'd shove it up him worse than ever. You can't help but like the cheeky little bastards though, he thought. He jammed his hands a bit further into the pockets of his track-suit top as he strode on into the light rain. Still, he'd be more than glad when this Kilby caper was over and done with. The thought of being stuck in that room for another three days didn't appeal. Already it felt like he'd been there a month.

Norton was turning out to be a pretty good customer by now, so the Greek in the hamburger shop gave him a big, oily smile when he walked in. He whipped up the steak sandwiches with plenty of extra onions while Norton got a large bag of fruit and some magazines from a shop across the road.

By the time he arrived back at room 9 the boys had switched the TV on and were laughing like drains at an old Marx Brothers movie, *Duck Soup*.

'Hey grab a seat, Les, and have a look at this,' roared Tjalkalieri as Norton placed the food on the table. 'It's the funniest thing you've ever seen in your life.'

'Yeah,' giggled Mumbi. 'There's a big, boofheaded heavy running around trying to get Groucho — and he looks just like you.'

The rest of the afternoon was spent eating, drinking tea and watching a special run of Marx Brothers movies on Channel 10. Despite himself and the rotten day Norton found himself laughing like a hyena along with the others. Maybe because it was such a miserable bastard of a day outside it made the movies seem funnier than ever.

At ten past four Les turned the TV down just a little and switched the radio on, telling the boys it would only be for a minute or two as it was the second leg of the double and he'd backed one of Price's horses. By the time they'd swung round the turn and Dealer's Choice was fourth on the rail heading into the straight, Norton had the $250 each way at 8-1 counted, folded and in the bank.

The sky had blackened noticeably as the southerly picked up, and so had Norton's face when Dealer's Choice got beaten in a photo finish for third. He switched the radio off, almost snapping the knob from the dial, and resumed his seat. Somehow the Marx Brothers seemed to have lost a lot of their humour. Medicine men or not, Tjalkalieri and the others didn't have to be mind-readers to know what had just happened. Norton's face was showing about as much mirth as the public executioner in Tehran, not that this was going to stop them from a stir.

'What's up, Les?' asked Yarrawulla, with mock innocence. 'Don't you like the Marx Brothers?'

'No Yarra,' hissed Norton. 'They're my fuckin' favourites.'

'That's good,' chuckled Mumbi. ''Cause you're gonna love the next one.'

'Yeah Mumbles. And why's fuckin' that?'

'It's called *A Day At The Races*.'

If looks could have killed, Numidi, Natjinin and Mammanduru would have been waiting a long time for their men to come back to Binjiwunyawunya.

It certainly wasn't the best day in Les Norton's life. It was raining, cold and miserable, he was stuck in a room in a grotty hotel in Redfern, and now he was $500 down the gurgler as well. The only two things Norton could find to give him any sort of cheer were: one, he didn't come across a TAB when he went out to get lunch or he probably would have put more on Dealer's Choice; and two, when the boys sent him out for more pizzas he lied and told them the shop was closed so he'd have to get Chinese food again instead, which he knew the boys hated. Especially the prawn chow mein, of which he got four extra serves. Norton wasn't real keen on the local version of Chinese food himself, but even though it was a bit like cutting his nose off to spite his face it was worth it just to hear the whingeing and see the looks on the faces of the boys as they forced themselves to eat it.

But despite an annoying day and a boring night watching TV, Norton managed to sleep well enough. In fact he was almost nodding off in his seat by the time John Wayne finally got Maureen O'Hara's pants off in *The Quiet Man*.

Sunday was almost a repetition of Saturday. The rain had eased up slightly, but Norton noticed it was definitely colder as soon as he stepped out of the hotel to get the boys their steak sandwiches and the Sunday papers. The only variation after that was every now and again one of the boys would get up to make a fresh pot of tea.

By lunchtime Norton had read every paper twice. He had steak sandwiches coming out of his ears and he swore that if he never had another cup of tea again as long as he lived it would still be too soon. The others, however, kept pouring it down their throats like they owned Ceylon. All Norton could think of was his comfortable home in Bondi, his nice big double bed and how every Sunday Warren used to grate a big heap of potatoes and onions and they'd have a late breakfast of hash browns and ham and eggs. With percolated American-style coffee that strong you almost needed a whip, a chair and a gun to keep it down in the cup.

Meanwhile the weather added to Norton's blues. You couldn't open the door to let in a bit of air because the wind blew the rain in on the carpet. Besides which all the extra onion on the steak sandwiches was beginning to work and every two or three minutes one of the boys would let go a fart that would've won an Olympic gold medal. Norton did his best to fight back but with three on to one it was no contest. During one particular volley if anyone had walked past the room they would have thought there was a Salvation Army band in there, tuning up. And if the noise was bad enough the smell would stop a wildebeest. Mumbi let go one particular scorcher that stung Norton's eyes and he swore that if Mumbi had let it go out in the hallway it would have set off every sprinkler in the hotel.

Raining or not, Norton ran to the balcony door, tore it open and shoved his head outside, only to be hit with a violent chorus of 'Close the bloody door, you stupid big prick. It's freezing.'

'Right. That's it,' Les said, closing the door behind him and wiping rainwater from his face and hands. 'Those bloody steak sandwiches are definitely off the menu.'

'Yeah. Pig's arse they are' replied Tjalkalieri. 'They're about the only things around here worth eating.'

'In fact to tell you the truth,' chimed in Yarrawulla, 'we were just thinking of sending you up to get some more. It's after lunchtime you know.'

'Yeah? Well too bloody bad.' Les resumed his seat and began flicking through the Sunday paper once more. 'You want more steak sandwiches. You can go up and get 'em your bloody selves.'

'Fair enough' replied Tjalkalieri casually. He folded his paper, stretched his legs out in front of him and clasped his hands behind his head then smiled over at Les. 'But no steak sandwiches. No chant tomorrow morning.'

Norton glared at the smiling Tjalkalieri, then at all three of them. 'Fair bloody dinkum,' he cursed. 'You three have got to be the most obnoxious little turds I've ever come across in my life.' He rose to his feet and once more zipped up his tracksuit top. 'No bloody wonder old Bjelke won't have a bar of you.'

As he opened the door to step outside Mumbi called out to him. 'Hey Les.'

'Yeah?'

The grinning little Aborigine lifted one cheek of his backside off the lounge and let go with a fart that made the others sound like the tinkling of a wind chime.

'Don't forget the extra onions — will you,' Mumbi added.

Norton knew he was a beaten man as he trudged off into the rain once more. And it was further emphasised when he returned and wanted to watch the *Wide World of Sport*. He was ruthlessly vetoed in favour of an absolutely diabolical Elvis Presley movie. The girls in it all had those horrible beehive hairdos and wore bikinis about a metre wide on the sides. Elvis mumbled his way through several inane songs and carried on like some pimply faced adolescent you'd expect to see hanging around a pinball parlour near a Western Suburbs railway station. And if that Elvis movie wasn't bad enough there was another one, an even worse one, on straight after it. And the boys insisted on watching that also.

It was obvious it was going to be Annoy Les Norton Afternoon. All they did was fart, eat, watch Elvis and do everything they could think of to goad Les into blowing his stack. But Norton persevered and did his best to ignore them. The climax came, however, after Les had gone up and got their pizzas for tea and they were all settled back watching the news on Channel 2.

As they sat there, stuffing themselves with tea and pizzas, the news flashed onto an anti-apartheid demonstration outside the South African Embassy in Canberra. A small crowd of beefy-looking, crewcutted women dressed mainly in overalls were screaming their lungs out, burning flags and making horrible noisy arseholes of themselves while they did everything possible to provoke a number of cold, frustrated young policemen into arresting them. The young cops having to take all the abuse and grit their teeth looked like they would have liked nothing better than to take their caps and badges off and thump the stuffing out of the lot of them. Norton thought this might be as good a time as any to have a go back at the boys, who were watching the demonstration with looks more of contempt than anything else.

'Fair dinkum' said Les sarcastically. 'Fancy those silly sheilas sticking up for you Aborigines. You'd think they'd have more bloody sense.'

'What was that?' said Tjalkalieri.

'I said those sheilas sticking up for you Aborigines. They're wasting their bloody time.'

Tjalkalieri looked at Norton in both disgust and amazement. 'Do you really think those... those so-called women are sticking up for us?'

'Yeah. Well of course they are,' replied Les. The tone of Tjalkalieri's voice had taken him back slightly. 'Anti-apartheid. South Africa. Aborigines. Same bloody thing isn't it?'

'Have another look at them, Les.'

Norton studied the demonstrators for a few moments. One of them — a particularly sour Slavic-faced blonde in a Levi jacket — had just flung red paint on one of the police and was now on her back, kicking and screaming as she was getting dragged off by the arms to a waiting paddy-wagon. 'Paula. Paula,' she was screaming out to one of her equally sour-faced girlfriends as if she was in mortal agony. 'Help me. Help me.' She wasn't in all that much pain and it was obvious she was putting an act on for the cameras.

'Notice anything about them?' asked Tjalkalieri.

'They all look like they could do with a good wash,' he shrugged.

'Yeah,' snorted Tjalkalieri. 'And they're all bloody lesbians too.'

From his observations around the Cross Les had to agree. 'Yeah, they're all dykes. That's fairly obvious. So what?'

'And you think those dykes are sticking up for us do you?'

'Well... I...' Norton was beginning to wish he hadn't said anything now.

'Now have a look at the cops. They're nearly all young blokes. Right?'

Norton kept his eye on the screen. 'Well... yeah.'

'Well that's how the dykes get their rocks off, you dopey big clown.' Norton could sense the bitterness increasing in Tjalkalieri's voice and the others weren't looking too happy either. 'Those man-hating dykes couldn't give a stuff about Australian Aborigines. Demonstrating against South Africa is just an excuse to pick a fight with those young cops and look like heroes at the same time. They love it.' Tjalkalieri turned from Les back to the TV. 'Have a look at that thing they're dragging into the wagon. She's just about blowing in her pants. Once she gets in the back of the wagon she'll start fingering herself.'

'Oh come on. Turn it up.'

'Turn it up my arse,' snorted Yarrawulla. 'Heaps of mugs like you tumble in and think they've got the interests of our people at heart. Balls. They wouldn't give an Aborigine the time of day. You won't get your head on TV sticking up for Abos.'

'All right. I just...'

'Hypocrites. They give me the bloody shits,' continued Tjalkalieri. 'One of the only blokes in this country who's fair dinkum about helping Australian Aborigines is Peter Garrett.'

'That bloke out of Midnight Oil?'

'Oh you do know bloody something Les. That's a change.'

Then it was on. Somehow, just looking for a joke, Norton had unsuspectingly touched a nerve with the boys, especially Tjalkalieri. And it wasn't funny. They sat on the lounge very sourly, gesticulating amongst themselves and arguing in their native tongue. Then Tjalkalieri reached over and abruptly switched the TV off, after which you could have cut the air with a knife.

Christ, what have I done, thought Les as he sat there in the almost inflammable silence. Every now and again one of the boys would mutter something under his breath to the others and they'd all glare murderously at the blank TV. Norton couldn't ever remember seeing the boys in such a foul mood. What he'd said was only meant as a joke, and a very mild, back-handed one at that. He didn't dream it would be so provocative. But evidently those lesbian protesters had rubbed the boys right up the wrong way, especially where it concerned their people.

After about five minutes or so of uncomfortable silence Norton had had enough. He thought it might be a good idea if he got out of the room and left the boys alone for a while.

'Look,' he said. 'I, ah... might go for a walk for a few minutes. Get a can of Coke or something. You blokes want anything while I'm up the road?'

There was an almost imperceptible shaking of heads and

113

more sour looks followed by continuing silence.

'All right. Well I'll only be about fifteen minutes or so. I'll see you when I get back.' The door clicked quietly and he was gone.

Norton didn't see anybody else in the hotel as he trotted down the stairs and when he got out on the footpath he had a quick look in the bar. There was no sign of Bailey and no more than half a dozen people in there. The streets were quiet also. A few cars swishing past and that was about it. Satisfied it would be safe to leave the boys alone in their room for a while, Les started walking; straight up Regent Street.

I don't know about a Coke, he thought, as he trudged along in the soft glow of the neon signs and shop lights. I wouldn't mind a beer after that little caper. Should've had one in the bar, I suppose, but I might've bumped into the owner and I sure don't feel like talking or trying to crack jokes with anyone at the moment.

After he'd crossed the next intersection and got a bit further down the street, Les noticed a couple of people standing beneath a red canvas awning in a lane off to his right. In the darkness he could just make out the words Redfern RSL. Hello he thought, the local 'rissole'. That'll do just nicely. I'll have a couple of schooners and a lash at the pokies. Wonder if I can get in wearing my tracksuit and joggers. Round here? Can't see why not.

Just like the Kelly Club, he laughed to himself as he stepped under the small, canvas awning and through the wood, panelled door. Don't think it'll be quite the same clientele though.

Apart from a woman using a red phone in the foyer there was no one else around and no one at the reception desk. A red and brown carpeted hallway, flanked by a large photo of the Queen, led inside, so he followed that along to what appeared to be the main bar.

It was a typical, fair-sized RSL bar, with poker machines around the walls and another circle of machines in the middle. There was a restaurant selling Asian food plus a menu of hamburgers, pies and chips for the local plebians. In front of him were a blank video screen and a small stage with a sign on it — 'Lester And Smart Next Show 9 p.m.' Les didn't think he'd bother staying for the floor show. The place was happily noisy, however, fairly crowded with boozy, casually dressed whites and almost the same number of Aborigines. No one approached Les for membership as he stood there, so he eased himself through the drinkers, the rattle of the poker machines and the cigarette haze, finding an uncrowded spot right in the corner of the bar. There didn't appear to be any Fourex on tap or in the fridges, so he settled for a schooner of Tooheys new. A skinny tired-looking barman had it in front of him pretty smartly and it was cold and crisp and hit the spot almost straight away. Norton downed most of it and got ready to order another.

Well this isn't too bad, he thought, propping himself up on his elbows with his back to the bar after the second schooner arrived. And it sure is nice to get out of that room for a while. He took another huge slurp of his schooner. I'll finish this, get another and run a few bucks through the pokies.

Norton was almost lost in pleasant thoughts as he leant against the bar checking out the heads on the locals. Although he wouldn't be able to stay too long, it was good to get a break out of the room away from the others and in a place where no one knew him and he could lean back and enjoy the pleasure of his own company over a nice, cold beer. He took another hefty swallow. And there's nothing wrong with the Tooheys on tap either.

But unbeknown to Les there was one person in the club that did know him. A tall Aborigine in a tracksuit similar to Norton's had been watching him intently, almost from the moment he had ordered his first beer. He was standing off to Norton's left, where the bar cornered round in front of the Men's Toilets, drinking with two other Aborigines from the local football team — one about the same size, the other shorter but more solid. He said something to the two men who looked over at Les, nodded grimly, then looked away again. The tallest one turned slightly side on to Norton while he sipped his beer but never took his eyes off him.

So, thought Frank, Vernon Stroud the chartered accountant, eh? Or is it Les Norton? Price Galese's so-called bloody heavy. Well you don't look so heavy to me, you red-headed goose. And you're right out of your territory. I think we might just be having a little word or two before the night's over. And it won't be about donations for South bloody Africa either.

Norton finished his schooner and placed the glass on the bar.

'Same again mate?' said the barman.

'Yeah. But make it a middy this time will you? And take

it out of that. I'm going for a leak.' Norton nodded to some change on the bar and moved towards the toilets. That beer's nice all right he thought. But shit! It goes through you like a packet of bloody Epsom Salts. Easing himself through the other drinkers, Les still didn't notice the three pairs of brown eyes watching him stealthily but intently as he entered the toilets. They gave him a minute or so then Frank nodded to the other two and they followed him inside.

Alone in the men's room, Norton had just finished and was standing in front of a long mirror above a row of hand-basins, while he rinsed his hands and splashed a bit of water on his face. A movement to his left caught his eyes and the hairs on the back of his neck bristled as he immediately recognised Frank. A quick surge of adrenalin hit the pit of his stomach. The sour look on Frank's face and the way his two associates were swarming behind him like a pair of hungry barracudas told Norton something wasn't quite right. Casually, he moved to the roll-towel on his right, pulled it down, and acting blasé, began drying his hands. Frank and his mates moved a little closer to Les, surrounding him yet not quite crowding him. Frank stood in the middle with his arms folded.

'How're you goin' there mate. All right?' sneered Frank, menace dripping off his every word.

'Yeah, not bad,' replied Norton breezily. His back was to Frank who couldn't see his eyebrows bristling as he continued slowly wiping his hands.

'How're all the chartered accountants these days?'

Norton looked at Frank quizzingly and shrugged his shoulders. 'I don't think I know what you're talking about.' He finished drying his hands and turned to face the three of them.

'Don't give me the fuckin' shits,' continued Frank. 'You know what I'm talking about, you prick. You were snooping around in our office the other day with your shitpot $250. Weren't you. Les Norton.'

At the sound of his own name, Norton couldn't help but look surprised. How the bloody hell did he find out who I am, he thought. But it was too late now. The game was definitely up.

'You're about as much a fuckin' chartered accountant as what I am,' hissed Frank. 'You're one of Price Galese's bumboys aren't you? Come over to try and put the frighteners on Perce.'

Norton didn't say anything. He just stood there rocking

116

slightly on the balls of his feet, his eyes moving across the three faces in front of him as he sussed out the situation and set himself up.

'So you think you're gonna put shit on us do you,' Frank continued. 'Well you're in the wrong part of town. Arsehole.'

Frank had now unfolded his arms and the other two had bunched their fists. Les knew he had about two seconds to make a move.

'Look mate,' he said, turning his hands palms up to Frank in a gesture of helplessness, 'I honestly don't know what you're talking about.'

Frank was about to say something else before they moved in, when quick as a snake Norton closed his left hand and hooked his massive fist into the face of the solid Aborigine to his right. It caught him flush under the nose, ripping apart his top lip and caving in most of his front teeth. From the shock that ran up his arm Norton knew it was a knockout punch.

As the solid thug yelped and spun along the washbasins before he hit the far wall and dropped to the floor, Les swung a quick short right, hitting Frank on the jaw. He was a bit crowded though and couldn't get his shoulder properly behind it. It hurt Frank and flung him against the toilet doors, but it didn't drop him. By now, though, the last hood had swung into action.

As Norton was about to step in and follow up on Frank with a left hook he just detected a movement out of the corner of his eye. He managed to tuck his chin in and move his shoulder up as a solid right thumped in behind his ear and a left caught him above the eye. That was all hood number two had a chance to get in. Norton spied an opening, bent slightly at the knees and let go a monstrous right uppercut that caught the tall Aborigine right under the chin, shattering his jaw like a sledgehammer hitting a housebrick. He let out a little shriek of shock and agony, made a grab for the towel-rack for support and brought the lot crashing down noisily on top of him as his knees went from under him. That now left only Frank, whose confidence had taken quite a dive at the sight of his two friends out like lights on the men's room floor. But he was tough, fit and an ex-heavyweight fighter; plus he had a slight drop on Norton who was just turning around after dropping hood number two.

Frank tore into Les, throwing lefts and rights which nearly all landed and stung. But one on one, even for an ex-pro it was no match. As soon as he got settled Norton swung a peach of a left into Frank's face that completely mashed the tall Aborigine's mouth and made his already broken nose 'even broker'. A short right, straight after, split open his cheek and flung him back against the toilets. It was almost lights out time for poor Frank. But instead of following through with another barrage of punches Les took him by the front of his tracksuit, moved slightly to one side as he jerked him forward, and in almost the same movement grabbed Frank by the scruff of the neck, shoving him face forward up over the washbasins and into the full-length mirror. Frank's big, bony forehead split open and sent cracks splintering along the glass at the same time. The linen handtowel was still rolled out all over the floor and as Frank began to slide to his knees, Norton grabbed a length of towel, wrapped it around Frank's neck and began choking him. With Frank turning blue and gagging for his life, Les dragged him to his feet, spun him around and forced him up over the basins again.

By now Frank's face wasn't the most appetising sight in the world. His hair was matted with blood and tears were streaming out of his eyes, running into the blood pouring from his nose and mouth and the wicked zigzag cut in his cheek. 'Now listen — you fuckin' yobbo,' hissed Norton, his eyes about an inch from the barely conscious Aborigine's. 'I didn't come here looking for any trouble. I'm over here for another reason altogether. But if you, or your smartarse boss want trouble, I'll give it to you. By the container load. You understand?' Les jerked the towel around Frank's neck. Kilby's offsider was in too much pain and discomfort to say anything, but the terrified look in his eyes said the message had got through. 'Good,' smiled Norton. 'Now, Frank, you're a bit of a mess old mate. I think we'd better get you cleaned up.'

He dragged Frank across to the nearest toilet, pushed him through the door, shoved his head down the bowl and pushed the flush button. Frank coughed and spluttered as Les kept his head down and the smelly water sloshed up his nose and into his mouth, turning a weird purple as the blood blended in with the blue flushmatic. Norton dumped him casually in the cubicle, checked on the other two, who were still snoring soundly, and with a grunt of satisfaction walked out of the men's room.

With all that noise and shouting, thought Norton, it's a wonder nobody's come in to see what's going on. As he opened the door he saw why. Another Aborigine, big but more over-weight than anything else, had been left standing outside to make sure Frank and his two cohorts weren't disturbed. The blackman didn't actually turn white when he saw Norton suddenly appear out of the men's room unscathed. But he certainly went a very milk coffee colour.

'You a mate of Frank's are you?' grinned Les. The Aborigine gave two very short, very quick nods. 'Well he needs you inside. There's no toilet paper and he wants you to hold his legs while he does a handstand under the blow dryer.' The Aborigine blanched even more, gave Norton a double blink, then turned and ran inside.

There was no blood on Les's face; he'd made sure of that in the mirror as he walked out. Apart from a sore knuckle, a sore ear and a thickening above his left eye, he hadn't been hurt. For a fairly willing fight with three big men he'd hardly raised a sweat. But he hadn't lost his thirst. His middy was still sitting on the bar with his change, so he downed that and ordered another, drinking it pretty smartly while he watched the shocked looks on the faces of the small group of men surging around the front and coming in and out of the men's room. Oddly enough, apart from the goon who'd been left standing outside, nobody seemed to know who did it. But Les surmised that it would only be a matter of time before someone said something. He finished his middy, delib-erated on whether or not to get another, then decided to leave.

Walking back to the hotel, Norton's amusement at the funny side of belting Frank and his mates started to wear off and a few worrying thoughts began to enter his head. Frank was a twenty-four carat mug and deserved to get flattened, there was no two ways about that. And so did his two mates. But from another angle that little incident back at the RSL could cause some repercussions. Price had been adamant that nothing was to happen to Kilby or any of his associates because of the newspapers. And knowing Frank's type and how they operated there would be no way he would tell the truth about what happened. It would come out more like Norton and a few of Galese's heavies jumped him outside when he was drunk and gave him a kicking. And now that they'd found out who he was — how they did was still a mystery to Norton — what would Kilby's reaction be? He'd have to interpret this, along with Les calling into the AWEC office, as Galese trying to put pressure on him. The one thing Price didn't want. Now Kilby could dig his heels in and demand more money. He could go to the papers with Frank and scream assault and intimidation. It was only their word against Norton's and Kilby could do any bloody thing. If this bone-pointing thing didn't work out, and Les was getting dubious about that, he could find himself right up shit creek, without a paddle and with a rather large hole in the bottom of the boat as well.

Norton's mood grew gloomier and gloomier as he approached the hotel. And it grew even more so after he'd told the boys what had just happened.

They'd turned the TV back on and were sitting in the same spot watching a Bryan Brown movie when Les walked in. At first they didn't appear to take all that much notice, but when he explained to them who Frank was Tjalkalieri reached over and turned the TV off and the three of them sat there staring at Les — incredulous, almost horrified looks on their faces.

'And one of the men you just beat up. This Frank,' said Tjalkalieri. 'That's Percy Kilby's offsider?'

Norton nodded glumby.

'And he's in the AWEC office with Kilby nearly all the time?'

Norton nodded again. 'I imagine so.'

Tjalkalieri turned to the others. 'Shit!' he cursed. The looks on Mumbi and Yarrawulla seemed to echo Tjalkalieri's sentiments precisely.

Norton stared at the three of them for a moment or two. 'Why, what's the trouble?' he shrugged. 'It's not going to make any difference to what you blokes are up to . . . is it?'

'That's where you're wrong, Les,' sighed Mumbi. 'It's going to make a difference all right. A lot of difference.'

Norton's jaw dropped slightly. After the other thoughts that had been running through his mind this was all he needed. He stared at them for want of an explanation.

'You see, Les,' said Tjalkalieri quietly and seriously. 'Kilby can draw strength from this.' He gave a brief, sympathetic smile at the dumb, hurt look on Norton's face. 'It's hard to explain to an outsider. But with Frank in the office all day next to Kilby, and us trying to take away Kilby's Kurinata, his Kurinata can draw not only on Frank's pain, but the revenge and hatred that would be inside him for you.'

'Yeah,' added Yarrawulla. 'And this . . . this aura of hatred and violence entering right into where we're pointing the bone. It could bugger things up completely for us.'

'Shit!' cursed Norton.

'This pointing the bone is a very involved, very complicated ceremony Les. I know we tend to make light of it and make it look easy. But there's a lot more to it than what you think. There's a hell of a lot of things can go wrong. And this is one of the worst things that can happen.'

Norton closed his eyes and shook his head. 'Shit!' he cursed again. 'So what happens now?'

'We honestly don't know, Les,' sighed Tjalkalieri, giving his head a bit of a shake. 'And I don't want to alarm you. But ... it's not looking too good.'

'Bloody hell,' cursed Norton once more. 'Just my fuckin' luck.'

Everyone was silent for a moment. There was just the noise of the wind against the balcony door and the gentle spattering of the rain on the tiles.

Mumbi rubbed a little warmth into his arms and got to his feet. 'I'm going to make a fresh pot of tea. We'll talk about it over a cuppa.'

Mumbi made the tea and they sipped it slowly while they talked between themselves, mostly in their own language. Les just sat there, cursing himself for going into the RSL in the first place. The boys stopped talking. For a few moments there was complete silence. Then they had another quite excited burst, nodded solemnly to each other and turned to Norton.

'We may possibly have just one card left up our sleeve,' said Tjalkalieri. 'It's a dicey one, but it might work. But if it doesn't ...' Tjalkalieri shrugged his shoulder at Norton.

'What is it? Tell us.'

Mumbi shook his head. 'We're tired and we're going to bed,' he said as they all got to their feet. 'We suggest you do the same, and we'll talk about it in the morning.'

Norton nodded his head and stared disconsolately at the floor for a little while. In fifteen minutes they were all in bed. Despite what Tjalkalieri had just said, the big Queenslander felt pretty ordinary as he lay there, staring up at the ceiling. It was a very worried Les Norton who finally got off to sleep about an hour after the others.

The rain appeared to have stopped when Les walked out into the main room around seven the following morning. The southerly was still blowing, though not as hard and nowhere near as cold. Through the open balcony door Les could see several small patches of blue in the grey lumpiness of the sky. The empty cups on the table next to the teapot told him the boys had been up for a while. They were stripped down to their tracksuit pants, daubing themselves with ochre and feathers, and while Les's eyes were grainy and he felt a little tired from not sleeping so well, the others looked fresh and relaxed.

'G'day fellas' he said with a slight yawn. 'How are you?'

'Not too bad, Les,' replied Tjalkalieri. He was standing side on to Norton as Mumbi daubed his back with yellow ochre. The others, who were already painted, gave Les a cheery greeting also.

Despite their freshness, Norton could detect a very businesslike manner, almost a sense of urgency. He studied them for a moment or two then walked towards the table.

'Any tea left?' he said, placing a hand on the still warm teapot.

'There might be one cup left in there,' replied Yarrawulla.

There was, just, so Norton poured it and took a seat.

'So what's doing? You want me to go and get you some breakfast?'

'Not this morning,' replied Tjalkalieri. 'We might have some fruit for lunch. That's about all.'

'Whatever.' Norton took a sip of tea while the others continued to daub Tjalkalieri with symbols. 'So what's the story anyway? You said something last night, Chalky, about having one last card up your sleeve. What is it?'

'I'll tell you in a minute. Just wait'll we finish doing this.'

Norton continued to sip his tea, watching intently as Mumbi finished painting a pair of braces in white circles and yellow dots across Tjalkalieri's back. The others were painted in fairly similar fashion, only in red and brown. All had blood-smeared parrot feathers in their hair and tucked up under their stringy black headbands. After a minute or two Mumbi stepped back and nodded to Tjalkalieri.

'Yeah. I reckon that ought to do,' he said.

'Right then,' replied Tjalkalieri. 'We'll have time for another cup of tea then we'll get stuck into it.

Yarrawulla went to the bathroom as Mumbi put the kettle on and Tjalkalieri walked over to Norton.

'Righto, Les,' he said, 'I'll try and give you an idea about what's going on. We're going to have to chant like buggery today. All day. Probably right up till about five. Then we've got to be left alone in the room for about an hour while we go into a trance and summon up the serpent spirit.'

'The serpent spirit?'

'That's right. And I'm not even going to bother trying to explain it to you.' An air of brittle politeness crept into Tjalkalieri's voice. 'In the meantime, you've got to arrange a confrontation with Kilby for us. Can you do that?'

'A confrontation?'

'Exactly. And not in his office, and not right up close to him. It's got to be about twenty feet away. Can you arrange that?'

Norton took another sip of tea. 'I'll have to won't I,' he shrugged.

'If you want this to work you will.'

'When do you want to see him?'

'About an hour after we finish our trance. Say six thirty. But no later than seven.'

'Okay. I'll work something out.'

Yarrawulla re-entered the room just as Mumbi finished making the tea. He gave the others a cup each and looked at Les who shook his head.

'Now you got all that?' said Tjalkalieri. 'We have to front Kilby no later than seven. And it's absolutely vital that we do.'

'As a bean,' nodded Les. 'I'll sort something out.'

'Good on you. Now,' Tjalkalieri turned to the others, 'Kilby and Frank are in their office. We'll finish our tea then I think we'd better get stuck into it.' The others nodded in agreement.

Norton got up from his seat, walking across to the open glass door and looked out over the balcony. There didn't appear to be any cars or movement around the AWEC office. He scratched his chin thoughtfully for a moment and turned to the others. How would they know if Kilby was in his office yet or not, he wondered. I still don't know about all this bloody mental telepathy bullshit. And what's all this about summoning up the serpent spirit? Norton shook his head. If you ask me, this is turning into one big shemozzle all around. Why did I open my big mouth in the first place?

He sat back down on the lounge chair and let the others move to the balcony door. The bone was on the floor wrapped in the cotton sheet. Tjalkalieri picked it up, handed it to Mumbi, who had slipped on the Kurdaitcha shoes, then after nicking all their arms with the sharpened piece of quartz and bleeding onto the bone they started chanting and dancing once more; Mumbi with the bone in his left hand and the hair chord in his right playing it towards the AWEC office.

Deep in thought, Norton watched them from his seat, pondering how he was going to organise the confrontation with Kilby, and with him somewhere in the background. It was a bloody tricky one again, and no Eddie to help him this time. It was nine-thirty and each of them had taken a turn on the bone before Les made a move. He picked at his chin, nodded to himself, checked his pockets for change and went down to the yellow phone in the foyer.

When the phone rang Percy Kilby was sitting in his office feeling angry, ill and completely mystified. He was angry because of what had happened to Frank the night before. His illness, although nowhere near as bad as it had been, had started not long after he walked into the office. Which was why he was mystified. How could you feel like a million dollars all weekend, then feel like a shithouse as soon as you start work? This had to be the weirdest case of flu, or whatever it was, he'd ever had or ever heard of. He was definitely going to see a doctor that night. Kilby was crook all right. But he didn't feel anywhere near as bad as Frank, who was sitting opposite him, looked.

His lieutenant's mouth was puffed up and full of stitches. There were stitches in his cheek and a large portion of hair was missing just above his forehead, where the nurses at Prince Alfred had shaved it to add a few more stitches. Frank felt like he had more stitches in him than a wedding gown. And his two mates hadn't fared that much better. One had a broken jaw. The other had about the same amount of stitches in his mouth as Frank, and all his front teeth were gone. Frank's larynx wasn't in the best of shape either, from where Norton had tried to tie a Windsor knot around his throat with the towel. Which was why Kilby, sick and all as he now was, had to answer the phone. Frank's voice sounded like a Sydney silky with bronchitis. His discomfort, however, was matched by his hatred for Norton. And his hatred was matched equally by his fear. Frank had met some tough boys in his time, in the ring, in the street, and on the football field. But he'd never come across a punching machine like Les. No one could possibly fight like that. Nevertheless, it was quite a different version of the battle in the Redfern RSL men's room that he'd related to his boss.

Kilby reluctantly looked at the ringing phone for a few moments before finally reaching over and picking up the receiver. 'Yeah hello. AWEC', he growled.

'Is Percy Kilby there?' Norton crossed his fingers on his end of the line and hoped the plan he had in mind would work.

'This is Percy Kilby.'

Norton couldn't help but hesitate for a second or two before he answered. 'My name's Les Norton. I work for Price Galese.'

There was a shocked pause for a moment, then Kilby exploded. '*What!*' he roared. 'You — you cunt. You've got a fuckin' hide ringing me. After what you and your mates did to my assistant last night.' Kilby put his hand over the receiver and looked at Frank. 'It's that prick from last night. Les Norton.' Frank gave a double blink. 'I can't believe your front ringing me after what you and your team did to Frank. What do you want anyway? You arsehole.'

'What did your mate Frank say happened to him last night?'

'You and a couple of other clowns jumped him outside the RSL when he was half full of piss and gave him a kicking.' Kilby stared over at Frank, who swallowed hard and looked away.

Despite his apprehension Norton couldn't help but chuckle to himself: he hadn't been too far out in his summing up of Frank. 'Is that what he told you, is it? I think you'd better pull him aside later and find out the truth.'

'Ohh look, don't start coming on with that shit.' Kilby dismissed Norton's last statement with a contemptuous wave of his hand. 'Anyway, what do you want, you flip?'

'I want to see you. I want to have a word with you.'

'You want to see me, do you? Well I don't particularly want to see you. You cunt. And you can tell that old prick you work for, Galese, that the price has just gone up to $650,000 too.'

'That's what I want to see you about,' lied Les. 'Price has agreed to your offer.'

There was a sudden pause at Kilby's end of the line. 'He has?'

'Yeah. Look, what happened last night was just a mistake. But Price is prepared to give you $250,000 tonight. And another $250,000 next week. I'll have to get back to him about the other $150,000 though.'

Kilby drummed his fingers on the desk for a moment while he had a think. Coming on top of what happened to Frank, this took him completely by surprise. 'So you want to give me $250,000 tonight?'

'That's right.'

'What's wrong with bringing it round here? Right now.'

'No. It has to be on neutral territory. And there has to be other people around. We're talking about quarter of a million dollars you know.'

Kilby's eyes narrowed. 'I don't know. This all sounds a bit funny to me.'

'There's nothing shifty going on. I just don't trust you in your office — that's all.'

'Ohh don't give me the shits.'

'Look,' said Norton. 'What about I meet you up in the RSL tonight? I'll be on my own, and I'll have the money in a blue overnight bag. I'll put it on the bar and order a drink. What can possibly go wrong?'

'I don't know. It just don't seem right to me. You could have a bomb in the bag.'

'Ohh don't be stupid. You can open the bloody thing in front of me. And you can have as many mates with you as you like. But don't get any ideas in your head about giving me a serve, cause you won't get the rest of the dough.'

Kilby thought about it for a few seconds. What could go wrong? Norton would be on his own in a crowded RSL. And he'd make sure Frank and some of the boys were around. There'd be no point in giving Norton a serve over Frank and bombing the other $250,000. Plus possibly the extra $150,000. Fuck Frank if it came to that, anyway. Norton was right. What could possibly go wrong?

'Yeah all right,' agreed the AWEC boss. 'I'll see you up there when we finish here. About five.'

'I can't get there before six-thirty, seven.'

Kilby tapped on the desk for a second. 'Yeah righto. But no later than seven. I'm not too good and I want to get home to bed.'

'You're what?' Norton couldn't hide his surprise.

'I said I've had the flu or something the last few days. And I want to get home to bed.'

Norton's face broke into a grin. Kilby had been crook the last few days. Maybe this thing was working. 'No worries mate. I'll see you there about six-thirty. Seven at the latest.'

'Just make sure you are. And on your own. Or you and Galese can shove your money and I'll go straight to the papers.'

'Sweet as a nut. I'll see you up there.'

126

Kilby hung up abruptly.

Well thought Les, gazing absently through the door of the foyer in the direction of the AWEC office. That's that. I just hope to Christ I've done the right bloody thing. He sucked in a breath of air and let it out again. I think I have. Oh well. Too bloody late now. Anway, I'll go and get that fruit, then I s'pose I'd better tell the boys what's going on.

In room 9, Tjalkalieri, Mumbi and Yarrawulla were chanting away like there was no tomorrow. They didn't stop or even turn around when Les walked in, so he guessed they didn't want to be disturbed. He placed the fruit on the table, and still feeling a little tired, walked quietly into the bedroom and lay down staring up at the ceiling. Even though a multitude of thoughts were swirling around in his mind, the steady, low buzz of the boys chanting seemed to relax him as it drifted through the open door. It wasn't long before he'd dozed off.

He came to with a bit of a start just before twelve. Shit! What time is it? He blinked groggily at his watch, stretched, then went into the bathroom and splashed some cold water on his face. Back in the main room the boys were still chanting and dancing away steadily. He peeled and spread the fruit out on the table, then sat down on one of the seats and watched them. Before long it was afternoon and they abruptly stopped.

'Ohh shit!' said Tjalkalieri, flopping down on the seat nearest Les, while the others almost collapsed on to the settee. 'I'm buggered.'

Norton could see from the flushed looks on their faces and the trickles of sweat beneath their headbands that they were obviously quite exhausted. 'Hard work eh?'

'It is this time,' said Mumbi. 'We've really got to concentrate.'

'Yeah. I understand.' Norton felt more than a little self-conscious because it was mainly his fault. 'I'm sorry about last night.'

'That's all right' said Yarrawulla. 'You couldn't help what happened.' The little Aborigine tilted his head back and closed his eyes. 'Listen Les. What about making us a cup of tea. We're dead-set too fucked to move.'

'Yeah, sure mate,' replied Norton, getting to his feet. 'There's fruit on the table too if you want it. Do you want me to run out and get you something to drink? Some orange juice, or lemonade or something. What do you want?'

'Just a nice cup of tea'll do, Les,' said Tjalkalieri. Like

the others, he had his head tilted back and his eyes closed.

Norton made a pot of tea and after the first cup they seemed to have freshened up a little, so he poured them all another and made a fresh pot. While the kettle was boiling he told them about his phonecall to Kilby and what he'd organised. He hoped it suited them because if he had to ring Kilby back and change the arrangements there was a good chance he'd smell some sort of a rat and back off.

'Meeting him up the RSL was about the best thing I could think of fellas.' Norton threw the tea leaves in the pot, poured in the boiling water, then folded his arms and looked hopefully at them while he waited for it to draw. 'If I'd have arranged to meet him somewhere where there was no-one around, and I walked in with you, or you were already there, he'd get suspicious. He's a real shifty bastard.'

Tjalkalieri gave Norton a tired wink. 'Actually that's perfect, Les.' Which cheered Norton up immeasurably. 'It's best there's some people around. Even though what's going to happen will be over in a matter of seconds. With people around it will help to hide it. A small group, or one or two people would take notice. In a crowd there'll be confusion. No-one will be sure what's happened. You've done well, Les. It'll work out good.'

'Just what is going to happen?' asked Norton.

Tjalkalieri looked earnestly at Norton, looked for a second at the others, then back at Norton.

'Les,' he said slowly. 'What you're going to see briefly tonight . . . No white man in Australia, or the world for that matter, will have ever seen before.'

'Yeah?'

'We're going to fleetingly make contact with the Otherworld tonight Les. We can't, and we won't, explain it to you. But you must swear you'll never, ever, tell a soul what you'll see tonight. If you're quick enough to see it.'

Norton nodded solemnly. 'Yeah, fair enough.'

'There's forces in this world, Les,' chimed in Yarrawulla, 'that you and any other white man know nothing about. Even we're not too sure of them.'

'I can appreciate that. I've known you blokes, and about you, all my life.'

Tjalkalieri got up, took a piece of rockmelon from the table and chewed on it for a moment when he sat back down; as if he needed to get a sudden dryness out of his throat before he could continue.

'We're going to raise an evil spirit tonight, Les, and hope he'll do something for us. He's called Mungoongali. He's one of the evilest there is. The thing is, Mungoongali feeds on the weakest. If we don't insure that Percy Kilby's Kurinata is weaker than ours, Mungoongali will turn on us.'

Norton stared at the three of them and blinked. It all sounded like some sort of fairy tale. But their usual light-hearted banter had completely disappeared and the nervous looks on their faces told him they were deadly, even fearfully serious.

'If Mungoongali doesn't wish to do what we want him to do after we raise him from the Otherworld. He'll kill us.'

'What Tjalkalieri's trying to say,' said Mumbi, 'is we're laying our lives on the line tonight.'

'Jesus!'

'We'll need more than him to save us if this doesn't work out Les,' said Yarrawulla.

Norton stood there staring at them. Motionless. Absolutely lost for words.

'But don't worry, Les,' smiled Tjalkalieri. 'We're fairly confident our Kurinata's good.'

'Look,' said Norton, and he pointed at all three of them. 'I don't know much about all this spirit thing. But I know you blokes, and I know you've always been fair dinkum. If this is getting a bit beyond what you can handle, and there's any sort of danger to you, I want you to knock it on the head. That's fine by me. And I'll still give you your money. It's not worth it to lose three old mates.'

'No. Everything's going to be okay,' smiled Tjalkalieri. 'We've come this far. We can handle it.'

'Okay, suit yourselves,' shrugged Norton. 'But if you want to pull out — no sweat. It was a good try. And all this fuck-up's my fault anyway.'

'She'll be sweet, Les,' winked Mumbi.

'Anyway. I think we've got time for another cup of tea,' said Tjalkalieri. 'And then we'll get into it again. I'll tell you what. This rockmelon's all right.'

'Yeah I was just watching you,' said Yarrawulla. 'I might grab a bit myself.'

The boys finished their tea and most of the fruit. Then after using the bathroom they started chanting again. Yarrawulla took first turn at holding the bone.

There wasn't a great deal Les could do now. The fresh linen had been left outside the door so he made the beds

129

and cleaned up what little mess there was from lunch, doing his best to keep quiet and out of the way while the others continued their chanting. Tjalkalieri told him that when they'd finished their trance and went up to the RSL to do whatever it was they were going to do, they would still have to wear their body paint and their headbands with the blood-smeared feathers stuck in them. Their tracksuits would cover their bodies, but they would need some beanies or caps. So Les went out, found a K-Mart and bought three Khaki cotton, army-style bush hats. Back in the hotel he phoned Kingsley Sheehan, putting him on standby for Tuesday. That was no sweat said Kingsley. The rest of the afternoon Norton spent reading and half-dozing in the bedroom and before long it was five.

He folded his magazine, then went out to the main room and sat on one of the lounge chairs, watching as the boys gave it one last frantic burst before finishing just on ten past five.

'Shit! I reckon that ought to do it.' Tjalkalieri was the last one holding the bone. He placed it carefully on its sheet and they all flopped down in pretty much the same state of exhaustion as before. Eyes closed, heads back. Two on the settee, Tjalkalieri on the spare lounge chair across from Norton. 'What time is it Les?' he asked.

Norton couldn't help but feel for the little Aborigine. His arms dangling loose by his sides, feet spread out in front of him. Tiny streams of sweat were still trickling down his face. He was obviously buggered.

'About quarter past five, Chalky.'

'Righto. We'll take a break for five or ten minutes, then we'll get in touch with Mungoongali.' Their eyes still closed, the others nodded in agreement. 'This is where we're going to have to ask you to leave us for about an hour. What we're about to do now, you can't see. Sorry mate.'

'That's okay. I understand.' Norton got to his feet. 'I may as well get going now. I'll see you in about an hour.'

Well there's not a great deal I can do, thought Norton, standing outside the hotel. The rain had stopped but it was cool and starting to get quite dark. The Regent Street traffic was thick and noisy and exhaust fumes and other smog hung in the air, frozen momentarily by the headlights of passing cars. I'd better not go too far though. He had a quick glance through the drinkers crowded around the public bar. And I'd better not have anything to drink either. Oh well, guess

I'll just have to take in the sights of beautiful downtown Redfern for an hour.

If Norton had stepped out of the hotel about ten minutes earlier, he more than likely would have seen two shadowy figures walking up the opposite side of the road towards the RSL. A shorter, stockier one who wasn't feeling all that well and kept coughing and spitting into the gutter as he walked along. And a taller, rangier one who wasn't sick at all, but certainly didn't look too healthy.

'You reckon the prick'll turn up, Perce?' asked Frank, as they shuffled along the RSL side of Regent Street.

'Dunno for sure.' Kilby shrugged. 'But I reckon he will. He sounded fair dinkum over the phone.' Kilby hawked and let go another gob into the gutter.

'You reckon he might try and pull something clever?'

'Dunno about that either. But I made a few phone calls and there'll be six good boys up there with us.'

'Seven counting me.' Frank spat into the gutter also. 'And just quietly, I hope the big cunt does.'

'Just cool it up there Frank — till after we get this 500 grand. Then after that. Well, wouldn't it be a shame if Mr Les Norton was to get knocked down by a hit-and-run driver.'

'Or accidently copped a shotgun blast in the face.'

Kilby laughed and spat in the gutter again. 'Right now I wouldn't mind giving him some of this bloody flu I'm getting back. But with half a million dollars in our kicks, anything could happen to him.'

'Yeah. Anything.'

They both laughed and continued walking.

Norton continued with his stroll around Redfern, but after half an hour of grimy terrace houses, equally grimy shop windows and not much more in the darkness, he ended up back in the Greek's having a coffee and raisin toast over the evening papers. When the hour was up he folded his newspapers and headed back to the hotel.

Tjalkalieri, Mumbi and Yarrawulla were sitting on the settee dressed in their tracksuits and hats. Each of them looked quite subdued and serious, as if they'd just undergone some sort of strain. They looked up expressionlessly at Les as he crossed the room.

'How're you goin' now fellas?' he asked quietly. 'Everything all right?'

131

'Yes,' replied Tjalkalieri. 'We've done everything we had to. And everything we could do.' He snatched a nervous look at the others next to him. It was the first time Les had ever seen him look like that. 'We can only hope for the best now.'

'You guys all right yourselves?'

'Yeah we're okay,' nodded Mumbi. 'We're absolutely knackered and we're a bit frightened about what we just done. But we're okay.'

'It's still not too late to pull out if you want to.'

'No Les,' said Tjalkalieri, giving him a tired smile. 'We've come this far. We may as well go through with it.'

Norton nodded as he folded his arms. 'Okay. Now how do you want to work this?'

Norton explained roughly the layout inside the club. He said he'd prop in the same spot he was drinking last night. He'd put his overnight bag — which would have nothing in it but dirty clothes — on the bar. He guessed Kilby and his team would probably be standing at the other end of the bar where it formed a bit of an alcove in front of the men's room. That was where Frank and his two mates must have been standing when they saw him walk in before, and it was the sort of place where shifty characters usually like to congregate when they want to have a drink and do a bit of side-of-the-mouth talking.

The boys said that that would be ideal for them. They'd enter the club behind Les, but not with him, then stand at the bar to his left and order their own drinks. He could discreetly point Kilby out to them, then stand back out of the road. As soon as it was all over the boys would leave the club and wait outside for Les.

'How long do you reckon this will take? Once we're inside,' asked Norton.

'From as soon as you point Kilby out to us. No more than a few seconds,' replied Tjalkalieri.

'Yeah? I thought you said I'd be seeing something weird. Something I'd never seen before.'

'You will,' said Yarrawulla. 'But you'll want to keep your eyes open.'

'And you'll want to be quick,' added Mumbi.

Norton nodded and looked at his watch. 'Well. It's getting on for six-thirty. We get going?'

Norton got his bag out of the bedroom and opened the front door. The next thing they'd left the hotel and were walking slowly and silently, four abreast, heading for the showdown at the Redfern RSL. For all his own nervousness and uncertainty about what was going to happen, Norton couldn't help but feel like Gary Cooper in *High Noon* or one of the Earp brothers heading for the gunfight at the OK Corral. All that was missing was someone playing a lone harmonica in the background. He was going to mention this to the others, but the worried, almost fearful looks on their faces told him this was not the time to be flippant.

Once again there was no one at the reception desk so they ambled straight in and up the hallway to the bar and auditorium. The place wasn't quite as crowded as Sunday night, but it was just as smoky and just as noisy. Keeping a discreet distance, the boys followed Les around the circle of clattering poker machines and stopped in the corner at the bar, just down from him. Before long the tired-looking barman from last night came over. He took Les's order, a middy of new, and turned to the boys slightly down to his left, who ordered three of the same. To all appearances it didn't look at all like they were together: the drinks came; they paid separately. Norton started looking around the bar, spotting Kilby and the others about a minute after they'd seen him.

Les was fairly spot-on about Kilby and his associate's drinking habits. He couldn't miss Frank's tall frame propped up in the alcove near the men's room. I'll bet that's where they were standing last time I was in here thought Les. And I didn't even notice them.

Even at that distance Norton couldn't mistake all the stitches sticking out of Frank's mouth and cheekbone like a lot of little flies' legs. And he couldn't help but smile at the way the AWEC thug was gingerly sipping his middy to one side of his swollen mouth. Frank was looking absolute daggers back at Les. Standing just to Frank's left — wearing brown trousers, matching shirt and stylish leather jacket, and more-or-less surrounded by another six big Aboriginal heavies — was Percy Kilby. He stared impassively at Norton, who stared back for a moment before picking up his overnight bag and placing it on the bar. He then stared back at Kilby and nodded to it with his head. Very casually, Norton picked up his middy, moved his head slightly to his left as he took a sip, and leant a fraction towards Tjalkalieri.

'That's him at the other end of the bar. The solid bloke in the tan leather jacket and brown shirt.'

'Gotcha,' replied Tjalkalieri urgently. 'Now move back from the bar Les.'

Norton did that, keeping his head straight but not taking his eyes off the boys. Kilby and Frank didn't notice him say anything or see anything suspicious; they were too interested in the bag which was supposed to contain $250,000. What happened next, Norton still isn't sure of and he still keeps it to himself.

The boys had all turned in Percy Kilby's direction, except that each had their eyes closed. After a second or two they opened them and when they did their strange blue eyes now had a bright, luminous green glow. The intense glow pulsated for a second, then seemed to radiate a few centimetres from their eyes where it formed a thin ribbon of emerald-green light. Quickly, the ribbon of green light beamed along the bar before materialising behind Kilby and his associates like a small, flat cloud of tiny sparkling crystals. It closely resembled a mist or a handful of glowing grains of green sand, suspended in mid-air.

In the smoky light of the club and the heaving throng of drinkers, no-one noticed anything. Norton was watching intently and he only just saw it. Kilby and the others, who were too interested in watching Norton and his overnight bag, didn't notice a thing.

The sparkling crystals, or whatever they were, hung in the air behind Kilby and his associates for barely a second before they began to take the shape of an unbelievably muscular man. A man almost eight feet tall. But instead of skin he had thick, lumpy green scales. And where the figure had a man's torso the head was a cross between a snake and some kind of lizard — possibly a goanna but much more evil, with piercing orange eyes. Across the creature's shoulders and chest were body markings identical to those Tjalkalieri had on back in the room. The wicked, horrible mouth opened slightly and a thin forked tongue, black like wet tar, seemed to dart out and briefly touch Kilby on the back of his head.

There was no noise, no sound at all. Only the hubbub of the drinkers and the rattle of the poker machines. Kilby and his gang still hadn't noticed anything. Their eyes were glued on the overnight bag, though they were probably a little curious at the now wild-eyed look on Norton's face.

The monster, or apparition, or whatever it was, had no sooner touched Kilby when the tongue vanished back into the huge, scaly mouth. The figure then dissolved into the glowing crystals, then into the thin beam of green light which raced back down the bar and swiftly vanished into the glow still radiating from Tjalkalieri's, Mumbi's and Yarrawulla's eyes. The boys closed their eyes for a moment and when they opened them again they were as clear, blue and piercing as ever. They picked up their middies and continued drinking as though nothing had happened.

The whole strange, horrifying incident had taken no more than six or eight seconds. No-one really saw it. The one or two drunks that did could only shake their heads in disbelief and forget about it. Even Norton, who was prepared for and saw the whole thing, wasn't sure what he'd just witnessed. But he was certainly stunned.

Eventually Norton shifted his gaze back to Kilby and Frank, who were staring back at him, curious about the odd look on the big Queenslander's face. Kilby pointed towards the bag, said something to Frank, and still had his left arm out in Norton's direction when he began to blink rapidly. His jaw swung open and a look of shock and disbelief spread across his face as his gaze switched to the boys standing quietly at the bar. From where he was standing, Norton could see Kilby's mouth and throat moving as he made several short, choking gasps. He clutched at his chest with one hand and turned to Frank for support with the other. Frank's face screwed up with worry at the look on his boss's. But now it wasn't a look of pain. It was a look of peace. A smile of understanding, as if a great mystery had just unfolded itself to him, and although he knew what was just about to happen to him he was glad that it was. He gave one small, final gasp and collapsed at Frank's feet.

All eyes immediately focused on the stricken AWEC boss. Norton glanced over at the boys who were now finishing their beers. They put their empty glasses down and headed for the door.

'We'll see you out the front, Les,' said Tjalkalieri as they walked past. Still a bit dumbfounded at what was going on around him, Norton could only nod.

He turned back to the other end of the bar where Frank and several others were crouched over Kilby. Through the confusion and hubbub Norton heard someone yell out. 'Quick. Get a doctor.' Les picked up his overnight bag full of dirty T-shirts and walked up for a better view.

The chances of finding a doctor drinking in Redfern RSL are pretty remote. But as is often the case there was an off-duty nurse in the club, a plump, apple-faced woman in her early fifties who now worked part time and was in there having the odd middy or ten before she switched over to brandies and soda. And go easy on the soda. She huffed and bustled her way through the crowd. Not really enjoying having her drinking disturbed, though relishing in her brief moment of importance, she told Frank and the others to move aside while she undid Kilby's collar and loosened his belt. Professionally she picked up Kilby's wrist and held it for a second before placing his hand back on his chest. She placed her hand on the side of his neck, waited a moment, then put her ear on his heart. Grim faced and tight lipped the sister next peeled Kilby's eyelid back with her thumb: his pupils were just widened, dark pools of nothing. The sister shook her head and placed Kilby's hand down by his side, before getting slowly and a little unsteadily to her feet.

'I'm afraid he's dead,' she shrugged, looking helplessly around her.

'*Dead*!' said Frank, who was still kneeling by Kilby's side. He leapt to his feet and stared accusingly at the slightly swaying nurse. 'What do you mean dead? There's got to be something you can do.'

'I'm sorry young man. But it's too late. There's no pulse. No heartbeat. No respit . . . no resp . . . He's stopped breathing and his pupils are dilated.' She shrugged again. 'Call for the paramedics. But they won't be able to do anything. He's dead.'

'But . . . but,' protested Frank, 'he was only standing there having a drink two minutes ago. How can he be dead?'

The sister, now keen to get back to her drinking shrugged and made a helpless gesture with her hands. 'It looks like he's had a heart attack. Or a massive stroke.' She looked down at Kilby. 'Or both.'

Frank's mind was immediately filled with confusion and dread. Percy. Dead. He couldn't come to grips with it. Not as quickly as that. His eyes darted towards the other end of the bar. What about that bloody Norton? Could he have something to do with this? No. He was standing on the other side of the room. Besides. Perce had been sick the last few days. Very sick. The poor bastard was dying and didn't even know it. And he thought all he had was the bloody flu. In the surrounding silence, broken only by the distant clunk of someone playing a poker machine, Frank stared down at his late boss. Before she went back to her table, the sister had closed Percy's eyes and now he looked like he was in a deep restful sleep. Even the smile was still on his face. The next thing, Frank felt a tug at his elbow.

136

'Hey Frank. You got a minute?' said Norton.

Frank didn't know what to do when he turned around and saw Les. Immediately he was filled with hatred and fear. Yet at the same time his boss had just collapsed dead at his feet making him a hotbed of helpless grief and confusion. He glared grimly at Norton, completely speechless.

'Well Frank old mate,' said Norton, giving his overnight bag a tap. 'Looks like all bets are off. Sorry about your boss. But that's the way it goes.'

Norton paused to run his eyes across Frank's mates, who were glaring at him over the small crowd gathered around the prostrate Percy Kilby. The looks on their faces weren't at all friendly and they appeared to be edging towards him. Norton ran his eyes over them again, then turned back to Frank and looked him right in the eye.

'Now Frank, I'll give you some real good fuckin' advice. Firstly, don't you or any of your boofheaded mates get any ideas of following me out of the club for a square up and to try and get this money. We've got two blokes with guns waiting outside and they won't think twice about blowing you and the rest of them to bits. You got that?'

Frank nodded briefly.

'Good. Now secondly.' Norton nodded his head in the direction of the railway station. 'Be out of that building by Thursday morning. Typewriters. Furniture. Your poster of Michael Jackson. The fuckin' lot. If you're not,' Norton looked down at the body of Percy Kilby, 'that's how you'll finish. Only you won't go out with a smile on your face. You'll have no head. You got that too?'

Frank nodded sourly again.

'Good.' Norton smiled at the tall thug. 'Well I guess I'll be seeing you, Frank. Don't know when though.' As Les turned to walk away the smile on his face spread into a huge grin. 'In the meantime. Keep those stitches dry, won't you.'

Frank clenched his fists with rage, but he didn't say or do anything.

Outside the club the boys were waiting impatiently. 'Come on Les,' said Tjalkalieri. 'We want to get out of here.'

'You want to get out of here,' replied Norton. 'So do bloody I. And I want to have a word with you three back at the bloody hotel.'

They reached the Thames Tavern as an ambulance came screaming up Regent Street, its red light flashing as it shot through the traffic lights outside the front door.

Back inside their hotel room, the boys took their hats and headbands off and flopped down on the settee to watch Norton clumsily making a cup of tea. He was still wide eyed and still obviously in a state of mild shock.

'Right,' he said, pointing a finger accusingly at the three of them once he'd managed to get the kettle filled and switched on. 'Did I see what I thought I saw back in that bloody club?'

The boys just stared up at him, slight smiles flickering around the corners of their eyes.

'Just what in the bloody hell was that thing?'

'That,' smiled Tjalkalieri. 'That was Mungoongali.'

'Christ!' exclaimed Norton.

'Yes. He's an ugly big bludger, isn't he?' said Mumbi.

Norton shook his head and stared at the three little Aborigines on the lounge.

Norton made the tea, waited in silence till it drew, then poured them all a cup. Norton took his over to the balcony where he opened the door and stared out at the city skyline for a few moments before coming back inside. He closed the door behind him and stood in front of the others.

'I still don't believe what I saw back at that RSL.'

'Good,' replied Tjalkalieri, slowly sipping his tea. 'Keep it that way, Les. Forget you were ever up there. Forget the whole thing. Just put in down to your imagination.'

'That wasn't my imagination. I saw some bloody thing in there. Either that or you hypnotised me.'

A titter of laughter ran across the lounge.

'Les,' intoned Yarrawulla. 'There's a lot of things about our people the whites will never understand.'

'Yeah,' nodded Mumbi. 'We're not all like those morons hanging around Redfern. Sucking on flagons of plonk and trying to look like they just got off a boat from Jamaica.'

'I know that Mumbles.'

'You ever heard of the Strehlow Collection, Les?' asked Tjalkalieri.

Norton nodded his head. 'Yeah. There was something on TV about it just the other week. They call them Australia's crown jewels. They're sacred relics, thousands of years old. Is that right?'

'That's them,' nodded Mumbi. 'Professor Ted Strehlow conned the Aranda elders into letting him take them for safekeeping about fifty years ago.'

'Did it say on the TV about the Canadian anthropologist

who got a look at them and it scared the shit out of him?' said Yarrawulla. Norton nodded slowly again. 'Well that'll give you an idea why. And we've got an identical set back at Binjiwunyawunya.

'How about another cup of tea Les.' Tjalkalieri held up his empty cup. Norton topped it up and the others as well. Tjalkalieri took a sip and smiled up at Norton. 'We're the only people in the world that worship the earth. Did you know that Les?'

'Hey. I know a fair bit about you,' replied Norton. 'And I know that.'

'Other people and tribes worship the moon. The sun. Stars. Gods. Buddha, Mohammed. We worship the earth.'

'And where do you think Mungoongali comes from?' smiled Mumbi.

'I don't know what to think. But I'll bet he doesn't come from the local women's softball team. Anyway,' Norton drained his cup and put it on the table, 'I've got to go and make a phonecall. Do you want anything while I'm down there?' There was a general shaking of heads. 'Righto. I'll be back in about ten minutes.'

A skinny woman — in her fifties and obviously a wino — had just got off the phone when Norton came down into the foyer. After waving away the cigarette smoke and brown muscat fumes, he was able to get straight through. Price was sitting in the lounge room of his Vaucluse home discussing something with Eddie Salita when the phone rang.

'Hello,' he said into the receiver.

'Price? It's Les. How're you going?'

'Les!! Shit! I've been waiting for you to ring. What the bloody hell have you been up to?'

'Nothing. Listen, I want you to ring Redfern RSL and ask for Percy. Here. I'll give you the number.'

'What! You're bloody kidding aren't you? What do I want to talk to that arsehole for?'

'I just want you to ring up and ask for him,' laughed Norton. 'That's all.'

'You're off your bloody head,' replied Price, jotting down the phone number. 'What am I bloody well going to say to him? He's got to be the last prick in the world I want to talk to.'

'You won't be talking to him. I just want you to ring up and ask for him. I've got a surprise for you.' Norton laughed out loud again. 'I'll tell you what though. If he does answer the phone — hang up quick. I'll ring you back in five minutes.'

'Yeah righto,' mumbled Price reluctantly.

'What'd Les want?' asked Eddie.

'He wants me to ring Redfern RSL and ask for Kilby.'

'You going to?'

Price shrugged. 'I may as well I suppose. Don't know what I'm going to say to him though.'

Price pushed the buttons and was through. It seemed like a while before a rather anxious voice answered the phone.

'Hello. Redfern RSL.'

'Yes,' said Price slowly. 'Could you page someone in the club for me.'

'Yeah sure. Who is it?'

'His name's Percy Kilby. He runs the local Aboriginal office.'

There was a pause for a moment. 'Are you a relative of Mr Kilby's?' came the careful voice at the other end.

'Well, I'm a pretty close friend of his. I have to talk to him about something. Is he there?'

The voice on the other end began to sound very strained.

'Look. I ah ... don't know how to put this to you. But Mr Kilby just had a heart attack in the club.'

'He what!'

'He had a massive heart attack at the bar. Barely thirty minutes ago.'

'A heart attack?' Price's face lit up and a huge grin spread across it. 'Fair dinkum. How is he?'

There was another pause. 'You are a friend of Mr Kilby's are you?'

'Yeah, of course I am. We're like brothers. Hey, what's going on?'

'I'm afraid Mr Kilby died in the club before the ambulance could get here.'

Price couldn't help but burst into laughter. 'Did you say he's dead?'

'Yes. I'm very sorry.'

'You're sorry,' roared Price. 'Mate, I'm fair dinkum heart-broken.' Price roared laughing again and hung up.

'What's going on Price?' asked Eddie.

With a huge grin on his face Price stared at Eddie in amazement. 'Kilby's just had a heart attack. He's as dead as a dodo.'

'What!!?' Now it was Eddie's turn to stare. 'How did it happen?'

'I don't know,' shrugged Price. 'But I will as soon as Les rings back.' The mercurial casino owner rubbed his hands gleefully in front of the phone. 'Come on you big red-headed prick. Where are you.'

Right on five minutes later Norton phoned back.

'Hello Les?' said Price, snatching up the receiver.

'Yeah. Did you ring the RSL?'

'I sure did. Kilby's brown bread. He had a heart attack in the club.'

'Yeah I know. It happened right in front of me,' chuckled Norton. 'It's a shame isn't it. That's why I said if he answers the phone hang up for Christ's sake.'

Price burst out laughing again. 'Hey fair dinkum Les. How did you bloody do it?'

Norton gave a tired laugh. 'Ohh, it's a long story, Price. But look. I'm not quite finished over here yet. Will you be home tomorrow afternoon?'

'Yeah. For sure.'

'Well I'll call over about four. I'll tell you all about it then.' Norton paused for a second. 'Or as much as I can.'

'Fair enough. Eddie'll be here. We'll see you then.'

'Okay. See you tomorrow Price.'

Back in room 9 the boys had turned the TV on and were sitting in front of it watching the figures on the screen more out of habit and indifference than anything else. Mumbi had his eyes almost closed and Yarrawulla wasn't far behind him. Tjalkalieri looked up and let out a cavernous yawn as Les walked in.

'Make your phone call Les?' he asked.

'Yeah. I just rang Price.'

Norton told them about his brief conversation, which had them all smiling despite their heavy-lidded tiredness.

'So your boss is quite happy eh?' yawned Mumbi.

'Yeah. Happy as the proverbial pig in shit. I reckon he'd like to meet you blokes, too, before you go back.'

Tjalkalieri shook his head. 'Sorry Les. We'd like to and all that. But we want to get going as soon as we can tomorrow. It's been a big five days for us — and we're starting to miss home.'

'Fair enough, Chalky. Anyway,' Norton clapped his hands together and grinned, 'what do you want for tea? How about something grouse tonight. Anything you want.'

Tjalkalieri smiled then yawned as he shook his head. 'Les.

141

We couldn't eat a thing. We're too stuffed.'

'You sure?' Norton looked surprised. 'All you've had all day has been a bit of fruit and a few cups of tea.'

Yarrawulla shook his head and yawned. 'Thanks all the same, Les. But we're dead-set rooted. We'll probably be in bed in another five minutes.'

And they were. Leaving Norton in front of an almost inaudible TV, staring absently at it on his own. After a few minutes he went down to the bottle shop and got a couple of cans of Fourex, then came back and propped in front of the TV sipping them slowly. Very slowly. He wasn't really watching the TV either. Just staring at it. The thing may as well have not been turned on for all the notice he was taking. There was a lot more on Norton's mind besides *A Country Practice* and *Hill Street Blues*.

Ancient Aboriginal ceremonies. Vicious fights in men's toilets. Subterfuge in the AWEC office. That bloody Mungoongali or whatever it was. And when it was all boiled down, he'd just been an accessory to another murder. Yeah. Like Tjalkalieri said, it certainly had been a big five days. Or at least very bloody strange ones. Hard to believe it's finally all over. Oddly enough, Les began to feel quite tired himself after the second can of beer. He turned the TV off and was in bed by nine. Five minutes after his head hit the pillow, he hardly moved for almost ten hours.

They were all up and showered and dressed by not long after eight the following morning. Although a little stiff at first, Norton felt good after all that uninterrupted sleep. But everyone was in high spirits. It was the relief, more than anything else, that the job was finally over and almost like a great burden had been lifted from all their shoulders. Especially with the boys. Where they had been noticeably tense and strained, especially the last day or so, now they were positively jubilant. What they'd come all this way to accomplish had been done, they'd soon be paid and in a few hours they'd all be home with their loved ones. Norton made a pot of tea and they drank that while they gave the room a bit of a tidy and the boys carefully packed up their Tjuringa boards and the bone, etc. Norton made a quick trip downstairs to ring Kingsley Sheehan to confirm they'd be out there about eleven or so. The cheerful pilot said that suited him as he had a bit of bookwork to catch up on and he'd see them when they got there.

'Well. Everything's arranged,' Norton said happily when

he got back to the room. 'You fly out around eleven and you should be home in Binji by four.'

'That's good Les,' smiled Tjalkalieri.

'The girls know what time you'll be there?'

'We let them know last night before we went to sleep,' winked Yarrawulla.

'Saves the price of a phone call,' nodded Norton.

The room was cleaned up now and the boys were standing next to their bags sipping the last of their tea while they waited patiently to leave.

'Well,' said Norton, smiling at the three of them. 'I suppose you're going to miss room 9 eh?'

'Yeah,' replied Mumbi. 'Like you'd miss Johnny Holmes belting you over the head with his cock for a couple of hours.'

'It was starting to get like a prison,' added Yarrawulla. 'And those bloody beds. You'd be more comfortable sleeping on a sheet of corrugated-iron.'

'Yeah. You're pretty right,' smiled Les. He jangled his car keys in his hand after he slipped off the key to the door. 'Anyway. What about breakfast? How about we slip up to the San Francisco Grill at the Hilton. Or the New York Deli at Double Bay. Have some eggs benedictine and hash browns. Tell you what. We'll go down to Pancakes on the Rocks. Have some blintzes and pancakes with maple syrup. What do you reckon?'

'Les,' smiled Yarrawulla. 'You know what we'd like for breakfast?'

'No. But name it Yarra baby and it's all yours.'

'McDonalds.'

'McDonalds?'

'Yeah. Too right Les. That's just what I feel like.'

'Bloody oath,' added Tjalkalieri. 'Quarter pounder with cheese. French fries. Coca-Cola. And one of those grouse chocolate fudge sundaes. Les, I can taste it now.'

Norton smiled at them almost in disbelief. Fancy wanting to go to McDonalds when he would have taken them anywhere in Sydney they wanted to go. And hang the expense. But actually McDonalds suited him. There was one at Bondi Junction just down from the bank. He could kill two birds with the one stone, so he wasn't going to argue.

'Come to think of it Yarra. That's not a bad idea. I might even have a Big Mac myself.'

'Have a nice day. Enjoy your meal,' grinned Mumbi.

The boys picked up their bags. Les took his, plus the big

black one, and they walked down the stairs to the foyer. Norton asked the girl in the bottle-shop where Bailey was; she said he was out in the parking area washing his car. When they got out there, Ross was running a hose over a green Ford Station-Wagon parked two down from Les's old sedan. He smiled as soon as he spotted the four of them.

'Hey. How're you goin' there George? All right?'

'G'day Ross,' replied Norton. 'How's things?'

'Pretty good.' The hose had one of those little plastic guns for a nozzle; Bailey dropped it and walked over to where Les was unlocking his car. 'So how did the ad go. Everything sweet?'

'Yeah. Good as gold,' replied Norton easily. 'I'm just taking the boys out to the airport now. Fellahs,' he said, turning to the others. 'This is Ross. The owner of the hotel.'

The boys nodded briefly and gave Bailey a half smile.

'Nice place you've got,' said Tjalkalieri.

'Yeah. Just bonzer,' nodded Yarrawulla.

'Great view,' added a po faced Mumbi. 'Pity we've got to go home so soon.'

'Yeah,' winked Bailey. 'She's a beaut little pub the Thames. I thought you blokes'd like it.'

'Anyway Ross,' said Norton. 'We'll just shoot our swags in the car and I'll fix you up.'

'When you're ready George.'

They put their gear in the boot, being especially careful with the bag containing the bone and the Tjuringa boards. Then Tjalkalieri got in the front and the others in the back, winding all the windows down quickly because although it was quite sunny now, after five days being locked up out the back of the pub in all kinds of weather, the inside of Norton's old Ford smelt like bath night in an English boarding house.

'Righto Ross,' said Norton, dipping into the back pocket of his jeans. 'This should make us square.' He handed the hotel owner $500 plus the key to the room.

Bailey slipped the money straight into his own pocket without bothering to count it. 'Thanks George. I hope everything suited you.'

'Couldn't have been creamier,' replied Norton, climbing in behind the wheel. 'They've never had it so good.' He smiled at the others, whose faces reflected about as much expression as the statues on Easter Island.

'Well, make sure you have a safe trip home.' Bailey leant

his hand on the roof above Les and absently tapped it. 'And take it easy. I lost one of my good customers last night. I don't want to lose any more,' he added, with a bit of a chuckle.

'How was that Ross?' asked Norton, starting the motor and giving it a gentle rev as it idled.

'One of my regulars had a heart attack just up the road last night. Poor bastard. He was only forty-three too.' Bailey peered into the car at the others. 'You blokes might've known him. Percy Kilby? He ran the Aboriginal affairs office just over the road.'

Tjalkalieri shook his head. 'Can't say as I have. What about you blokes?'

'Never heard of him,' said Yarrawulla.

'Me neither,' added Mumbi.

'Oh well, doesn't matter. Funny thing though. He was only in here on Saturday having a drink. Said he had the flu bad but he'd managed to shake it.' Bailey shrugged his shoulders. 'Just goes to show, eh. You're drinking with a bloke on Saturday. Then you're going to his funeral on Thursday.'

'Yeah. That's the way it goes Ross,' nodded Norton. 'You're a rooster one minute, a feather duster the next. Anyway. We've got to go. We've got some more filming to do.'

'Yeah? What are you doing now?' asked Bailey.

'An Aboriginal kung-fu movie' replied Norton.

'Fair dinkum. What's it called?'

'Enter the Flagon.'

'Oh. That sounds all right. Anyway, I'd better let you go. I might see you again George. See you fellas. Nice meeting you.'

The boys smiled thinly back at the owner as Norton reversed out then drove over to the entrance of the parking area. 'Don't suppose you'll be wanting to stay for the funeral,' he asked as they waited for the traffic in Regent Street.

'Not particularly,' replied Tjalkalieri.

'Funny thing,' said Norton slowly. 'I only just saw an Aboriginal funeral going past the balcony this morning. I thought it might've been his.'

'How did you know it was an Aboriginal funeral?' asked Mumbi unsuspectingly.

'The first four garbage trucks had their lights on.'

Cracking up inside at his two corny jokes and the stoical looks on the faces of the others, Norton laughed like a drain all the way to McDonalds.

Les sat the boys down against the window facing Oxford

145

Street, then got them everything they wanted. Big Macs. Quarter pounders with cheese. McFeasts. French-fries — stacks of them. Gallons of Coca-Cola. Ice cream sundaes. Apple pies. Anything they wanted and more. Even Les had a Big Mac and a thick shake and some French-fries. The boys were laughing and giggling like three little kids as they tore into all the fast food. They were equally fascinated at what, to them, were some very strange looking people walking past and getting on and off the bus just in front of the window.

'You sure you wouldn't like some party hats?' asked Les, as he watched a giggling Mumbi rip into his second quarter pounder with cheese. 'Maybe the manager might find some little cakes with hundreds and thousands on them for you.'

'Good thing you mentioned hundreds and thousands honkey,' said Tjalkalieri. 'Because you're just about to fork out fifty big ones.'

'Plus the 17.5 per cent loading,' laughed Yarrawulla.

'The only loading you three cheeky little pricks'll be getting is when I load you onto that bloody plane out at Mascot.' Norton washed the last of his hamburger down with orange juice. 'Anyway. The bank's only over the road. I may as well go and get the money, then I can piss you off.'

'Grab us another chocolate sundae each before you go,' said Mumbi.

Les did; then walked up to the bank.

Norton only had to wait a couple of minutes before he was ushered into Mr Sturgess' office. The manager didn't ask too many questions, Norton signed a couple of documents to close the account, there was a brief handshake, and before long he was back out in Oxford Street with the remainder of the cash in his overnight bag, holding onto it tighter than a rope-ladder. Before he went back to get the others Les took a small note pad and biro from a side pocket in the bag and did a bit of quick adding and subtracting.

After taking out Murray's $10,000, the pilot's $9,000, the hotel bill, the AWEC sling and various other expenses, there was around about $75,000 left. Of which the boys were to get $50,000. Leaving $25,000 — Norton's whack if he wanted it. Not a bad earn for being stuck in a hotel room with three cheeky Aborigines for five days. And he thought it would take closer to three weeks. Not that it had been the best five days in his life. Far from it. But in that time he'd developed an affinity with the boys that had never been there so completely before. And at one stage the three cheeky little bludgers had laid their lives on the line for him. He was convinced they were sincere about that. Norton absently tapped the biro on the pad for a few moments before putting it in the bag and walking back to McDonalds.

The boys were still at the window, surrounded by paper cups and food wrappings and laughing like drains at two punks arguing over something just out the front. A pimply-faced girl in an oversize leather jacket, tartan miniskirt and holed black stockings tucked into a pair of boots that looked like they belonged to Mammy Yokum. Her boyfriend, or whatever, looked pretty much the same except that the rips in his trousers were held together by thin chains. Both their acne-riddled faces were topped by gelled up, spiked red hair that made them look like a couple of floating mines.

'Jesus, Les,' said Mumbi as he walked in and noticed what they were laughing at. 'What bloody tribe do they belong to?'

'They don't belong in a tribe, Mumbles,' smiled Norton. 'They belong in a zoo.'

'A circus'd be more like it,' said Yarrawulla.

'You wouldn't have to worry about buying them a clown's outfit,' added Tjalkalieri.

They watched the two punks arguing till they were eventually joined by another pair; just as pimply and just as ugly. Finally Les spoke.

'Well. If you've had enough to eat and you've seen enough of the sights in beautiful downtown Bondi Junction, we might get cracking, eh.'

'Yes. I think that might be a good idea, Les,' said Tjalkalieri. 'We've certainly eaten enough. And we've certainly seen enough to last us for a long time.'

'Binjiwunyawunya's never looked so good, eh?'

'Never,' the three of them chorused.

They walked down to the car and headed for the airport. Norton took his time driving out to Mascot. The weird five days, with their bantering and roasting, were over now and soon it would be time to say goodbye to three old friends he'd known and respected all his life. When he'd seen them again Les didn't know. But he hoped it might be soon and in more comfortable, relaxed circumstances. A week or two out at Binjiwunyawunya after the smog and noise of Sydney would be unbelievable to say the least.

'If you blokes want to wait here, I'll race up and get the pilot. I won't be a minute.'

'Righto Les.'

There was a general nodding of heads and the boys waited in the flight facilities hangar with their bags while Norton rattled up the stairs to the Boomerang Aviation office. Sheehan was in his usual position, sitting beneath the window at the end of the office. He must have finished whatever bookwork he had to do because he had his feet up on the table and was reading a copy of *Hustler*. He looked up when Norton knocked and walked straight in.

'Well, if it isn't me old mate George,' he grinned cheekily, dropping the magazine on the table. 'How are you?'

'Not too bad squadron leader,' replied Les just as cheekily. 'We ready to scramble are we?'

'We certainly are boss. I'll just grab my logbook.'

Kingsley picked up a leather briefcase and followed Norton down to where the others were waiting in the hangar.

'Hello fellas,' he said cheerfully. 'How's it going? Looking forward to going back home?'

The boys nodded and smiled.

'Well, if you want to grab your gear, you can follow me and we'll get on board.'

Les took the big bag and they followed Sheehan over to the plane. Kingsley climbed aboard and let them hand the bags up to him. He figured they'd all want to say goodbye, so when what little there was was loaded he left them on their own.

'I'll go and warm the engines up, George.' He winked at Les before he disappeared inside the plane. 'You've got a few minutes yet.'

'Righto wing commander. And this fella here's got your money,' he added, resting his hand on Tjalkalieri's shoulder. 'He'll fix you up when you land. Okay?'

'No Cloncurries George.'

There was an awkward silence for a moment as the boys smiled at Norton and he smiled back at them.

'Well. What can I say?' he finally said, the smile on his face breaking into a huge grin. 'Just what can I bloody well say?'

'Yes,' grinned back Tjalkalieri. 'That's about it Les. What can you say?'

'I can't say it was the best five days I've ever spent. But . . . it's definitely got to be the most memorable.'

148

'Yes. It certainly was different, old fella. Wasn't it?' said Yarrawulla.

'It certainly was,' agreed Norton. He stared at his three Aboriginal friends for a few seconds, then slapped his hand hard against his thigh. 'I hate to have to say this. But I'm gonna miss you three little pricks.'

With the grin back on his face bigger than ever, Norton shook hands with each of them. And the handshakes were warm and firm and lasted quite a bit longer than your normal handshake.

'I'll tell you what Les,' chuckled Mumbi. 'We've got to admit. We did everything we could to stir you up.'

'Fair dinkum. Did you?' replied Norton innocently. 'Well I'd never have noticed.'

'You noticed all right,' replied Yarrawulla. 'In fact at one stage there I thought you were going to choke Chalky.'

'Now would I do a thing like that?' grinned Norton.

The boys were about to say something when the two engines whined and kicked over, sending a dusty blast of propwash swooshing over them. They moved a little away from the plane to escape the wind and noise.

'Anyway,' said Norton, having to raise his voice a little over the noise of the engines. 'It's all over now. And to show there's no hard feelings. Here.' He opened his overnight bag and took out a small, black plastic bag which he handed to Tjalkalieri. 'There's your fifty grand. Plus that fuckin' loading you've been whingeing about.'

Tjalkalieri studied the bag of money for a second, then bounced it up and down in his hand as if he was weighing it mentally. 'Exactly what do you mean by that, Les?'

'There's about $75,000 there Chalky. Plus the four grand you've got to give the pilot. Bit of a bonus for you.'

'But... just a second Les,' protested Tjalkalieri. 'Didn't you say something in the hotel, that what was left after paying us and all was to be your share?'

'Yeah,' shrugged Norton. 'But who gives a shit. I couldn't really take it and I'd only end up giving it back to Price. Not that he'd want it. So you blokes may as well have it. Price won't miss it anyway. He takes ten times that on a good Saturday night.'

'Jesus, Les,' said Tjalkalieri, awkwardly expressing the sentiments of the others.

'Anyway,' said Norton, nodding towards the plane. 'I just saw the pilot wave to me. So I reckon it's time to go boys.'

They shook hands briefly again when Mumbi's face broke into a huge grin. He looked at the others for a moment, then back at Norton before he spoke.

'To tell you the truth,' he said. 'It's not as if we didn't think of you either. In fact we brought you down a little present too. We've just been waiting for the right opportunity to give it to you. And I reckon this is it.' He put his hand in his tracksuit pocket and handed Norton a tiny leather pouch made out of emu skin. 'There you go, Les. A present from the boys.'

Norton opened the pouch and inside were what looked like two pieces of clay-covered gravel about the size of sultanas. He tipped them into his palm and studied them curiously for a few seconds.

'What are these?' he asked, looking at all three of them.

'Lucky stones,' smiled Tjalkalieri.

'Lucky stones?'

'Yeah.'

'What am I gonna do with them?'

'Keep them. They're lucky,' said Yarrawulla.

'Fair enough,' shrugged Norton. 'If you blokes say they're lucky they've got to be. Thanks a lot. I appreciate it.'

'If they don't bring you any luck,' grinned Mumbi. 'Throw them at the pigeons out your way.'

'Yeah,' nodded Yarrawulla. 'Make yourself a slingshot and fire them at any pigeons in your backyard.'

The three little Aborigines grinned at each other, then burst out laughing as if they had some private joke going amongst themselves.

Norton continued to study the two pieces of gravel before finally putting them back in their pouch. 'Lucky stones? Pigeons?' he said shaking his head. 'Buggered if I know what you're on about. But thanks anyway.'

'Don't worry about it,' said Tjalkalieri. 'You'll work it out. Anyway, we've got a plane to catch.'

'Yeah, you lucky bludgers. I wish I was going with you.'

They moved over to the steps where they said their last goodbyes. Kingsley gave Norton a bit of a wave and pulled up the hatch, leaving Les walking back alone to the hangar. He turned around to see three beautiful white grins almost shining at him from the portholes. With a bit of a lump in his throat he waved back then stood there as the Beechcraft taxied out to disappear momentarily amongst the other planes taxiing around. A few minutes later he saw it take off and bank towards the ocean. Subconsciously he gave another wave then headed back to his car.

Just before he started the engine Norton pulled the little pouch out of his pocket and tipped the two pieces of gravel, or whatever, into his hand. He studied them intently for a minute or two before putting them back. So that's my earn for five days of living like a pig in that sleezy hotel in Redfern eh? He chuckled to himself. Two pieces of blue metal. Oh well, you never know, they might be lucky. I'll take them down to the paper shop with me on Friday, when I put my Lotto tickets in.

After sharing the one mildewed shower — and not all that often — with three others for almost a week, Norton's shower at home was like sheer, oppulent luxury. Plenty of steaming hot water. His own special soaps. His own shampoos and conditioners. His own backscrubber. And all Warren's imported aftershave lotions and deodorants. He took his time in the bathroom, changed into a clean pair of jeans and a sweatshirt, unhurriedly made a pot of tea and some sandwiches for lunch, did his laundry, then pottered around the house doing not much more than just enjoying being back home.

At about half past three, he headed over to Price's place.

Price's gardener, cum caretaker, Vince, an ex-sergeant in the Welsh Guards and still ramrod straight despite it being over twenty years since he'd left the army, waved him through the security gates with a smile.

'G'day Vince,' said Norton, smiling back at the grey haired, rosy cheeked Welshman. 'Price is expecting me. Where is he?'

'He's out the back by the pool boyo,' replied Vince. 'Eddie's with him.'

'Righto mate.'

Les cruised up the white concrete driveway to the front of the mansion where he pulled in between Price's Rolls and Eddie's Mercedes; Myra's BMW was nowhere to be seen so he figured she must be out somewhere. The huge front door was open but instead of walking through the house Les cut around the side. Price and Eddie were seated at one of those white, wrought-iron outdoor tables sipping coffee. Price had just got off an extension phone when they both spotted him coming towards them.

'Hello, here he is,' beamed Price. 'The man of the bloody hour. Grab a seat old son, it's good to see you. We've missed not having your big boofhead around the last few days.'

'Our man in Redfern,' grinned Eddie. 'Les Norton. Undercover agent extraordinaire. How are you mate?'

Norton returned their grins and after a brief handshake pulled up a seat facing away from the glare of the swimming pool. 'Any coffee left?' he asked, nodding towards the silver pot.

'Help yourself,' smiled Price. 'Eddie only brewed it five minutes ago.'

Price and Eddie were obviously delighted to see Les and were all smiles as they started firing questions at him the moment his bum hit the seat. It wasn't hard to see they were breaking their necks to find out what had happened in that hotel in Redfern. Especially Eddie. However, the smiles on their faces were well and truly gone about thirty minutes later when Norton refused to elaborate on what had happened back at room 9 in the Thames Tavern. In fact the look on Eddie's was downright rancorous. Les explained, and in detail, where all the money went. He told them about the fight with Frank and his two mates and about meeting Kingsley. But he wouldn't disclose where the boys came from, nor give out too many details about the ceremony. Not that he would have told them about the finale in the RSL. No-one would believe that. Les still wasn't too sure about it himself.

'So that's about it fellas,' said Norton, taking a sip of his second cup of coffee. 'The boys made me promise I wouldn't let on what they did. And that's it. Sorry. But I gave them my word.'

Eddie was almost fuming. Price was still quite curious but more-or-less glad just to have Percy Kilby out of the way. Both, however, knew Norton was as staunch as they come; the big Queenslander's word was his bond and if he'd been told to keep something to himself he would. They respected him for it, though in this case it was exasperating to say the least.

'But Jesus, Les,' pleaded Eddie. 'Surely you can tell us something. I mean. All you've told us is about getting that blood. They point a bone out the window. Sing and dance a little bit — and Kilby has a heart attack four days later. Come on.'

'Well that's all you need to know anyway,' replied Norton. 'Look Eddie. I started asking that pilot mate of yours a few questions about you. And he soon clammed up. So...'

'Fair enough,' sighed Eddie grudgingly.

Price leaned back and clasped his hands behind his head. 'Anyway, who gives a stuff? The job's done and that's the main thing.'

'That's right,' nodded Les.

'I still reckon you're a mug though,' said Price 'for not keeping that twenty-odd grand that was over.'

'Doesn't matter,' shrugged Norton. 'They deserved it more than me.'

'Suit yourself,' said Price, shrugging his shoulders also. 'But no good putting yourself out of pocket.'

'I'm not out of pocket.'

'You've done a week's wages.'

Norton screwed up his face. 'What do you mean? I've done a week's wages?'

'I've had Danny bloody McCormack up the club the last four nights. You don't think I can afford to pay him and pay you as well while you're galavanting around Redfern.'

Norton shifted his gaze out across the pool and shook his head.

'But don't worry.' Price winked over at Eddie. 'See George tomorrow night at work and if you're going bad you can sub him for a few bucks till payday.'

Norton smiled and went to pour another cup of coffee but it was cold. 'That's not the only money I've lost, too, come to think of it,' he chuckled. 'I also done $500 on that rotten horse of yours. Dealer's Choice.'

'That's right,' grinned Eddie. 'You're into the Brute for five hundred aren't you?

'Poor old Dealer's Choice,' intoned Price. 'He fell in a bit of a hole halfway down the straight. He's in again next week at Rosehill. He should win then.'

'Mmhh! Now you tell me.'

'So,' said Eddie slowly. The grin on his face had widened. He was still dirty on Les for not telling him exactly what happened in the hotel and now he was getting a bit of a buzz out of seeing him squirm. 'You could say it wasn't the most profitable week you've ever had mate.'

'Yeah. I suppose you could,' smiled Les. 'But I did finish up with something out of the wreck.' He dipped into the front pocket of his jeans and took out the tiny, emu-skin pouch. 'I finished up with these.' He tipped the two pieces of gravel out into his hand and held them out in front of Price and Eddie. 'Lucky stones.'

'What did you say they were?' asked Eddie, holding a piece

153

of gravel between his forefinger and thumb. Price held the other.

'Lucky stones. The boys gave them to me just before they left.'

Price still hadn't said anything. The smile on his face however had completely disappeared as he peered almost transfixed at the small greyish brown piece of stone in his hand. Suddenly he reached across the table and almost snatched the other out of Eddie's fingers. 'Give me a look at that other one,' he muttered gruffly.

With slightly amused smiles creeping across their faces, the other two watched as Price carefully rolled the tiny pieces of stone around in his fingers. He jiggled them around in his cupped hands as if he was trying to weigh them before licking the edge of one and scratching at the wet part with his thumbnail. Finally he held that one up to the light and squinted at it with one eye closed.

'Where did you say you got these?' he asked, turning and staring almost accusingly at Les.

'The boys gave them to me as a going-away present, just before they got on the plane,' replied Norton indifferently. 'They said they were lucky.'

Price's eyes darted back to the little rocks, then back to Norton. 'Yeah. What are you going to do with them?'

'Keep 'em,' shrugged Les. 'Take 'em with me when I go to buy my lottery tickets. You never know. They might just be lucky and I won't have to put up with you anymore.'

Price ran his tongue around the inside of his cheek for a moment. 'How about leaving them with me for the night.'

'Yeah, okay,' shrugged Norton. 'What are you going to do with them?'

'I just want to have a good look at them — that's all.'

'Go for your life.' Norton handed Price the skin pouch. 'Don't lose them, though, will you?'

Price didn't say anything. But after another look at the stones he put them back in their pouch and tucked it carefully into the fob pocket of his trousers.

They sat around talking for another twenty minutes or so before Norton said that he might make a move. Price meanwhile hadn't said a great deal. His mind seemed to be somewhere else and every now and again he would subconsciously run his fingers across his fob pocket. Finally Les stood up and said goodbye, saying he'd see them at the club tomorrow night.

Norton bought a couple of pizzas on the way home and waited for Warren, who arrived around six, all ears and all excited at seeing Les. About twenty minutes later he'd got less information out of Norton than Price and Eddie had. So what exactly the big Queenslander had been up to for the last five days was still a mystery to him. But knowing Les's line of work he reluctantly copped it sweet.

Wednesday wasn't too bad a day. The light cloud cover and the onshore breeze had taken the edge off it for a day on the beach, but it was ideal for training and Norton was up and roaring at six. He ran eight laps of Bondi, then did an hour in the gym, hitting the heavy bag with left and right combinations that loosened half the tiles on the roof and frightened every starling out of the building plus the blocks of flats across the road. He topped this off by borrowing a surf-ski and paddling six laps of the beach. By ten-thirty the two kilos he'd put on were gone, and so was Norton.

He went straight home, decided to skip breakfast and held out for lunch instead, which consisted of a slice of rump about as thick as a house brick swimming in a lake of mushroom gravy surrounded by a mountain range of mashed potatoes. Plus enough tossed salad to feed Southern California. Normally Les had a sleep for an hour or so late in the afternoon before going to work. But with all that food inside him he could hardly move, so he lay down on his bed like a blueribbon hog at the Easter Show and crashed out till four o'clock.

Blinking groggily, he got up, yawned and stretched for a few moments before splashing some cold water on his face in the bathroom. He then drifted slowly into the kitchen and made a cup of coffee. He was sitting in the lounge room quietly sipping it, not fully wide awake and still a little stiff and sore when the phone rang. He blinked at it for a few seconds before picking up the receiver. It was Price.

'Is that you Les?' he almost barked.

'Yeah. How are you Price?'

Price didn't answer straight away. There was a laboured pause as if he was having trouble getting the words out. 'Listen. Where did you say you got those two pieces of rock from?' he finally managed to blurt out.

'Off those three mates of mine,' yawned Norton. 'I told you didn't I. They gave them to me as they got on the plane.'

'And they told you they were lucky stones?'

'Yeah,' yawned Norton again. 'Something like that.'

There was another pause and more laboured breathing. 'You know what they are, don't you? You great red-headed galah.'

'No,' shrugged Les. 'What?'

'They're two pigeon-blood fuckin' rubies. That's all.'

Norton yawned again. 'What are they?'

Price sighed heavily on the phone. 'Fair dinkum. It's like talking to a brick bloody wall. You don't know anything about gemstones do you?'

'No,' replied Les. 'Not really.'

'No. I didn't think you did. You bloody wombat. Bloody lucky stones. I took them down to Consolidated Diamonds this morning. Got the boss there to have a look at them, knowing a dubbo like you would be arsey enough to fluke something like this. He split them, cleaned them up a bit and bloody near fainted. They're two eighteen-carat, pigeon-blood rubies. They could be worth anything. At least $30,000.'

'Did you say pigeon blood Price?'

'Yeah. That's what the best rubies in the world are called. It's a real dark, deep rich red.'

'So that's what the boys meant,' chuckled Les.

'What?'

'Nothing.'

'Bloody lucky stones,' snorted Price. 'You . . . boofhead. They're two of the best rubies I've ever seen in my life.'

Norton shook his head and took a sip of coffee. Despite Price's outburst he still wasn't fully wide awake and a lot of this was still going in one ear and out the other.

'Hey but hold on a second, Price,' he said. 'There's no rubies in Australia. Is there?'

'That's what I'm getting at, you imbecile. They're as rare as rocking-horse shit. These'll be the first of their kind ever found here.'

There was another pause on the line and Norton could hear Price breathing deeply as if he was trying hard to control himself before he spoke.

'Now listen, Les,' he said tightly. 'In all seriousness. I know you don't want to tell me too much about those Aborigine mates of yours. And you won't tell me what they got up to in that hotel room. That's all right. I don't really give a stuff. But surely to Christ, Les, you can tell me where those rubies come from.'

Norton paused for a moment, then chuckled to himself as his thoughts drifted off to a rambling, old wooden house built into a mountain full of spa water right on the Tropic of Capricorn. Where more than likely at that very moment three wise old Aboriginal men would be sitting on their verandah with their beautiful young girlfriends, watching the Queensland sun go down over their landscaped garden dotted with lily-covered ponds full of tropical fish. The peace and tranquility disturbed only by the noise of the countless native birds. Norton chuckled again as a whimsical smile spread over his face.

'Price,' he said slowly. 'I can't tell you that mate. But there is one thing I can tell you.'

Norton let his gaze wander across the lounge room to his open back door. Through his backyard and over the top of the house behind he could see the countless red-tiled roofs of the other houses and the cramped rows of home units and flats. Their silhouettes crowded each other through the car fumes and smog of Old South Head Road towards Bellevue Hill.

'If they come from where I think they do, it's a bloody long way from here.'

St Kilda Kooler

It was a dud pinch, there was no two ways about it, and Norton was entitled to blow up. But not quite to rant and rave to the extent that he did, and definitely not to make dire threats against the life of a poor, hard-working Highway Patrol officer. Not at eight-thirty on a fine Monday morning in July anyway.

Ordinarily, Norton always liked Monday mornings. After four late nights at the Kelly Club, getting to bed almost at dawn and getting up close to lunchtime, Mondays were almost a revelation to the big red-headed Queenslander. He'd get to bed before eleven on Sunday night, then be up by six the following morning feeling fresh as a daisy. Sometimes, depending on the weather, he'd have a run in Centennial Park, but mostly he'd do a few laps of Bondi, have a workout and a hit on the heavy bag in North Bondi Surf Club — sometimes with Billy Dunne, sometimes without — then top this off with a swim and a shower. He'd get back home around eight-thirty, wait for Warren to leave for the advertising agency, then cook up a monstrous feed of bacon and eggs, chops, toast, muesli or whatever, and take his time eating it over the morning paper. It was a good way to start the week and this particular Monday morning looked like being no different from any other; better if anything.

It was fresh but not cold. The usual westerly wind wasn't up and didn't look like coming up. There was no pollution, not a cloud in the sky and for mid-winter it was almost like early spring. Norton was up, finished his mug of tea and honey and down on Bondi Beach before six-thirty. He did six laps on the hard sand and two on the soft, had a workout in the surf club, almost punching the heavy bag into another dimension, following this with a swim in what seemed the icy cold ocean to an old Queensland boy like Les. Then he had a long hot shower. He had a laugh and a bit of a mag with some of the old regulars while he changed back into his tracksuit, and after stopping for the paper in Campbell Parade was whistling happily to himself feeling on top of the world as he drove up Lamrock Avenue listening to Mike Carlton on 2GB. Les felt good, great even, and glancing up into the clear blue sky it looked like being a great day too. The last thing he was expecting was to be pulled over by a traffic cop barely half a kilometre from home.

Actually Les noticed the traffic cop heading the opposite way and was somewhat surprised when he did a U-turn a little further down from him. He was even more surprised when he zoomed up behind and absolutely astonished when he briefly hit his siren and flicked his headlight on and off. What the bloody hell's goin' on here, thought a mystified Norton. He wasn't speeding, his seat belt was on, he didn't have his arm out the window, the old Ford's muffler was okay and it wasn't blowing smoke. Oh well, better pull over and see what this wombat wants. It's probably just someone I know. Looking in his rear-vision mirror, Les realised as soon as the cop got off his bike it definitely wasn't anyone he knew; and he also knew, by a sinking feeling in his stomach, that he was in some sort of bother.

The cop didn't just swing his leg off the new BMW, he alighted dramatically, like he was Wyatt Earp dismounting at the Last Chance Saloon in Dodge City hot on the trail of the James gang. He gave his balls a scratch while he stood there, then adjusted his service revolver for a bit more effect. After taking his own sweet time getting his infringements book from the metal saddlebag he swaggered over to Norton's old Ford with a walk that made John Wayne look like Sir Robert Helpmann.

'What's up mate?' said Norton as he wound the driver's window right down. 'I wasn't speeding was I?'

The cop stared impassively down at Les. Because of the helmet and sunglasses, Norton couldn't make out his face, but he did notice a sour turned-down mouth topped by a thick ginger moustache. 'Do you have a letter of permission from the Department of Motor Transport allowing you to drive without your seat belt on sir?' said the cop in a monotone, almost expressionless voice.

'Seat belt?' replied Norton, screwing his face up slightly.

160

'It's on.' Les gave the buckle a tap and strained against the strap to prove his point. The belt restrained him before he could reach the steering wheel.

The cop stared morosely at Les as if he had committed a worse crime by having his belt on, thus depriving him from getting a booking. 'Mmhh,' he grunted unhappily, 'it's a bit loose.'

'Well, I don't like having it too tight,' shrugged Les, half smiling now because he knew he'd done nothing wrong. 'You can't see out the side windows properly.'

The cop didn't agree or disagree but gave him another dirty look before moving to the front of the car where he gave it a quick once-over and took a note of the licence number. He stood there for a moment then came back to the window.

'May I see your driver's licence sir?' he asked with brittle politeness.

'Yeah sure.' Norton dipped into the side pocket of his tracksuit, then remembered he'd left his wallet at home. 'Ah shit! I've just been for a run down the beach and I didn't want to take my wallet with me. The bloody thing's at home. But I can tell you the number.' Norton recited his licence number to the cop, who wrote it down on the back of his notepad. 'And my name's Les Norton. I only live just up the road in Cox Avenue.'

Without saying anything, the cop stared at Les for a second before walking back to his motorbike where he picked up the receiver and related Norton's licence number and numberplate back to base to be fed into the computer. Oh well, he's only doing his job I suppose, thought Les as he watched the cop in his rear-vision mirror half sitting on and half standing against his BMW. Still, it would be nice to see that bike fall over and break one of the miserable prick's legs. I wouldn't mind accidentally backing over the other one either.

After a few moments the cop came back to the window. 'That checks out Mr Norton,' he said.

'Yeah. That's me all right mate,' smiled Les, trying for half a joke with the still expressionless cop. 'I'd know me own face anywhere.'

The smile on Norton's face quickly faded as the cop flipped open his infringements book and began making out a ticket.

'Hey what's goin' on?' asked Les.

'I'm giving you a ticket for not producing your driver's licence,' replied the cop, almost ignoring Norton as he continued to write away.

'But I just gave you the number,' blurted Les. 'I mean. I only live about 500 yards up the road. If you want to follow me up I'll show you. I'll even give you a cup of coffee and a toasted ham sandwich.'

'You are required by law, sir,' said the cop as he continued writing, 'to have your driver's licence with you at all times when operating a motor vehicle.'

'Yeah, but Christ. I only live up the road,' pleaded Les. But it was to no avail. The cop continued to pencil away totally ignoring him. 'Ohh you're kiddin'', muttered Les, and threw his hands on the steering wheel.

'What was that?' snapped the cop suddenly.

'I said you're kiddin' aren't you?'

The cop stopped writing and glared down at Les like he was a child molester or a heroin dealer or both.

'Do you want to argue with me?' he said, his voice rising noticeably. 'Well do you? Do you want to argue?'

Les looked up at the cop and realised he was in a no-win situation. If he said another word Red Moustache would more than likely start going over his car for defects then he'd finish up having to go over the pits at the Department of Motor Transport and if they didn't put him off the road it would at least cost him a fortune to get things fixed. The cop was obviously only out to get his revenue for the morning and would probably love to do it. Norton clenched his teeth, shook his head and copped it sweet — but inside he was seething. With his hands on the steering wheel he sat there and stared grimly out the windscreen.

Finally the cop finished writing. 'You ever had one of these before?' he said, handing Norton his part of the ticket. Les nodded his head. 'Good. Then you know what to do.'

With Norton looking daggers at him, the cop closed his infringements book, slid his biro back down the side of his boot and walked back to his motor bike. Then, like Wyatt Earp climbing back on his horse after shooting it out with the James gang, he swung his ample backside across the seat, hit the starter button and did a U-turn back the way he had been going originally.

Steely-eyed, Norton watched him in the rear-vision mirror hoping he might hit a patch of oil or run into a truck; but it didn't eventuate. After a few moments he checked out his ticket. Failure to Produce Driver's Licence . . . $35. Well, well, well he chuckled tightly, that was an expensive run and a morning paper wasn't it. He folded the ticket neatly, then put it in his pocket and continued home.

If Norton was seething when he got booked, he was absolutely ropeable by the time he got home. He barged through the front door like Elliot Ness, slammed it behind him and then stampeded down the hallway to confront an unsuspecting Warren, dressed and sitting at the kitchen table finishing a last cup of coffee before leaving for work.

'G'day Les,' he said cheerfully. 'How was the run?'

Norton glared at Warren as if he'd just called his mother a whore. 'How was the run?' Here's how the fuckin' run was.' He took the traffic ticket from his pocket and tossed it across the table to Warren.

Warren nonchalantly took another sip of coffee and unfolded the brief. 'Oowaah,' he said, a hint of a smile working at the corners of his eyes. 'You've been a naughty boy, Les, haven't you. That'll learn you.'

'A naughty boy!' bellowed Norton. 'You should have seen the greasy fat turd that pinched me. Fuckin' jumped up telegram boy. I should've booted him right in his fat arse.' Les then went on to relate what had happened to him, his craggy face growing darker all the time.

Warren kept sipping his coffee and looking up at him impassively. He could see Les was in a vile mood and it was almost killing him to keep a straight face. He would dearly have loved to give Les some sympathy, but this was a golden opportunity for a stir. Warren waited until Norton had finished his tirade, then leisurely sipped some more coffee, slowly shaking his head from side to side.

'Well, Les,' he said, very matter-of-factly, 'you can't really blame the police officer. What's his name?' Warren checked the brief. 'Constable Kennewell. You can't blame Constable Kennewell for doing his duty. They do have to check identifications these days you know.'

Norton glared at Warren like he couldn't believe his ears. 'Check identifications? What are you talking about. That cunt knew who I was. Whose side are you on anyway?'

'I'm not on anyone's side,' replied Warren. 'But how was he to know you were a law-abiding citizen? You could've been anyone. You could be some thug working at a casino in the Cross and an associate of known criminals for all he knew.'

'Oh you're a funny cunt at times aren't you?' Norton waved his arm towards the front door. 'Listen mate. All that prick wanted was to fill his bloody, lousy book for the morning.

Fuckin' thievin' bastards they are. Fair dinkum, they put those old World War II German airforce uniforms on and they think New South Wales is Poland in 1939. The cunts.'

'Hey hold on a minute Les,' protested Warren. 'When have you ever been dirty on the cops? You play touch football against the TRG and Armed Holdup blokes every second Tuesday. You were wrapping them the other day when they caught those brothers that raped and killed that nurse out at Fairfield. You reckon the RBT's good 'cause it helps keep the drunks off the road. And it wasn't all that long ago you almost got yourself killed saving one's neck up in Bondi Junction. Now they're all Nazis.'

'Yeah, but they're good blokes. This thing was just a... just a motorised bloody parking cop. A jury fucker as the detectives call them.'

'Ahh turn it up Les.' Warren got up from the table and rinsed his cup in the sink. 'Look, you got done. Pay the $35 and cop it sweet.'

'Cop it sweet, eh.' Norton tore the ticket up from the kitchen table, rolled it in a ball and flung it in the kitchen tidy. 'There. That's how much I'm gonna cop it sweet. I won't pay the fuckin' thing. How's that grab you?'

Warren folded his arms and leant against the sink still trying hard not to laugh. 'All right,' he shrugged. 'Don't pay the bloody thing.'

'I won't!'

'Don't then. Go to gaol.'

'I will!'

'You'll what?'

'I'll go to gaol.'

Now Warren had to laugh. 'Ohh bullshit. Listen Les. You'd last about five minutes out in the nick. There's no Sealy Posturepedic mattresses and mugs of Ovaltine before you go to bed of a night out there old fella.'

'That wouldn't worry me.'

'Yeah?' Warren continued laughing. 'What about all those old lags out there? They'd just love a big spunky redhead like you landing in their midst. They'd be into your blurter before you could whistle the first two bars of 'Oh If I Had the Wings of an Angel'. Jesus you do carry on at times Les.'

Norton's face set and he stared at Warren evenly. 'You reckon I wouldn't be game to cut out that fine in Long Bay do you?'

'Ohh you'd be lousy enough. But not game enough. Any-

164

way, you're being silly now.' Warren moved across the kitchen towards the door. 'And I've got to get to work. I'm running late.'

'Hey hold on you little weazel,' said Norton, half blocking the door. 'You reckon I'm not game enough to cut that fine out eh?'

Warren gave Les a tired smile as he pushed past him and moved on down the hallway. 'I'll see you when I get home,' he called out.

'Yeah. Well you just wait and see what happens — you little prick,' shouted Les.

'Yeah terrific Les,' Warren shouted back. 'I'll come and visit you.'

'You needn't fuckin' bother.'

'See you tonight — Wally. Be careful if you're thinking of driving your car again today.'

'Get stuffed.'

The front door closed and Norton was alone in the house. Slowly nodding his head he kept glaring down the hallway before turning back to the kitchen tidy with the crumpled-up traffic ticket still sitting on the top.

'All right, you smart little prick,' he muttered to himself, still slowly nodding his head. 'We'll just see what happens. We'll just see what happens.'

And so, about two and a half months later, Les Norton, owing to the due process of the law, plus his own rather crass inexorability tinged with possibly a little parsimony, found himself at two-thirty in the afternoon on another Monday at Waverley Police station. Waiting to be finger-printed, hand-cuffed, flung bodily into the back of a paddy-wagon, and taken out to Long Bay Correctional Centre to be a guest of Her Majesty in the Central Industrial Prison for two days.

Norton got the message that he was required at Waverley lockup the previous Friday morning. He hadn't been long out of bed and was in the kitchen making a coffee when the phone rang.

'Hello,' he said, still feeling a little sleepy.

'Is that you Les? It's Des Smith, up at Waverley.'

'Oh g'day Des. How you goin'?' Desmond Smith was a young fair-haired cop who played centre for Eastern Suburbs. Norton had got to know him through football and some other cops he knew.

'Not bad,' replied Des. 'Listen Les. There's a bluey up here for you.'

'Really,' smiled Norton. 'What's it for Des?'

'Failure to produce driver's licence,' chuckled Des. 'It's $53 now.'

'Go on eh? I must've forgotten all about it.'

'Yeah. It's a shitty one isn't it. Anyway — when do you want to come up? Or if we're going past your place we can call in. Save you a trip.'

'No. That's all right Des. But look, I won't come up over the weekend because of work. How about I call in Monday 'arvo?'

'Good as gold Les. I'll be on duty then. I'll have a yarn to you.'

'Okay Des. Hey, you had a good win on the weekend.'

'Ohh, I didn't. The other blokes did. I pulled a hamstring when I scored that try in the first half.'

'Yeah. How is it now? You playin' this weekend?'

'No. I'm still getting physio.'

'Oh, bad luck. Anyway Des, I'll see you on Monday.'

Yes, thought Norton, a strange half smile forming on his face as he stared at the phone for a few moments after he'd hung up. I'll see you on Monday all right Des. But unlike what the blokes say on TV, I won't be bringing my money with me.

Late the following Sunday afternoon Les and Warren were in the lounge room watching the first half of *Countdown* while they waited for the replay of Parramatta versus Balmain to start. Norton was into his third can of Fourex, Warren had just smoked a joint and was into his second Jack Daniels and Coke. The music had stopped and Molly Meldrum was umming and aahing his way through Humdrum when Les spoke.

'Well Woz, old buddy old pal,' he smiled, 'are you going to come out and visit me on Monday?'

Warren's eyebrows knitted as he looked at Les. 'Visit you? Why, where are you going?'

'I'm going out to Long Bay to cut out that fine.'

'Fine? What fine?'

'That one I got down the road for not having my driver's licence.'

Warren stared at Norton in slight amazement. 'That was months ago. Haven't you paid the bloody thing yet?'

Norton shook his head. 'I told you Warren. I had no bloody intentions of paying it.'

Warren eased back in his chair and stared at Norton sprawled along the lounge. 'Are you fair dinkum?'

Norton nodded slowly.

'You mean to tell me, you're going out to Long Bay Gaol to cut out a lousy $35 fine?'

Norton nodded again.

Warren continued to stare at the big Queenslander, then shook his head. 'Fair dinkum Les. If you're going to go into Long Bay Gaol rather than pay a $35 fine, you would have to be the meanest man in Australia. No, hold on. I take that back. The meanest man in the world.'

Norton stared back at Warren. Then his face broke into a grin and he nodded again.

The following morning Norton was up early as usual and did his training. Warren had left early for work so he missed him when he got back. But there was a note on the kitchen table:

'Les. I still don't know whether you're fair dinkum about cutting out that fine. But don't expect me to come and visit you. You can rot in chains for all I give a stuff. But if any of those old lags finish up rooting you, don't come back here with AIDS. Warren.'

Norton laughed to himself then screwed the note up and tossed it in the kitchen-tidy. Cheeky little prick he chuckled. After breakfast he pottered around the house. It wasn't much of a day so he watched the midday movie then had some lunch. He asked himself once or twice whether he should still go through with it, but he'd made up his mind to do it and he would. Before he knew it, it was two. He changed into an older tracksuit and took no more than $20 with him, plus an old Seiko watch. He left a note on the kitchen table saying 'Thanks Woz. You're a real mate. See you Wednesday.' Then he locked up the house, walked down to Campbell Parade, and caught a cab to Waverley Police Station.

Des Smith was behind the counter with a sergeant and two other cops when Norton walked in.

'Ah g'day Les,' he smiled. 'You here to pay the bluey?'

Norton smiled back at him. 'To tell you the truth Des, I'm not going to pay it.'

Des returned Norton's smile with a strange look. 'What do you mean — you're not going to pay it?'

'I'm not paying it. I'm gonna cut it out.'

'You want to cut it out? Ohh don't be bloody crazy, Les. Look, if you're going bad I'll pay it and you can fix me up. Christ, it's only fifty-odd bucks.'

167

Norton shook his head adamantly, 'No Des. A bloke bet me I wasn't game to cut it out, so I am. Anyway, it's only a couple of days,' he added with a shrug.

'Les, it wouldn't matter if it was only a couple of minutes. Have you ever been out to Long Bay? It ain't the Sebel Town House, I can tell you.'

'Don't matter Des. Just handcuff me and drag me away. Do what you want. Torture me. Starve me. Apply electrodes to me nuts. I don't care. I can handle it.'

Des looked at the other cops then back at Les. 'Are you sure you know what you're doing?'

Norton nodded his head.

'Suit yourself,' sighed Des. 'All right come down here.'

Norton was led to the charge room. Trying to keep a straight face in front of his fellow officers, and at the same time hide his bewilderment at Norton's wanting to spend time in Long Bay, Des checked Norton's warrant and shook his head once more at the amount: $53. He stood him in the dock and entered the particulars in the charge book. Norton was then searched, his valuables removed and placed in a large envelope.

'You're travelling very light Les,' said Des, entering the contents in a register before he sealed the envelope.

'Yeah. Not much there for you to knock off while I'm inside eh,' Les winked.

'Ohh I dunno,' replied Des. 'That watch has got to be worth ten bucks.'

'Have a bit of a heart Des. It was a present from me mother.'

'I see you're not wearing a belt.' Des nodded at Norton's tracksuit, then at his sneakers. 'If I let you keep your shoelaces, will you promise me you won't hang yourself.'

'If I do you can keep the watch. Fair enough?'

'Fair enough. Anyway, come on. We've got a nice room down the back for you.'

Norton was led through a barred door and along a passageway that led into a corridor facing four cells. Des opened the nearest cell and Les stepped inside.

'There'll be an air conditioned coach leaving in about fifteen minutes,' said Des as he locked the cell door. 'If you should require any light refreshments, coffee, biscuits, anything like that. Don't hesitate to call will you.'

'I wouldn't mind a cappuccino and a toasted ham sandwich.'

'Coming right up,' smiled Des. 'Don't go away now will you.' He gave Norton a wink then turned and left.

As far as comforts go, the cell didn't have a great deal

going for it. Grey painted bars, grey speckled walls, a half-dozen sort of wrestling mats were scattered around the floor and about twice that many blankets. A stainless-steel toilet bowl sat in the corner furtherest from the door.

There were two other men in the cell, sitting on the floor across from each other. One had long blond hair, the other's was black and cropped close to his skull. Both looked to be in their early twenties and both were wearing jeans, T-shirts and V-neck jumpers. Norton gave them each a smile and a nod before he sat down. They gave him an almost imperceptible nod in return.

Norton plonked himself down on one of the mats, leant back against the wall and had a bit of a look around. So this is life in the can eh, he chuckled to himself. I've only been in a couple of minutes and I can't say I'm over rapt in it already. His two cellmates continued to stare silently at the floor or into space.

After about five minutes Norton turned to the fair-haired one on his left. 'What are you in for mate?' he asked.

The blond continued to stare at the floor for a few moments. 'Can't remember,' he finally answered.

Norton looked at him for a few seconds, then turned to the other. 'What about you mate?'

'I'm in for the same thing,' he muttered.

Norton nodded and stared up at the ceiling. 'Yeah righto,' he said to no one in particular.

They sat there in almost total silence, broken only by the hum of a large overhead air-duct. After about fifteen minutes a door opened and a beefy sergeant and a young red-haired constable walked into the corridor. 'Righto,' the sergeant called out as he unlocked the cell door. The other cop stood behind him holding three sets of handcuffs. Norton's cellmates shuffled out first and automatically held their hands out in front of them; it was obvious that they'd been there, done that before. Then it was Les's turn. The ratchets clicked and Norton was well and truly cuffed and booked. And although one side of Les was finding it rather amusing, to the other side it was a distinctly alien and unpleasant feeling.

'Righto. This way,' growled the sergeant.

They were led out into another corridor and down some steps to a paddy-wagon waiting at the rear of the courthouse. The red-haired cop opened the back door and stood next to it; he didn't say anything but the three of them knew what to do. Crouching slightly the others got in first. Norton was about to climb in when he heard a voice behind him. He turned around to face Des Smith; hatless and a big grin spread across his face.

'Hey Les. Before you go,' he said to Norton, almost half in the door. 'Remember when I was playing reserve grade for Souths and I had my first run in firsts. It was against Easts at Redfern Oval. You were playing second row.'

'Yeah. I think I remember Des.'

'I was playing centre. I'd just got the ball and you came across and hit me with a tackle that almost cut me in half. I tore all my rib cartilages. I was out for nearly a month.'

'Ohh yeah,' smiled Norton. 'Now I remember.'

'Good,' grinned the fair-haired young cop. He stepped back, brought the sole of his police boot up and reefed Norton in the rump, propelling him to the other end of the wagon. With the handcuffs spoiling his sense of balance, Norton sprawled against the rear of the cabin. Only a desperate grab at the canvas roof stopped him from hitting the floor as the door slammed behind him.

'Sorry about that Les,' came Des's voice from outside. 'But it was too good an opportunity to miss.'

'Dirty mug copper,' bellowed Norton. He got his balance back and sat down next to the crim with dark hair. 'Fuckin' coppers,' grunted Norton. 'They're all cunts.'

'You're not wrong,' was the laconic reply.

The next thing, the motor started and they lurched up the driveway, bumping and weaving their way to Long Bay Gaol.

How long the trip took, Les wasn't sure — fifteen, twenty minutes? But through the grill on the back door he could see Charing Cross fading into the distance, then Randwick Junction, Maroubra Junction, and before long they were cruising along Anzac Parade with still nobody saying anything. Les noticed a set of lights and a sign saying Beauchamp Street; there was a bit of a lurch as they turned left up another driveway, a boom-gate opened, then they stopped at the sound of a huge gate opening. A shadow seemed to fall across the wagon as they went a little further and stopped with the motor still running. Peering out the back of the wagon it looked to Les as if they were inside a monstrous grey birdcage; to his left he could make out a huge brass bell. For whom the bell tolls, mused Norton, his thoughts going back to an old Ernest Hemingway story he'd read at school. Another gate clanged open to the sound of different voices. The wagon eased forward again, stopped, then reversed up to an open doorway and the motor was turned off as the two police climbed out of the wagon and went inside.

After a few moments Les turned to the crim sitting next to him. 'Looks like we're here,' he said.

'You'd better fuckin' believe it.'

They sat there in the gloomy silence of the wagon. Through the canvas walls Norton could hear voices coming from somewhere and the sounds of more gates or heavy doors opening and slamming shut. After what seemed quite a while the back of the paddy-wagon opened and they were motioned out. The same cop that had put his handcuffs on undid them and took them off. Norton rubbed his wrists, scratched his back and had a good look around him.

He was standing in some sort of a large reception room, with a step-down shower area off to his right. It was all painted a faded yellow and everything, from the tiles in the shower to the dull yellow paint on the walls, looked and even felt old. There was a short counter to his left and a longer one in front of him fronting rows of shelves stacked with cartons and green or brown prison uniforms. Even from where he stood the shower area seemed to smell almost overpoweringly of bleach and strong disinfectant. Someone had painted some sort of a country-scene mural on a wall above the showers and above his head several old-fashioned wooden fans stood motionless against the equally ancient wooden ceiling.

The two police officers handed over Les's personal effects to a guard, signed something and disappeared. But there was no shortage of prison officers; all very solid and stony faced, though oddly enough having a cheerful banter amongst themselves.

Along with the two others, Les was told to strip. Then, after being searched thoroughly they were asked if they wanted a shower but all three declined, Norton mainly because it was too cold and he was convinced that the smell of disinfectant and bleach would knock him out. He was then given his prison clothing — green trousers, fawn shirt, green jacket and brown jumper; they let him keep his joggers and the Speedos he was wearing as underwear — and told to fill in a blue Description Sheet. Name, aliases, whether he was an Aborigine or not, previous convictions, distinguishing marks, etc. He signed this and they took a fingerprint of his right forefinger on the bottom corner of the sheet. While

171

he was being printed a male nurse asked him if he had had any drug problems or illnesses. Norton replied that he was a bit hungry, that's all.

If Les appeared to be a little flippant about it all, underneath he was feeling trapped, degraded and beginning to find it all rather distasteful. It was his own stubbornness and I'll-show-him attitude that had got him in here and a couple of times, especially when he was being searched, he regretted his foolishness. But it was only for a couple of days so what the hell. However, if Norton was being a bit casual about it all, his travelling companions were quite the opposite. They were completely humourless and listless and moody when filling out their forms or taking instructions from the warders. It was a sure bet they were in for something a bit more than traffic warrants and Norton was curious what for and for how long.

Finally Les was given two woollen blankets, a towel, a yellow pamphlet entitled *Information Booklet for Inmates of the CIP* (Central Industrial Prison), and told to wait to be allocated a cell. That was when it dawned on him what he was. An inmate. A prisoner. And standing there in his drab prison garb with his blankets under his arm he looked and felt it. Nothing fitted, it all smelled of mothballs or something and soon he was going to be dumped in a cold, dank cell. Immediately he began to think of his nice warm house at Bondi and all the food and beer in the fridge. What a nice dill I must be, he thought. Warren and Des were right. Oh well, at least there's no one here to see me looking like this. He was just about to flick through his information booklet when he heard a mystified voice behind him.

'Les Norton. What the fuckin' hell are you doin' in here?'

Norton brought himself around slowly. Ohh no, he thought. Not in here. Not like this. Please.

He turned around to face a tall, half-smiling guard standing behind him with his hands on his hips. He was somewhere in his early fifties and built not unlike himself, only with slightly more of a paunch. With a mop of thick steel-grey hair he had one of those lived-in, Robert Mitchum type faces, only a little fuller and a little jowlier.

'Les Norton,' he said slowly. 'It is you. What have you been up to?'

'Ohh g'day Bernie,' replied Norton sheepishly. 'How's things?' Shit, Les cursed to himself, not another bloke from football. I wish to Christ I'd never laced on a boot.

The guard was Bernard Cottier. Les had got to know him through his brother Michael, who was a boner in the meatworks at Ultimo Les worked in when he came down from Queensland and first started playing with Easts. Bernie had been a pretty useful front-rower for Newtown in the early 'sixties and since he'd retired he spent most of his time coaching juniors. However, his main claim to fame, apart from football, was having a wife that ugly she'd run second in a one-woman beauty contest. But Bernie was one of those blokes that loved kids and he'd had eleven to her, nearly all girls.

Bernie continued to stare at Les, then picked up his charge sheet from the desk. He looked at it briefly and shook his head in disbelief. 'Are you fair dinkum?' he said. Norton couldn't quite look Bernie in the eye as he nodded his head at the floor. 'Christ! Mick always said you were tight with a quid, Les. But mate. This is ridic.'

Norton nodded again, red-cheeked. 'I think you're pretty right Bernie.' He paused while Bernie kept looking at his charge sheet as if there was some mistake. 'Are you going to take me to my cell?' he asked.

'Yeah. I may as well I s'pose.'

'Good. I'll tell you about it on the way over.'

Bernie replaced Les's charge sheet and handed Les a name tag which he was to wear during all musters. He then told the other guards he'd take the prisoner to his cell. 'You right Les?' he said, picking up a clipboard. With his name-tag pinned on, his pamphlet in one hand and his blankets and towel in the other, Les nodded sheepishly again. 'Okay. Follow me.'

They went out the open doorway and across a yard past the big grey birdcage Les had seen when he first came in. By the time they'd reached yet another barred gate Norton had explained the reason he was there. Bernie was still shaking his head though he couldn't help but laugh.

'I always said you were a stubborn big bastard, Les. Even when you were playing. But a couple of days in here won't hurt you.' He gave Les a slap on the back. 'Might even give you a bit of an idea about what goes on. From both sides,' he added.

They stopped at the gate and Bernie told Norton to wait while another guard looked across to make sure the main gate was locked before he unlocked his. Even in the short time he'd been there, Les noticed that only one gate was opened at a time. They stepped through into another reception area with a two-tiered row of cells running off it to their right.

'In their?' Les nodded towards that wing.

'Turn it up,' smiled Bernie. 'At least those blokes are in for something useful. You're only in the shitty warrants section. Come on ... crim.'

Although he felt terribly embarrassed at first, Les was glad now that he'd bumped into Bernie. At least he knew one person in there, and the big, rough prison guard wasn't a bad bloke underneath. They moved past the desk in the reception area onto a concrete strip that ran around a huge patch of dry, sandy grass about 200 metres square and flanked by other buildings.

'That's the exercise yard,' said Bernie. 'Or as it is affectionately known — the square.'

There were about fifty or so men in the square, some jogging around it, some walking; all of them under the eye of what looked like a similar number of guards. Most of the joggers were wearing green shorts, the rest their green and brown uniforms, and they were the hardest faced, toughest looking men Norton had seen in quite a while. Even some of the joggers going past, who had to be in their fifties, were square jawed with steel-grey crewcuts and built like tanks. Apart from their tough appearance, one slightly amusing thing did stand out to Norton. Several groups of men walked briskly, four or six abreast, from one side of the square to the other. They walked and talked as if they were on a ten mile hike in the countryside, but when they'd reach the side they'd all turn on the spot completely in step, not even disrupting their rhythm, their pace or a word of their conversation. Norton had been standing there only a short while and the men would have done at least six laps.

Bernie noticed the curious look on Norton's face. 'Like to join the lads for an afternoon stroll?' Norton smiled and shook his head. 'Righto. Well come on and I'll show you to your motel room.'

They went into another reception area full of guards, through a doorway and out into the warrants section.

The warrants section, or wing, consisted of about twenty yellow washed cells running off to the right, with an open area in front of them and a covered area supported by poles in front of that. Bernie pointed out the white-tiled shower area at the far end and behind them a servery where you got your food. There were about fifteen men of all shapes and ages milling around, trying to get a bit of sun in front of their cells or standing under the covered area. Some were potting balls on a pool table while others were drinking coffee from a hot water machine next to the servery. All looked fairly bored and listless except for one long-haired bloke tunelessly banging on a cheap guitar; he was getting stuck into it like he was Jimi Hendrix. Raised above them in the covered area was a colour TV, blaring loud enough to drown out Jimi Hendrix, and a book-case full of books stood underneath this. Rocking slightly in the light wind was an almost-new black Ring-Master punching bag hanging on chains from a beam in front of the shower area.

'Can you still thump as hard as you used to Les?' asked Bernie, noticing Norton eyeing the punching bag.

'I hope so,' replied Norton. 'I might end up losing my cherry in here if I can't.'

'I think you'll be pretty safe mate,' chuckled Bernie. 'You're too ugly anyway — even for some of these desperates. Come on, I'll show you your room. I mean cell.'

They moved across the yard to the row of cells. Norton's was about four from the servery end. Number 602. The door was open and in one of two brackets above it was a piece of paper saying: Gatenby, 20 days. Bernie took another slip of paper and slid it in the bracket. It said: Norton, 2 days.

'After you Les,' smiled Bernie, motioning to the open cell door.

Des Smith at Waverley Police Station was right when he said Long Bay wasn't the Sebel Town House. Apart from being musty and dirty the cell didn't have anything going for it at all. It was around ten feet by eight with a toilet bowl in the corner and two narrow beds almost alongside each other. The light came from the open door and from an enclosed fluorescent tube that played dim shadows of a mug, a jar of coffee and a few other odds and ends across the top of an ancient wooden cabinet in front of one of the beds. The cell's one outstanding feature was the graffiti. There was hardly a square inch of wall or ceiling that didn't have something scrawled or drawn on it.

'Like your new digs, do you Les?'

'Yeah,' muttered Norton. 'It's just peachy.' He nodded towards the mug and the jar of coffee. 'Who's in with me? Some axe murderer I suppose.'

'No. His name's Max. He's a truck driver.'

'What's he in for?'

'Warrants. The same as you. That's all this wing is. In fact Max is one of our regular customers. It's weird really. He doesn't mind it here at all. Sometimes I even think he likes it.'

Norton continued to gaze round the cell, shaking his head. 'He must be weird if he likes this. I've only been here five minutes and I can't stand it already.'

'Well, you know the old saying Les,' smiled Bernie. 'If you can't spend the time, don't do the crime.' The prison officer glanced at his watch. 'Anyway I've got to get going. I'm knocking off in a few minutes and they'll be mustering you for dinner shortly. I'll probably see you tomorrow.' He paused at the door for a moment. 'And a bit of advice, Les. Take it easy. It's a different ball game in here and if you get into any strife there's not much I can do for you.'

'Strife? Jesus Bernie, I'm only in here for two days and one's nearly over already. What could happen?'

'Not much I suppose. But in here, you never know Les. You just never know. I'll see you tomorrow.'

'Yeah. See you Bernie.'

The bed closest to the door was half made, Les tossed his stuff on the other and tested the springs with his hand. It wasn't the best, but it wasn't all that bad. Any more than two days, though, and you'd need to know a good chiropractor. He spread his blankets over it, gave the pillow a scrunch, then sat down on the edge and looked around him. So this is it eh. Long Bay Gaol. His eyes wandered from the graffiti to the chipped walls and ceiling to the chipped floor. Christ they must've built this joint in 1800. I wonder where those pricks on the radio and in the papers get all those ideas about motel-like accommodation. I don't see any colour TV or stereo in here. I'd like to stick some of them in here for a few days — see what they think. Especially that flip in Melbourne with the beard. No wonder he was crying when he looked like going in for six weeks. Oh well, Norton smiled to himself, maybe it's not all that bad and it's not as if there's nothing to do. I can go outside and watch TV if I want to. I can join the lads for a nice stroll in the square. I can have a game of pool or read a book. I can even have a workout on a punching bag if I want. Or I can spend two days reading all this graffiti. He picked up his yellow information booklet. I think I might just see what this says instead. Norton started flicking over the pages.

Introduction. You are in the Central Industrial Prison. Well I certainly bloody know that, Norton smiled to himself. If you have been sentenced in court you will be held in the CIP until you are classified and transferred to another gaol. There are also some prisoners here who are appealing against their sentences and others serving sentences for non-payment of fines. Hey that's me. Well what do you know? I'm on page one already. Norton read on about Reception Tobacco. Passing Information With Care. Daily Routine. Vegetarians. Library. He was smiling at the section on Visits when in walked his cell mate, who looked like he'd just come from the shower.

'G'day mate,' he said breezily, tossing his towel on the bed. 'How's things?'

'Not too bad,' replied Norton, looking up from his pamphlet. 'What about yourself?'

'Can't complain.' He looked at Norton evenly for a moment. 'My name's Max, anyway,' he said offering his hand.

'Les,' smiled Norton, half rising from the bed and accepting Max's firm but brief handshake. 'Please to meet you mate.'

Max was a wiry sort of bloke, shorter than Les and in his late forties or early fifties with a bit of a potbelly. He had thinning sandy-coloured hair adorned with a pair of huge side levers spreading over his square jaw. He seemed to have those ever-smiling eyes and a lopsided smile that opened up to reveal a set of discoloured buckteeth that looked like a mouthful of broken paddle-pop sticks.

'I see you're only in for a couple of days,' he said. 'Goin' a bit bad are you?'

'No. Not really. It's a bit of a funny story to tell you the truth. I noticed you're stuck in this dump for twenty bloody days though. Shit!'

'I don't really look at it like that, Les. I reckon it's all right in here actually.'

Norton screwed his face up at Max. 'Are you fair dinkum?'

Max nodded enthusiastically from where he was sitting on his bed. 'Mate, this is the grouse in here. All you've got to do is stick to yourself and mind your own business and you're sweet. It's the tops, I'm tellin' you.'

Norton continued to stare at Max almost in amazement. Bernie was right about the truck driver. He definitely had to have a loose cannon rolling around on the top deck to come out with a statement like that. He was about to elaborate on it when he heard voices outside.

'That's muster,' said Max, clapping his hands together.

177

'They check our names, then we get dinner.' Max smiled at Les, winked and ran his tongue over his lips. 'The food's great too. Come on.'

Still shaking his head, Norton got up and followed Max outside. Along with the rest of the inmates they stood in front of their cells while two guards with a clipboard walked past and called their names, which were answered with a 'yo' or a 'yay' or whatever. After they were satisfied everyone was there they let them form a queue outside the servery.

Norton got behind Max and was given a tray with his eating utensils and a mug. Then came the food. Fried lamb-chops, peas, carrots, mashed potato and pumpkin; plenty of gravy and a lump of bread. Sweets were some sort of rice pudding with stewed fruit and custard, plus a mug of tea. There was plenty of it and although it wasn't quite as cordon bleu as Max made out it was okay. The only fault, if any, was that it came from the other side of the gaol and was a little cold by the time it got there. Some of the men took their meal into their cells, but Max and Les ate theirs seated at a bench near the pool table. After they'd finished Norton returned his plate and cutlery but kept his mug for another cup of tea.

'You were right about the food, Max,' he said. 'It wasn't half-bad.'

'Wasn't half bad?' replied Max. 'Mate, those lambchops and vegetables were bloody beautiful. And I haven't tasted sweets like that in years.'

Norton looked at the side-levered truck driver and smiled; he'd barely known him a few minutes and already he couldn't help but like him. He was open and friendly, without being a crawler, and incongruously happy at the same time. Yet there definitely had to be something wrong with someone who referred to a cell in Long Bay Gaol as the grouse and plain food as bloody beautiful. In the short period he was going to be there, Norton was determined to find out why.

'So what happens now Max?' asked Norton as they sat beneath the blaring television, sipping their mugs of tea.

'What happens now? Not much,' replied Max. 'They lock the wing off after five o'clock muster then you can sit around and watch TV or whatever till they bundle us into our cells at ten. Then you can do what you like. Read, think. Listen to the radio. Have a pull if you like. Or you can put your head down and have a good eight hours of beautiful, unbroken sleep. Which is generally what I do,' Max added with a wink and his lopsided smile.

'Sounds ... just great,' Norton smiled back.

'It is, it's heaven.'

The more Norton spoke to Max, the more curious he became. Now the truck driver actually referred to being locked up in that filthy graffiti-ridden cell for nearly ten hours as heaven. Where the fuck had Max come from? Devils Island? A North Vietnamese prison? It was a funny one all right.

Most of the other prisoners had drifted back out and were sitting around staring vacantly up at the TV. Now that the sun had gone they nearly all had their blankets over their shoulders and sipped at mugs of coffee and Ovaltine to keep warm. Jimi Hendrix had resumed his spot outside his cell, and guitar in hand was mercilessly putting the cleaners through 'The Times They Are a-Changin' ' before absolutely crucifying 'Hey Jude'. Luckily the TV still drowned most of it out so no-one seemed to take much notice. Norton nodded and half smiled to some of the blokes seated around him; and got a half smile back for his efforts. They were a pretty average looking lot, no real heavies amongst them. Except maybe for two rugged-looking blokes standing unsmiling as they earnestly discussed something out of earshot down by the bookcase.

Before long another two guards came in and did a quick muster before a rattling noise told Norton they'd locked off the wing as they left. Norton bummed a bit of coffee and sugar from Max and with his blanket across his shoulders watched the news and some boring shows on TV. Between checking out the faces around him and watching programs that he didn't at all like Norton felt like going into his cell and reading. But he'd be getting locked in there before long and wasn't actually relishing the thought, so why hurry. Before he knew it, that time had arrived.

The same two guards returned and the taller one switched off the TV. 'Righto girls,' he said, rattling a large set of keys. 'Time for beddy byes. Come on. Let's go.'

There was a general discontented muttering, a few quiet curses and they all shuffled into their cells. Max was already laying on his bed reading a *Penthouse* when Les walked in.

'Thank Christ they've turned that fuckin' TV off,' he said as Norton stood in the muted light with his back to the door.

A queasy feeling suddenly hit Norton as the door slammed shut behind him and the locked turned; much queasier than the ones he'd already experienced. It was a feeling of finality. Now he was well and truly locked in and he couldn't get out if he wanted to. A few little butterflies gave a slight but noticeable flutter in the pit of his stomach.

'Ahh! Peace and quiet at last,' said Max, resting his head back on the pillow and momentarily closing his eyes. 'Isn't it lovely?'

Norton looked at him for a moment or two before sitting down on his bed. 'Yeah. If you say so,' he shrugged.

'You sleep like a top in here, Les. I'm tellin' you.'

Norton noticed that the truck driver's head was only going to be about two feet from his own. 'Hey Max, how do you get on if you get some cunt in here that snores?'

Max reached behind him to the cabinet and handed Norton a plastic container. 'I use these. Anti-noise wax earplugs. Do you snore Les?'

'I've ... been known to get a bit of a rhythm going now and again. What about you?'

Max nodded. 'Yeah. I saw up a few logs on the odd occasion.'

'All right if I borrow a couple of these?'

Norton started to soften up the cotton wool covered earplugs in his fingers while Max did the same. 'Hey what time do they turn the light off?'

'They don't.'

'What do you mean — they don't?'

'They don't. They leave it on all night.'

'Christ.' Norton frowned at the dull fluorescent tube above their heads. 'How do they expect you to get to sleep?'

'Easy. Just shut your eyes. In fact it's way past my bedtime, so if you want to watch me I'll show you.' Max stuffed the earplugs in his ears, closed his eyes and lay back on the pillow with his blanket up under his chin. 'See you in the morning.'

Norton stared at Max lying there as if he was having the time of his life. 'Yeah. See you then Max,' he finally said.

It seemed like no time at all and Max was snoring away softly, almost like a baby. Norton watched him and shook his head. Well if that don't take the cake, he chuckled to himself.

Norton had been up early that morning and he made sure he trained extra hard, so by now he was starting to feel more than a bit tired himself. He gazed absently at the earplugs sitting in the palm of his hand and started to think. I dead-set must be an idiot to do something like this for the sake of a lousy $53. But a bit of a taste of this won't really hurt I s'pose. And you never know, something might come out of it. Can't see what though. Except maybe that lousy $53.

Anyway. Who gives a stuff? I wouldn't mind knowing Max's secret to life though.

His tired eyes drifted up to the graffiti on the wall in front of him. Most of it was obscene or cursing the screws and Long Bay in general. One lot did catch his eye though. A few lines of verse with a rough drawing of a bong next to it:

> I used to pull cones.
> I used to suck piss.
> How the fuckin' hell will I
> ever handle this?

Easy, chuckled Les. He put the earplugs in, lay the edge of his towel across his eyes and rested his head back on the pillow with the blanket up under his chin; just like Max. Before he knew it he'd managed to switch himself off and he too was snoring away, dead to the world.

Norton woke up a few minutes earlier than Max, just before seven. Apart from a little stiffness in his back and neck he didn't feel all that bad. They both had a leak and Max suggested that if either of them needed a crap, to bake it until they opened the cell door as the odour from two men in a ten-by-eight cell hung in the air for hours, like mustard gas. They lay there listening to Max's tiny radio for a while before the guards unlocked the cells.

It was a little cloudy and cool when they stepped outside, blinking into what sunlight there was. After a quick muster they got cleaned up and it was time for breakfast. Porridge, cereal, toast, it was nothing marvellous but there was more than enough and it filled the gap. Before long, the TV was blaring again, Jimi Hendrix had his guitar out and was mutilating 'The Long and Winding Road' and it was just another day in the warrants section at Long Bay.

Les asked Max what he intended doing.

'Absolutely nothing. Maybe read a book,' Max replied. Norton thought that was as good an idea as any and ambled over to the bookcase. They were mostly hardbacks. Classics, biographies, early Australiana and that. There were one or two paperbacks. Norton picked one up. Franz Kafka. *Stories, 1904-1924.* That'll do, he thought. I can handle a few short stories.

He walked back to his cell, got his blanket, and folded it on the ground outside, made himself as comfortable as he could and opened the book up in the sun. This story looks okay he mused. 'Metamorphosis'. Didn't Roxy Music have an album out called that. Oh well, sounds all right anyway.

He was about to start when an old sweeper came though pushing a broom. He was a wizened little bloke with a broken nose like a piece of squashed putty sitting on a thin, lined face. He had heavily lidded eyes that seemed to be darting everywhere at once, like a small animal in the wild expecting predators to pounce on it at any time.

Norton had his legs stuck out in front of him. 'Sorry mate,' he muttered, pulling them in so the sweeper could get around him.

'Sweet pal,' was the clipped reply, straight out the side of the old sweeper's mouth.

Norton smiled to himself and started reading.

It wasn't all that easy to concentrate with the TV blaring; and Jimi Hendrix sounded like he was saving his ghastly best for 'Hey Mr Tambourine Man'. Norton went into his cell, got his earplugs and jammed them in before resuming his original position. That was a bit better, the noise was no more than a blur now. He continued reading.

'Metamorphosis' was definitely nothing to do with the Roxy Music album, and Kafka would have starved to death trying to make a living as a gag writer. It was about a bloke that wakes up one morning in his room and finds he's turned into a giant dung beetle. It was awful — and the writer's style, although excellent, was pure misery. Christ! What a place to read something like this thought Les. I'll have bloody nightmares tonight. I'll dream I'll wake up in the morning and find I've turned into a giant cockroach. Fat chance, he snorted. A cockroach wouldn't live in that cell. He read on.

Les was almost halfway through the story when he felt someone kick one of his outstretched legs. He looked up and the two toughs he'd noticed talking by the bookcase the previous night were standing over him. Apart from one being a shade taller than the other they looked identical. Sour, florid faces. Bushy black hair and equally black and bushy Pancho Villa moustaches. Their arms were covered in tattoos. Gravestones, panthers and dragons with great blue spiderwebs wrapped round their elbows. The taller one seemed to be snarling something down at him.

Screwing up his face, Norton stared up at him for a moment before taking out one of the earplugs. 'What was that mate?' he muttered.

'I said how about gettin' your feet out of the fuckin' road. Are you deaf or something?'

'I didn't hear you,' replied Norton. 'I had these earplugs in.'

'You oughta clean your fuckin' ears out now and again,' said the shorter hood.

'Oh yeah,' replied Norton slowly. He put down the book and his eyebrows started to bristle slightly.

'Yeah. Fuckin' yeah,' snarled the first hood.

There was a bit of a Mexican stand-off for a few moments as they all glared at each other. The hoods were pretty confident; they looked tough and Les was on his own. Les glared back up at them for a few seconds before finally putting his earplugs back in, picking up his book and continuing with his story. The hoods said something else to him which he couldn't hear, then went over to the pool table, abruptly interrupting the two smaller men playing on it and started up a game of their own.

Norton's eyes had narrowed and his face had darkened. What a nice pair of mugs, he thought. I might just go over and shove those pool cues right up their tattooed arses. Then he remembered what Bernie had said to him: 'Take it easy, Les. It's a different ball game in here.' He snorted and continued reading, but he wasn't at all happy.

He finished the story and it only made him worse. Jesus! What a lemon of a book, he thought, slamming it closed and dropping it down beside him. God, I can't see myself reading any more of this. I'll end up slashing my wrists. All I need now is for Jimi Hendrix down there to start playing some Neil Young. He worked the earplugs out and couldn't believe what he was hearing. Jimi was getting stuck into 'Southern Man' like there was going to be no tomorrow. Ohh no. Norton closed his eyes and slumped back against the wall. I don't bloody believe this. He opened his eyes up towards the sky. You wouldn't do it to me boss. You couldn't be that cruel.

But he was, and all Norton could do was sit there shaking his head. He slipped the earplugs into his pocket and tried to figure out what he could do. The boredom of prison life was starting to get to him already, plus he was still more than annoyed at the gobful he'd had to cop from the two hoods with the Pancho Villa moustaches. Looking up he noticed they were having another earnest conversation next to the bookcase. After drumming his fingers on the concrete for a few moments, Les decided this would be as good a time as any to put Franz Kafka back where he'd found him.

The hoods stopped their conversation. They bristled slightly when they saw Norton approaching and gave him a sour look. Les returned this with a strange half smile as he stepped in between them and carefully placed his book back in the case. In the space between the bookcase and the shower block the punching bag was moving very gently on its chain. Les ambled over, stood about a metre or so away and studied it for a moment or two. There were no bag mitts around but this wasn't going to worry the two calloused legs of ham that passed for Norton's fists. The hoods frowned and exchanged dark glances just as Les bent slightly at the knees, and with a whack that made everybody in the wing look over from what they were doing, drove a murderous right rip up into the heavy bag. The bag jackknifed in the middle and flew back with a great rattle as far as the chains supporting it would allow. While it was still suspended in midair Les slammed in a left hook that spun it crazily towards the shower block; this was followed by another sizzling left hook, just as hard and just as loud. Another right rip jackknifed the bag again and another two left hooks spun it back towards the showers. As the bag spun back Norton stepped back and let go with a thundering straight right that nearly tore it and the chains holding it off the wooden beam. He then moved away and left the heavy bag rocking and bucking violently as if an earthquake had just hit the place.

After a nod of his head and a little grunt of satisfaction, Norton turned and, calm and quiet as a cat, walked back past the two hoods, now very wide-eyed, giving them an evil grin and a little wiggle of his eyebrows as he did. They didn't say anything, but somehow their droopy moustaches seemed suddenly to droop a lot further. Norton resumed his original position on the concrete outside his cell as every eye in the wing settled on him. He gazed briefly back at the fifteen or so faces around him before closing his eyes and leaning back against the wall.

It wasn't much longer and they were mustered for lunch. Sandwiches. Norton walked down with Max to join the queue at the servery. The two moustachioed hoods were about to join in a step or so in front of him when the taller one turned around and noticed Les. 'After you mate,' he said, letting Les and Max get in front of both of them. Norton gave them both a thin smile. It wasn't hard to see they'd got the message.

After several corned beef and salad sandwiches, washed

down with plenty of prison tea, Norton returned to his position outside his cell. The sun wasn't all that warm and he was soon bored and fidgety again. Ah bugger this, he thought, I may as well have a fair dinkum workout on that bag, do some exercises and have a shower. Better than sitting around here like a battery bloody hen. He got his towel from his cell, walked over to the bag and slipped off his brown prison jumper. He was about to do some loosening-up exercises when he heard voices, curses and slapping sounds accompanied by short cries of pain coming from inside the shower block. Curious, he stopped what he was doing and walked inside to have a look.

It was the old sweeper Les had seen earlier. He was lying on the floor with his back against the wall, hands and arms around his head, his broom on the floor next to him. Another powerfully built prisoner, with his back to Les, had hold of him by the shirt with one hand and was punching into him with the other. The sweeper was trying desperately to protect himself but he was about a third the size of his assailant and having absolutely no luck at all. Norton stood there for a moment trying to figure out the best thing to do. It was none of his business and the first thing they tell you when you go in the nick is never stick your head in where it doesn't belong. But he couldn't stand there and watch an old man being beat up. He had to do something.

'That's two ounces of tobacco you owe me now, you old cunt. And I want it. Where is it?' The big prisoner had just said that and given the sweeper another couple of thumps when Norton tapped him on the shoulder.

'Hey take it easy old mate,' he said quietly. 'He's an old man. You don't want to kill him.'

The crim doing the bashing let go of the sweeper and turned around. It didn't take Les long to realise he was bad news. He was a brute of a man, and even though he had to be at least fifty there was hardly an ounce of fat on him. A steel-grey crewcut topped a bony head sitting on a massive neck and about four day's growth was spread across a rock-solid jaw. The crim's eyes narrowed when he saw Les and venom dripped from his voice when he spoke.

'You,' he snarled. 'Fuck off!' He emphasised this by shoving a huge paw in Norton's chest and pushing him away.

If he hadn't laid a hand on Norton, Les may have left him alone. But now the crim had made it personal.

'Well I'm telling you boofhead,' replied Les, giving the

crim a shove back, 'you fuck off. And leave the old bloke alone.'

That was the end of their conversation. Straight away the crim threw a solid right at Norton, and if it had landed it would probably have taken Les's head off. Fortunately he slipped slightly on a patch of water where he was standing and the punch was wide of its mark.

Norton could see there was no mucking around now and the bloke he was confronting was probably a hate-crazed lifer who did nothing but train all day. He jammed a right, backfist across the crim's neck and followed it with a sizzling left hook. The crim slammed into the wall above the old sweeper, who was still lying on the floor. He bounced off the wall straight into one of Norton's short rights, which sent him cannoning into another wall at the end of the shower.

Les stood there with his fist still vibrating from the force of his punch, expecting the crim to drop, or at least start wobbling around. Instead, he shook his huge head, mopped some blood from his mouth and glared at Norton.

'You fuckin'...' He cursed something else and charged at Les like a Brahman bull.

Christ, thought Norton. This bloke's built like Joe Frazier and his head's just as bloody hard. I'd better do something pretty drastic or I'm gonna be in trouble.

Just as he reached him, Les bent down and shoved his right arm through the huge crim's legs, taking hold of his shirt front with his left hand at almost the same time. He then straightened up with the crim over his shoulders in a cross between a fireman's lift and a judo throw. The momentum of his charge flipped the crim over Norton's head and he slammed heavily onto the floor, banging the back of his head with a sickening crunch as he landed. He gave a little gasp of pain, tried feebly to rise, then slumped back unconscious. Almost immediately a pool of blood oozed across the tiles from beneath his head. Norton gave him a hefty kick in the ribs to be sure he was out of it, but the crim didn't move.

'Thank Christ for that,' thought Norton out loud. He turned to the old sweeper who was on his feet, leaning a little unsteadily against the wall as he dabbed a skinny finger at a trickle of blood in the corner of his mouth. 'You all right mate?' asked Les.

'Sweet pal.'

'What was all that about anyway?'

The sweeper was about to reply when Norton noticed him look nervously across his shoulder. Les turned around expecting to see some of the unconscious crim's mates, but instead it was Bernie and another equally florid-faced guard.

'What in the fuckin' hell's goin' on here?' bellowed Bernie, looking first at the crim bleeding on the floor, then back at Norton.

'He fell over and hit his head on the floor,' said the sweeper straight off.

'Bullshit!' Bernie jabbed a huge forefinger at the sweeper. 'Mousey. You take your broom and fuck off.'

'I'm tryin' to tell you . . .' protested the sweeper.

'You heard what he said,' barked the other guard. 'Piss off.'

The sweeper made a futile gesture with his hands, that mirrored the look he gave Les, before picking up his broom and scurrying out.

Grim faced, Bernie turned back to the crim laying on the shower block floor: the puddle of blood underneath his head was increasing all the time. 'Jesus, what have you done, Les? You bloody great dill. Do you know who that is?' Norton shrugged his shoulders and gave Bernie a blank look. 'No. I didn't think you did.'

The other guard had bent over the unconscious crim and turned back an eyelid with this thumb. 'His skull could be fractured,' he said.

'Shit!' Bernie paused for a moment then turned back to Les. 'Right,' he said, taking Norton by the arm. 'Come on.' He half pushed, half led Norton back past the other prisoners to his cell. 'In there.' He shoved Les inside and without another word slammed the door behind him and locked it.

Left alone in the sickening enclosure of his cell, Norton began to worry a little. It had all happened so quickly he still couldn't quite believe it. What had started out to be a bit of a lark had turned into a nightmare, though once again it wasn't really his fault . . . all he'd done was try to stop an old prisoner from getting beaten up. But now another prisoner was unconscious and possibly had a fractured skull. Les could be looking at an assault charge. And what if he died? Then it could be manslaughter. He could be in here for God knows how long. Norton's mouth went dry as the smell of disinfectant, the bleached hygiene and the muffled sounds of shuffling, captive men seemed to come crowding in on him. A dreadful emptiness hit the pit of his stomach and it wasn't caused by hunger. He flopped down on the edge of his bed and angrily banged his fist into his palm. 'Shit!' he cursed out loud. 'Shit! Shit! Shit!' His only chance was somehow to get word to Price. But wouldn't Price think him a bloody idiot for being in there in the first place? And could the casino owner's influence, powerful as it was, reach over prison walls?

After what seemed like five hours to Norton, but was closer to one, there was the dull rattle of a key going into a lock and his cell door opened. Les looked up at Bernie. The big guard didn't say anything at first, he just sat down on the opposite bed and stared at Norton.

'Well,' said Les, after staring back at him for a few moments. 'What's goin' on?'

'We spoke to Mousey.'

'The old sweeper?'

'Yeah. He told us, more or less, what happened.'

'Well there you go.' Norton made a gesture with his hands.

'Yeah. But it's not quite as simple as that.'

'Oh?'

'You don't know who that other bloke was, do you?'

Norton shook his head.

'That was "Chopper" Collins.'

'He was a nice tough bastard,' shrugged Les. 'I know that.'

'He's a nutter too. He used to go around chopping off people's fingers with a meat axe. That's how he got his nickname.'

'Nice bloke.'

'He got sick of chopping off people's fingers. So one day he decided to chop off some heads instead. Now he's doing life.'

Norton reflected on the crazed look the crim had given him before he charged and didn't disbelieve what Bernie was telling him.

'The thing is, Les,' continued Bernie. 'He runs all the rackets in here with four other blokes — just as nutty as him.'

'Rackets?'

'Yeah, you know. Tobacco, drugs, protection. All that rattle. And when his team find out what happened they'll be looking for you. With prison-made knives.'

Norton shrugged again. 'Yeah, but I should be out of here

188

by this time tomorrow — shouldn't I?'

Bernie gave a tight smile and shook his head. 'Chopper's in the prison hospital — he's not too good on it. And you're on an assault of a fellow prisoner charge.'

'*What!*'

'That's right,' nodded Bernie solemnly. 'I told you, Les. It's a different ball game in here.'

'So what the bloody hell does all this mean?'

'It means you could be in here another month waiting to face the charges. And if you're found guilty, you could get anything. Six months to two years.'

'Jesus Christ!' Norton sucked in his breath and turned to face the wall. Suddenly he felt helpless and physically ill. He spun back to Bernie. 'Surely there's got to be something I can do. Christ, I only tried to help some old bloke.'

Bernie stared at Norton evenly. 'There is something — and I can fix it. But by the living Harry, it's going to cost you.'

Norton stared back at the guard almost in disbelief. So Bernie Cottier was no different from the rest of them. Cops, politicians, judges. Now prison guards. It seemed everybody was on the take. Price wasn't far out when he used to say that corruption in the N.S.W. government was like lights on a Christmas tree; it went all the way from the bottom to the top. But Bernie Cottier? Bernie had to be the straightest, most honest bloke Les had met since he'd arrived in Sydney. But then again, maybe it was a good thing Bernie was bent. At least there was a chance of getting out of here now.

Norton nodded his head slowly. 'Yeah, righto. Fair enough. What's it gonna cost me?'

Bernie reached across and jabbed his banana-like forefinger in Norton's chest. 'Saturday fortnight,' he said, 'I've got the Bondi Sharks, under fourteens, going into the semi-finals. Mate, they can attack like a brigade of Ghurkhas. But they're just a little shy in the tackling department. Especially a couple of the forwards.'

Norton screwed up his face as if he couldn't quite believe what he was hearing. What was bloody Bernie on about?

'Now Les,' continued the big prison guard emphatically, 'I'm not trying to kid to you by telling you this. But you were one of the best tacklers ever to lace on a boot for Easts. They still talk about some of those hits you made against Manly and St George. The kids know you and so do their parents. I want you up at Waverley Oval this Saturday morn-

189

ing, to give the kids a pep talk and show them how to tackle. Les Norton style.'

Norton gave Bernie a double, triple blink. 'That's it?' he asked, incredulous.

'That's it. That's the ask. Just be up at Waverley Oval at nine-thirty this Saturday morning to lecture the kids and I'll sort all this "Elliot" out with Chopper. 'But,' and Bernie emphasised the 'but' with his forefinger, 'let me down and I'll come looking for you. And I don't give a stuff how good a scrapper you are. You might beat me. But I'll guarantee you'll know you've been in a fight.'

Norton's face lit up in a grin as he straightened up on the bed. 'Bernie,' he said, 'I'd rather do another six months in here than tangle with a tough old rooster like you.' He reached across, took Bernie's massive paw and shook it warmly. 'Thanks mate,' he said.

'That's okay. Anyway, I've got to go. In the meantime keep your eyes open. I've told the guards out the front to keep a look out for any of Chopper's crew, though I don't think they'll do anything yet. It's too soon and they don't know for sure what happened. And there's not much chance Chopper'll be telling them about it for a few days. But keep your eyes open just the same.'

'I will. And thanks again Bernie.'

'No worries. I'll see you in the morning.' Bernie gave Les a wink and left.

The sunshine coming in through Norton's cell door was like a tonic to him. Sunshine had never felt so good and daylight never looked better. Santa Claus was real and so was the Easter Bunny and the tooth fairy. And Bernie Cottier was honest too. Christ Norton sighed as he moved to the front of the cell, I'll be glad when I get out of this prick of a joint all the same.

Bernie was right about Chopper Collins; none of the gang came near him all afternoon. If anything it was the complete opposite. The entire warrants section saw the guards take Chopper's bleeding, unconscious body out on a stretcher and Norton was given a wide berth by everyone, especially the two hoods he'd had words with earlier. It was the same when they were mustered for their roast beef and vegetables, tapioca and custard that evening. Sweet smiles all around and Les and Max were given all the seats they wanted. One prisoner even took Norton's plates back for him and the taller of the two moustachioed hoods asked him if there was anything in particular he might like to watch on TV. But even though the front was locked it was a little too shadowy in the warrants section for Norton's liking, so rather than risk a knife in the back he went into his cell not long after tea and read — with one eye on the door. Max joined him shortly afterwards and it didn't seem long before the guards locked them in for the night.

They were lying on their bunks reading, listening to Max's radio and not saying a great deal when Max put his magazine down and turned to Norton.

'I hear you had a bit of trouble today,' he said, smiling over at the big Queenslander. 'Is that right?'

'Ohh yeah,' drawled Norton, putting down his book also. 'Some bloke was bashing up that old sweeper in the shower. We ended up in a bit of a scuffle and he hit his head on the floor. That was about it,' he added with a shrug.

Max gave a bit of a chuckle at Norton's laconic description of how he'd put one of the toughest men in Long Bay in hospital. 'Les, this mightn't be any of my business,' he said, a little hesitantly, 'but you don't seem to be the kind of bloke that's so hard up he has to spend two days in the Bay to cut out a $50 fine.'

Norton chuckled to himself also then smiled over at his cellmate. 'You're about half right Max. I suppose I may as well tell you about it. But promise you won't laugh too much.'

With Max's little radio playing softly in the background, Norton told the friendly truck driver a little about himself and exactly how he came to be in Long Bay. Including the challenge from Warren and his description of the Highway Patrol cop who booked him in the first place.

'So that's about it, Max old mate,' Norton concluded. 'I can be a stubborn bastard at times. But I'm pretty bloody sure I won't be doing this again,' he added with a shake of his head.

Max chuckled. 'Fifty-three bucks isn't actually the end of the world is it? Still. The money's better off in your kick than in the rotten government's.'

'Yeah,' Norton agreed reluctantly. 'I suppose that's about the best way I can look at it.'

Apart from the music on the radio there was silence between them for a while, then Norton folded his arms across his chest and stared the truck driver right in the eye.

'All right Max,' he said solemnly, 'I've given you my story.

191

Now what about bloody yours? I want to know how you can possibly like it in here. I mean — this place is a shithouse. And by calling the food edible, that's givin' it a wrap. But you go on like it's Lindeman Island with a team of French chefs. What's your story?'

Max grinned back at Les. 'You really want to know do you?'

'Fuckin' oath I do,' replied Norton, with an emphatic nod of his head.

The truck driver sat up with his back against the wall and folded his arms across his chest like Norton had. He gave his chin a bit of a thoughtful scratch before he started.

'Les,' he began. 'I've been married to the ugliest, fattest, most horrible drop kick of a wife for over twenty years.'

'Crook sort is she?'

'Crook sort. Mate she's so ugly we haven't even got our wedding photos developed yet, because no photographer's game enough to lock himself up in a darkroom with the prints. Six gynaecologists gave up medicine after she visited them, and went back to driving cabs.'

'Jesus. That is a dud wrap,' chuckled Norton. 'But if she's so ugly, how come you married her in the first place?'

'She was about the first root I ever had. Besides,' Max pointed to his face, 'I'm not actually Mel Gibson myself. Am I?'

'Well . . .' Norton looked at Max's weathered face and lop-sided jaw full of rotten teeth and gave a non-committal shrug of his shoulders.

'Now,' continued Max, 'besides having a miserable bag of a wife that can't light a bloody stove let alone cook anything, I've got three kids I wish I'd drowned at birth. My two sons are around twenty. Both fucking mules. Long ears, buck teeth, the lot. They've been on the dole and not done a stroke of work since the day they left school. They sit around the house all day and night, picking their arses, smoking bongs and listening to blaring loud, head-banging heavy-metal music. Iron Maiden and all that shit. Where these two morons get their money from I don't know and I don't bloody care. The only redeeming feature they've got is I know they'll never become heroin addicts because neither of them would have the strength or the brains to use a hypodermic syringe.'

Norton blinked and smiled at the truck driver almost in amazement. He didn't have a bad sense of humour and this was one of the best yarns Les had heard in years. It was also starting to become obvious that Max was enjoying getting a few things off his chest as well. 'Go on Max,' nodded Norton avidly.

'I've got a daughter nineteen. She's pregnant. To ... I don't know who, and I'm positive she doesn't either. But if I did, I'd run and shake his hand. Because she's twice as fat and ugly as her mother and it's nice to know there's some blokes in Australia more desperate for a root than me.'

'Jesus, Max. You can't talk about your own flesh and blood like that.'

'Can't I?'

'Yeah,' shrugged Norton. 'I s'pose you're right.'

'Okay. So that's my home life, Les. Two boofheaded sons sitting around smoking dope all day listening to shit music. A slug of a daughter propped in front of the TV twenty-four hours a day farting, whingeing and stuffing her fat pimply face with chocolates. And a wart hog for a missus that couldn't cook anything to save her bloody life. Not that it would worry the other idiots, because they only eat McDonalds and pizzas anyway. And it won't be long and I'll have a screaming baby on my hands as well.'

'Yeah,' agreed Norton. 'I guess it's not much to look forward to.'

'So that's my wonderful home life. Now I'll tell you about work. As you know I'm a truck driver.'

Norton nodded slowly.

'It's a prick of a job. Forget all that crap about modern-day cowboys and the romance of the open road. That's all bullshit. You're stuck behind the wheel of a monstrous, noisy, smoke-belching rig day and night, popping pills to try and stay awake with your eyes hanging out of your head. Fuel, running costs and taxes are crippling. You've got to speed, overload and dud up your logbooks just to try and make wages. And as soon as you drive out of the yard some prick on a motor bike pulls you over for anything, just to fill his fuckin book up.'

'I know exactly what you mean there,' agreed Norton.

'I chalked up about $5,000 worth of fines last year. I just laugh at the pricks and tell 'em to give me another one. I've got about $1,500 so far this year — which I'm cutting out now. There's no way I can afford to pay them anyway. Besides, most of the pinches are just rorts to get money out of you so they can pay the wages for all the bludging public servants in this state.'

'You're not far out there neither,' agreed Norton again.

'So I just come in here, cut out my warrants, save my money and get a bit of peace and quiet and good tucker at the same time. And that's my story, Les. This is the best rort ever if you ask me. I'm laughing.'

Norton stared at Max for a few moments, chuckling as he shook his head almost in admiration. 'Yeah Max,' he conceded, 'I guess with your home life this wouldn't be half bad to you. The only thing you'd miss in here is a bit of sex I suppose. But from the description you gave me of your wife, I imagine you're not worrying too much about that either.'

'Hey, don't worry about sex. I get the best blow jobs I've ever had in my life in here.'

'Blow jobs? In here. Where?'

'Off the drag queens. They've got their own section where they can wear women's clothes and do their hair up and all that. One of the screws is a relation of mine. I give him the dough and he brings me in bottles of perfume and make-up and that, and I swap it with the drags for a polish.'

Norton was dumbfounded. 'You're kidding?'

'No way José,' replied Max enthusiastically. 'I get blow jobs down there that almost stop your heart beating. Your legs go to jelly and your head spins around like a chocolate wheel. I've been having two or three a day, too,' Max added with a sly chuckle.

'So that's where you get to of a day is it?'

Max winked. 'Why do you think I sleep so well of a night? It's not just these bloody earplugs, I can tell you.' Norton unfolded his arms and shook his head at Max's last statement. 'Well Max,' he laughed, as he settled back on the bed, 'I reckon that might just about do me. I don't think I need to know anymore so I'm going to shut my eyes.'

'Yeah. Me too. It's way past my bedtime.' Max reached over and turned off the radio. 'I'll see you in the morning.'

'Yeah. See you then.'

There was silence between them for a few moments, then Norton propped himself up on one elbow and stared over at the wily truck driver.

'Hey Max,' he said. 'Before we go to sleep. Just tell me one thing.'

'Yeah, what?'

'If your missus is such a beast and your kids are so horrible. Why don't you get a divorce and piss off?'

Max opened one eye. 'Are you kidding, Les? Move out

of my grouse big home at Regents Park and leave it to those useless, loafin' bastards. While I go and live in a stinkin' one-bedroom unit somewhere. Not a chance.'

'Fair enough,' nodded Norton. 'It was just a thought, Max. That's all.'

Norton settled back down on his bed, pulled his blanket up and got ready to go to sleep when Max spoke again.

'But I'll tell you what I am gonna do,' he said, a noticeable coolness creeping into his voice. 'And I'll tell you this because I reckon you're the sort of bloke who'd keep it to himself.'

'Go on Max.'

'About a year or so from now, you'll be reading the name Max Gatenby in all the newspapers.'

'Yeah. Why's that?'

''Cause I'm gonna blow the cunts up.'

'You're what?'

'I'm gonna blow 'em up. The house, their dog, the fuckin' lot. I've had this planned for a while now. You see, those arseholes in my house all watch *A Country Practice*. They love it. I hate the show myself. Especially that doctor and the cop. Anyway, they're all gonna be watching it one night and I'm gonna leave an overnight bag full of dynamite in the lounge room with a timer device. I'll go down the road. Have a few schooners, a game of pool and whooshka. Up she'll go. Chocolates, bongs, heavy-metal records. The lot.'

'You're kidding.'

'Not a chance. But that's only part of the plan. Just after I do it, I give myself up to a reporter on the Willesee show on TV. I'll get maximum coverage while I make out I'm mad as a meat axe. The cops'll come and drag me off on prime-time TV. They'll put me in Morisset. Pleading insanity and diminished responsibility, the most I'll get is ten years, and some social worker'll have me out in two. Mate. Two years of rest, medication, good tucker and blow jobs every day. Be like winning the lottery.'

Norton was even more astounded now. The tone in Max's voice told him he was deadly serious. 'Yeah... well,' said Norton. 'Whatever.'

'They'll let me out of the rathouse after two years. The house'll be gone but I'll still own the land. It's worth eighty-odd grand. I flog it and buy a weekender up the North Coast — Forster or somewhere — and spend the rest of my life on the pension, fishin' everyday. And none of those pricks to annoy me. What's wrong with that?'

'Nothing — I don't suppose Max. You've certainly got

your head screwed on better than what I thought.'

Max gave an evil chuckle. 'I'm not just a pretty face Les.'

'Indeed you're not. Anyway, I'll see you in the morning mate.'

Norton didn't know whether to laugh or what after that. So he went to sleep instead. And he managed to surprise himself, despite the circumstances of the day, by sleeping quite well.

It wasn't too bad a morning when the guards unlocked the cells and mustered them for breakfast; cool but not much cloud around. After his porridge and toast and whatever, Les drifted back to the front of his cell to wait for Bernie or whoever it might be to come and let him out; which Norton figured would be around lunchtime. The TV was blaring as usual and Jimi Hendrix was once again giving 'Hey Jude' a punishing serve. Although it was sunny outside, Norton decided he'd wait in his cell, read some of Max's magazines and keep a weather eye on the door at the same time. He was propped up on his bed, thumbing his way through some old *People* and *Penthouses* when a sudden movement at the door made him tense up and drop the magazine he was reading. It was the old sweeper, Mousey or whatever they called him. He stood in the doorway for a moment or two without saying anything.

'G'day mate,' said Norton eventually. 'How're you feeling?'

Standing framed in the light above the door, Norton could see the sweeper had the makings of a black-eye and his bottom lip was swollen. 'Listen pal,' he said. 'I've been in here twenty years. And I'll be here another twenty fuckin' years. I won't get out of here alive.'

The sweeper didn't acknowledge Norton's greeting but went straight into some sort of a preamble, almost like a well-rehearsed speech, and every word was squeezed tightly out the side of his mouth. Norton had met a lot of old blokes like the sweeper since he'd moved to Sydney. Shifty old blokes especially from around the Eastern Suburbs and Balmain. For some reason they all loved to talk out the sides of their mouths. Some seemed to be able to talk out of both sides of their mouths at once and Norton swore that one old ex-wharfie he knew from up the Cross could talk out of his ears. The sweeper continued with his side-of-the-mouth sermon.

'No one's ever done a fuckin' thing for me since I've been

in the puzzle, pal. I've been robbed, stood over. Bashed by both the screws and the other crims, and no-one's ever given me so much as a kind word — let alone jump in and stick up for me.'

'Ahh, that's all right mate,' shrugged Norton. 'Don't worry about it.'

'So here. I want you to have this.'

The sweeper handed Les an envelope. It was sealed, there was nothing written on the front or back and it appeared to contain a couple of sheets of paper inside. Norton examined it for a second or two, then looked back up at the door not quite knowing what to make of it.

'Well . . . thanks mate.'

But the old sweeper had vanished even quicker than he'd appeared. Norton moved across to the door and had a good look around the wing, but he was nowhere to be found. With a shrug of his shoulders Les resumed his original position on the bed. He had another look at the mysterious envelope. He gave it a sniff. It didn't appear to contain any drugs and a shake verified there was only a sheet of folded paper inside. Norton decided against opening it and slid it inside the yellow pamphlet he'd been given on his arrival. Well that's a funny one. Oh well. He continued with his reading. He'd barely got another two or three pages when a loud knock on the door revealed the jowly but smiling face of Bernie Cottier.

'Righto L. Norton, 6102,' he boomed. 'This is your big moment.'

'Don't tell me I'm finally getting out of this prick of a joint,' grinned Les.

'Yep.'

'What time is it?'

'Around ten-thirty.'

'Well how about that. And I wan't expecting to get out until at least lunchtime. Looks like I got an hour and a half off for good behaviour.'

'You got all your belongings?'

Norton had already folded his blanket and towel. He slipped them under his arm and picked up the yellow pamphlet with the letter inside.

'I might just keep this for a souvenir,' he smiled.

'Suit yourself. Come on.'

They walked fairly quickly through the warrants section. Les had a last look around for Max, but he was nowhere to be seen. That figures, Norton chuckled to himself. They were through the small office near the servery and heading towards the square when Norton turned to Bernie.

'Hey Bernie,' he said. 'That old sweeper I had the stink over. What's he in for?'

'Mousey? Old Mousey Thomas. He shot two cops in Newcastle, around 1950. He's in for life is the Mouse.'

'Fair dinkum?'

'Yeah. He's bladed other prisoners. He hit a guard over the head with a piece of pipe in Goulburn, nearly killing him too. He's pretty harmless now. But he can be a bad old bastard — don't worry about that.'

'Evidently.'

'He originally came from Melbourne. They reckon he was involved in several murders and bank jobs down there. But they could never pin them on him. They got him for the Newcastle ones though. He's lucky he didn't hang.'

'Yeah. Anyway, I was just wondering — that's all.'

They went past the square, towards reception, when Bernie made a motion with his head. 'Come over this way for a sec, Les. There's something I want to show you.'

He led Norton through another gate which opened out onto a yard with a row of high bar-fronted cells running off to their right. They were about three or four metres across and almost twice that in height. Rubbish and other articles were strewn around the front and they seemed to be dark and gloomy inside, despite the light coming through the bars. At first appearance they reminded Norton of the monkey cage in a zoo. There looked to be only one man to a cell listlessly moving about and calling out to the prisoner in the next cell over the high wall separating them. Except for a lumpy red-haired crim with a bushy red beard in the end cell. He was screaming out at the top of his voice a non-stop torrent of the most vile abuse Norton had ever heard in his life. The abuse was directed at an older guard in a freshly dry-cleaned zip-front jacket with some sort of rank or insignia sewn onto the sleeves. He was accompanied by a worried looking brown-haired man in a sports coat and glasses carrying a clipboard and biro.

'What's this?' enquired Norton.

'Protective custody, Les. This is where you would have finished up if Chopper's boys were after you. Stay next to me and don't get too close.'

'Who are those two blokes?' Norton nodded to the nervous looking man in the sports coat and his accompanying guard.

'That's one of the directors of the gaol — and I think the bloke with him's from TV.'

'Who are the blokes in the cells?'

'Child molesters. Perverts. Kid killers. Prisoners giving evidence against other prisoners. We've got to keep them in there or the other crims'd kill them.'

'Shit!'

The bearded crim in the end cell was really serving it up now to the director and the TV journalist. The language would take the paint off a wall. Norton wasn't averse to using a few four-letter words now and again, not in mixed company of course, but the bloke with the beard made Rodney Rude sound like a choirboy.

'What are you fuckin' lookin' at cunt,' he roared at the journalist. 'You greasy fuckin' big poofter. Where's your fuckin' gun screw,' he bellowed at the director. 'You got the fuckin' thing shoved up your fuckin' arse have you. You've both been sucking too many cocks that's your trouble. You cunts. Get fucked.'

Now and again one of the prisoners in the adjoining cells would call something out also. 'Yeah. Come and have a look at us,' yelled one. 'We're the animals.' 'Yeah. This is the boneyard,' yelled another. 'Have a good look. We're the shit. We're the animals. Have a look.'

The journalist's face was a mask of shock and disbelief, like he'd burst into a timewarp and didn't quite know where he was. The director had more of a bemused look on his face with his hands stuck snugly in the side pockets of his fur-collared jacket. If it was at all possible, redbeard's voice seemed to rise in a further crescendo.

'You pair of fuckin' greasy cunts You cock sucking pair of fuckin' poofters.' Even from where he was standing Norton could see the veins standing out on his neck and forehead. Hatred and rage dripped from every word. 'You want something to fuckin' look at do you. You greasy fuckin' big poofter,' he screamed. 'Well have a fuckin' good look at this.'

Redbeard turned his back to the cell bars and pulled down his trousers. Still screaming abuse he spread the cheeks of his backside apart to reveal the dirtiest, smelliest, blotch covered bum Les had ever seen. It looked like two great lumps of white dough, covered in red wood shavings, with a big burnt donut jammed in the middle.

'There,' roared Redbeard. 'How about sticking your tongue in there.'

'Holy shit!' exclaimed Norton. 'What an awful looking blurter.'

'How would you like it stuffed and hung over your fireplace?' chuckled Bernie.

Norton shook his head. 'Come on Bernie,' he pleaded. 'Get me out of here. I've seen all I want to see.'

'No, hold on a sec.'

Despite the continuing torrent of abuse the journalist approached Redbeard's cell to ask a reasonably polite question. Redbeard immediately spun round and spat all over him. As the shocked journalist stood there looking at the spit all over his coat, glasses and clipboard, Redbeard cupped his hand over his bum, bent slightly and strained. It was obvious he was trying to crap in his hand and fling that at the journalist as well.

'Ohh bugger this,' said Norton in disgust. 'I'm pissin' off — whether you like it or not.'

'Seen enough have you Les?' laughed the big guard. 'Righto. Come on.'

They were almost at the reception when the non-stop torrent of abuse was suddenly interrupted by a high pitched shriek. Norton slowed down but he didn't look back.

'Sounds like he got him Bernie.'

The big guard stopped and turned towards the cells. 'Yep,' he nodded. 'All down the side of his nice tweed sports coat and trousers. Not a bad shot either — considering it was through the bars and he had the sun in his eyes.'

'Get me out of here Bernie. For Christ's sake.'

'Well Les. What do you reckon.' Norton had been discharged, changed back into his tracksuit and signed for the return of his watch and $20. He and Bernie were walking towards the main gate, and despite feeling dirty from not showering for almost three days, Norton still couldn't seem to shake the smell of disenfectant from himself. 'Did you enjoy your little stay at Malabar Mansions?'

Norton paused before another guard unlocked the door in the main gate. 'I'll put it to you this way, Bernie. I don't feel clever or glad about coming out here. But I don't regret it.'

Bernie nodded solemnly. 'Fair enough.'

'But after having a bit of a look around and a taste of what goes on here. There is one thing I do reckon.'

'What's that Les?'

'I reckon they ought to get all those smart-arsed young

kids, that are running around thieving and vandalising things and that, and bring them all out here and give them a look at how they're gonna finish up.'

Bernie smiled and nodded his big head in agreement.

'And if that didn't wake them up — nothing would. Because I reckon I can handle myself all right. And I've seen quite a few hairy things in my time. But mate. That's a dead-set horror show in there.'

'You don't think you'll be back, Les?'

'Not if I can help it.'

Bernie took Norton's hand and shook it. 'I'll see you up Waverley Oval on Saturday morning Les.'

A door opened in the main gate and Norton stepped outside into freedom. Somehow even the sunshine seemed to feel different on the other side of the wall. He walked briskly past the guard on the boom gate, almost expecting to be stopped and taken back inside, but he was scarcely given a second look. There were no taxis around in Anzac Parade so Norton caught a bus to Maroubra Junction and a cab from there to Bondi. When he stepped inside his humble semi it had never looked so good.

Norton was going to jump straight under the shower but decided he'd get a bit of exercise and have a think first, so he slipped on a pair of running shorts and drove down to Centennial Park. Running alone around the park in the bright winter sunshine seemed to add a whole new dimension to the word freedom. As he sped past the ponds full of water birds and swans his thoughts drifted back to those stony-faced men he'd seen jogging around and walking backwards and forwards across the square at Long Bay. An uneasy feeling hit him in the stomach as he thought how easily in the past he could have finished up doing a stretch out there. And possibly, if it hadn't been for Bernie Cottier, he could still be out there now. Norton quickly shook those thoughts from his mind. The last three days he would keep to himself, except of course for Warren and George Brennan and the boys at the Kelly Club. Especially George Brennan who was forever roasting him about being tight-fisted with his money. Wouldn't George have some ammunition to fire at him when he found out Les had spent three days in the can rather than pay a $53 traffic fine. He finished his run off with a series of stretches, push-ups and sit-ups; then went home.

Norton's first shower since Sunday was like a stroll through paradise, and the grilled T-bone after it was heaven from the first bite. Warren hadn't left a note, but there was a copy of Monday's *Sun* near the kitchen sink. Les flicked through it until two familiar faces and a couple of paragraphs on page three made him put down his coffee and blink:

'Stephen George Yiagnou and Vincent Brian Swales were arrested earlier today by members of the Armed Holdup Squad in connection with a series of hotel and service station robberies in the inner-city and Eastern suburbs. They have also been charged with possession of two shortened firearms and an amount of heroin . . .'

Next to the article were two mug shots of the youths who had travelled out to Long Bay with Norton. So that's what they were up to mused Les. Forgot what you were in for did you boys. Yeah. I'll bet. Then Les chuckled over his cup of coffee. I wonder what Max is up to right now? Probably over visiting his drag queen friends. Mad bloody Max. I wonder if he's fair dinkum about blowing up his family? Norton shook his head. Wouldn't bloody surprise me. Suddenly another thought dawned on Norton, almost like he'd been hit over the head by a piece of four-by-two. The old sweeper's envelope. Mousey's present or whatever it was. He rose from the table and retrieved it from inside the CIP booklet he'd tossed on the table.

A knife soon had the envelope open and next thing Les had a sheet of foolscap paper spread out on the kitchen table. It was divided in two by a line of biro, and the sections were two roughly drawn maps with even rougher printing on them. The smaller map was a half-circle with Melbourne written across it and four lines representing roads radiating out of it. Norton could make out Hume Highway on one, what looked like Upper Harrisburgh on another; the others he couldn't read. The top map was a continuation of the Hume Highway with roads running off it, a little row of dots and more printing. Mousey's printing was woeful to say the least. You had to be a professor in Ancient Egyptian hyroglyphics to make it out. There was an unreadable road running off the Hume Highway towards a circle saying what looked like Yin Yoe Residence. Follow this one mile. Turn left onto some other road at twin pine trees. Norton shook his head. Follow this half a mile to other twin pine trees. At least that's what it looked like. Fifty yards south of pine tree on right. Dig here. The pine trees were signified by four circles. Next to dig here was a large X.

Dig here eh, mused Norton, drumming his fingers on the edge of the paper. Bloody Mousey. He must've read *Treasure Island* or something. Pieces of eight. Spanish doubloons. Argh! There he be cap'n. Poor little bastard he's been in the nick too long. What'd be there anyway? A case of Victorian Bitter? Some of those Four n' Twenty pies they all eat? A little disappointed, Norton chuckled and shook his head again. Besides, it's in bloody Melbourne and I don't think there's much chance of me ever going down there. Thanks anyway, Mousey. Still I suppose the poor old bugger meant well. Norton replaced the map in its envelope and put it in a draw in his bedroom. He then finished his coffee and cleaned up.

Feeling a little tired after the run and the big meal, Les decided to have a nap. But he must have been tireder than he thought, or his own bed just felt good, because it was almost six when he woke up.

He was a little groggy when he half-stumbled into the shower. But an extra close shave and a few bursts of cold water had him all bright eyed and bushy tailed when he got out. He made a toasted sandwich and a cup of coffee and was in the kitchen thinking Warren was a bit late when he heard the front door open. Next thing the fair-haired young advertising executive was standing in the kitchen doorway, a pizza carton under his arm, staring at him.

'G'day Woz,' said Norton casually. 'You're home late.'

Warren blinked. 'Yeah. Well...' he replied slowly. 'I... had to work back.' He stared at Norton in silence for a few moments while he put his pizza in the oven. 'There... were a couple of phone calls for you,' he said hesistantly. 'Hey,' he blurted. 'Have you really been out in Long Bay?'

'Fuckin' oath I have,' intoned Norton. 'Three punishing days. And not a visit. Not even a letter — or a card. You're a nice mate Warren. Thanks a lot.'

'Well... I...' Warren made a self-conscious gesture with his hands. 'Ohh look, bugger it. Anyone that's mean enough to spend two days in the can rather than pay a lousy $53 fine doesn't deserve a visit. So fuck you. Besides. I've been flat out at work anyway.'

'Hmmph!' grunted Norton. 'It's nice to know who me mates are.'

Warren continued to stare at Les, then his face broke into a huge grin. 'So what was it like anyway. What happened?'

'Piece of piss,' shrugged Norton. 'I'd do it again any time.'

While Warren made himself a coffee, Les told him most

of what happened to him and what it was like in the Bay. He didn't mention the fight or the sweeper's envelope but he told him about Max, omitting his intended bombing of his family. In all, Norton made it out to be a fairly easy time actually; just sitting around reading, watching TV and eating good prison food.

'So that's about it roughly, Woz. I wouldn't really recommend it. But it ain't all that bad. The thing is though. The bastards never got my $53 did they? So it was definitely worth it — on principle's sake. Anyway,' shrugged Norton, 'I'll tell you a bit more about it tomorrow. I gotta get to work soon.'

Warren shook his head. 'Fair dinkum Les. You never cease to amaze me. I still reckon anyone that'd go in the can for three days, rather than pay a lousy $53 fine has got an empty breadbin for a head.'

'Oh well. That's your opinion and you're welcome to it,' replied Norton indifferently. 'Anyway. What's been happening while I was away? Any phone calls? What've you been up to?'

'Billy rang a couple of times. I just told him you were out.'

'Fair enough.'

'Apart from that — nothing. I've been flat out at work on this new campaign we've got going.'

'Ohh yeah. And what are you and all the rest of your North Shore yuppie pals up to this time?'

'Mate. This is going to be bigger than mastadon turds. Wait here and I'll show you.'

Warren went to his room and came back with a six-pack of wine cooler which he placed on the kitchen table. Norton took a bottle out. It was green with a white label. Across the label in mauve and lime was St Kilda Kooler, superimposed on a drawing of a fun pier. Along the side of the six-pack was: St Kilda Kooler. Kool Off With A Kilda.

Norton rolled the smallish bottle round in his hand. 'So what's this shit?'

'This shit,' replied Warren dryly, 'is going to be a very big selling drink in Victoria this spring and summer.'

'I can just imagine.'

'It will — don't you worry about that. Here. Why don't you try one?'

'It's warm.'

'There's some cold ones in the fridge.' Warren took a bottle from the refrigerator, opened it and handed it to Les. 'Try it Les. See what you think.'

Norton took a hefty swallow and nodded slowly, without changing the expression on his face.

'Well,' beamed Warren. 'What's it taste like?'

'Rat's piss. With a dash of pineapple flavouring.' He took another sip. 'No, hold on. I think it's tom cat's piss. With turnips in it. Or is it potato peelings?'

'Ohh you'd have to say that wouldn't you — you nark. It's sparkling white wine with pure mango juice.'

'Mango! Listen mate...'

'Yeah yeah. I know. You come from Queensland and they invented mangoes in Queensland. And if there's any mango in there...'

'Yeah that's right. You can shove that six-pack up my arse.'

'After three days in Long Bay it'd probably fit.'

'What was that?'

'All I know,' said Warren, pointing to the six-pack, 'is that St Kilda Kooler's going to be a big seller. And the kids are going to love it.'

'Oh of course they will,' snorted Norton. 'By the time you unscrupulous pricks have finished with them. They'll be brainwashed into thinking it's uncool not to drink this crap.'

'That's right,' grinned Warren. 'There mightn't be a market there. But we'll soon create one. You should be in advertising Les.'

'And what's your ad going to be like?' asked Norton sarcastically. 'Dawn shots of horses galloping along the beach in slow motion. Bored looking bags in bikinis wearing big sunglasses. Pretty boys in white sports coats with their sleeves rolled up to their elbows. What about a few slim young men in dressing-gowns? What's the new image Woz? Tell us mate I'm all agog.'

'Actually, we're shooting it in Melbourne. We're using a big Aussie Rules player.'

'Well that figures,' sneered Norton. 'Aussie Rules players'd drink this shit.'

'Well they're not all beer-swilling thugs like you League players. Or should I say ex-League players?'

'You've got me again Woz,' conceded Norton. 'There is definitely no matching your rapier-like wit. Anyway,' Les picked his tuxedo jacket up from where it was sitting on the back of a kitchen chair, 'this beer-swilling thug has to go to work and punch a few heads in up the Cross.'

It wasn't long after Les had let everyone know he was at work that he and Billy Dunne were standing outside the door, waiting to welcome the punters and discourage the mugs. Billy finished the apple he was eating and turned to his taller workmate.

'I rang you a couple of times to see if you wanted to go for a run. But Warren kept saying you were out. What've you been up to?'

Norton grinned sheepishly down at the footpath for a moment or two before turning to face Billy. 'If I tell you,' he chuckled awkwardly, 'you promise you won't laugh?'

'Well,' Billy had to think for a second, 'I won't promise. But I'll certainly do my best. Where were you?'

'I was in Long Bay cuttin' out a warrant.'

'You were what?' The ex-prizefighter screwed up his face as if he didn't quite believe what he'd just heard.

'I was in Long Bay. I went in Monday arvo, and got out this morning.'

'How much was the warrant?'

'Fifty-three bucks.'

'How much?'

Billy didn't laugh, he almost cracked up. He fell against the wall behind them clutching at his ribs as he tried to get his breath; tears were starting to squeeze out of the corners of his eyes. Several patrons entering the club and a number of passers-by thought he was having a violent asthma attack. Finally he managed to regain his composure.

'Fair dinkum, Les. Give me a break,' he gasped as he massaged the aching sides of his throat. 'You're unbelievable. Does George know about this?'

'Not yet,' replied Norton. 'The fat cunt's going to have a picnic when he does though.'

'Is he what?' chuckled Billy. He shook his head as if he didn't quite know what to say. 'So what happened? What'd the coppers just catch you out in your car or something? Why didn't you ring one of us. You wouldn't have gone out there just to save fifty-odd bucks, would you?' Billy gave Norton a suspicious look. 'Surely?'

Norton shook his big red head and had to look away. 'I'm almost too ashamed to tell you Billy,' he chuckled.

Norton told Billy how he came to be in Long Bay. He didn't say anything about what happened out there, just that in retrospect he wished he hadn't done it and he swore he'd never do it again. When Norton had finished Billy didn't quite know whether to laugh or cry but he settled mainly for laughter. He wasn't all that amazed, though, because most of the outrageous things Norton did had ceased to amaze him long ago — especially where it concerned money.

'Fair dinkum Les,' said Billy. 'You are unbelievable.'

'Yeah,' agreed Norton. 'I certainly have my moments at times — don't I? But like I said, Billy, I don't think I'll be doing it again.'

'No. Long Bay's a prick of a joint ain't it. I spent a week in the remand yard out there on an assault charge. Years ago.'

'Did you?'

'Yeah. Price squared it all up for me. That was about when I first met him. Does he know you were out there?'

'No.'

'Christ! Wait till he and George find out. Hey you're going to have to let me do the lead up work when we knock off for a drink. It'll make Brennan's week.'

'Fair enough,' grinned Norton. 'Go for your life. I deserve all I get anyway'

The night went fairly uneventfully, as Wednesday nights usually do. Not even a cross word let alone a push and a shove or a fight. By three-thirty they had all the punters and most of the staff out and were seated in Price's office having their customary after-work drink.

Billy winked across the top of his bourbon and Coke at Norton sipping on a Fourex before turning to George.

'Hey George,' Billy said slowly. 'Have you heard about Les's latest little effort?'

'No,' replied the corpulent casino manager. 'What's the big goose been up to this time?'

'It concerns money.'

'Money.' This was George's cue. Immediately his ears pricked up and a grin spread across his face. 'Hullo. What've you done this time Les?' he said, looking directly at Norton. 'You found a box of corn plasters, so you bought a pair of shoes a size too small for you?'

'Worse than that George.'

'His mother visited him over the weekend and he hid her false teeth so she couldn't eat between meals.'

Billy turned to Norton. 'I think you'd better tell him Les.'

Norton looked up at George. 'It was nothing really,' he sniffed. 'I've been out in Long Bay since Monday cutting out a traffic warrant. That's all.'

'You what!'

'He went into Long Bay for three days,' chortled Billy, 'rather than pay a $53 fine.'

Brennan's jaw dropped. He stared firstly at Billy, then at Norton. 'You miserable big prick. Is he fair dinkum?'

Norton nodded his head impassively.

Suddenly Price sat bolt upright in his chair and even the normally reticent Eddie Salita came to life in the corner.

'Hey hold on a sec Les,' he said, tapping his index finger on the desk. 'What you do in your own time is your business, but I don't like the idea of my employees spending time in the can. Bit of an explanation here son. And it better be good.'

Once again Les told his story about how he came to be in Long Bay and what it was like. Again he didn't mention the fight with Chopper or the sweeper's envelope, but the way Norton was telling the story and the inferences to his meanness had the others cracking up. With a bit of prompting he told them a few more things, especially about Max and his being sprung by Bernie Cottier and him promising to help train the kids this coming Saturday. But mainly, only for George's sake, Les made out he did it rather than pay the $53.

'So that's about it George,' concluded Norton when the laughter was replaced by amazed looks. 'It was a piece of piss to tell you the truth. I'd do it again any time.'

Price closed his eyes and rested his head back on his seat. 'I'm completely lost for words.'

'Me too,' added Eddie.

Billy remained silent but Brennan was nowhere near finished. 'Les Norton,' he intoned, 'you are without a doubt the meanest man in Australia. Possibly the world. You wouldn't help a blind spider back to his web.'

'Whatever you say George,' shrugged Norton indifferently. 'But one thing I do know.' He winked slyly across at Billy and pulled exactly $53 out of his coat pocket. 'They never got my money though — did they George?' Norton waved the money at the others before putting it back. 'And there it is. Right bloody there,' he added, giving his pocket a pat.

Nobody could think of anything to say, except George. 'Well good on you Les,' he sneered. 'Whatever turns you on. Now what are going to do with it? I'll bet you you don't spend any of it.'

'I won't either. Don't worry about that,' agreed Norton.

'This'll go straight into the Building Society.'

'Yeah bullshit. You'll probably bury it.'

'I might even do that too,' shrugged Norton.

'Hey!' An excited look came across George's face. He grinned and turned to Price. 'Remember when the big hillbilly first started work here? He hadn't been down from Queensland all that long and you told him to back that horse of your's. The two-year-old. Poker Face.'

'Yeah. I remember,' smiled Price. 'We almost had to put a gun to his head to get him to have a hundred on it.'

'That's right,' chortled George. 'His hands were shaking and he was sweating like he had malaria when he handed over the money. And it got up at 12–1. And Les had thirteen hundred dollars in his hand. He near shit himself. And you said to him, I suppose you'll put that straight in the bank Les? And the miserable big prick said, "Ohh I don't know, I think I might hold on to it for a while. I don't trust banks." I don't trust banks. Hah!' George was laughing almost fit to burst.

'So?' Norton shrugged his shoulders. 'I still don't.'

There was silence for a few moments then George got up dabbing at his eyes. 'I'll tell you what, Les,' he said while he was getting drinks all round. 'Are you fair dinkum about going out there again rather than pay a fine?'

'Bloody oath!' Norton nodded his head enthusiastically, slipping Billy a wink at the same time.

'Well next time, see if you can get a cell with some dirty old lag doing life.'

'Why's that?'

"Cause while you're there, you can get him to root some sense into that empty big red head of yours. Fifty-three bloody dollars. Fair dinkum — you are a wombat Les.'

Norton smiled and copped it sweet. And with the big Queenslander the butt of a few more jokes they stayed drinking till four-thirty then locked up and went home.

Apart from Billy giving a young drunk a backhander on Thursday night and Les having to cop a bit of a bagging every now and again, the rest of the working week went smooth as honey. Les and Billy did their training in the daytime and Warren was too involved in his agency's new campaign, getting home late every night, for Norton to see much of him either. George Brennan's football team, the Balmain Tigers, had just lost their third game on the trot and looked like missing out on the semis, so Norton had a little bit of ammunition to fire back at the overweight manager. Although George lived near Bondi Junction he originally came from Rozelle and was still a red-hot belligerent one-eyed Tiger supporter and loathed it whenever his team lost. However, Norton wasn't really in the mood for any verbal jousting when they finished work on Friday night. He still had his promise to keep to Bernie Cottier early that morning so he left the others to have a drink without him and came straight home.

Bernie was all smiles at Waverley Oval when Norton arrived, still a little tired from not enough sleep and still a little hungry from not enough breakfast. The big prison guard had taken a slight advantage of the situation also. Besides Bernie's team there were three others, plus a horde of parents and the other coaches. By the time Norton finished talking, lecturing, shaking hands with parents and teaching the kids his way of tackling, plus getting tackled about one hundred times himself and watching the teams go through their paces afterwards, it was getting on for one when they finished. Then Bernie and the other coaches insisted on shouting Les a few beers at the bowling club across the road, where they ended up swapping old football yarns and swallowing schooners till three. Norton generally didn't like drinking through the day, especially if he had to go to work that night, and he wasn't all that pleased with himself when he arrived home around four still tired and still hungry. The Kentucky Fried Chicken he'd bought on the way home was a bit greasy too; but he tore into it and crashed out till six-thirty.

It was just as well Warren wasn't home when Norton got up because with his headache and indigestion Les was about as much company as Frankenstein as he stumbled half asleep between the bathroom and the kitchen. It was just as well there was no trouble at work that night either, because Norton would have been about 50-1 on to thump first and ask questions later. In Price's office after work the big Queenslander was almost nodding off over his first can of Fourex as he told the others about what sort of a day he'd had with Bernie and the kids and all that.

'So. It's been a bit of a big week for me,' he concluded, after finishing his beer. 'In fact I might make this one cobbler's.' He tossed the empty can in the office tidy, stretched and yawned. 'About the only thing I've got to look forward to is knowing that Easts will beat Penrith. And Manly'll flog the shit out of Balmain.'

'You want to make a bet on that, bloodnut?' cut in George Brennan quickly.

'No.' Norton gave his head a tired shake. 'But I will have a bet with you next week, when Easts play that motheaten team of yellow tabby cats you're silly enough to follow.'

'You're on son. You are on,' said George.

'Anyway,' Norton got to his feet. 'I am dead-set stuffed. So I'm gonna hit the toe. I'll see you on Wednesday. I'll give you a ring early on Monday about training Billy.'

'Righto mate.'

There was a chorus of sympathetic goodbyes and goodnights and Norton left.

Well thank Christ that's over he thought as he trudged slowly and wearily to his car. I am absolutely stuffed. If they threw a pillow and blanket down on that dirty footpath, I reckon I could doss there and not move for ten hours. He reached his car and got his keys out.

The car parked in front of him was a huge blue Mercedes with a personalised numberplate: AG something-or-other. As he stepped between the two cars Norton noticed one of the rear tyres on the Mercedes was flat. Well at least I'm having a better night than him he mused. Shit! Fancy trying to change a flat tyre right now. I'd leave the bloody thing and get a cab home. As Les stepped between the two cars, an object, almost invisible in the gutter, caught his eye. He reached down and picked up a black leather wallet — and a very fat one at that. Norton put it straight in his pocket. Good thing I picked that up he thought. Lying around in the Cross it'd only finish up in some junkie's arm. It's a wonder it isn't in there already. He started the car and headed home.

Warren's door was closed and there were no women's shoes or handbag in the loungeroom when Norton climbed out of his tuxedo into his tracksuit, so he figured the little bloke must've had a quiet night. With the kitchen radio playing softly in the background Norton made himself a mug of Ovaltine. Now I wonder who this bloody thing belongs to he yawned as he sipped his drink and examined the contents of the wallet.

It opened with a driver's licence belonging to a Mr Abraham Goldschmidt of Birriga Road, Bellevue Hill, on one side, and a photo of a smiling overweight man standing next to a smiling overweight woman and two smiling overweight boys on the other. The men were wearing yamulkas and standing in front of a menorah candelabrum.

Well, well, well Norton chuckled. This wallet belongs to one of God's chosen people. And a goyim has found it. My my. Doesn't God work in mysterious ways.

A further examination of the wallet revealed several business and credit cards. A card from a synagogue and several others written in Hebrew. It also revealed $1,650 in cash.

Norton chuckled to himself again as he counted the money for the second time. The good Lord certainly does work in mysterious ways, doesn't he? One minute I'm in Long Bay cutting out a lousy $53 parking fine. Now I've got $1,650 in cash. But the thing is, should I keep it? Norton drummed his fingers on the table and sipped his Ovaltine for a moment or two. Well, he mused, I look at it this way Abe Goldschmidt, old buddy old pal, I'm not anti-Semitic. But if you can afford a new Mercedes with personalised number plates, and a Bellevue Hill address, you won't miss $1,650. Besides, what were you doing in filthy Kings Cross at four a.m.? Trying to change a flat tyre and your wallet fell out? Yeah, pig's arse. Tooling around on the side'd be more like it. And you with such a fine wife and sons too. No, Abraham old mate. Keep this money is what the Lord Jehovah tells me I should do. And let this be a bitter lesson to you too — a heartless adulterer is what you are.

Now, thought Norton, smiling happily at the stack of banknotes. What'll I do with it? I certainly don't need any clothes. I don't get much chance to wear what I've got as it is. I just bought a bloody compact disc player. S'pose I could get a few CDs. The hum of the refrigerator suddenly cutting in over the radio made him switch his gaze in that direction. Down one side of the fridge Warren had stuck a long poster-type calendar for a record shop in San Francisco he'd brought home from the agency. Every day of the year was numbered and around one particular day, which was next Monday, was a circle with a number of arrows pointing to it. Next to it was printed, 'The Big Day'. That's right. Norton snapped his fingers. Monday's Warren's birthday. That's what I'll do. We'll get a couple of sheilas and I'll shout Woz out for dinner. And hang the expense.

Despite his tiredness, Norton was beaming as he rinsed his cup and put it in the dish rack. Yeah. First thing Monday morning I'll put Abe's wallet in the mail and shout Woz to a grouse feed for his birthday. A heart of gold I've got. He yawned and headed for bed, where his last thoughts before he fell asleep were, Jesus I'm a terrific bloke. I really am you know.

212

Les felt like a bit of extra sleep so it was well after lunch when he got out of bed. The Sunday papers on the kitchen table and a couple of dishes in the dish rack told him Warren was up and gone. A quick look out the back door told him it wasn't going to be much of a day either. After a cup of coffee he had a run on Bondi to shake off his tiredness, then just pottered around the house taking it easy.

He popped a pork and veal roast and some vegies in the oven around three and by the time it had cooked Warren was back home.

'You going to the Sheaf tonight Woz?' asked Norton over dinner.

'No. I think I'll brush it,' replied Warren. 'I got to get up early again tomorrow. What about yourself?'

'No. It'd be freezing out the back there tonight. I'm going to stay home and watch TV.'

'Hey Woz.' Norton paused for a moment to give his mate time to look up from his food. 'It's the big day for you tomorrow — isn't it?'

'How do you mean?'

'It's your birthday isn't it?'

'That's right. How did you know?'

'Well you'd have to be blind to miss it. It's written on the side of the fridge in letters eight feet high.' Les chuckled at the self conscious smile on Warren's face. 'So what are you doing for your birthday?'

'Dunno really. I've been that busy at work the last couple of weeks, it just about slipped my mind.'

'How would you like to go out for dinner? I'll shout.'

Warren's jaw hung open and he dropped his knife and fork by his plate. 'What was that again Les?' he blinked.

'How about we get a couple of sheilas and I'll shout us all out for dinner?'

Warren kept blinking. 'Please Les. Not while I'm eating. You're starting to make me giddy and I'll end up being sick.'

'I'll even buy some French champagne.'

'French champagne? Shit! Did someone break a chair over your head last night? That stuff costs money. Besides, you reckon you hate the frogs for letting off atom bombs in the Pacific.'

'I do. They're cunts, and they always will be. But seeing as it's such a momentous occasion, and you're me mate, I'm willing to bitterly swallow my pride and get a few bottles.'

'Bloody hell. All right Les, you've got me.' Warren looked at Norton a little suspiciously for a moment. 'You're not going to take us down to the No Name are you?'

'No. I'll shout you to the best fish restaurant in Sydney.'

'Zino's?'

'You got it baby.'

Zino was the Italian mate of Gary Jackson, Norton's sometime fishing partner. He was a bloody good cook, and being a fisherman himself and having Gary on side, if the fish were any fresher they'd swim off your plate.

'Okay Les,' Warren nodded enthusiastically. 'You're on. Who're you going to take?'

'I'll give Lou a ring.'

Lou was Louise. A tall copper-haired New Zealand barmaid Les had met at a barbecue. Lou was no oil painting but she had one of those inquisitively happy faces that was compensated for by a figure that would have stopped John F. Kennedy's funeral. Like a lot of New Zealand country girls, she also had a bubbly, cheeky personality that Norton dug — always calling him 'fella' and never his name. Except when he'd do something dumb; then she'd call him a big dill pickle. In fact if it hadn't been for Norton's night job and Louise wanting to do a bit more travelling, there was a good chance they would have been seeing a lot more of each other than they were. Both in and out of bed.

'So you're going to bring big Lou are you?'

'Yep. What about yourself?'

'Probably that sheila that was last month's *Penthouse* Pet. Lisa — with the blonde hair.'

'Fair enough.' Norton tossed Warren a wink. 'So, mate. It looks like it could be a good night, tomorrow night.'

'It sure does Les,' agreed Warren, still not quite sure about Norton releasing all the money. 'It sure does.'

And it was. Billy called round early in the day to go training and Les told him about finding the wallet. On the way to the gym he dropped it in the post box with a note saying: 'Dear Abe. You left your wallet at my flat. Thanks for the drink and Yom Kippur. Love Deidrie.' After training he starved himself all day and when they hit Zino's at eight he was growling like a polar bear. They had a few drinks with the girls earlier, and on departing Norton left three bottles of 68 Pol Roger in the fridge and took three with him plus a bottle of Tasmanian 1977 Heemskerk Chardonnay. Warren nearly went into a trance.

Zino knew Norton through Gary and he liked the big Queenslander. As soon as they walked in the door they were given the best table and treated like long-lost relatives from the old country. The wine flowed and to describe Zino's cooking on the night as good would be like describing the Mona Lisa as not a bad drawing. Barbecued king prawns. Tasmanian scallops and mussels in white-wine sauce. Lobster. Blue swimmer crabs. A filleted snapper dish in garlic and some other wine sauce that almost brought tears to their eyes. Then there were pancakes smothered in cream liqueur and fresh strawberries. They all got roaring drunk, including the owner, and cut into 'Santa Lucia'. That's 'Amore'. And the whole restaurant, including the staff and Zino's Filipino wife, ended up singing Warren a happy birthday.

Back home more champagne flowed, a couple of joints went around and they danced and sang and played the guts out of the latest Midnight Oil and Spy Vs Spy albums. Apart from it being his birthday and the fabulous food, it was still one of the best nights Warren had ever had. Louise kept coming out with all these ridiculous corny down-home expressions. Norton's usual, bone-dry sense of humour was right up to scratch. And Lisa, the absolutely stunning *Penthouse* Pet, who was generally just a pretty face at the best of times, came out with a couple of gags that cracked everyone up. It was a great night all right.

But as Warren settled back on the lounge with Lisa's head on his shoulder — drunk from the champagne, mellowed out from the pot and getting into the music — he gazed fondly across the lounge room at Norton cuddled up next to Louise and the enigma of it all suddenly hit him. There was a man who'd just spent three days in Long Bay rather than pay a paltry fine. Yet now he'd turned around and cheerfully forked out the best part of $700 on food and drink. And although Norton tried to hide it, Warren saw him leave a fifty dollar tip on the table. Warren continued to stare at his mate in both wonder and admiration and two thoughts dawned on him. Les Norton was one hell of a man. But he'd also never figure him out as long as his arsehole pointed to the ground.

Norton and Louise were still in bed and Warren was running late for work when he dropped Lisa off at her Watsons Bay home unit on his way to the Paddington agency the following morning. The bright young advertising executive was a bit seedy but in an extra good mood when he breezed into the office just before ten. The faces on the three partners that ran Wirraway Advertising, however, were more like heroin dealers sitting on death row in a Malaysian gaol. They were pure misery. From their neatly trimmed beards down through their collarless shirts and leather jeans to the tips of their alligator skin cowboy boots.

'Hello fellas,' he said a little hesitantly. 'What's ... doing?'

'What's doing Warren? Frank Johnstone's broke his fuckin' jaw in a fight last night and can't do the ad. That's what's fuckin' doing.'

Warren blinked. 'Are you fair dinkum?'

'Ohh no Warren. We just made it up for something to fuckin' do. Of course we're fair dinkum. The fuckin' big imbecile.'

'Shit!' Warren flopped down on a brown velvet lounge chair. 'What are you going to do?'

'What are we going to do?' The partner on the end threw his hands up in the air. 'Well you're the fuckin' executive producer. You fuckin' tell us.'

'Shit!' Warren shook his head and stared, crestfallen, at the white carpet. 'I don't bloody well believe it.'

'Neither do we.'

'When did this happen?'

'Last night at training.'

'Shit! Have you tried to get someone else?'

'We've rung every fuckin' agency in Sydney. Anyone that even resembles that moron in Melbourne is either doing something else or working on that bloody stupid war movie in Frenchs Forest. We've just rung Bedford and Pierce — they're going to ring us back at eleven. If they can't find anyone we're stuffed.'

'But it's only Tuesday,' said Warren. 'We're not shooting till Saturday.'

'Warren,' said the partner in the middle. 'It wouldn't matter if it was only bloody pancake day. There's no way we're going to find someone that looks like Frank Johnstone in that space of time. It took us six weeks to cast that imbecile.'

Warren nodded despondently.

The partner on the end leant back on his seat and ran his hands across his face. 'Ohh Christ!' he exclaimed. 'Can you believe this? Johnno might be a bloody big pain in the arse. But he's unique. He was ideal for that ad. Big but not too big. Plenty of red hair and just enough personality. The contrast between him and the others would have been perfect. Perfect.'

'Perfect,' agreed the partner on the opposite end. 'And now the whole shoot looks like going down the gurgler. Where will we find another big red-headed bloke that looks like him? Where?'

Those last two descriptions hit Warren straight between the eyes. 'Where?' he said quietly.

'That's right Warren. Where?'

'How about I go into my office,' he said cautiously, 'and phone around till B and P ring us back.'

The others nodded silently in agreement.

Warren went into his office, sat at his desk and stared at his phone. A big red-headed bloke with a bit of personality. There was a bloke answering that description lying in bed not far from there at that very moment. But there were several things to be taken into consideration and several ways of looking at this that had Warren in a gigantic wrestling match with his conscience.

If he tipped Les into this commercial and it turned into another riot like that Bowen Lager one he wouldn't get a job in advertising selling space on the sides of garbage tins. But if Les pulled it off without wrecking the place Warren would be flavour of the month at Wirraway for years to come. They'd even let him drive the company Porsche. However, there was every chance Les would knock it back anyway. He swore after that Brisbane episode that he'd never do another one of those stupid bloody things as long as he lived. And he'd had offers. And how much chance was there of him wanting to go to Melbourne anyway. He wasn't all that wrapped in Sydney, so he'd positively loathe Melbourne. But the thing was worth $3,000 and if that wasn't a big enough magnet nothing was. Les would rollerskate through a stampede of wildebeests for that sort of money. And if he did take it, what could go wrong? There was only ten in it. All half baked fairies sipping fizzy wine in an old pub in St Kilda. Les could do it standing on his head. Les was the man all right.

Warren drummed his fingers on his desk. There was a way of going about this. He'd offer Les the ad to make up for him spending all that money last night. If he knocked it back, too bad. If he went down and killed it Warren would be a hero. And either way, Les would think him a good bloke for giving him a chance to get his money back. Warren decided to have a coffee and think it over between then and eleven.

Around eleven, a still very seedy Les Norton was sitting

in the kitchen next to a pot of tea and convincing himself he'd do some training later that afternoon. Louise had to start work at twelve, so he'd dropped her off at her place and got the paper on the way home. In the paper shop, Les had noticed a fold-up road map of Melbourne and surrounding districts that he'd bought out of curiosity. Now he'd finished reading the paper, and with the map spread across the kitchen table, he was comparing it with the map Mousey had given him. Pieces on the two maps were beginning to match up.

The road Mousey had written as Upper Harrisburg was Upper Heidelberg. The almost unreadable suburbs or towns were starting to make sense. Thomastown. Merang. Yarrambat. And what at first looked like Yin Yoe Residence was a dam. Yan Yean Reservoir, next to a town called Whittlesea. Other roads and streets on Mousey's map became identifiable also. Norton's mind slipped into overdrive, because suddenly the little sweeper's map began to make sense. He'd definitely buried something near some pine trees next to that Yan Yean Reservoir. But what? And it looked like it was around eighty kilometres out of town, although Mousey had written everything in yards and miles. It was obvious the little sweeper hadn't quite come to terms with the metric system yet. Norton drummed his fingers along the side of his teacup. He still had about a $1,000 left from that money he'd found. It'd be almost worth taking a trip down to Melbourne one Monday, hiring a car and seeing just what was buried out there. It could be anything. It was certainly worth a thought sometime in the future.

Norton was still mulling it over when the phone rang. 'Hello,' he said, after striding into the lounge room to pick up the receiver.

'G'day Les. It's Warren. How are you feeling?' Wirraway Advertising had struck out with Bedford and Pierce, so he'd decided to take the risk.

'I'm as seedy as a tin of raspberry jam,' smiled Norton. 'What about yourself?'

'I'm only running on two cylinders. I hope I can see the day out.'

'It was a good night though.'

'Was it what. And thanks for that too Les.'

'No worries.'

They chatted about the food and the drink and one thing and another for a while, then Warren casually began to edge the conversation around his way.

'You know. That must've cost you a bundle last night, Les,' he said cagily.

'Ahh, that's all right Woz. The day I can't pull a few bucks out of the bank to celebrate my mate's birthday, I'll give up,' lied Norton.

'Well, I still appreciate it Les. And if you're interested, I can give you a chance to get your money back. Plus.'

'Yeah,' said Norton. 'How?'

Warren crossed his fingers on the other end of the line. 'Are you interested in doing a TV commercial?'

'A TV commercial. Ohh mate, I dunno about that.'

Warren winced slightly at the tone of Norton's voice. He definitely didn't sound too enthusiastic. 'Yeah. I didn't think you'd be too keen. It's in bloody Melbourne of all places, too.'

'Melbourne!' Norton's ears pricked up and his eyes flicked across to Mousey's map sitting on the table. 'Shit! I've never been to Melbourne, Woz.'

'You haven't missed much.'

'Mmhh.' Norton stroked his chin thoughtfully and an odd smile crept over his face. 'Well, tell us about it anyway,' he said easily, 'and I'll let you know what I think.'

Warren brightened up a little. This was a definite nibble and he still hadn't mentioned the money. Norton would bite at that like a Tasmanian Tiger, especially after dropping $700 on a night out, so he gave Les a run-down.

First, he told Les how Johnstone had broken his jaw and the agency was stuck. He'd be doing them a big favour if he could do it. It was being shot in Melbourne in an old pub in St Kilda. There'd be a mixed bunch of sweet young things at the bar sipping St Kilda Kooler. Norton would front up to the bar and someone would offer him a bottle. Norton would then pick up the bottle, look all mean and nasty, and come out with the big line, 'That's a sheila's drink.' Then with all the little ponces terrified and looking as if they were expecting him to wreck the place, Norton was to take a big swig, smile, nod his head, then order a six-pack and walk out. And the spiel was, everybody can kool off with a Kilda. He'd go down Friday afternoon. It was a six a.m. shoot Saturday. They'd probably shoot all day. He'd stay there Saturday night and return Sunday afternoon.

Norton thought without a doubt it was one of the greatest loads of shit he'd heard in his life. He wondered just what these advertising yuppies were into when they got these ideas.

But for $3,000 he'd keep his opinions to himself.

He forced a laugh. 'Sounds like it might be a bit of fun, Woz. I'll give it a shot if you like.'

'Good on you Les.' Warren was beaming. He was taking a risk with Norton, but he just might have saved the day. 'You know where the agency is. Can you be in here, say one o'clock?'

'Yeah sure.'

'Okay. See you then.'

Warren went into the main office where the three partners were looking more dejected than ever. 'I think I might have found someone for you.'

'Yeah,' grunted the partner in the middle. He sounded about as keen as Les did when Warren first rang up. 'Has he ever been in front of a camera before?'

'He did a couple of beer ads in West Aussie.'

'Oh? So he has got some ability?'

Warren nodded enthusiastically.

'Well, I suppose that's a plus,' said the partner on the end.

When Norton, dressed in a shirt, jeans and cardigan, walked into the agency at one, Warren led him straight into the main office and the partners brightened up noticeably. Norton certainly looked the part — if nothing else. Warren quickly introduced him around but the names went straight in one ear and out the other and they all looked the same anyway. Like Kenny Rogers before all his hair turned grey. They handed Les a script and let him study it for a while.

'Warren has explained to you what's going on?' said the partner in the middle.

'Yeah,' nodded Norton, glancing up from the script.

'Have you tried the drink?'

'Yeah,' nodded Norton again. 'Warren gave me some the other day.'

'What did you think of it?'

Norton looked po-faced at Warren. 'Nice. It's easy to drink.'

'Good. Anyway, would you like to have a go at the line?'

'Sure.'

The partner on the end handed Les a bottle. Norton chucked a mean look and came out with the line. Then did it another three or four times. The partners had sat up, but they didn't seem all that enthusiastic.

'Can I make a suggestion?' asked Les.

'Sure. Go ahead.'

'Well. Don't you think "sheila's drink" is a little bit . . . how do you people like to put it? Ocker. Is that the word?'

'Go on.'

'Well. Why not try it like this?' Norton picked up the bottle and said, 'That's a girl's drink.' Only with more of a sneer and more curling of the lip.

Fancy having to go through this shit thought Norton. Larry, Curly and Mo here in the leather pants wouldn't know their arseholes from a wombat burrow in a river bank.

The partners looked at each other, then at Les. 'Say that again Les,' said the partner in the middle.

Norton repeated the performance, really giving the sneer the full on Sylvester Stallone treatment this time.

'I'll tell you what,' said the Kenny Rogers look-alike on the end. 'He could have something there.'

'Yeah,' nodded the one on the other end. 'After all. It is Melbourne, and they are a little more, shall we say, conservative down there in VB territory.'

'Do it again Les.'

Norton repeated the performance a couple more times. It went over like a bunch of roses on Mother's Day.

Smiling to each other the partners took some polaroids of Norton and thanked him for coming in. Warren did the same and walked him to the door, thanking him again and saying he'd either ring him or see him when he got home that night.

Norton was shaking his head in annoyance as he walked back to his car. God. What about those three clowns? They ought to be locked up. That's it for me. Never, ever again. They can stick their ad up their arse.

'Well?' said Warren, as he walked back into the office. 'What did you think?'

'Not bad,' conceded the partner in the middle.

'I reckon he looks more like Frank Johnstone than Frank Johnstone does,' chuckled the one on the end.

'If nothing better turns up,' nodded the remaining partner, 'he just might do.' He turned to Warren. 'Not bad Warren. You did well.'

Later that evening, when Warren got home from the agency, Les was in the kitchen having a cup of coffee. He was dressed and getting ready to take Louise to the movies. A pot of curry he'd made earlier was sitting on the stove.

'G'day Les,' Warren smiled as he stepped into the kitchen. 'How's things?'

'Woz,' nodded Norton. 'How's it goin'? You had tea yet?' Warren shook his head. 'There's some curried chicken on the stove. Get into it.'

'Good. I'm bloody starving.' Warren went across to the stove, took the lid off the pot and had a sniff.

'So,' said Norton, eyeing Warren from across the top of his coffee, 'what're those three yuppies with the beards doing? Do they want me to do that ad, or what?'

'They haven't quite made up their minds yet,' replied Warren, ladling some curried chicken onto a plate.

'What do you mean, haven't made up their minds yet?' frowned Norton. 'I went in there. They checked out my melon. I even brushed up that stupid bloody line for them. What do you want for $3000. Paul fuckin' Newman?'

'Les, it doesn't quite work like that,' replied Warren.

'What do you mean — doesn't quite work like that? You told me over the phone this morning you were desperate. And I'd be doing you a favour by coming in.'

'We were. But another couple of blokes have turned up since then.'

'Oh I see,' nodded Norton sourly. 'One minute I'm flavour of the month. Now I get shoved on the reserve bench. Thanks a lot mate.'

'I know just how you feel Les. It's a ruthless world, modelling.' Warren pulled out a chair and sat down with his dinner. 'But you can't blame me for this Les. These blokes just happened to turn up and they've got heads rougher than yours. I know, it's hard to imagine, but it's true.'

Impassively, Norton watched Warren getting into his food for a few moments. 'How's that curried chicken?' he finally said. 'All right is it?'

'Yeah. It's beautiful. The banana and pineapple really give it that extra something.'

'That's good. How would you like the rest of it over your fuckin' head.'

It was almost the same the following evening when Warren came home from work and Les was getting ready to go to the club. They'd narrowed it down to Les and just one other bloke, but the three bosses still hadn't quite made up their minds yet. However, Les was the front-runner, if that was any consolation.

Norton was almost going to tell Warren he could tell his

three bosses in their black leather jeans they could shove their ad, mango flavoured wine and all. But he copped it reasonably sweet. He did say, however, that they'd better make up their minds because he'd have to give them some sort of notice at the club. Warren agreed and apologised. He told Les he'd let him know one way or the other by lunchtime Thursday.

After work that night, Norton hinted that he might be going away for the weekend and could they get Danny McCormack in. Price said that was no problem. It was rare that Les ever took any time off and Danny was always keen to earn a few extra dollars, especially with five kids hanging round his neck. Despite a barrage of questions Norton didn't say where he might be going. George Brennan said it was obvious. The big goose was going back to the Bay to cut out another fine.

At training with Billy Dunne the following day, Les told his workmates more or less what was going on. He said he wasn't relying on getting the ad and it didn't really worry him one way or the other, but the lazy $3000 would be nice. He didn't tell Billy his ulterior motive for wanting to go to Melbourne. Billy replied by saying he wouldn't spend a weekend in Melbourne for $103,000. Billy didn't elaborate on this and Norton didn't ask him any more on it either.

About four that afternoon Norton was getting ready to have an hour or so's sleep before going to work. He'd just finished a cup of tea when the phone rang.

'Les. It's Warren.' He gave a little laugh over the phone. 'I just rang to tell you — you little starlet you — that you've got the ad.'

'Yeah.' Norton was pleased, but he wasn't all that enthused. After two days of indecision it was a bit of an anticlimax.

'Yeah. I'm sitting here with the bosses of the agency now, and they're keen for you to do it. And they're sorry we had to muck you around a bit, but this is a fairly big promotion with quite a lot of money involved and everything had to be spot on.'

'Ahh that's okay Woz,' drawled Les. Then a thought hit him. 'Hey. Are you sitting there with Larry, Curly and Mo now are you?'

'Ah . . . yes. Why?'

'Well tell those three yuppie wombats that seeing they didn't mind fucking a big star like me around all week, they can do me a favour.'

'Sure Les. What is it?'

'I've found out I've got an old uncle lives out of Melbourne a bit and I'd like to go and visit him,' Norton lied. 'Can they get me the loan of a car while I'm down there? In fact tell those three clowns I demand it. Or no red-headed ocker for their dopey fuckin' ad.'

'Yeah that's okay Les. No problems.'

'Good.'

'Well look Les. I'll probably miss you before you go to work tonight. I've got quite a bit to finish off here yet. So I'll see you about lunchtime tomorrow. Don't forget, you fly out at six-thirty tomorrow night.'

'No sweat Woz. I'll see you tomorrow mate.'

Well, thought a smiling Norton, it looks like I'm going to Melbourne for the weekend eh. This could be very interesting. Very interesting indeed. He went into his bedroom and lay down. Just before he put his head on the pillow he had another look at Mousey's map. He chuckled for a moment, then closed his eyes and dozed off.

In Price's office after work that night he told all the others, besides Billy, where he was going and what he was doing for the weekend. Without mentioning Mousey's map of course.

'So, Price, I thought bugger it. Three thousand dollars is three thousand dollars. I'll give it a shot. And I've never been to Melbourne either. So why not?' he added with a shrug.

There was a bit of an amused silence for a moment as everyone took a sip on their drink and the story Les had just told them began to sink in. Naturally, George Brennan was the first to speak.

'So,' he said with a cynical smile. 'The teenage heart-throb's off to Melbourne for the weekend is he?'

'Yes,' replied Norton, running a finger delicately across an eyebrow. 'Just a brief modelling assignment in one of our capital cities, George. Then it's back to Sydney. It's all very boring really.'

'One of our capital cities eh,' chuckled George. 'You know what Melbourne is don't you?'

'What?'

'Dubbo without the glamour.'

'You read the Bible, Les?' chimed in Billy Dunne. 'You know how God made the world in six days and on the seventh day he rested. You know what he did on the eighth day?'

Norton shook his head.

'He gave the world an enema. And Melbourne's where he stuck the pipe.'

'You know all that a person from Melbourne is?' guffawed Brennan.

Norton grimaced and shook his head again.

'A Tasmanian on his way to Sydney.'

'Did you hear...'

'Ohh look fair dinkum,' cut in Norton. 'You blokes are just jealous. It wouldn't matter where I was going. You'd still bag it. The place can't be all that bad.'

'You're right Les,' said Price. 'Melbourne's not all that bad. Me and Eddie often pop down there — and we always have a good time. Don't we?'

'Yeah Melbourne's all right,' chuckled Eddie. 'Apart from Vietnam, I couldn't think of a nicer place to shoot someone and bury the body.'

'You'll see some good-looking women down there Les,' added Price. 'And well dressed too. The best clothes in Australia come from Melbourne. I still get most of my suits and shoes from down there.'

'Price is right about the clothes,' giggled Billy. 'They certainly like to dress up down there. You even wear a coat and tie to go and have a shit. Don't let them catch you sitting on the crapper with only your underpants on. They'll never talk to you again.'

'Look,' said Norton, draining his can of Fourex, 'let me sort the joint out for myself. All I know is, I'll be there till Sunday. I'll do this silly fuckin' TV commercial and whether the place is good or bad, I'll just cop the money and run. Now,' Les got to his feet, 'anyone want a drink while I'm up?'

There was a chorus of laughter and orders and Norton started pottering around behind the bar.

'Hey while you're on the subject of money, film star,' said George Brennan slowly. 'You're forgetting a little something aren't you?'

'What's that George?' replied Norton, his head stuck in the bar fridge.

'That team of poofs from up Bondi Junction play the Tigers this Saturday. You still want to have a bet?'

'Ohh yeah. That's right. The semi-finals start this weekend. Whoever loses gets the arse till next year.' Norton spread the various drinks across the bar and began adding the splits.

'Yeah I'll have a bet with you mate. How much?'

'How game are you? You've been bagging Balmain all year.'

'I dunno,' shrugged Norton. 'Hundred bucks?'

'Why don't we make it five?'

'Five hundred,' said Les. 'Shit!'

'Come on,' goaded Brennan. 'Show a bit of ticker. It'll be the last game of the year for one of them. I know which one too.'

Norton thought for a moment. 'I'll tell you what I'll do, you fat cunt. Why don't we make it an even thousand. Anything to shut you up — once and for all.'

'Did you hear that? Did you hear that?' George rose in his seat and looked excitedly around the room at the others. 'Ebenezer Scrooge wants to back Easts for a thousand bucks. You're all witnesses.' He turned back to Norton. 'Righto you miserable big Queensland bastard. You're on.'

'No sweat George,' replied Norton casually. He still had a thousand of the money he'd found, plus the money he'd earn on the weekend. So he wouldn't really miss it. And Easts were a good chance to squeak in against Balmain anyway.

'Fair dinkum,' said Price, shaking his head as Les handed him his Dimple Haig and soda. 'A thousand bucks on a game of bloody football. You blokes are off your bloody heads.'

George turned to Price. 'How much did you have on Kelly Girl last Saturday?'

'Fifty thousand each way.'

Brennan raised his Bacardi and grapefruit juice. 'The defence rests,' he smiled.

They hung around drinking and cracking jokes till well after four. Everyone, including George, wished Les all the best in Melbourne and they'd see him next week. Then they closed up and went home.

Beside lecturing Les all the way from Bondi to Mascot when he drove him out to the airport the following evening, Warren also gave him his last-minute instructions on what would happen when he arrived in Melbourne. A girl named Pamela would be waiting for him at the Ansett counter; she knew what he looked like and she would drive him to his motel and fill him in on the Melbourne end of it.

'Now for Christ sake Les,' Warren pleaded as they pulled up in the parking area, 'don't get into any trouble down there. I'm begging you. Just be cool.'

'Jesus you're a fuckin' old sheila Woz. From what they tell me, Melbourne's the most conservative place in the world.

I'll be one day doing this ad and that's it. There's no chance of me playing up tonight because it's a six o'clock start tomorrow. And there's no chance of me getting drunk, because I wouldn't drink that shit you're advertising if they held a loaded gun to my head. What could possibly go wrong?'

'Knowing you, Les. Anything. So cool it — okay?'

'Ohh arseholes.'

Norton picked up his bag and they began walking across to the departure terminal. 'Hey just tell me one thing Woz,' he asked.

'What's that Les?'

'How come they're shooting this silly bloody thing in Melbourne. Yet all the organising seems to be done in Sydney. It just doesn't make sense to me.'

'Les,' replied Warren. 'That is just one of the intricacies of advertising. I'll explain it to you when you get back. In the meantime Les, all you have to do is take the money and run.'

Norton gave the side compartment on his travel bag a pat where Mousey's map was folded up inside the road map. 'Yeah. I guess you're right mate,' he smiled.

They had time for two drinks in the departure lounge. The next thing Norton was winging his way to Melbourne.

Norton was struck a bit of a body blow on the plane trip down. No Fourex. But there was an abundance of Victoria Bitter and Tooheys and as he was in the first-class section it was free. Consequently Les was in a pretty good mood when they touched down at Tullamarine. Whistling and smiling to himself, he picked up his travel bag from the conveyor belt and with that in one hand and his small overnight bag in the other, he headed for the Ansett counter.

A tallish woman in her late twenties was standing there and straight away Norton tipped she was the one he had to meet. She was strikingly attractive, in a heavily but tastefully made up sort of way. Long dark hair parted on the side and flicked casually across one eye billowed across the top of a loose-fitting silver and black patterned trouser suit that seemed to conceal what to Norton looked like quite a full-breasted figure.

A smile creased the corners of her dark brown eyes as she saw Norton approach. 'Hello,' she said pleasantly. 'You must be Les.'

'Yeah. Are you Pamela?'

She nodded and extended her hand. Les shook it briefly and it was a warm, firm handshake.

'So. How was the flight down?'

'Good,' replied Norton. 'You no sooner seem to be on board than you're here.'

'That's good. Well, if you'd like to follow me out to the car, we'll get going? Do you want a hand with anything?'

'No. I'm right thanks.'

'Okay. No worries.'

Norton followed her out of the terminal across to the parking area where a shiny red XJS Jaguar was sitting. Pamela unlocked the doors and Norton threw his bags on the back seat.

'What sort of work do you do on this ad Pamela?'

'I'm Mr Leishman's secretary. He owns the agency. This is his car.'

'Not a bad heap,' smiled Les. 'There must be some dough in advertising.'

'The agency does all right.' Pamela started the motor and they moved off.

'I'll tell you what,' said Norton, sounding a little surprised. 'It doesn't seem like a bad night. I was expecting it to be freezing.'

'I know. It's only early spring and we've had a heatwave the last couple of days. It's almost unbearable. But they're expecting a big storm on Sunday that should cool things down.'

'I don't know about it being unbearable,' said Norton. 'But it's not too bad.'

Pamela smiled at Les. 'And what do you do in Sydney, Les? Are you an actor or some sort of a stuntman or something?'

'Hardly,' laughed Norton, easing his neck into the headrest. 'I got this thing more or less by accident.'

As they cruised comfortably along the straight, wide streets that make up the sprawling flat suburbs of Melbourne, Norton told Pamela what he did for a living and where he lived. How Warren tipped him into the ad, including the last-minute casting, and how he told the three bosses at Wirraway Advertising what he thought of their line. He could have lied to her and told her anything. But he thought what would that prove? Besides, he was still revved up from all the free booze on the plane, and the way the stories were coming out by the time they reached downtown Melbourne and crossed the

228

Yarra into St Kilda Road, Pamela was laughing unashamedly and enjoying Norton's easy-going company.

'It certainly sounds like you and your friends lead a pretty good life up there in Sydney,' she grinned.

'Yeah, it's all right. Can't complain.'

'Fair enough. My word, you've got a good tan for this time of the year.'

'Yeah, we've got a spot behind the Pavilion at Bondi where we, sit on our fat arses of a day. It's out of the wind and you sort of stay brown all year round. You should see some of the other blokes. They look like they just come down from New Guinea.'

'You've certainly got a good life up there Les.'

'Wouldn't be dead for quids Pamela,' winked Norton.

They followed the traffic down Fitzroy Street, then turned into a wide, palm-tree dotted boulevard. A marina full of boats and a vast expanse of inky blackness beyond that told him they were near the ocean. From what he could see in the darkness, it reminded Norton a little of Brighton le Sands and Botany Bay in Sydney.

'Where are we Pamela?' he asked, peering curiously out the window.

'St Kilda. That's Port Phillip Bay out there.'

They turned up some small side street, did a U-turn and pulled up in front of a classy-looking motel overlooking the ocean. A discreet red, white and black neon sign out the front said St Moritz Motel. It was only a couple of stories high but wide, with plenty of tinted windows, sandstock bricks and white balconies covered in lush green vines facing out across the bay.

'This looks all right,' said Les.

'It's the best motel in the area and very private,' replied Pamela. 'Besides. It wouldn't be very civil to put a big star like you in the YMCA for the night, would it?'

'I'd be exceptionally pissed off if you did, Pamela,' said Norton, reaching over for his bags.

'Do you need a hand with anything?'

'No. She's sweet.'

'No worries.'

An automatic door opened and Les followed Pamela into a tastefully and expensively furnished foyer. Thick, brown carpet, matching furniture, lush indoor plants and a nice collection of paintings and mirrors around the walls. A haughtily attractive woman, not unlike Pamela only more into her thirties and with her thick dark hair bobbed up at the back, was standing at the desk. She was wearing a colourful, three-piece woollen outfit, the extra long knitted top tied in the middle with a matching sash. Behind her a younger girl in a black uniform was working at a switchboard.

'Les. This is Mrs Perry, the owner,' said Pamela. 'Mrs Perry, this is Mr Norton.'

Mrs Perry gave Norton a very heavy once up and down. She blinked a couple of times and stared at him for a moment before answering. 'Why hello Mr Norton,' she smiled, gushing just a little. 'Pleased to meet you. You're the gentleman from Sydney down to do the television commercial.'

'That's right,' said Norton, returning her smile.

'Well I hope you have a very pleasant stay with us.'

'I'm sure I will Mrs Perry. Your motel looks very nice too.'

'Why thank you Mr Norton,' she breathed, with more fluttering of the eyelids.

'Well I might leave you to it Les,' said Pamela, exchanging an even look with the motel owner. 'I've got quite a bit more running around to do tonight. You know it's a six a.m. start tomorrow.' Norton nodded again. 'So we'll probably call you at five-thirty. I'm not trying to tell you what to do. But it might be an idea if you got an early night. It's going to be hectic tomorrow.'

'To tell you the truth Pamela,' smiled Les. 'I was up early myself this morning and I'm pretty rooted as it is. I intend doing just that.'

'Okay then.' Pamela held out her hand. 'I'll see you first thing tomorrow.'

Norton gave her hand a quick, warm shake. 'See you then Pamela. Nice to have met you.'

'No worries.' Pamela exchanged another even look with Mrs Perry, smiled thinly at her then disappeared out the door.

As he watched her leave Norton swore he could feel two eyes burning holes in the back of his neck. He turned around and Mrs Perry was staring at him like he was a TV set tuned to her favourite program.

'If you'd like to follow me Mr Norton,' she cooed, 'I'll show you to your room.'

'Thanks.'

'No worries Mr Norton.'

Light background music was playing when they stepped

inside the lift for the short ride to the first floor. Admittedly the lift wasn't very big, but if Mrs Perry had stood any closer to Les she'd have been inside the fob pocket of his jeans.

'So you've just flown in, Mr Norton,' she said as the door closed.

'Yeah,' replied Norton. 'Only about half an hour ago.'

'And what do you think of Melbourne?'

Norton looked at her for a moment as the door swished open again. 'You've got nice roofs.'

He followed her down a carpeted hallway to room 19. Mrs Perry unlocked it, switched on a light, and Les followed her inside.

Norton couldn't help but be impressed with the room. It was beautiful. A huge, pink double bed pushed against one wall and, facing it, a matching suede ottoman with a full-length wall mirror above it, reflecting oil paintings on every wall and indoor plants beneath them. There was a kitchenette and a bar with a stereo. A remote-control colour TV sat on pure white carpet that thick you almost needed a dog-sled and a team of huskies to drag you over it. Mrs Perry moved across to the balcony and drew the curtains to reveal the darkness of Port Phillip Bay, broken here and there by the flickering lights of fishing boats dotted against the blackness like distant campfires.

'Christ, there's nothing wrong with this room Mrs Perry. It's the grouse.'

'Yes, we like our guests to be happy here Mr Norton.' Mrs Perry glided across the carpet and stood directly in front of Les, peering deeply into his eyes. 'You will be happy here. Won't you Mr Norton,' she almost crooned.

'Happier than a hunchback that's just seen another hunchback with a hunch bigger than his Mrs Perry,' replied Norton.

Mrs Perry nodded and smiled softly. 'There's a fully stocked bar there,' she indicated with a delicate hand. 'Champagne in the fridge. A coffee machine. And we always leave a bowl of fresh fruit for our guests.'

Mrs Perry edged in a little closer to Les. 'But of course, should you require anything else. Anything. Don't hesitate to ask,' she breathed.

'Righto. Just ring for room service do I?'

'No. You ring for me personally.'

'Okay.' Norton eased back from the motel owner just a little. 'Say Mrs Perry,' he asked. 'Do you run this motel on your own or with your husband?'

'With my brother. I'm divorced.'

'Oh, I see.'

Mrs Perry gave Les another heavy once up and down, then moved across to the door. 'Don't forget Mr Norton,' she smiled. 'Anything you want. Just call.'

'I'll do that. Thanks Mrs Perry.'

'No worries Mr Norton.'

The door closed softly and she was gone, leaving Les standing there stroking his chin thoughtfully. Is that bloody sheila fair dinkum, he mused. You will be happy here won't you Mr Norton. Ring for me personally Mr Norton. He gave a bit of a chuckle. Nah. They're just different down here, that's all. Christ, imagine if I did have a lash at her and she blew up. Warren'd have a stroke. You're only in the place five minutes and you tried to rape the woman that owned the motel. Yeah, that'd be my luck. He shook his head, unpacked his bag and changed into a dark blue tracksuit and joggers. Now. Let's see what they've got in the Lightning Ridge.

There were numerous bottles of spirits and liqueurs on the bar, two bottles of Veuve Cliquot, splits and a couple of dozen beers in the fridge. Some of it was imported, but no Fourex. Les settled for a can of VB. He tugged the ring-pull off and stepped out onto the balcony.

It was cool but not cold. He watched the cars zooming past on the wide road below and noticed that the marina he'd seen earlier was almost in front of him. There were other buildings near the beach, but at that angle he couldn't quite make out what they were. Further in the distance he could see what seemed to be some sort of an amusement park. Might finish this, he thought, and go for a bit of a walk. Give my legs a bit of a stretch. It's only about nine-thirty. He finished his beer and did just that.

Mrs Perry wasn't in the foyer but the girl in the black uniform gave Les a smile which he returned as he went past. The door opened and he went down the steps, hesitated for a moment and then turned towards some shops and hotels he'd seen on the way in.

He hadn't walked far when he turned a corner into a blaze of neon lights and wide footpaths teeming with people taking advantage of the unusually warm spring weather. After about two hundred metres it reminded Norton of Kings Cross; a little roomier, a little more laid back, but pretty much the same scene. Pizza shops, milk bars, and neon-spattered restaurants. Hotels, motels, rock palaces and amusement arcades. Voyeurs on foot, voyeurs in cars. Skinheads, straights and vacant-looking night types propped in doorways. Christ. I can't see myself lasting too much longer here he mused. It reminds me too much of work. The only redeeming feature was that the green-and-white numberplates on the cars reminded him a little of Queensland. He paused for a few moments outside a German restaurant full of drunken patrons hiccuping their way through a Nordic drinking song to a German band on stage. Then he strolled on past a hotel called the Duke of Kent and on to a bigger one that seemed to be in the process of being torn down. One bar on a corner was open. He put his head in there but it was full of seedy types you'd expect to see in a seedy hotel in any seedy part of any town in Australia. No thanks thought Norton. I might have one beer in that other pub then hit the toe.

He walked down to the Duke of Kent, went in one bar, through another and into a third. A jukebox was playing in one bar and a video screen going in another. It was smoky and fairly crowded with nearly everyone dressed to kill, and if the majority of the patrons weren't gay, they were that happy it didn't make any difference. In his blue tracksuit and suntan, Norton stood out like a black with a banjo at a Ku Klux Klan rally, and was already getting pretty much the same looks. Ohh bugger this he thought. I think I'll leave the St Kilda dag rattlers to drink on their own. I'm going to head back to the motel, drink what piss is in the fridge and hit the sack. I've got to be up around five anyway. He had one last look around the bar and headed back to the St Moritz.

He returned the smile of the girl on the switchboard and went straight to his room, tuned the stereo to some local FM station, kicked off his joggers and socks and opened another beer. He lay back on the bed to give it a test; it was firm yet wonderfully comfortable. Jesus, how did I manage to fluke this he chuckled as he took in the opulence of the suite. There was a TV guide sitting on the smoked-glass coffee table in front of the ottoman. That's what I'll do. I'll watch the late news and check out Mousey's map again before I go to sleep. He finished his beer and was about to get another when there was a soft knock on the door. He opened it and there was Mrs Perry.

Norton was taken slightly aback. 'Oh hello Mrs Perry. What... seems to be the trouble?'

'There's been a complaint that some of the phones aren't working properly. Do you mind if I come in and have a quick look?'

'No. Go for your life.' Norton stepped back from the door and closed it behind her.

He stood near the bed as Mrs Perry made a great fuss about picking up the receiver, pressing the buttons and clicking the switch hooks up and down with her finger.

'Yes — well. That seems to be working properly now.' Mrs Perry was acting sophisticated and businesslike but all the time her eyes kept darting nervously around the room, always coming back to rest on Les.

'Well that's real good, Mrs Perry,' smiled Les. 'Is there anything else you think you ought to check while you're here?'

Mrs Perry moved over and stood right in front of Les again. 'I don't know Mr Norton,' she breathed. 'What do you think?'

'What do I think?'

Norton looked at her. This is getting absolutely ridic he thought. This sheila's doing everything but send up smoke signals; and she's a bloody good sort too. If I don't make some sort of a move she'll either think I'm a bigger mug than what I look, or a poof. Bugger this. I'll have to have a lash.

He reached out and took Mrs Perry by the knot in her cardigan sash and drew her gently towards him. She gave about as much resistance as the Italian Army in 1943. Eyes swimming, she looked up at Norton who smiled, stooped his head slightly, and kissed her softly on the lips.

That was all Mrs Perry was waiting for. She wound her arms around Norton's neck, moaned quietly and kissed him back, avidly, hungrily, her tongue darting into Norton's mouth and around his ears and neck. It wasn't long before Les had a horn hard enough to break an icepick. He drew her in a little closer, ran his hand up over her ribcage and across her firm well-rounded breasts. Mrs Perry began kissing him more passionately than ever. Steadily, Les eased her back against the edge of the bed. She gave another little moan as he sat her down on it, spread her legs apart and stepped in between. Mrs Perry was only too willing to oblige and opened her legs up more, sitting her knees up on her chest. Norton pushed her long, woollen dress up over her stomach and ran his hand tenderly across her backside and her thighs.

It was then that Norton, much to his disgust, found that

234

Mrs Perry, ladylike owner of the classy St Moritz Motel, was a bit like the girl in the Holeproof ad on TV. For Mrs Perry was wearing no knickers. She was wearing no knickers at all. No underwear. Nothing.

Well I'll be buggered, he thought. Sophisticated, conservative bloody Melbourne eh. At least the sheilas in Sydney wear pants. He had a quick look to make sure. Yeah. Smooth white skin, neatly trimmed pubic hair. But definitely no knickers. You filthy little devil. It was revolting.

It was also very convenient. The next thing, Norton's tracksuit and Speedos were off quicker than you could yell 'Up Collingwood'.

Norton eased her right to the edge of the bed, lifted her legs up a little more and entered her, slowly and gently. Mrs Perry let out a long moan of agonised ecstasy.

'Ohhh yessss,' she gasped. 'Yessss.'

Well, that definitely doesn't sound like no to me thought Norton — and away he went.

In a word, it was sensational. Mrs Perry got into it with him like there was going to be no tomorrow. She bucked and squealed. Norton lifted her legs up further till her ankles were up behind her ears. The sudden unexpectedness of it could have had something to do with it but there was no two ways about it, Mrs Perry was one hell of a woman in bed. She went off like a Chinese new year. Norton would have liked to have gone on for ages, for both of them. But it was just too good and Mrs Perry's ted was too warm, tight and delicious. With his knees going like the pistons on the Spirit of Progress, Norton slipped into top gear with Mrs Perry screaming encouragement. Finally Les had to clench his jaws to stop from screaming out himself, and with his eyes virtually spinning around in his head he arched his back and with a huge shudder poured himself into her. Mrs Perry let out one long wail that ended with a choked-off scream.

Eventually Norton slowed down and withdrew, just as his knees buckled on him. He went to sit on the edge of the bed, missed and fell on the floor. Blinking groggily, he sat there for a few moments before climbing back up on the bed. Mrs Perry was lying there, legs spread apart, one arm over her face the other out at her side. An explosion of woollen dress and cardigan up over her stomach.

Panting quietly, Norton sat on the edge of the bed staring at her in disbelief. This was one of the weirdest things that had ever happened to him. Mrs Perry oozed sophistication, grace and good manners, but underneath she was a mad raving case. He had to say something, though without offending her. But what? Norton was almost lost for words.

He got his breath back and stared at Mrs Perry lying next to him, her chest still heaving slightly underneath her woollen top. Finally he took in a deep breath and ran his hand through his matted, sweaty hair.

'I tell you what,' he said sincerely. 'It is hot for this time of the year — isn't it?' He rose a little unsteadily to his feet and lurched towards the bar. 'You want a drink?' Norton reached into the fridge, grabbed the first can of beer he could find, ripped the ring-pull off and swallowed almost half of it in one go. His eyes watered and after a second or two he belched. The belch seemed to sting Mrs Perry back into life.

She jumped to her feet and began straightening her dress. 'Yes. Well... Mr Norton,' she said, tidying her hair and looking everywhere around the room but at Les.

'Well what Mrs Perry?' shrugged Norton, leaning against the bar completely naked, his old fellah still wet and shiny and flopping around in front of him like a broken arm.

'Well. Everything seems to be in order here Mr Norton,' she flustered, but she still couldn't seem to look at Les when she spoke.

'Everything's the grouse Mrs Perry,' smiled Norton, raising his can of beer. 'Couldn't be creamier.'

'Yes, well. That's very good isn't it, Mr Norton.' She continued to straighten her dress and tidy her hair.

'Good?' replied Les. 'Mrs Perry. If this is your idea of room service. You leave anything else I know for dead. You sure you won't have a drink?'

'No thank you,' she sniffed. 'I, ah... think it might be best if I got going. Seeing everything's all right in here now.'

'Okay Mrs Perry,' shrugged Norton, a little mystified. 'Suit yourself.'

Mrs Perry moved across to the door. Norton opened it for her and extended his hand. 'Well Mrs Perry,' he grinned, 'thanks for fixing the phone anyway.'

Commanding as much dignity as she could, and acting completely oblivious to Les's nakedness, she gave his hand a discreet shake. 'That's quite all right Mr Norton. Anytime. Now I really think I should be going.'

Norton raised his can. 'Thanks again, anyway.'

'No worries Mr Norton,' she replied with a quick toss of

her head. Norton closed the door and she was gone.

He drained his can of beer, got another one and leant against the bar, head spinning slightly and still not quite convinced of the last twenty minutes' events. Christ, did that really happen or am I just imagining things? I'll just check your phone for you Mr Norton. Check my phone. Jesus, Telecom could sure learn a lesson from her.

He still wasn't quite convinced it had happened when he got out of the shower about ten minutes later. But a spreading wet patch on the edge of the quilt told him it had. Christ, what a funny old night. This definitely calls for something a little stronger than beer. He went to the bar, searched around for a moment and made himself a good, stiff Old Grandad and Coke... Ah yes. I certainly could do with that.

There was a digital clock radio next to the bed. He sipped his drink while he fiddled around setting it for quarter past five; it was almost eleven. And Billy and George want to bag Melbourne. They're kidding. I've only been here two hours and I reckon it's the best place I've ever seen. He finished his drink, switched off the bed lamp and went straight to sleep.

A languid studio mix of Peter Frampton's 'Do You Feel Like I Do?' gently woke Norton. He blinked around the still darkened room not quite sure where he was, then switched on the bed lamp and it all came back to him. Christ, what a funny old night. He yawned and chuckled at the same time, spun out of the bed, stretched for a few moments, then got under the shower. I won't bother having a shave he thought. Seeing as I'm the heavy in this bullshit they'll probably want me looking like Clint Eastwood in *A Fist Full of Dollars*. He was towelling off next to the bed and feeling pretty good when right on five-thirty the phone rang.

'Hello,' he said, picking up the receiver. 'St Moritz House of Bondage.'

There was a stunned pause at the end of the line. 'Les. Is that you?'

'It sure is. How are you Pamela?'

'I'm... very well. You sound all bright and breezy this morning. I was expecting you to be still asleep.'

'No. I had a nice early night and I've been up since quarter past. I'm showered and just about ready to go.'

'Oh. Good on you. Well I'll meet you in the foyer at ten to six.'

'Okay Pamela. See you then.'

'No worries.'

Norton made a cup of coffee and had a couple of pieces of fruit while he threw on his jeans, black R. M. Williams riding boots, a sweatshirt and the black leather jacket he had on the night before. There was no-one in the foyer when he went down, but just as he got there Pamela pulled up in the Jaguar and gave the horn a quick bip.

'G'day Pamela. How's things?' he said, climbing in next to her.

'Good.' Pamela was wearing a brown corduroy skirt, boots and a loose-necked brown pullover that, even though it looked to be three sizes too big for her, still couldn't hide something about her figure that had Norton intrigued. 'Looking forward to the big day?' she asked.

'Reckon. We got far to go?'

'No. It's just up the road.'

Norton no sooner had his backside in the car when they pulled up outside a big white hotel barely 500 metres away. The area in front of the hotel was roped off for the film crew. There were several trucks packed with equipment and generators and a number of chords and cables ran up the staircase into the hotel. A battered old truck at the end had Black Rock Catering written on the side. It was a beautiful morning when Norton stepped out of the Jaguar — crisp and clear, and through the palm trees by the water's edge the sun coming up over Port Phillip Bay seemed to turn the water a shimmering, golden pink.

'The Boulevard Hotel,' said Norton, looking up at the name above the door.

'Yes,' replied Pamela, as a tram rattled past in the background. 'It's ideal for the ad. Wait till you see it inside. Come on.'

Les followed her up a fake marble staircase to where two blue-uniformed security guards were standing just inside the foyer. Pamela explained who she and Les were and they smiled politely and stepped aside.

The red and black carpeted foyer was large and high ceilinged with a bit of old-world charm about it. There were black vinyl cubicles against the walls and black vinyl chairs and tables at the bay windows overlooking the water. A set of stairs ran either side of a reception desk at the end of the room and a blackboard next to a cigarette machine almost in front of them had the names of the bands playing there that week.

Norton followed Pamela through another door with Neptune Room written above it. Like the foyer, it was spacious and high ceilinged with the same red and black carpet. A red carpet-fronted bar faced them and there were more cubicles and a number of chairs and tables full of people in front of the bay windows. A few potted palms were propped in the corners and large, framed posters of old St Kilda adorned the walls. To the left of the bar was a small stage with the amps and speakers from the previous night's band still sitting there. Behind that was a bistro or dining area.

There were around thirty or forty people present and the place was a hive of activity. Technicians, gaffers and other film crew were running around everywhere, dodging between lighting set-ups, sound systems, camera tracks and other equipment. For a booze ad, the whole scene had an aura of bustling fashion about it and Norton tipped they must be spending plenty of money to give St Kilda a sophisticated, up-market image. Everybody, including the crew, was dressed pretty swish, especially about half a dozen young couples seated in front of the windows. Everybody, that is, except one short-ish, dark-haired guy walking around peering at things through what looked like a little black monocle which he'd then check on a digital light meter hung around his neck. He was one of the greatest grubs Les had ever seen. He wore filthy white jeans, an equally filthy Breaker Morant sweat-shirt and the undone laces of his gym boots trailed behind him like squashed strands of spaghetti. He'd managed to top this off by not having a shave for at least a week and it looked like he'd combed his hair with a gardening fork. It turned out later he was the cameraman and he came from Sydney.

'Come on,' said Pamela. 'I'll introduce you around.'

The first person Les met was the director, Richard. An overweight, fair-haired guy in baggy jeans and some sort of an expensive battle jacket. Despite his air of bored amusement he gave Les a good, firm handshake and seemed happy to see him. Then came the writer, the soundman, someone else and someone else and finally B.O. Plenty the cameraman. Except for the director, Les couldn't remember their names. Pamela then led Norton over to the young couples who were to be the drinkers at the bar and told them who he was. They were all about a third Les's size and dressed to kill. However, they weren't at all stand-offish and appeared to view Les with an air of amicable curiosity. Les had been expecting a bunch of half-baked queens and gushing would-be starlets, but they all seemed to be capable young performers, keen to get the job done, get paid and go home.

Pamela then led Norton over to the make-up woman, who immediately went into a screaming tailspin when she saw Les's suntan and howled for the director. Richard soothed her by explaining to her that for the purpose of the ad Les was supposed to be a bit of a rough type, like a building worker or a wharfie, and these kind of people did go brown from working out in the sun, so the tan was okay. Just a little bit of make-up to take the shine off his broken nose, that's all. The wardrobe lady let him keep his riding boots and jeans, but he had to wear a St Kilda Aussie Rules guernsey: red, white and black. It fitted well and didn't look half bad on. Norton immediately made a mental note to souvenir it after the shoot.

Pamela brought him over a cup of coffee, which he sipped while the make-up lady gave him a last detail. The wardrobe lady took a polaroid, and before he knew it Norton was set to go on.

'Well Les,' said the director, giving him a nod of approval. 'If you're ready we'd like to have a crack at it. What do you reckon?'

'Sure. Why not?' Norton shrugged.

Richard explained they were going to shoot his part with the bit of dialogue first. It was the most difficult and Les was only there for the day. They should have it all sorted out by late that afternoon and if there were any problems they could bring the others back tomorrow. Norton promised he'd do his best.

They led him over to the bar, picked out which trendy would offer Les the drink and positioned the other trendies around him. The camera was ready, the lighting was set, the soundman nodded approval and a bit of silence fell across the set.

'Okay Les,' said Richard. 'Let's try a rehearsal. Quiet everyone. Annnnd . . . action.'

Les moved to the bar. The trendy nervously offered him a bottle of St Kilda Kooler. Norton looked at it and frowned and said. 'Turn it up mate. That's a girl's drink.'

Richard, B.O. Plenty and the soundman all exchanged pleasantly surprised looks.

'Tell you what,' said Richard.

'Looked good to me,' said the cameraman.

'Sounded okay to me. No worries.'

'Why don't we go for a take?' Richard turned to Norton.

'Les. We'll make this a take. Can you do exactly the same thing again?'

'As a bean, Richard.'

'No worries. Righto. Roll film. Roll sound. Annnnd... action.'

Norton repeated the performance. The trendies had just the right amount of horror on their faces and it went over like a baked dinner on Sunday. They shot it another four times and that was it. Richard was astounded.

They moved the camera slightly and shot the looks on the trendies' faces when Norton picked up the bottle, then moved it around for his expression when he took a mouthful: from a sneer to grudging approval. Les hit it like an old pro. Sir Laurence Olivier couldn't have done a better job. The St Kilda Kooler was chilled and although it was a little sweet it wasn't all that hard to drink. After the equivalent of about four bottles before breakfast, Norton wasn't drunk but he was in a happy, easy-going mood which seemed to rub off on the others and they all got along famously.

They did some shots of Norton walking towards the bar looking rough and mean, some wide shots of the trendies, and some of Norton picking up his six-pack and walking out. It went like clockwork. The next thing it was just after nine and they wrapped for breakfast in the bistro.

Norton got some fruit, coffee, a bit of scrambled eggs and sausages, and sat out at a table underneath the windows next to the front door. He had just about finished his meal when Pamela and the director came up. Pamela had taken off her loose fitting top and was wearing a white, brushed cotton shirt that almost fitted her. Norton immediately realised what it was about Pamela that kept intriguing him. She had one of the best set of tits he had ever seen. They made Samantha Fox's look like a pair of cocker spaniel's ears. Les tried not to make it too obvious, but he nearly bit the side out of his paper plate.

'Les,' Richard smiled as he and Pamela sat down opposite him. 'I just came to tell you, you're going absolutely sensational. You've no idea what a difference that makes to us. I just had a look at the video, and it looks great. Just great.'

'Ohh good. I'm glad.'

'With a bit of luck you'll be wrapped by lunchtime.'

'Fair dinkum.'

'Yep.' Both Richard and Pamela smiled. 'Also. We're having a bit of a drink in town tonight, if you'd like to come.'

'Sure,' shrugged Norton. 'I'm not doing anything.'

'Good. Well, I'll go back inside. Pamela will tell you all about it.'

Norton waited for a moment till Richard went back inside. 'So,' he said, turning to Pamela, 'what's the story about tonight?'

'We're all going to a disco in the city. It's called Richard's. It's in Collins Street. You can't forget it. It's the same name as the director.'

'In Collins Street eh. What do I do? Just lob up?'

'That's all. We probably won't be there till about nine. Half past.'

'Okey doke. Sounds good.'

'We'll probably have a bit of dinner. Rock on for a while. Then if you like, I've got a flat at Sandringham. You can come over and have a drink.'

'That sounds good too. You live on your own do you Pamela?'

'The flat belongs to Mr Leishman. He lets me stay there,' she added with a wink.

'Good one.'

'And if you get a bit drunk and you don't feel like driving back to the motel, I might even be able to find somewhere for you to sleep,' she purred.

'That sounds even better Pamela.'

Pamela smiled seductively and took a deep breath that nearly sent a shower of buttons all round the foyer. 'Oh. By the way. This is for you too.' She reached into her pocket and handed Norton $300 in cash.

'What's this for?'

'Your expenses. $100 a day.' Norton looked a little bewildered. 'And that car you asked for is in the parking lot at the motel. A white Ford Falcon. The keys are at the reception.'

'Ohh beauty.' Norton pocketed the money. 'Well, I certainly can't complain about Melbourne hospitality.'

Pamela got to her feet and gave Les another seductive smile. 'We do our best. And you never know, Les. The best might even be yet to come. I've got to go. I'll see you inside,' she added with a wink.

'Yeah ... righto.' Norton was almost speechless.

Christ-all-bloody-mighty, he thought as he watched her shapely backside disappear into the Neptune Room. Is this for real? I've been here one night and I've emptied out the woman who owns the motel. The ad's a piece of piss. I'm another $300 in front. And that glamour's just invited me back to her flat for a drink. I don't believe this. I think I'd better have another look in the mirror, I must be a better sort than what I think. Or Pamela needs new glasses. And Billy and George want to rubbish the joint. They're kidding. They wouldn't know sheep shit from baked beans at times.

Norton felt like he needed a bit of a walk after that; besides, it was getting a little hot and smoky in the foyer. He gave the two security guards a nod, trotted down the front steps and stood on the footpath stretching his legs while he watched the traffic, the people and the odd tram go past. He had a bit of a sniff around the trucks parked out the front; maybe he could have a bit of a mag with some of the crew, but everybody still seemed to be inside eating. One truck caught his eye. It had South Melbourne Special Effects painted on the side. Now what would they be doing here? Oh that's right. He remembered something on the script they handed him about lights and coloured smoke going off at the end. He walked around and had a look in the back. There was no-one inside. Tools, rolls of wire, pieces of pipe, cans of nails and other equipment were either hanging from the roof, sitting on benches or scattered around the floor. Jesus, what a rat's nest thought Les. A small cardboard box covered in red lettering and lying on the floor next to a coil of rope caught his eye. Hello he thought. What are they doing there? They must've fallen down. I'd better put them back on the shelf or some kid walking past might pick them up. Bloody electric detonators. It's a long time since I've used these he mused as he picked up the carton. Then one of Norton's usual, bizarre but diabolical thoughts occurred to him.

George Brennan had bought an old home unit at Coogee he wanted to do up and sell. But a team of punks were living in there and refused to budge. Les and Billy were going to go round and put the bustle on them. But a couple of them were young girls and they weren't all that keen. The old exploding-bag-of-shit-trick should help the punks change their minds.

It was a low caper to pull. You broke the glass off round a light bulb and attached an electric detonator to the filament. Around the filament you placed a small plastic-bag full of shit, which you taped to the ceiling. The victim came home, switched on the light, and bang! They got shit splattered from one end of the room to the other. Which you could only remedy by repainting and recarpeting the room.

With a devilish grin on his face, Norton slipped two of the little, bullet shaped detonators out of their polystyrene packing and into his pocket before placing the carton back on one of the shelves. Whistling innocently, he walked back up the stairs of the hotel, nodded to the two security guards and stood inside the foyer waiting for them to call him.

He was standing there, gazing around absently, when he noticed a young girl walking from the Neptune Room towards the cigarette machine. She had a mop of straggly blonde hair, the dye starting to go off in parts, and heaps of chains round her neck and rings on her fingers. She was wearing a minidress made out of recycled jeans, black lace stockings and Peter Pan kind of ankle-length boots. She didn't have a bad figure but Norton noticed she was a bit on the pale side. He recognised her as one of the caterers. She must have had her mind on the food because she didn't notice a cable on the floor and tripped over it. She pitched forward and would have gone straight on her face, only Norton reached out quickly and grabbed her arm. None too gently, but it certainly saved her from a nasty spill.

'Whoops. Hold it there kid,' he grinned. 'Just stay on your feet another round and you'll get a draw.'

'Ooh,' she squealed. 'Thanks.'

'That's okay,' Les smiled chivalrously. 'Don't tell me you've been getting into that bloody St Kilda Kooler too.'

'Hardly,' she smiled back, running a hand through her hair. 'Just watching you drink it's enough.'

'Yeah I know,' replied Les. 'Then I gotta eat your food on top of that. They ought to be paying me danger money.'

'Hey hold on, digger. There's nothing wrong with our cooking.'

'No. If you were doing twenty years in a Russian gulag, you'd probably get to like it.'

'Jesus you're a cheeky big mug,' she said, half turning her back as she pumped some coins into the cigarette machine. 'Are all Sydneysiders as cheeky as you?'

'Actually, I'm from Queensland,' smiled Norton.

'Ohh Christ. That's even worse.'

She lit a smoke, offered Les one which he declined, and they started having a bit of a friendly chitchat. Norton was just about to ask her her name when Pamela came to the door.

'When you're ready Les,' she said politely.

'Righto.' Norton turned back to the catering girl. 'Well.

I'd love to stay and talk to you, mate,' he grinned, 'but I gotta get back inside and play movie stars. I'll see you anyway.'

'No worries. Nice talking to you.'

Norton's next few scenes were even easier than the first ones. A few pick-ups here and there and a few shots of him from different angles. Half the time he spent just hanging around talking to Pamela or Richard; it couldn't have been easier and Les was ready to kiss Warren when he got back to Sydney. Though after about an hour or so of gooning around the set he did make himself one promise. The next person that said 'no worries' — be it man, woman or child — he was going to kick fair in the groin. The Melbournians were pretty heavily into rhyming slang, and he could handle that okay. But the 'no worries' every two minutes was starting to get to him.

Check the gate. No worries. How's the sound? No worries. Bit more light. No worries. Bit less smoke. No worries. Would you like a sandwich? No worries. Russia's just invaded Europe and half of California's been washed into the sea by an earthquake killing fifteen million people. No worries.

Still, he supposed, in Sydney, everyone says 'sweet' all the time. And in Queensland they say 'eh' after every sentence. But he'd never heard the expression 'no worries' flogged to death like it was on this set.

But the big Queenslander needn't have worried, because they wrapped him at eleven-fifteen. And everyone was tickled pink with his work. The director thanked him. B.O. Plenty thanked him. The whole crew, including the trendies, gave him a big cheer and wished him all the best. And they told him he could keep the St Kilda guernsey, which saved him having to steal it.

'Well come on,' said Pamela, after Norton had scraped off what little make-up there was. 'I'll run you down to the motel.'

'That's okay,' replied Les. 'I'll walk. It's only just down the road.' He stuffed the guernsey into his overnight bag, palming the two detonators in there at the same time.

'Are you sure?'

'Sure I'm sure. No bloody worries.'

'Okay.' She shrugged her shoulders, oblivious to Norton's sarcasm and they moved across to the front door. 'You're still coming tonight. Aren't you?'

'Are there shamrocks in Ireland?'

'Good.' Pamela gave Les another one of her seductive, shirt

splitting smiles. 'Then I'll see you tonight. And I'm looking forward to it.'

'Me too,' winked Norton. He paused and smiled at her. 'I'll see you tonight Pamela.'

'No worries.'

Norton winced slightly as he turned and walked down the steps. I'll give you no worries tonight when I get you back to your place, you big titted thing. When I'm finished with you, Pamela, you won't have a bloody worry in the world.

He headed briskly for the St Moritz. The sun was shining brightly and it was a beautiful day. What a bloody ripper he chuckled to himself. I was expecting to have to do that other business tomorrow. I can do it today. I'll have a quick bite to eat, pick up the car and head out to that reservoir or whatever it is. I should be back by six. Get a couple of hours sleep, then it's disco down tonight with the lovely Pamela. He grinned out across Port Phillip Bay. Melbourne. Don't believe what those mugs in Sydney say about you. You're a great little town.

Les smiled and said good morning to the girl in the office as he walked past. She gave him an odd sort of smile in return, as if possibly she may have known something about the previous night's episode with her boss. He got the lift to his room, made a cup of coffee and changed into his tracksuit and sneakers; very un-Melbourne gear for Saturday afternoon, but Les wasn't shopping for clothes or hanging around the coffee shops in Toorak Road, South Yarra.

He spread his road map of Melbourne and the outer suburbs on the bed and lay Mousey's map next to it. The little sweeper's map began to make more sense than ever now, and Whittlesea and that Yan Yean Reservoir didn't look all that hard to get to. From his travel bag he took a carpenter's retractable tape measure and a small azimuth compass he'd bought before he left Sydney and placed them on the bed too. He'd been counting on stealing or borrowing a shovel from somewhere, but seeing it was still early Saturday he should be able to find a garage or hardware store open somewhere and buy one. Nodding his head slowly, he gazed at the objects on the bed for a few moments while he sipped his coffee. Well, he thought. No good hanging around here like a stale bottle of piss. That won't get it done. Nothing to it now but to do it. He took the St Kilda guernsey out of his overnight bag and put the maps and the other little odds and ends in, then finished his coffee and went down to the foyer to pick up his car keys.

A casually but well dressed man of about fifty, thinnish with grey hair and a neat moustache, was standing behind the front desk. Norton tipped him to be Mr Perry.

'G'day mate,' said Les breezily. 'I'm Mr Norton in room 19. Is there a set of car keys here for me?'

'Yes there is,' smiled the man with the moustache. 'Here you are.' He took a set of keys from a pigeonhole and handed them to Les. 'You know where the carpark is?'

Norton nodded. 'You must be Mrs Perry's brother?' he asked.

The man looked at Norton blankly. 'Brother? I'm her husband. Whatever gave you the idea I was her brother?'

Norton gave him an equally blank look in return. 'Oh. Just something the girl from the film company said. I must have got it mixed up.'

'You must have,' smiled Mr Perry.

The girl on the switchboard gave Les the same odd smile she gave him when he walked in earlier. Just then Mrs Perry stepped out of an office down from the switchboard. She baulked only slightly when she saw Les, but not a muscle in her face moved.

'Good morning Mr Norton,' she sniffed.

'G'day Mrs Perry,' replied Les dryly. 'How are you this morning?'

'Fine thank you Mr Norton.' She gave Les a brief smile as she picked up some papers and began busying herself behind the desk.

'Well, I guess I'd better get going,' said Norton, giving the keys a jangle.

'Have a good day,' smiled Mr Perry.

Norton smiled back. As he got to the front door he stopped and turned around. 'Oh Mr Perry,' he said slowly. The owner looked up. 'There might be a couple of phone calls for me this afternoon. Could you take a message?'

'Certainly.'

'And the phone's been playing up in my room. Could you get someone to take a look at that too?'

'Certainly,' replied Mr Perry. 'I'll get my wife to take a look at it. In fact I'll do it myself.'

'You will, will you.' The smile on Norton's face turned into a rotten great grin. 'I sure can't complain about the service here.'

'We do our best,' smiled Mr Perry.

'You certainly do indeed.'

Mrs Perry still managed to keep her composure and not a muscle in her face moved. But there was a distinct colouring in her cheeks. The girl on the switchboard had no luck at all, though. She sniggered and nearly wet herself. Filthy old thing thought Norton as he walked out to the carpark. Not only did she rape me. She lied to me as well. And me a stranger in town too. Rotten bitch.

There was a Melbourne *Gregory's* in the Falcon, which Les compared to the map he'd bought in Sydney and the sweeper's. This looks easy as cake he mused. Fitzroy Street onto Punt. Punt goes into Hoddle, which goes into High Street which takes me straight out to Woodstock. A snack. He started the car, found a radio station playing reasonable music and headed north.

There wasn't all that much traffic and it was a good clear day for driving. Before long he'd found Punt Road, gone under an overpass, crossed the Yarra somewhere and was on High Street going through Richmond. Just before North Fitzroy he found a hardware store and bought a shovel and a small trenching tool. He had plenty of time and there was a Greek milk bar next door, so he had a doner kebab, a couple of baclavas and a chocolate malted. With that under his belt and the tools in the boot, he headed north again.

The streets were wide and the suburbs flat; there was scarcely a rise or a gully let alone anything remotely resembling a hill. It was nothing like driving in the congested sprawl of Sydney with a set of traffic lights on nearly every corner. Oddly enough, the lack of high rise and the old wooden buildings on either side of the road reminded Les of Townsville of all places.

As he drove on a few thoughts began to occur to him. When it all boiled down, his chances of finding whatever was buried on this obscure map were pretty slim. And Mousey had been in the nick for over twenty years, so all this could be changed anyway. And if he did find it, what would it be? After all this time it might be rotted away. Then again, it could be somebody else's loot Mousey had got onto. Oh well, who gives a stuff? Win, lose or draw. He was still over $3,000 in front. Plus a top root and a big chance for an even better one tonight. So what the hell. He'd go out there, get as close as he could to the directions on the map, and dig a few holes. If he didn't find anything, stiff shit. It was still a bit of fun driving around the Victorian countryside in a new car anyway.

A sign on the other side of a place called Epping said, Woodstock, 11 km. The countryside had opened up a bit now and houses were gradually starting to disappear. It was still a pleasant, sunny day but on either side of the road the flat sparsely-treed plains stretching out to a few low hills seemed more desolate and barren than ever. Suddenly those plains started to get hilly with more clumps of trees. Les was a bit lost in thought, listening to the radio as the miles slipped past and had to hit the brakes quickly at a sign saying, Donnybrook Road. Whittlesea, 15 km. He checked Mousey's map and smiled. This was it all right. The tyres squealed, gravel spurted and he sped up Donnybrook Road.

The road was one gentle sloping hill after another, dotted with farms and strung haphazardly with fences. The fields still looked a little dry and sparse, home to a few cows and horses and mobs of dumb-looking black-faced sheep. Around these animals were scattered rolls of hay and stock food bound tightly like bundles of roofing batts, only instead of being pink or yellow they were a dull khaki green. He topped a rise and about five kilometres in front of him was a huge, shimmering expanse of water. That's got to be the bloody reservoir. A sign on a shed saying Yan Yean Stables confirmed this. Down the bottom of that rise he came to a roundabout where Donnybrook Road met Plenty Road. A set of street signs said Melbourne to his right, Whittlesea 5 kms to his left, Reservoir Road straight ahead.

Norton checked Mousey's map again. 'This is it,' he said out loud. 'This is bloody it.' Despite his early pessimism, Norton was becoming quite excited. 'Now. What's it say here again? Follow Reservoir Road two miles. Big tree on right. Cross bridge. Four pine trees on right. Fifty yards direct south of end pine tree. Dig here.' Norton rubbed his hands together gleefully and drove on.

Mousey's map was in miles and yards but Les soon judged when he'd gone the distance. There was no big tree on the right. But there was a huge dead one bleached grey by the sun. A chipped circle around its base said that years ago someone must have got sick of seeing all those nice green leaves stopping soil erosion and giving shade and shelter to the birds; so they ringbarked it. But that could be the tree thought Les. Because if Mousey buried stuff out here years ago, before he went in the nick, that tree would have been all lush and green then. Yeah, that makes sense. He moved on and sure enough there was the little bridge. It was rickety, wooden and old, so that made sense too. He went on further and nearly couldn't believe his eyes. Just off the road to his right, before it meandered up the hill to the reservoir, was a row of pine trees. Instead of four there were closer to twenty, but the four on this end were noticeably bigger than the others. Well that bloody well makes sense too, thought Norton. There could have been four there to start off with and somebody's planted a few more. That's why they're smaller. Well I'll be buggered. This is dead-set bloody it all right. This is fuckin' it. You little bloody beauty. Hardly able to control his excitement, Norton did a U-turn, pulled up in the shade of the pine trees, got out of the car and had a look around.

There were a few farm houses a kilometre or so from where he stood, the fields fenced off in front to keep the stock from wandering onto the road. Unexpectedly, there was a church just off the road about fifty metres the bridge side of the end pine tree. That's funny, thought Les. It doesn't say anything on the map about a church. Then again that church doesn't look all that old and probably wasn't built when Mousey buried whatever it is out here. In fact, thought Norton, twenty or so years ago there probably wasn't much here at all. Only the reservoir and that bridge. There wasn't anyone around so Les walked over to the little church for a closer look.

It wasn't very big and was made of whitewashed wooden panelling built up on concrete piers. The front door was locked but there was a two-door open vestibule built over that with two sets of wooden stairs running into it. Above the vestibule was a wooden cross bolted to the panelling and below that was painted the figure of a man standing legs apart, arms outstretched, in a circle inside a triangle. Above all of this was painted, in red, Church of Scientific Achievement. Can't say I've ever heard of this mob of bible-bashers thought Norton. Oh well. God bless them, whoever they are. Anyway it's time I got to work. Norton went back to the car, got the map, the compass and the tape measure from his bag, and with his adrenalin starting to pump a little now, walked across to the end pine tree.

For such an unusually fine spring day, Norton thought there might have been more cars or people around. He'd only seen a couple on the road in and none since he'd pulled up. Just as well I s'pose, he thought. Whistling happily he flipped open the azimuth compass. The needle spun round and Norton adjusted the points. Due south was directly towards the church. Les checked it again. Yep. That was due south all right. With a big grin he tacked one end of the tape measure to the pine tree and began running out fifty yards. The tape was in both yards and metres so that was no problem. It was easy. Easy. Norton kept grinning and following the compass needle and running out the tape measure in the direction of the little church, which was suddenly starting to get closer and closer to the fifty yard mark.

Yes, it was easy all right. Too bloody easy. Norton's grin had started to disappear and he couldn't quite believe it when he found fifty yards due south of that end pine tree was spot-on with one of the corners of the Church of Scientific Achievement. He looked at the spot, frowned, wound the tape up and measured it again. One of the concrete piers supporting the church was right where fifty yards south was. Les measured it out again, even allowing a few inches for the growth of the tree over the years. But Norton could have allowed for the rotation of the planets over the last twenty or so years: fifty yards due south of that pine tree was smack-bang on line with one corner of the church. And whatever Mousey had buried here, twenty years ago or whenever it was, now had a dirty-great concrete pier sitting on top of it, and a fairly soundly constructed wooden church built on top of that.

Ohh no I don't believe this, Norton cursed to himself. I just don't bloody well believe it. But after futilely checking it out one more time, even wriggling the tape measure around in desperation, it was true. As true as God made little apples.

'You fuckin' idiot Mousey,' Norton cursed out loud. 'Why couldn't you have buried it fifty yards north? Or west? You stupid little prick. You deserve to be in bloody gaol.'

But you couldn't blame the Mouse. How was he to know that someone would build a church on that spot.

Norton gave the side of the church a good boot. 'Fuckin' bible-bashin' bastards,' he bellowed. 'Why couldn't you build your rotten, fucking church somewhere else? You brainwashed bunch of hypocrites.'

But you couldn't blame the brethren of the Church of Scientific Achievement for building their house of worship there. It was a beautiful little valley they'd picked just down

251

from the Yan Yean Reservoir. Peaceful, green, secluded and almost in the shade of those lovely pine trees. An ideal place for worshipping the Lord or whoever it was the disciples worshipped. And the elders of the Church probably got the land for next to nothing, too. So there was no way in the world that you could blame them.

'Bugger it,' Norton cursed again. 'I should have known something would go wrong.' His darkening brown eyes moved balefully towards the sky. 'You're crooked on me aren't you. I know it. You always have been.'

Then a thought occurred to him. Maybe he could dig around it. He checked out around the pier. No, there was a big rock just on the pine trees side of it, so that stopped that. And he didn't know how far the pier went down. If he dug down and got underneath it, the bloody thing could collapse on him. He'd be there a month no matter what he did. The only way he could get to that loot would be to dynamite the bloody thing. And that was just out of the question.

Norton stepped back, shaking his head as he let go with another string of curses. 'Well, that's bloody that ain't it. Thanks anyway Mousey. You wombat.'

He rolled up the tape measure, walked back to the car and threw it and the compass back in his overnight while he dumped his backside heavily down on the driver's seat. He'd put some fruit from the motel in the bag so he picked up an apple and started chewing on it morosely while he stared glumly out the windscreen at nothing in particular. The way he was chewing, the apple didn't last long so he put his hand back in the bag to find the two mandarins that were in there somewhere. While he was groping around another two little objects caught his eye. The pair of electric detonators. And another thought suddenly hit Norton like a light bulb of pure diabolical wickedness shining above his head.

I'm out in the bush. I've got the detonators. Why don't I make a home-made bomb and blow that bloody pier to the shithouse. This is farming country. I could get the stuff and knock one up in no time. He checked his watch. It was just after two. Jesus, with a bit of luck I might be able to find a hardware store and a chemist still open. Bloody oath. Why not? He hit the starter, jerked the car into drive and sped off in the direction of Whittlesea.

A toboggan hire, set into the hills on either side of Plenty Road, was the first thing Norton saw that told him he was getting into Whittlesea. The local hardware store, still open, was a little further on. A ramshackle old house, a pub and a garage were next to it. Jesus, thought Les, I hope there's a bit more to the place than just that. He turned right at a saddlery opposite a roundabout and drove down a few hundred metres to where a statue of a soldier faced the main street from in front of another row of pine trees.

Turning left at the war memorial, Norton could see Whittlesea was a typical Australian small country town. One wide street flanked by various old wooden shops. The only one that seemed to stick out was the local barber shop complete with a red-and-white striped pole out the front. A St Vincent de Paul opportunity shop sat next to it, its windows full of old clothes and other bric-a-brac. The whole place had that sleepy appearance of a town that hadn't changed much in fifty years; like something out of a book on early Australiana. Nice little town mused Norton, but I'm not here to play *Ask the Leyland Brothers*. It's down to business. The chemist shop and supermarket are still open, but I'll go to the hardware store first.

The two front windows were dusty and full of dead flies and everything else you'd expect to see in a country hardware store. As he got out of the car Norton noticed that the owner was an agent for the ANZ Bank and for Australian Explosives and Detonator Company. Bloody hell, he thought. Look at that. That'd make things a bloody sight easier. But then again, a stranger in town buying dynamite... Anyway, if I can remember the recipe, this'll work just as well. A little bell above the flyscreen rang as he entered the shop.

Inside, the little store was just as dusty and cluttered as the front windows. Tins of paint and gas bottles were stacked haphazardly next to chainsaws, primuses, rolls of fencing and water pump parts. A wizened old man in a grey dustcoat and flanelette shirt appeared from out of nowhere at the sound of the bell. With his unruly hair and glasses perched on the end of his nose he looked just as dusty and cluttered as his shop.

'You just caught me young fella,' he said with a wheezy smile. 'Another two minutes and I'd've closed up.'

'Good on you mate,' winked Norton.

'So what can I do you for?' The owner hobbled around behind the counter.

'Well mate. I need a bag of superphosphate and a can of thinners for a start.'

'No worries.'

Norton shook his head. 'You'd have to say that, wouldn't you.' The owner reached down behind the counter, got what Les ordered and placed them on top. 'Righto. I'll tell you what else I want,' nodded Norton.

He ordered the other materials for his home-made explosive, materials that can be bought in just about any hardware store. The owner found a cardboard carton and began stacking them in it.

'I'm gonna need about ten metres of copper wire too,' said Norton.

The owner shook his head. 'Can't help you there lad. The most I can give you is about twelve feet. I ran out on Thursday and I'm waiting for the truck from Melbourne on Monday.'

'Shit! Do you know where I might be able to get some?'

'There's a TV repair shop at the far end of town,' replied the owner, screwing his face up. 'You could try him. But I think he closes at twelve.'

'I'll try him anyway.' Norton gritted his teeth slightly and checked what was in the carton. 'Okay. Give us a plastic bucket, a pair of pliers and a can opener, and that should just about do me.'

'No worries.'

'Righto. Now what do I owe you?'

The owner itemised everything on the bill and rang up $87.80.

Norton paid him, thanked him and left the shop. He put the carton on the back seat of the Ford and drove up to the garage. He wanted a can of diesel fuel, but they could only give it to him in a plastic container. He got four litres and a large can of oil. These went in the boot.

Norton was a bit concerned when he cruised down the main street to find the TV shop closed. Three metres of copper wire was a bit too close for his liking. Maybe he'd find some somewhere else.

The chemist shop was easy and the skinny young chemist very helpful. He had everything Norton needed including the zinc oxide. The only thing that made the chemist a little curious was why Norton needed 300 grams. The six rolls of sticking plaster, the eye-dropper and two large torch batteries were a clue.

All Les needed in the supermarket was icing sugar and rubber gloves, plus a couple of Cherry Ripes to chew on while he was working. His only problem now was to find some more wire of some description. Three metres was definitely too close. If the bomb worked properly, and if it didn't blow his head off, at that distance it could possibly deafen him. He decided to drift around the shops and see if he could spot something while he chewed on one of his Cherry Ripes.

He strolled over to the St Vincent de Paul opportunity shop and gazed absently in the window. He was going to need a couple of old T-shirts or something to wipe his hands on and clean up that oil. Then something just inside the window caught his eye and solved his problem.

There were two apple-faced elderly women in the shop having a cup of tea and some scones when Les walked in. They had blue-rinse hair, twin-sets with pearl necklaces and were all matronly charm and smiles.

'Hello young man,' beamed one. 'What can we do for you?'

'I'll just have a bit of a look around,' replied Norton, returning the smile. 'I might find something I like.'

'No worries.' The two women went back to their tea, scones and conversation as Les drifted in amongst the racks of old clothes, tables of shoes, books, handbags and dozens of other odds and ends people had discarded.

An old three-in-one stereo had caught his eye from outside the window. Sitting on top of the speakers were two neatly rolled bundles of extension lead. Norton quickly ran his hands over them and judged them to be at least six metres long. Plenty. Jesus he thought. A man'd be a low bastard to steal something out of a St Vincent de Paul shop. I mean, that is about as low as you can get. With a deft tug he tore the two leads from the back of the speakers and dropped them down the front of his tracksuit top. The two old biddies, still munching away on their tea and scones, were completely oblivious to Norton's daring but heinous crime. On the way back to the counter Les picked up a couple of T-shirts.

'How much for these?' he asked, dropping them on the glass top.

'Those two,' said the woman closest. 'Oh a dollar. Is that all right?'

'Fair enough.' Les pulled out a fifty and dropped it on the counter.

'Oh, dear, I don't think we can change that.'

'Can't you. Ohh well. Don't worry about it. I like to give a donation to the church now and again anyway.'

'Ooh goodness,' said the other woman. 'That's a lot of money.'

'Ahh that's okay,' smiled Norton. 'I'm a good Catholic boy.'

'You must be,' beamed the first woman. 'Thank you very much.'

'That's okay.'

'There should be more young Christian gentlemen around like you,' she said. 'Not like some others in the district we know. Eh Doris.'

'That's perfectly right Thelma. Not like some others.'

'What do you mean by that?' asked Norton. He wasn't in all that much of a hurry and the almost shocked look on Doris had him curious.

'Those people up in Reservoir Road,' she replied with an indignant roll of her eyes.

'Reservoir Road?' That name rings a bell thought Norton.

'Yes. That church of scientific mumbo-jumbo. Or whatever it is they call themselves.'

'You mean the Church of Scientific Achievement,' said Les. 'What? They no good are they?'

'No good,' huffed Doris. 'They're absolutely disgraceful. They've broken up at least six families in the district with their brainwashing methods. They get the children you know.'

'Go on, eh,' said Norton, trying hard not to laugh.

'And poor old Mr Collier,' said Thelma. 'It was dreadful the way they got his land off him. He's almost ninety too. Poor old soul.'

Norton looked at the two gossipy old matrons. Christ, I'd hate to get on the wrong side of this pair. 'Oh well,' he chuckled, folding up the two T-shirts, 'the good Lord works in mysterious ways. You never know. These people might get their just deserts one of these days.'

'Oh they'll get their comeuppances one day young man,' intoned Doris. 'Mark my words.'

'I'm marking,' smiled Norton. He picked up the T-shirts and moved towards the door. 'Anyway. I must get going. I'll see you again.'

'Goodbye young man. God bless you. And thank you very much for the donation.'

For some reason Les couldn't help himself. He stopped at the doorway, turned around, grinned and stuck his thumb up. 'No worries,' he said with a huge wink.

Well that's about it I think, mused Les, dropping the T-shirts on the back seat of the car. He had a look at his watch, it was just after three. He still had plenty of time because it would be no good blowing up that pier till it was dark, which should be six o'clock at the latest. That should give him ample time to drive back to Melbourne, get cleaned up and be at that disco to meet Pamela by nine-thirty. Sweet, he thought. Or as they so often like to say around these here parts, no worries.

Les decided to grab a half dozen cans at the pub as he drove back out along Plenty Road. He didn't turn left into Reservoir, however. He went another five kilometres further on towards Melbourne, found a secluded little place just off the road under some trees and stopped there.

Now. How did me and Murray and the old man use to make these bloody things? I can remember the ingredients but I'm not too sure of the measurements he pondered as he spread some on the grass and others on the roof of the car. Christ, it's been bloody years. You start with the super-phosphate don't you. But how much did we use? The old man used to measure it in ounces. Was it a pound? Oh well, a bit more won't hurt. He threw closer to 800 grams in the plastic bucket and added half the icing sugar, then gradually added the other materials leaving the zinc oxide till last. Satisfied there was enough there, he gave it a good stir with his hands.

He opened the bonnet of the car, uncapped the battery and filled the eye dropper with battery acid. Now, how much acid do we use? Four drops? Ohh bugger it. He squirted the lot into the bucket. As soon as it hit the other elements it started smouldering and giving off poisonous fumes. Right. Got to hurry now. But what goes in next? The thinners, the diesel or the piss? And how much do I use? Ohh s'pose it doesn't matter all that much. He poured in nearly all the thinners and half the diesel and pissed about half a cupful on top of that. With the rubber gloves on now, he churned everything up in the bucket till it was about the same consistency as plaster of Paris. Looks a bit thick he thought. He added the rest of the thinners, most of the diesel and a little more urine. Which made it too thin. So he added more fertilizer and the rest of the icing sugar.

He tipped all the oil out of the can, opened the top half way around with the can opener, then wiped any excess oil off with one of the T-shirts and a bit of petrol. Watching to make sure he didn't catch his hands on the jagged edges, Norton started packing the mix into the can. When it was full, he got a thick piece of branch and pounded more in until it was packed solid. I don't know, he thought, looking at it while he had a swallow from his can of beer, there seems to be a lot more there than what we used to use. Oh well. As long as it works, that's the main thing.

With the pliers and a small pocket-knife he had in his overnight bag Norton managed to punch a hole in the middle of the top of the can. He wound the length of copper wire he'd bought at the hardware store to the small wire fuse on the detonator, then pushed the detonator down into the mix with a stick. He threaded the wire through the hole in the lid, then flattened it down. After that it was only a matter of binding the lid down tight with the sticking plaster, which he did over another can of Carlton Draught. Norton then had a crude, rather heavy home-made bomb, roughly the same size as a two litre can of oil.

Well if that don't work, thought Norton, nothing will. He had another look at it while he finished his beer. I dunno. It just seems a bit bigger and heavier than the ones me and the old man used to make. Still, that's a pretty solid pier I've got to blow. He gave his shoulders a shrug. Then again, the bloody thing mightn't work at all. Still, you can only try.

There were two cans of beer left. Les had another one, checked his watch and had a look at the sun. It would be dark in around an hour and a half. He put the radio on softly and decided to have a sleep on the front seat for a while. But the five beers must have put him in a bit of a coma and it was just after seven when he woke up.

Shit thought Norton, blinking at the dashboard clock. I'd better get bloody moving. He had a quick leak while he checked around the car to make sure he hadn't left any mess or incriminating evidence behind, then sped off back to Reservoir Road.

With the pine trees swaying gently behind it in the moonlight, the little church looked more peaceful and serene than ever when Les pulled up opposite and switched off his headlights. There was no-one around and the only signs of any life were the lowing of a few cows and the faint lights of some distant farmhouses. He drove down a little further, did a U-turn to bring him under the pine trees and killed the motor.

After standing cautiously in the shadows for a few moments, Norton opened the boot and took out the bomb, the trenching tool, the batteries and the speaker leads. He put the batteries in the pocket of his tracksuit top and walked across to the church, leaving the boot of the car open. He had a small torch with him, but the light from an almost full moon was enough for him to see what he was doing. It didn't take long, barely enough to raise a sweat, and he had a hole dug between the pier and the rock about a metre deep. That ought to be heaps deep enough he thought. He attached the leads to the copper wire, bound them with sticking plaster and placed the bomb in the hole, lid against the rock. He pushed it in firmly, then covered it with soil, patting that down firmly with his feet as well. There was a small culvert about midway between the church and the pine trees. Les ran the leads out behind him and lay down there. It didn't take him long to rip the batteries out of their plastic covering and tape them together with sticking plaster. The ends of the speaker leads were already exposed so that was it. He was ready to go.

Well, thought Norton, wedging the batteries into the soil and positioning the speaker wires just above the points. If this thing works properly it should just blow that pier away. And I can soon toss out any bits of concrete left over, then dig around a bit before anyone comes over to see what the noise was. Anyway, here we go. He held the leads above the batteries, had a last look around to make sure there were no passing cars, put his face down and touched the wires to the points.

Les was right that he knew the correct materials. But he'd certainly stuffed up the measurements. The charge went off like a car-bomb in Beirut. There was an almost ear splitting *Ka-Blam* that shook the ground around him and sent a tremendous thunderclap rolling and echoing through the surrounding hills and valleys. Wide eyed, his ears still ringing, Norton looked up just in time to see a huge orange and black fireball illuminate the surrounding countryside as it spiralled up into the night sky through the ashes, burning cinders and other debris raining down around him. In its glow Les couldn't quite believe his eyes. The concrete pier was gone all right. So was the vestibule and half the side of the church. What hadn't been blown away was burning and the fire was spreading fast.

'Jesus bloody Christ!' said Norton as he watched the tongues of flame licking hungrily up towards the roof of the church. 'I knew I shouldn't have used all that icing sugar.'

The fireball disappeared, and apart from the crackle of the spreading flames, there was a profound silence following the explosion. Then every dog on every farm for miles started barking. Terrified horses were whinnying and galloping through the fields among the startled, lowing cattle. Even the roosters and chickens started getting into the act as more lights from the farms in the area were switched on. It was pandemonium. Then a kerosene heater or something blew up inside the church, adding to the din.

Les couldn't believe what a balls-up he'd made of things. There shouldn't have been too much noise, but this sounded like a cross between the Edinburgh Military Tattoo and the Tet Offensive. It would only be a matter of time now and all the local farmers would be rushing over to see what was going on. Then the local fire brigade, and finally the police. He shoved the batteries in his pocket, grabbed the trenching tool and ran towards the church.

Norton didn't need a flashlight or the light from the moon to see what he was doing; there was more than enough light from the flames rapidly spreading through what was left of the church. The pier was well and truly gone. All that was left was a crater about a metre and a half deep by about two across. Not a brick or a piece of concrete was to be seen. The boulder was split in two and had obviously taken most of the blast. Jesus, it's a good thing that was there thought Les, or the whole bloody lot might have gone up. He jumped in the hole and started digging around frantically, knowing he didn't have a great deal of time.

The earth was moist and clingy but the explosion had loosened it up quite a bit. Norton dug away like a man possessed while panels and burning lengths of timber began crashing down from the church, sending sparks and glowing ash showering around him. Silhouetted in the flames of the burning church, the trenching tool rising and falling above his head, Norton began to take on the appearance of some madman in a B-grade horror film. You can bet your life whatever was buried here got blown away in the blast he thought as another shower of sparks and ash flew over him. But the big Queenslander's luck was in in one respect. He'd only been digging a minute or two when he hit something. Quickly he dug deeper as the light from the flames revealed a corner of rotted sack. Les grabbed it but it tore off in his hand. A few more digs revealed it was wrapped around something. Quickly he dug around it and pulled it out. The rotted sack was bound with equally rotted rope that crumbled in his hand. The old sack crumbled just as easily as he tore it away. The next thing, to both his joy and amazement Norton was standing holding an old black metal strongbox now covered by a thick film of damp rust. It was roughly the same shape as a telephone book but about half as big again; a heavy old-fashioned metal lock, now corroded solid, was attached to the front. Norton gave it a shake and something shifted inside.

'This is it,' he shouted out, eyes wide with excitement. 'This is bloody it. Mousey — you bloody little beauty.' With a big grin plastered across his dirt-caked face, Norton let out a cheer when a heavy beam crashed down from the church sending a shower of burning embers and hot coals over him; they burnt the side of his face and singed his hair as they stuck to his tracksuit and started smouldering. 'Oww, shit!' Les closed one eye and cursed at the pain.

He dropped the strongbox and started brushing the burning pieces of wood from his face and clothing. The pain down the side of his face hurt like a dozen wasp stings. The little church was totally ablaze now and the heat around Norton was intensifying. Les hadn't noticed it at first but he did now, especially with half his clothing almost alight. It was more than time for him to get out of there. He picked up the trenching tool and the strong box and sprinted for the car. Lights were approaching from the hills running up towards the reservoir.

The strongbox and trenching tool had hardly hit the floor of the boot when Norton slammed it shut. He jumped behind the wheel, hit the motor and without switching on the headlights did a U-turn and roared back up Reservoir Road. He made it to the other side of the little bridge just as an approaching utility reached it and could faintly see the startled look on the driver's face as he went past. He switched the headlights on as he reached the roundabout at Plenty Road and raced straight up the hills of Donnybrook past another two farm trucks speeding towards the burning church. In the rear-vision mirror it was an inferno now lighting up the countryside for what seemed like miles around. Les had turned left into High Street and was about two kilometres along it on the way back to Melbourne when he heard the sirens and the first fire engine roared past. A couple of minutes later another one went by, followed closely by a police car. He slowed down a bit then. All I need now is to get pulled over for speeding.

Before long Norton had reached the outer suburbs of Melbourne. He slowed down for some traffic and had a quick look at his face in the rear-vision mirror. What he could make out didn't look all that good and it also hurt like buggery; not to mention the holes in his tracksuit. But the bit of pain and some ruined clothing couldn't dampen his enthusiasm. He was grinning to himself like a kid in an ice-cream shop. He'd done it. He still wasn't quite sure what it was he'd done or achieved, apart from burning down some poor pack of bastards' church. But it was quite a caper and Les was rapt. He stopped not far from where he'd bought the tools earlier and got some vaseline and cotton wool at an all-night chemist's, then drove back to St Kilda.

The Saturday night traffic heading back into Melbourne was heavy and in the darkness Les took a couple of wrong turns. It was well after nine when he drove into the St Moritz Motel. There was a large commercial waste bin almost next to where he parked the car. He dropped the leftovers from the bomb in it, along with the trenching tool. The shovel, which he never used, he left next to some other tools standing in one corner of the parking area. No one would know where it came from. He jammed the strongbox as far as he could into his overnight bag, and with one hand covering his face, walked briskly through the foyer to his room. The girl on the switchboard had her head down and didn't even see him.

After stripping off Norton examined himself in the bathroom mirror. He didn't look too good at all. His hair was singed in front, the right eyebrow was almost gone and the skin around his forehead and cheekbone was blackened, red and blistered. And bloody painful. In a way he was lucky that burning piece of wood hadn't blinded him when it fell. Shit, he thought, screwing up his face in the mirror. What am I going to tell Pamela? I look like the phantom of the bloody opera. Oh well, I s'pose I'll think of something. And I'd better get moving too. It's getting late. He got under the shower and when he washed his dirt-streaked hair, the hot, soapy water stung his face like buggery. He couldn't lather part of it, either, when he got out to have a shave. Consequently, one half of his face looked okay, the other half looked rougher than five miles off Sydney Heads. Great red blisters, tufts of stubble everywhere, and a missing eyebrow to go with it. Jesus. I wonder what Warren's going to think when I get home, Norton chuckled to himself.

Despite his discomfort, Les was still on quite a high. He picked up the strongbox when he came out of the bathroom and gave it a good shake. There was something in there. But what? It could be anything. There was no chance of him opening it there. Apart from the huge old lock being corroded solid, the box was rusted shut as well. It would be a hacksaw, hammer and possibly electric drill job when he got it back to Sydney. Jesus I'd love to know what's in the bloody thing he mused as he dropped it back on the bed. Les was still thinking on it when the phone rang just after he'd changed into a white collarless shirt, dress jeans and his black R. M. Williams.

'Hello Mr Norton. There's a call for you from Sydney. A Mr Edwards.'

'Thanks miss.'

'Hello Les?'

'Yeah. Is that you Woz?'

'Yeah. How are you mate?' Warren sounded very bright and bubbly and loud over the phone. He also sounded like he'd had the odd drink or two as well.

'I'm pretty good Woz. How's yourself?'

'Sen-fucking-sational. Les. I had to ring up to thank you for what you did on the ad. Les, it's turned out absolutely sensational. Melbourne rang us straight after they'd seen the rushes. And they're ecstatic. Everyone's chuffed to the teeth.'

'Ohh well, that's good isn't it.'

'You can say that again.' Warren paused on the line for a moment. 'Les. I hate to say this. But I am relieved you know.'

'What do you mean, relieved?'

'Well. I was a bit worried you'd fuck everything up.'

'Ohh get stuffed will you. You rotten little nark.'

'Well you know what happened last time.'

'Yeah. But that was Brisbane. They're all hillbillies up there. Or so you keep telling me. This is Melbourne mate. They're all my type of people down here. All conservative and nice. And friendly. I was in my creative element.'

'Whatever,' chuckled Warren. 'Anyway, the shoot's turned out fantastic — and Les, you'll love this. There's another little bonus in it for you.'

'Fair dinkum.'

'Yep. The agency's going to give you $5000.'

'Go on. Well how about that? And so they fuckin' well should. I am talent you know.'

'Ohh yes Les. You're Sam Neill and Eddie Murphy rolled into one.'

The pair of them had a good laugh over the phone. Les

263

was happy for Warren and he also couldn't believe another $2000 had dropped in. Warren was happy because he knew his Jag-clad backside was as good as behind the wheel of the company Porsche; plus any other little lurks and perks his jubilant bosses would throw his way for sending Les along.

'So how's Melbourne treating you Les? Did you end up finding that old uncle of yours?'

'Yeah,' lied Norton. 'It turned out he was living just over in ah . . . South Melbourne.'

'How was he? Glad to see you?'

'Yeah. He was rapt. But you wouldn't believe it. He got me to clean up an old kerosene heater for him. And the fuckin' thing blew up in my face.'

'Shit! Are you all right?'

'Yeah. My face got a bit burnt, that's all.'

'Jesus. That's no good.'

'Yeah. I just hope it doesn't affect my career in modelling.'

'Ohh for God's sake don't ruin your movie star looks Les.'

They continued talking and laughing for a while, till Warren thanked Les again then hung up telling him he'd pick him up when he landed in Sydney on Sunday. Norton couldn't help but sit there and smile for a while after he'd put the phone down. Apart from his burnt face this Melbourne trip was turning out better and better. He had Mousey's strong box and whatever was in it, he was $5000 richer, and he had a date tonight with a dead-set glamour. Why wouldn't he smile? It wasn't long before Les was laughing out loud.

He made himself a nice strong bourbon and Coke and sipped it while he finished getting dressed. He wrapped the strong-box in his ruined tracksuit, stuffed it in his travel bag and shoved it under the bed. There was no point in taking the car into town. He'd probably get lost and Pamela would more than likely have one with her anyway. A quick call to the desk had a cab waiting outside for him ten minutes later. Norton finished his drink, put his black leather jacket on and was soon sitting in a Silver Top taxi heading for Collins Street and his date with the lovely and massive-breasted Pamela.

The Greek cab driver gave Les an odd sort of look when he got in the front seat, and an even odder one when he said he was going to Richard's. But Norton was completely oblivious to this, and oblivious to a number of other things as well. Like the bomb squad, the arson squad, TV crews, newspaper reporters, more detectives and other interested parties going over what was left of the Church of Scientific Achievement in Reservoir Road and asking questions around Whittlesea. Norton and the cabbie wouldn't have said more than a dozen words between them as they cruised through the night. Norton only had one thing on his mind. Or two things would be more like it. Pamela's tits. Before long they'd crossed Kings Bridge, turned down Collins Street and were outside the disco. Norton paid the cabbie and stepped onto the footpath.

Richard's was built on the corner of a sort of arcade leading into an international-class hotel built all around it like an old Gothic building you'd expect to see somewhere on the Rhine. There was a discreet neon sign above the huge door, lots of shiny brass railings, windows all over the place and several neat little trees out the front. A small set of steps and another brass railing led up to the disco. The whole place looked terribly, terribly pukka and mega-trendy. Norton figured this would be where every snob, scene-stealer and social cockroach in Melbourne would put on their glamour gear and make a beeline for it on Saturday night, hoping to see their photo in the papers the next day. But Norton couldn't have given a stuff who went there. He had a wallet full of money and Pamela waiting for him inside. He joined a small group of dressed-to-kill Saturday nighters and followed them up the stairs.

The Saturday nighters got in no troubles, even getting a half smile from the dark-haired girl on the door as they went through. But the steps were as far as Norton got. The girl on the door nearly had a stroke when she got her first glimpse of Les. If the wooden door hadn't been so big, she would have slammed it in his face. If there had been a moat around Richard's, she would have filled it full of alligators, raised the drawbridge and sent down a shower of arrows. Norton's friendly smile was met by a very frosty one.

'I'm sorry, it's members only in here.' She had hostile, overly made-up eyes and a tight, sour little mouth that was so small it looked as if she'd need a shoehorn to take an Aspro.

However, Les was expecting this. The old 'members' only dodge is the first thing people on doors put on you if they don't like the look of your head. Les and Billy used it plenty of times themselves. And Norton knew that at the moment his head wasn't the most likeable look in Melbourne either.

'Yeah, fair enough,' he smiled, 'but I've arranged to meet some people inside. They're expecting me. And I'm pretty sure they're members.'

The girl on the door ignored this, stepping back to let some people in and keeping a steely eye on Norton as she did.

'Miss,' said Norton politely. 'If you don't mind. I'm down from Sydney and these people are waiting for me inside. You'd probably know them yourself.'

At the mention of Sydney the girl on the door seemed to bristle. 'I don't care if you're down from Jupiter,' she sniffed. 'It's members only here. And you — are not coming inside.'

Norton gave a little exasperated sigh and a gesture with his hands. 'Look miss,' he pleaded, 'I'm not trying to be clever, or put something over you. But these people are expecting me. How about just letting me in for five minutes and I'll see if I can find them. They should be in the dining room. Or could you page them for me and let them know I'm here. The girl's name is Pamela. And one of the men's names is Richard. He's a film director.'

At the mention of Richard there appeared to be a brief flicker of recognition in the girl's eyes. However, she had made up her mind that Norton was off tap and that was it.

'We do not page people here,' she huffed. 'And you are not getting in. Now I'm getting busy and you are blocking the stairs. Would you please go away.'

The girl was just being unreasonable and bitchy now. Fair enough, Les did look like the wreck of the *Hesperus*, but he was being polite and he was dressed cleanly enough; it wouldn't hurt her at least to check some ID or get someone to escort him inside to see if he could find his friends. Billy and Les had done it plenty of times themselves for people at the Kelly Club when they'd come up looking a bit too casual but needing to see someone inside. But he was getting absolutely stonewalled by the girl and he could see what should have been a good night being completely stuffed up. Norton was also starting to get the shits.

'Ohh look, for Christ's sake, what's wrong with getting someone to go inside and see if those people are in the dining room. Jesus, it'd take you two bloody minutes.'

The girl on the door became more defiant and hostile than ever. 'I am not paging anyone for you,' she snapped. 'And you are not coming in. Now will you go away? I won't ask you again.'

'Ahh won't ask me again,' mimicked Norton. 'What are you? A wombat from Mars? You'd think I had two bloody heads or something.'

'Oh, you want to get clever do you.' She reached above her head. A few more Saturday nighters filed in and next thing two huge bouncers in short-sleeved white shirts and bow ties appeared behind her.

They weren't so much huge as they were tall. The dark-haired one with the moustache on Norton's right was six foot six. His mate had to be close to six foot ten. The taller one had a fleshy sort of mouth and a pinched nose that didn't look like it had stopped too many punches for a bouncer. But they both had long, powerful arms and neither was carrying much fat. Norton tipped them to be Aussie Rules players.

'What's the trouble Julia?' asked the taller bouncer.

The girl on the door jabbed a finger with plenty of nail polish on it at Norton. 'This... this person here. I've told him he can't come in, and he refuses to go away.'

Norton looked up at the taller bouncer towering over him two steps above. 'Mate,' he pleaded. 'I've arranged to meet some people inside, that's all. And the girl won't let me in for some reason.'

The taller bouncer shrugged his shoulders. 'Nothing I can do about it mate. She's the boss. If she says you can't come in, you can't come in. Sorry.'

'Yeah, but Christ.'

'Mate, she's in charge,' said the bouncer with the moust-ache. 'Whatever she says goes. Nothing we can do about it. Sorry mate,' he added with a shrug.

At least the two bouncers weren't putting any shit on Les and were showing a bit more commonsense and manners than the would-be glamour on the door. Not that that was going to do Norton's chances any good. It was futile and starting to become obvious that he was going to miss out on his date with Pamela.

'Ohh I don't bloody well believe this,' he said, shaking his head in exasperation. 'Fair dinkum. I've come down from Sydney and these people are waiting for me inside. What have I got to do to get into this joint?'

Full of cheek now that she had the two bouncers behind her, Julia gave Norton an extra supercilious look. 'You could try going back to Sydney and getting another head,' she sneered.

The two bouncers remained silent, trying not to smile as Norton rapidly came to the boil. But even through his rage and frustration, Norton could see the hopelessness of it all. The only way he was going to get into Richard's would be to go through the bouncers. Which didn't appear to be a particularly easy job as it was. And say he did manage to flatten them. You could bet there'd be more inside. And say he did fight his way to the dining room and found Pamela, he'd be covered in blood with all his clothing torn when he did. That would look good wouldn't it? Then he'd probably get lumbered with an assault charge on top of it. No. It was all over now. Norton's big Saturday night out in Melbourne had just gone down the gurgler thanks to one snooty girl on a door.

'Yeah righto,' he sighed, looking daggers at Julia. 'Thanks a bloody lot.' He turned on his heel and walked back down the steps, just as another half dozen Saturday nighters trotted happily up.

'Sorry old mate,' he heard one of the bouncers call out. Norton dismissed him with a wave of his hand.

Go back to Sydney and get another head, he muttered darkly to himself. Fuckin' smart arse. I'd like to go back and kick her right in the snatch, the rotten fuckin' bitch. The moll. She's certainly stuffed up my night. And got away with it. Norton let go another string of curses, then he suddenly propped and scratched his chin thoughtfully, his eyes sort of darting fiendishly from one side of his face to the other. He gave it a minute or two, then walked back to the disco.

Julia's eyes narrowed with anger and annoyance when she saw Norton at the bottom of the stairs. She was about to reach above her head when Les made an easy gesture with his hands.

'Hold on a second miss,' he smiled sweetly. 'I don't want to come in. I was just wondering though if you'd care to do me a favour?' Julia glared at him impassively as Les stepped up a little closer. 'If Richard, the film director I mentioned earlier, should happen to ask if I've been here looking for him, could I leave a message with you?'

The girl nodded curtly. 'Yes very well. What is it?'

'Would you tell him Nigel called and I'm going straight back to Sydney. And we're moving Monday's shoot from Manly to Spit Junction. Okay?'

'All right.'

Les smiled at her. 'Do you know where Spit Junction is?' he asked, almost melodiously.

'No I don't.'

'Well it's right here darling.'

Norton sucked some air in through his nose, hawked at the back of his throat and spat right in Julia's face. It was a mammoth gob. It didn't travel far but it splattered all over her face like lumps of a jellyfish that had drowned in Coca-Cola. Julia let out a piercing shriek and mopped at her eyes and what was left of her make-up.

'See you later — you miserable lookin' drop kick,' smiled Norton. He trotted back down the steps and walked briskly up Collins Street in search of a cab.

Norton was about a hundred or so metres from the disco when he heard a voice call out, 'Hey you.' He looked over his shoulder and the two bouncers were standing out on the footpath pointing at him. He ignored them and kept walking. 'Hey you with the red hair,' one of them shouted out again. 'Come here.' Norton turned around to give them the finger and noticed they'd started walking briskly towards him. He propped for a moment and debated whether it would be worth confronting them. Even though they'd both get an awful shock if they tried anything with him, would it be worth wrestling around on the footpath getting his shirt and good leather jacket ripped? Also, his face was sore enough as it was without having to cop a few punches on it. On the other hand, it would be nice to take out his ag on the two big palookas. They were probably thinking he was just some big slow-talking Wally and it would be an enormous laugh to see the looks on their faces when the shattering left hooks and upper-cuts starting landing. A tram rumbled past gathering speed as it lumbered up the hill in Collins Street heading towards the city. Ahh bugger it thought Les. He sprinted across the road and jumped on the running board.

He swung out the rear door on one arm like a monkey, grinned and gave the two bouncers the finger. 'See you next time I'm in Melbourne, you big pair of poofs,' he yelled out. 'Give my love to that moll on the door.'

The two bouncers stopped, looked at each other, then started sprinting after the tram.

'Yeah, come on you big pair of sheilas,' laughed Norton. 'See if you can catch the gingerbread man.'

Les was grinning confidently as he swung out the rear

door of the tram. It was a fair hill they were going up and the tram was doing around twenty or thirty kilometres as it rattled noisily along. Norton's grin suddenly turned to wide-eyed wonder. He'd underestimated the sprinting power of the two big Aussie Rules players. Not only were they keeping up with the tram, they were gaining on it rapidly. The taller one was galloping along like an antelope, taking strides about three metres long. Before Les knew it, they were almost at the door.

'Go up the front door Rick,' yelled out the bouncer with the moustache. Rick did just that as the other bouncer made a lunge for Les.

Christ almighty, thought Norton. How fit are these two big mugs? I could be in a spot of bother here. Oh well. No time now to be rooting around.

Just as the dark-haired bouncer made a grab for the rail, Norton stepped inside the tram a little, swung his foot back and punt kicked him straight in the face. The hardened toe of Norton's R. M. Williams riding boot caught him straight under the chin, shattering his jaw and almost ripping his head off his shoulders in the process. The bouncer screamed and flew crazily back from the doorway, clutching at what was left of his mouth and teeth. He fell heavily on his side, tried to get up, then pitched forward on his face, out cold on the road.

This left his mate Rick. The tall bouncer heaved himself up into the front compartment, sucked in a lungful of air and began advancing towards Norton. The dozen or so people in the tram, couples and parents with children, were beginning to wonder what was happening to their Saturday night as they rocked around in their seats. The eyes on the bleached haired conductress standing behind the driver's cabin were starting to bulge a bit too. She'd just seen one bloke nearly get his head kicked off, some big red-haired bloke cackling like a maniac as he hung out of her tram like a chimpanzee, and now some monster with hate-filled eyes had just lumbered through the door next to her. She didn't have to wait long for the action to start.

Norton met the big bouncer in the middle compartment, where the two pairs of double seats face each other, which was as good a time as any for the occupants to move. He zapped out a straight left which slammed flush into Rick's nose and if it hadn't been broken before, it certainly had now. It splattered across his face like a burst sachet of tomato sauce, flicking blood over the backs of the retreating passengers. However, the big Aussie Rules player got in a clubbing straight right into Norton's left eye at the same time. It hurt like hell and Norton saw stars as he slammed back against the brass rail behind him. Les knew the only way he was going to beat the big bouncer was to get in under him. He bounced forward, smashing horrible lefts and rights up into Rick's ribs and solar plexus. The relentless rain of punches didn't do the big bouncer's ribcage or internal organs one bit of good at all. He gasped and froze with pain as the air was gradually pounded out of his body. Norton banged his head up under his chin and slammed a knee into his groin; a couple of left-hooks opened up his mouth and shattered a few teeth. Rick suddenly found himself in one giant mess of trouble and wondered what sort of a beast he'd got hold of as Norton let go with another barrage of punches that seemed to get fiercer and heavier.

The kids on the tram were loving it; it made *Raiders of the Lost Ark* look like *Sesame Street*. Their parents were horrified. The young girls were screaming and hanging onto their terrified boyfriends. The conductress's face was starting to turn the same colour as her uniform — bilious green. She yanked frantically on the emergency chord just as some flying blood spattered across her and the advertising on the compartment behind her.

The tram lurched to a stop. Norton and the bouncer rocketed into the front compartment almost squashing the conductress up against the driver's cabin. Norton dragged Rick off the wall, sunk a right up into his sternum and another into his face, then spun him around and kicked him up the backside out the door of the tram. The big Aussie Rules player hit the roadway in a tangle of arms and legs. His head came up just in time to see Norton come leaping out of the tram and the Cuban heels of his boots land on his chest, with fifteen stone of enraged Queenslander behind them. If the onslaught of punches inside hadn't done Rick's internal organs much good, the final serve completely destroyed them. He gave one hideous moan and passed out.

Norton looked down at what was left of the blood-spattered bouncer and gave a little grunt of satisfaction. The passengers and the driver were hanging out of the tram staring at him. So was the conductress. Norton caught her eye and grinned.

'I'll get off here — if you don't mind. Thanks love.'

He gave her a wave and trotted round in front of the tram

just in time to flag down a passing taxi. It was the same driver who had picked him up at St Kilda earlier.

'Hey,' he said, as Norton plonked himself down in the front seat, 'didn't I just drop you off at Richard's?'

'Yeah, that's right,' grunted Les.

'What happened?'

'Ahh, the cunts wouldn't let me in.'

The driver laughed but didn't say anything at first. 'Can't understand why,' he finally said as he dropped the flag fall.

'No. Me neither,' grinned Norton. 'Oh well. It didn't look like much of a joint anyway to tell you the truth.'

The driver laughed again. 'So where to now?'

'Same place you picked me up in St Kilda.'

'No worries.'

The girl on the switchboard didn't notice Les or the condition of his head as he entered the foyer, which was probably just as well. He stormed past her to the lift and clomped down the hallway to his room. Well isn't that just great he cursed as he kicked off his riding boots and grabbed a can of VB from the freshly restocked fridge. Stinkin', rotten, snooty fuckin' Melbourne bitch. Gobbing on her wasn't enough. She's the one I should've belted. Not those two other silly big mugs. He gave a bitter chuckle as he sucked on the can of beer. I wonder how the heroes are feeling right now? Sore I hope. Norton noticed he was having a little trouble opening and closing his left eye. He went into the bathroom and checked his face in the mirror. If it had a bit of colour in it before, now it looked like a Ken Done T-shirt. There was some bark missing from the burnt side of his face, a gouge mark on the other, and his left eye was turning purple and starting to close. Christ almighty he muttered to himself. Have a look at me. It's a pity they're not casting for a horror movie down here. I'd be a walk-up start. He went back into the bedroom, flung himself angrily onto the bed and glared up at the ceiling. He started thinking about Pamela and her unbelievable body, the time he should be having right now and the time he could have been having afterwards. And what am I doing, he wailed to himself. Sitting in a stinkin' motel room, picking my bloody toes. He finished the can of VB, found a bottle of J and B and made himself a Scotch and dry strong enough to make you want to go out and head butt a mountain goat.

May as well get pissed and watch TV I s'pose. There's nothing else to do. I don't know anyone, and where can I go with my head looking like this anyway. There's no way in the world I'd go back to that pub I walked into last night. I'd be in there five minutes and end up getting bunned by poofs. And I sure as hell don't feel like walking around St Kilda. All it is is Kings Cross with seagulls. He took a healthy slug on his drink that made him cough slightly and his eyes spin around like revolving doors. Then a thought hit him.

What about the pub where we did that ad this morning? There's a band there tonight. It could be all right. I could find a spot where no one would notice me. Yeah. Bloody oath. Why not? He climbed back into his R. M. Williams, changed his shirt, tidied his hair and cleaned his face up as best he could. Then with the rest of the quickly-downed J and B warming his stomach he strolled down to the Boulevard Hotel.

The old pub looked pretty much the same at night as it did in the day, except there was a man selling hot dogs at the top of the stairs and two swarthy looking Europeans standing inside the door as you walked in. They were reasonably well dressed and Norton guessed they were either the owners or ran the place. They gave him a bit of a look as he ambled past and that was about it. Even with his burnt and battered head Norton was still as good a style as anyone in the place. For a supposedly ritzy hotel promoting a supposedly up-market drink on television, the actual clientele are a pretty seedy-looking bunch, thought Les.

The place wasn't packed but there was a fair crowd, mostly mid-twenties, early thirties. Some seated. Some standing. The men all seemed to have sallow faces and pale, oily skin that looked in need of a few hours of sunshine. Their clothes, especially their T-shirts, looked in need of a good dose of Rinso too. They were nearly all wearing faded blue jeans and jackets. Some had studded belts with some sort of animal skins hanging off them. The way they walked gave Norton the impression they were all trying to look and move like the lead singer of INXS.

All the women had dark hair: there wasn't a blond to be seen. Plenty of make-up, cheap silver jewellery, clothes made out of recycled jeans and black stockings with ankle-length boots appeared to be the order of the day or night. Whatever the case, the women all looked bored. The men looked half asleep. A gang of pimply-faced skinheads tossing empty beer cans at each other across the room was the only sign of movement.

It was much the same in the Neptune room, except for a small group of Aborigines in Akubra hats and moleskins. On the bandstand a man and a woman in cowboy hats, playing guitars and backed by a drum machine, were absolutely strangling 'On the Road Again'. If Willie Nelson had heard it he would have got the mafia to break both their arms. Norton winced and moved across to the bar.

The two barmaids were full of cheek as they ran up and down between the bottles and the taps and added a bit of life to the place. They were both as skinny as rakes. One had dark hair and a kind of French sailor's outfit on. The other had on a long white dress and strawberry-coloured hair and a sort of strawberry-coloured face. Perched on her head was one of those little fake leopard-skin pill-box hats, à la Annie Lennox.

'What'll you have love,' she said brightly as Norton walked up to the bar.

'Ohh. Just a glass of beer'll do thanks,' shrugged Les.

'There's a beer strike on and we've only got cans of VB or Carlton. The imported stuff's three dollars a bottle.' She stood there waiting for Norton's reaction.

Les looked at her evenly for a moment. 'Give us a Jack Daniels and Coke, will you. Make it a double. And plenty of ice.'

'No worries.'

Norton paid her, left a sizeable tip and moved away from the bar to have a look around. It was pretty ordinary and there didn't appear to be too many stray women about.

Not that any of them would have actually rushed Les, considering the state of his melon. Though if some of the lifeless-looking scrumbos propped round the place passing for men could get a girl, Norton, battered and all as he was, would still have to be a chance. The drum machine kicked into another beat and the duo took the hatchets to 'Islands in the Stream'. Norton winced again, finished his drink, got another and moved out to the foyer. Christ, I can't see myself lasting long here he thought.

He stood in the foyer gazing around and brooding a little about Pamela. But there was another thing he was trying to figure out, that had been on his mind almost since he got off the plane on Friday night. It was Melbourne women. There was something about them, apart from their clothes and white skin, that made them completely different from

Sydney women. What was it? More peering around and halfway through his drink Norton figured it out. It was the way they made their eyes up. All the women had beautiful, sensuous eyes. Even the ugliest, fattest, most unkempt scrubber in that hotel had her eyes made up to perfection. It had been the same with every girl or woman he'd met. Pamela, Mrs Perry, the girls on the film set, the girl on the door at Richards. Even those two old-birds in the op-shop at Whittlesea and that bleach-haired tram conductress. They all had beautiful, even fascinating eyes. Sydney might be a city of blondes, bikinis and suntans. But Melbourne's a city of brunettes and eyes. Don't know what they look like in the morning when they scrape the make-up off though, chuckled Les. Probably like two holes burnt in a sheet. Anyway, you can keep both of them, chuckled Les to himself again. Give me a good old Queensland girl with plenty of freckles any day.

His thoughts were running back to Dirranbandi and the banks of the Narran River when he heard a girl's voice from one of the cubicles behind him.

'Well, well, well,' it said slowly and sarcastically. 'If it isn't our big movie star from Sydney.'

Norton turned around slowly and suspiciously. He had to look for a moment or two to recognise the face. It was the young girl from the catering truck he'd been talking to earlier. The one he'd saved from falling on her face. She was sitting in one of the cubicles near the front door with two other girls, similar in appearance and dress to herself.

'Well I'll be buggered,' smiled Norton. 'It's the gourmet chef. The botulism queen of Victoria. How are you mate?'

'Not too bad handsome. How's yourself?'

'I'm pretty good. Probably because I got away before lunch.'

'Ooh, you're a smart big bastard, aren't you.'

'Only for getting away before you had a chance to poison me,' grinned Les. 'I've heard your cooking's killed more people than road accidents.'

'Listen digger, I told you before. There's nothing wrong with my food. It's the grouse.'

'Yeah. If you were in a lifeboat out in the middle of the Indian Ocean.'

The girl smiled and shook her head. 'What's the bloody use. Anyway. What are you doing in here, Wally? Just posing around are you? Letting everyone know the film star's back in town.'

'No,' shrugged Norton. 'I'm staying just up the road so

275

I thought I'd come in and have a drink. See what the place is like of a night. Can't say I'm over impressed. That band would give you corns on your ears.'

'Yeah. You're not wrong. If they were playing for meals, you wouldn't give them a paper plate. Anyway — George Hamilton, why don't you get your drink and join us? It doesn't worry you to drink with the peasants does it?'

'Well,' drawled Norton taking a glance around the room, 'I do have my image to think of. But I don't see any photographers around. So why not? Thanks.'

'I never got your name earlier,' said the young cook as Les plonked his behind down next to her facing the others.

'Les.'

'Well I'm Dixie, Les. And these are my friends, Mia and Penny.'

'Hello girls,' smiled Norton. 'Pleased to meet you.'

Neither girl said anything. They just nodded their heads and smiled. A smile of amused curiosity with a kind of confidence about it. They weren't bad looking. Somewhere in their early twenties. Mia, on Norton's left, had copper-coloured hair combed into an untidy bun on top of her head, a full, heavily made-up face, solid figure but no boobs. There was no shortage of silver chains and trinkets round her neck and wrists and underneath the sleeve of a black disposal store leather jacket. Norton thought he could see a tattoo of a mushroom or something on the back of her wrist. Penny had long, dark punked-up hair tinted with pink. Like her girlfriend, she too had a sensuous, heavily made-up face. But where Mia was wearing a denim mini, Penny had on a sort of white pinafore and a sleeveless Levi jacket with a Huxton Creepers T-shirt underneath. She didn't appear to be a grub, but Norton tipped that her Levi jacket hadn't seen any soap and water since the War of the Roses. Neither had the T-shirt.

They struck Les as either students or something to do with music or the arts. There was also something else about them that struck Les, but he just couldn't quite put his finger on it.

'So what's doing anyway girls?' he asked pleasantly. 'And how come you're down here?' he said, turning to Dixie. 'This your usual Saturday night hang is it?'

'No not really,' she replied. 'Mia and Penny live just up the road and I'm staying at their place tonight. I live at Footscray. You know where that is?'

Norton shook his head. 'No . . . not really.'

'You're lucky.'

Norton downed what was left of his drink, rattled the ice in the glass and looked at the others. 'Can I shout you a drink girls?'

'Sure,' said Dixie as the others nodded too. She ordered a Vodka and squash, the others a Scotch and dry. Les got three doubles, plus a Jack Daniels and Coke for himself.

'Anyway, cheers girls,' he said, holding up his glass when he sat back down at the table. 'It's nice to find someone to talk to.'

'Yeah. Thanks Les,' said Dixie. 'It's nice to sit next to a movie star.'

'Don't give us the shits.'

They all had a healthy pull on their drinks, with the girls giving a bit of a splutter and a comment as to the strength of them. Norton smiled and told them that if you're going to drink you may as well drink. He got no argument there.

'So how long have you been into modelling, Les?' Mia asked. Her voice was a little expressionless but sounded as if she was actually curious rather than just trying to make polite conversation.

Norton threw back his head and roared laughing. 'Me a model?' he grinned. 'You got to be bloody kidding. I think I'd better tell you girls the whole story.'

Les told them what he did for a living and how he came to be in Melbourne doing the ad. About Warren, the casting and how he had done one ad before in Brisbane. Pretty much the same story he'd told Pamela when she picked him up at the airport on Friday night. Dixie thought it a great hoot. The other two were amused all right, but still seemed a little reserved, almost distancing themselves from Les . . . as if, even though they appeared to be enjoying his company, it wouldn't have mattered to them that much if he'd got up and left. Norton asked them if they wanted another drink. They all said yes. Mia got them, doubles. Les paid.

The next round went down even easier than the first. It turned out Dixie was working casual on the catering truck. She was a silk-screen printer, but the factory where she'd been working had gone broke a couple of months ago. Penny had worked there too; she wasn't working at all now. Neither was Mia. She'd been playing organ in a band. The Boils. But the lead singer got killed in a car accident so the band broke up. She did do a little part-time work in a health food restaurant in Carlton. All three were on the dole, and all three were broke. Which was how they came to be sitting in the Boulevard, holding onto their drinks like hourglasses until Les came along. Norton didn't mind shouting the three battlers a drink. He still had more than half of Abraham Goldschmidt's money plus the $300 Pamela had given him, and there could be anything in that strongbox. Not counting the money he'd eventually pick up for doing the ad. So Les was releasing money easily enough. If he'd been paying for it out of his wages though, it might have been a different story.

'So girls,' smiled Norton, 'you could say between us we lead a pretty checkered sort of an existence.'

'Yes. We're not exactly what you'd call solid citizens are we,' agreed Penny.

Dixie looked at Norton with a derisive kind of smile. 'Hey Les,' she said slowly. 'There's something I've deadset got to ask you.'

'Sure. What is it?' shrugged Norton.

'Well, I'll try and be as tactful as I can about this,' she said, running a finger delicately around the rim of her glass. 'But what happened to your bloody head?' She had to laugh at the grin on Norton's face. 'No, fair dinkum, Les. Your head's pretty ordinary at the best of times. But at least on the commercial you could look at it without getting frightened too much. But now. Christ! It looks like a kicked-in shitcan.'

'Jesus you're bloody good,' said Les, trying not to laugh. 'I shout you drinks. Let you sit and talk to a big star like me, and what do you do? Turn around and insult me. Fair dinkum — are all Melbourne girls as horrible as you?'

'You're right Les,' nodded Penny. 'It was a tasteless thing to say.' Then she smiled. 'But Jesus. It does look rough. I was nearly going to ask you the same thing myself. You look like you've been playing water-polo against a school of piranhas.'

Norton chuckled like a drain. But now it was time for a bit of bullshit he thought. The kerosene heater story's a bit naff. And I can't tell them the truth. Tell them any bloody thing. They wouldn't know the difference.

'Well,' he drawled. 'It's a funny bloody story. You know that pub up the road, the Duke of Kent?' The girls nodded. 'Well I finished up in there this afternoon and I bumped into these girls and they invited me back to their flat for a drink and a smoke.' At the mention of the word 'smoke'

278

Penny and Mia's eyes lit up like birthday cakes. 'Anyway. They had this little bong there. I was half full of drink and picked it up and put a match to it before they packed it. One of the girls in the flat had been cleaning it and it was still full of methylated spirits. The rotten bloody thing blew up in my face. And when I've jumped up like a big mug, with my eyes closed, I hit my head on the door. That's how I got the black eye and the cuts on my face. I felt like a nice wombat, I can tell you.'

Dixie cracked up. Even the other reserved pair had to laugh openly at Norton's ridiculous, but by the look of his face, believable story.

'Ohh, that's one of the best ones I've heard,' said Dixie.

Norton smiled and nodded his head in agreement as they settled down a bit and sipped on their drinks. He was going to suggest another round when Mia spoke.

'You don't look much like a dope smoker,' she said evenly.

'Ohh, I have a puff now and again,' shrugged Norton. 'What's wrong with that?'

'Nothing,' replied Mia enthusiastically. 'In fact I could go one myself right now.'

'Yeah. Me too,' said Dixie. 'You ... haven't got any smoke on you. Have you Les?'

Norton shook his head.

'Skinny Jimmy's got some good deals of hash going for a hundred dollars,' said Penny. 'It's that grouse black putty too.'

'Yeah. But who's got a hundred bucks?' said Dixie.

There was silence for a few moments as the girls reflected into their drinks. Then Norton spoke.

'I'll tell you what we could do if you like, girls,' he said.

'What's that?' answered Dixie.

'Well you got to admit it's pretty boring in here, isn't it?'

'Are you kidding,' said Penny. 'You'd have more fun sitting around watching a plank warp.'

'Right,' nodded Norton. 'Well I'm staying at the St Moritz, just up the road. I've got a huge room with a bar stocked full of piss and a stereo. How about I buy one of those deals of hash and we all go back, have a smoke and a few drinks and sit around and have a bit of a mag for a while. It couldn't be any worse than sitting in here. Besides, I'm going back soon anyway.'

The girls looked at each other for a moment. You didn't need ESP to know what was going through their minds.

'Have you got a hundred dollars Les?' asked Mia.

'Here you are,' Norton slipped a hundred out of his wallet and palmed it across the table to Mia. 'Can you get that bit of Johnny?'

'I'll be back in about two minutes.' She got up and disappeared into the Neptune Room.

'Well, what do you reckon girls?' said Norton turning to the others. 'Is it a good idea or what?'

'Bloody oath,' nodded Dixie happily.

'You've got me,' said Penny. 'Thanks Les.'

'That's okay. Now why don't you insult me some more.'

'It's funny you should say that Les,' said Dixie. 'I was just going to say what a good looking bloke you were.'

They laughed and sipped their drinks while they waited for Mia. She was back in a little over five minutes.

'How did you go?' asked Les, as she sat back down. 'Did you get it?'

'No worries. It's right here in my bag.'

'Good.' Norton finished his bourbon and Coke and looked around the table. 'Well. Do you want to have another one here or will we hit the toe?'

'No. Let's piss off,' chorused the three Melbourne lovelies. They quickly finished their drinks and picked up their bags. The next thing they were out the front of the hotel heading towards the St Moritz.

Mia and Penny didn't say a great deal during the walk back to the motel, still distancing themselves from Les and preferring, it seemed, to keep to each other. Dixie however was all bright and bubbly and appeared to have taken a bit of a shine to him, even slipping her arm in his at one stage on the pretext of helping him along seeing he was all scarred and in pain. Norton was getting a little keen on her too. She had a good sense of humour and wasn't half a bad sort in a pale, punkish sort of way. Certainly different from a lot of other girls Les had met. Pity I couldn't piss those other two off he thought as they got closer to the motel. A man might be a bit of a chance with Miss Footscray once I get a few drinks into her. Can't see anything happening with those other two in the room. Then again my head isn't exactly a Rembrandt at the moment. Oh well, don't really matter. A few drinks and a laugh for an hour or two'll do. I'm starting to feel a bit buggered anyway.

The girl on the switchboard just blinked when she saw Les

280

troop past towards the elevator with the three girls. Les winked and gave her a cheesy grin. She tried to smile, but just blinked some more and shook her head.

'Jesus. How good's this joint,' said Dixie after Norton had switched on the light and closed the door behind them.

'Somewhere to throw your swag I s'pose,' he replied casually.

'I've heard about this place,' said Penny. 'But I didn't think it was this good.'

'You think I'd bring three good sorts like you back to a shithouse?' smiled Norton.

While the girls were gazing around the room, fiddling with the curtains, testing the bed and lounge, Norton got behind the bar. He tuned the stereo to some FM station playing good rock 'n' roll and brought up some glasses.

'What do you want to drink girls?' he said. 'Same as in the pub?'

'Yes. That'd be nice, Les,' said Dixie.

'Coming right up,' smiled Norton, rattling some ice into the glasses.

'Here's what you got for your hundred dollars Les.' Mia dropped the piece of hash on top of the bar. Norton gave it a cursory glance. It looked like a small piece of pumpernickel that had originally been wrapped in red cellophane, then folded up in glad-wrap.

'Looks all right,' shrugged Norton. 'You reckon there's enough there to get us stoned?'

'Shit. I bloody well hope so,' said Penny, giving it a little squeeze with her fingers.

'You got a bowl or a plate there Les? asked Mia. 'I might start rolling up a few joints.'

'Here you are.' Norton handed her a small plate with St Moritz Motel Melbourne stamped on it.

While he was making up the drinks he watched Mia sit next to Penny on the ottoman and place the plate on the coffee table in front of them. Mia broke off about a third of the block of hash, held a match over it for a few seconds to soften it, then crumbled it up onto the plate. Penny handed her a packet of cigarettes. She took a couple, emptied the tobacco out onto the plate then mulled it all up together. Being a non smoker, and not all that keen on hash, Norton could see these joints weren't going to go down all that well and his mouth would probably taste like Aunty Dora's window box when he got up in the morning.

By the time Les had made the drinks and handed them around, Mia had rolled two joints. He kicked off his riding boots, changed into a sweatshirt and dimmed the lights while she rolled another, then sat on the bed with his back against the wall. Dixie sat on the corner watching the others. Gangajang was playing on the radio and the drinks were going down quite easily. It was all very, very cosy.

'If you girls want another drink, just help yourselves. There's heaps there. There's even a couple of bottles of champagne if you want it.'

'Thanks Les,' replied Dixie. She turned around and smiled at Norton while she sang along with the music:

'Out on the patio we sit.
And the humidity, we breathe.
This is Australia.'

'Check it out, check it out,' smiled Les back at her.

'Well I might light one of these,' said Mia.

'Jolly splendid idea.' Norton moved down the end of the bed next to Dixie. Mia lit the number and went to hand it to him. He shook his head and made a motion with his finger for them to go first. When the joint came around to him he took a couple of tentative tokes. The hash didn't taste too bad but the tobacco wasn't the best and it made his head spin a little. It didn't seem to worry the others, however. They were sucking hungrily at it like it was the last bit of air left in the room. It wasn't long before it was gone and Mia lit another one.

'It's not bad Johnny this,' she said, passing the joint to Penny.

'Yeah. Not bad at all,' agreed Norton.

The second didn't last much longer than the first. Mia stubbed out the roach and immediately attacked the third. Norton declined when it came to him. He wasn't all that stoned, but the tobacco, apart from making him giddy, made his mouth taste like he'd just smoked an old army blanket. He moved back up against the wall, sipped his drink and watched the girls demolish joint number three.

Norton closed his eyes for a moment as the music almost immediately began to sound better — deeper, richer, every note crystal clear. The bed seemed softer, even his drink tasted mellower, sweeter. His black eye still felt thick but the pain in his face wasn't anywhere near as annoying.

'How are you feeling Les?' Dixie turned around as she passed the last joint back to Mia.

'Pretty good,' smiled Norton. 'Can't complain.'

Which was a fair assessment of his condition. He did feel good. Relaxed and in pleasant enough company. The hash may have made him a little drowsy, but that was understandable. He'd been up since five and had had a fairly hectic day. Filming, digging holes, fighting, drinking, etc. He put a pillow behind him and eased further back against the wall.

'If you girls want any more of that Johnny,' he said, 'just help yourselves.'

'Thanks Les.'

The girls whispered a few words between them and it wasn't long before joint number three was gone. Mia and Penny settled back on the ottoman. Dixie picked her drink up from the coffee table and moved up against the wall next to Les.

'How's your face feeling now?' she enquired softly.

'All right,' nodded Norton. 'A bit sore. That's all.'

'I've got a tube of lanolin in my bag. Would you like me to rub some in for you?'

'Ohh yeah, reckon. That'd be grouse.'

Dixie reached into her bag and produced a thick yellow tube of cream.

'It's getting a bit cool in here. I might turn the heater on,' suggested Norton.

'Okay.'

The controls were next to the bed. Norton switched it onto medium and in a few moments the fans on either side of the walls had quietly filled the room with warm air.

'How are you going down there girls?' he called out to the others.

'Good thanks Les.' In the soft light Norton could see them both smile and nod their heads.

'Why don't we get under the doona?' said Dixie.

'Yeah righto,' agreed Les. 'Not a bad idea.'

He was about to swing his legs straight under when Dixie pulled her jumper up over her head and slipped off her dress and stockings.

'No good crushing up all my good clothes,' she smiled.

Dixie may have been a bit pale but there was nothing wrong with her figure. In fact her smooth milky skin seemed to emphasise the light blue matching bra and panties she was wearing.

'That's a good idea too.' In an instant Norton had his jeans off and slid beneath the bed cover.

Dixie eased up next to him, smiled coyly, then squeezed

some lanolin out of the tube and began gently massaging it into the burns on his face. 'God that looks painful,' she said.

'Yeah. It hurts a bit,' replied Les. 'But what you're doing feels enormous. Thanks Dixie.'

'That's okay. Now why don't you just close your eyes and relax.'

Norton nodded dreamily and did just that. It was like a dream too. A dream Norton could scarcely believe. Wonderful shapes and colours were swirling around in his mind. The music, even though it was down low, seemed to fill the room and Dixie's gentle woman's touch was almost as if her fingers were dancing across his face in time to the music. The only difficulty was, as she was moving against him one of her beautiful firm breasts was almost bursting out of the bra as they both rubbed gently across his chest, and against his thigh Les could feel the soft bristle of her ted in the skimpy blue knickers. A noticeable stirring was beginning in Norton's loins and there wasn't a great deal he could do about it. Not that he really wanted to.

Norton slipped his hand up behind Dixie and started gently massaging the small of her back. He had his eyes closed but he was positive he could hear her smile; he could definitely hear her purr. She turned away from him to put the tube of lanolin down by the side of the bed. Norton was laying back, eyes still closed, half asleep when he felt a lovely, soft pair of lips on his. They were beautiful. Dixie began kissing him, gently at first, gradually becoming more eager, more intense, firmer. Her tongue, the sweetest, pinkest tongue Les thought he'd ever felt, darted inside his mouth and played around the corners. He ran his hand up and down her spine. Dixie sighed and arched slightly. A gentle pressure undid her bra and that same sweet tongue whipped into and around his ear. Norton felt as if he was going to burst into flames. A hand slipped down his Speedos as he kissed her delicate pink nipples and softly stroked her ted. Dixie spread her legs then brought them together as Norton eased her knickers down past her knees and over her ankles. Dixie did the same to him, kissing his neck and mouth at the same time.

Dixie was warm, firm and moist and ready for him. She lifted her knees and Les entered her, slowly, gently, then he gave a couple of thrusts and they began making love. Dixie shuddered and moaned in his ear. Norton had to bite into the pillow or he would have screamed out himself it felt that good. Before long they were moving almost as one.

Stoned or not, it was beautiful love-making. Whereas Mrs Perry the previous night had been a bit on the wild side and could be regarded as just an outrageous screw from out of nowhere, Dixie was sensuous and caring. She genuinely liked Les and he fancied her. It may not have been love, but there was quite a lot of affection there.

They writhed away beneath the bedcovers. Norton was in ecstasy, completely oblivious to everything around him; he could have been a million miles away when a sudden thought occurred to him. What about Mia and Penny? Taken right away by the smoke and Dixie's charms, he'd forgotten about them. This could be embarrassing.

Without stopping what he was doing, Norton slewed Dixie around beneath him to have a bit of a peek over his shoulder to see if they were watching. He managed to inch around to his right a little more when over the music he began to hear this slurping, sucking sound, interspersed with a lot of muffled moaning and groaning. It sounded like someone eating thick soup with a leaky spoon. Slowly, Norton slewed his head around further.

Someone had turned the lights down a little more and he had a bit of trouble focusing at first. When he did, Norton's eyes nearly fell out of his head. It looked like one white writhing form on the ottoman, then it began to take shape. He could make out a head at one end with a bum underneath it. And a bum at the other end with a head above it. Legs and feet were going everywhere. Hands and fingers were probing and squeezing. Mia and Penny were entwined on the ottoman, stark naked, having a furious sixty-niner. Who was doing what to who Les wasn't quite sure. But a burst of straggly pink hair at one end suggested Penny was on the bottom. Norton stared and blinked for a while, out of amazement more than anything else. Then the whole thing dawned on him. Mia and Penny were lovers. Liberated women. Gay ladies. Lesbians. Call them what you like. It was a scene Norton had never come across before. No wonder they seemed to distance themselves from him. But they didn't remind Les of the horrible-looking hairy-legged crew-cut things in army shorts and overalls he'd seen now and again hanging around pubs in Balmain and Surry Hills in Sydney. Mia and Penny had a certain amount of femininity about them. However, he could understand their indifference towards him. Fair enough. But conservative bloody Melbourne. Pig's arse. The place is a cesspool.

Mia and Penny's squeals and moaning began to grow louder

and their probing and clawing seemed to intensify. Beneath him, Les could feel Dixie starting to wind up too. Well he thought, they're certainly starting to get restless in the mounting yard aren't they. Oh well. If we're gonna go off, we all may as well go off together. He stiffened his legs and went for his life.

Dixie gave a little scream, wrapped her arms around his neck and kicked the bedcover up towards the ceiling. The next five minutes sounded more like a torture session at KGB headquarters than four people having a good time. It ended in a crescendo of screams, howls and writhing bodies, with a final 'aaahhhh shit!' from Norton. He rolled off onto his back with his arm around Dixie's shoulders. She threw an arm over him, dragged the bed cover back over them and snuggled into his chest while they got their breath back.

After a few minutes or so there was a discreet rustling from the ottoman, followed by a discreet rustling from under the bedcovers as Dixie wriggled back into her underwear. Norton slipped his Speedos back on. The sound of zippers being zipped came from across the room and then Dixie had her clothes on as well. Norton didn't bother about his. He just lay back with a grin on his face like a crack in a sheet of perspex. Dixie was on the edge of the bed running her fingers through the stubby red hairs on his chest and smiling down at him.

'We might get going soon Dixie. What do you reckon?' He heard Mia's voice.

'Yeah righto,' replied Dixie.

The two others got to their feet and Dixie joined them. Norton got out of bed and wrapped a towel around himself. 'You sure you wouldn't like another drink?' he said. 'Or a cup of coffee.'

'No thanks. It's all right,' smiled Penny.

'Okay. Suit yourselves.'

There was an awkward silence for a moment. Mia and Penny certainly didn't know what to say; they were certain Les had seen what was going on and weren't certain what he thought of them. Not that it would have worried them all that much what he did. Norton sure as hell didn't know what to say. It was definitely a new one on him. Though somehow a joke or a flippant remark didn't seem appropriate. He decided to keep his mouth shut and just smiled at them.

'Well,' he finally said. 'It hasn't been too bad a night I s'pose.'

'No. It was good,' said Penny. 'Thanks for the drinks. And the smoke.'

'That's okay. It was a pleasure.'

Mia looked at him for a moment. 'Hey...ah, Les,' she said.

'Yeah?'

'Do you think we could have a little piece of that Johnny. For a smoke when we get home.'

Norton glanced over at the piece of black hash sitting on the coffee table. 'Take the lot with you,' he said. 'I don't really want it.'

'Are you sure?' Mia sounded genuinely surprised.

'Yeah. Go for your life.'

'Gee, thanks Les.'

Norton smiled and shrugged a reply. Mia and Penny shuffled towards the door and Les opened it for them.

'We'll wait for you down in the lobby,' said Penny, turning to Dixie.

'Righto. I won't be long.'

'Well girls,' said Norton, framed in the light from the hallway. 'Don't know when I'll see you again. But it's been nice to meet you.'

Mia and Penny stood in the corridor looking evenly at Norton for a few seconds, then their faces burst into a grin.

'Hey Les,' said Mia. 'You're all right you know.' Both of them then grabbed him round the waist and kissed him on the cheek.

'Yeah. I s'pose there's worse blokes round than me.' He grinned.

'And it doesn't worry you about us at all. Does it?' said Penny.

Norton gave his shoulders a nonchalant shrug. 'Well, some girls I know in Sydney reckon lesbianism leaves a nasty taste in their mouths. But it's never bothered me.'

Mia and Penny shook their heads. Mia punched Les lightly in the stomach. 'Dixie was right. You are a cheeky big mug.' They tossed a grin each over their shoulders and skipped off down the hallway, leaving Dixie and Les alone. She moved into him and Les put his arms around her waist.

'Well Dixie old mate,' he said awkwardly, 'I don't know when I'll be seeing you again.'

'No, I don't suppose there's much chance of you coming to Melbourne for a while, is there?'

Norton smiled down at Dixie, unable not to feel a little

287

sad. She might have been a bit of a rough diamond, but there was no doubt she was genuine and had a good heart. Somehow the little Melbourne punk had managed to pluck at the big Queenslander's heart strings.

'Hey just hang on a sec,' he said.

Les broke away from her, went across to his overnight bag, shuffled around for a biro and something else then came back.

'Here,' he said, handing her a piece of paper. 'This is my phone number in Sydney. Ring me. Reverse the charges. And if you can find the time, come up for a few days. I'll pay your air fare. And you won't need to bring any money with you either. And here. Stick this in your kick too.' He pushed a hundred dollars into the front pocket of her recycled jeans skirt. A bit of a frown crossed Dixie's face. 'Now don't go getting the wrong idea. You're battling and I just got a big earn down here. You take it.' He stepped back a little from her and grinned. 'Even if you don't buy any food or clothes with it. At least buy a couple of cook books. Do Melbourne a favour.'

Dixie shook her head at him. 'God you're a cheeky boof-headed big bastard.' She then threw her arms around his neck and gave him a kiss that nearly took his face off. Norton immediately started to get ideas. 'You just stay near that phone Les Norton,' she said. 'You never know when it might ring.' Dixie kissed him again then danced off down the hallway.

Well bloody well beat that one thought Norton as he closed the door and came back inside. Does it ever bloody stop down here. I miss out on Pamela, and I get her. And I think I prefer ol' Dixie too, just quietly. He pulled a can of VB from the bar fridge and sucked on it lustily. Feeling sweaty and sticky he got under the shower, taking the can with him. He was still laughing about the night's events when he got out, towelled off and remade the bed.

And what about those other two? The two Jimmy Pikes. You're all right Les. All right? Why wouldn't I bloody well be all right. What other bloke would shout them drinks all night, buy them a hundred bucks worth of hash, take them back to his home and give them more drinks, then lay back and let them perform lewd and obscene sexual acts on his lounge? All in front of a girl he's trying to impress. All right? Norton chuckled out loud. I reckon I'm all right. But what about that poor little Dixie? Wasn't she a sweetheart. I wonder if she'll ring? I hope she does. Yawning like a cavern now,

Norton crawled under the sheets and switched off the light. His head was on the pillow about four seconds and he was dead to the world.

Norton woke up about eight-thirty. He was right again about the tobacco in the joints. After running his tongue around his teeth he couldn't decide whether his mouth felt like Typhoid Mary had pissed in it or her cat had shit in it. He blinked around the room for a few moments then got up, cleaned his teeth twice and had a very tender shave. A quick shower made him feel good and the happy memory of the previous night's events, plus the knowledge that he'd soon be flying home, made him feel even better. He also felt hungry.

No, said the girl on the desk, it wasn't too late to order breakfast. Sausages, scrambled eggs and just about everything else on the menu plus a Melbourne Sunday paper would be at his room before nine. The car company had picked up the Ford earlier and he didn't have to be out of his room until three. Thankyou Mr Norton.

Well that's okay thought Les. I can take my time getting ready, go for a bit of a walk around St Kilda, have a nice lunch somewhere, then piss off about two in time for my flight. A nice easy day.

He'd just got dressed when the phone rang. 'Hello,' he said, picking up the receiver.

'Mr Norton. A call for you from Sydney. A Mr Edwards.'

'Yeah righto. Is that you Woz?'

'Yeah. How are you Les?'

'Pretty good. What's up?'

'Ohh, nothing really. I was just wondering if you could catch a cab back from the airport when you get in.'

'Sure. That's no problem,' replied Norton. 'Just as long as you're paying for it, you little weasel.'

'Don't worry. I anticipated that. And the agency will reimburse you.'

'So they bloody well ought to. How come you've given me the heave?'

'I'm staying at the boss's weekender at Palm Beach. I'll probably be here till Tuesday.'

'Basking in the glory of all my hard work eh. Who's the sheila?'

'Rebecca,' laughed Warren. 'She's English. Works for *Cleo*.'

'Half your luck,' chuckled Norton.

'So how's things anyway. What's the weather like down there?'

'It's been unusually warm and sunny to tell you the truth.' Norton took a quick look out the bay window. 'Looks like it's gonna rain now though.'

'That'd be Melbourne.'

They chatted on for a few more minutes till Warren hung up saying he'd see Les on Tuesday.

Norton smiled at the phone. Bloody Warren. He pulls these sheilas out of his arse. He was still chuckling to himself when a knock on the door told him breakfast had arrived. He slung the girl a couple of dollars and put the tray on the bar.

Shit! this looks great he thought, and plenty of it too. He speared a piece of sausage with his fork and flipped open the Sunday paper. He'd just taken a bite when the front page made him drop his fork and his eyes bulge right out of his singed red head.

If Melbourne wasn't such a fanatical Aussie Rules town Norton would have made headlines. As it was, he got a banner across the bottom of page one and plenty of spread and pictures on pages two and three.

CHURCH BOMBING OUTRAGE was page one. Police link Whittlesea church blast to last week's bombing at Turkish Consulate in Toorak.

'Holy fuckin' shit,' said Norton. 'What in the fuck's this?'

The journalist's report went on roughly to say that a Middle East terrorist group with links with an Armenian cell in Sydney was alleged to have blown up the Church of Scientific Achievement because two of the founders were of Turkish parentage. The bomb used was equivalent to ten kilograms of gelignite, it went on. Police wish to question a tall solidly-built red-headed man in his late twenties or early thirties. Dark, olive complexion. Possibly of Middle Eastern appearance, the man was seen in the area earlier driving a late model white Ford or Holden Sedan.

'What?' said Norton, screwing up his face. 'Middle Eastern appearance. Me a wog? They're kidding. I'm as Australian as a Holden with the boot full of meat pies. I've even got a photo of Dawn Fraser in my bedroom. Haven't these pricks in Melbourne ever seen anyone with a suntan before?' The next paragraphs weren't so amusing.

Fearing more attacks, police have trebled airport and railway surveillance.

'Uh oh!' said Norton.

His eyes moved across to the travel bag under his bed. That means bomb squads with dogs and metal detectors. They'd pick that metal strongbox up in two seconds, take one look at my head, and bingo! Shit! This is going to be nice.

Suddenly Norton's appetite lost its edge. He quickly went through the story again, then looked at his watch. Just on nine. He left his food and switched on the TV. As soon as it focused Norton could see he was the main story on the mid-morning news. A teary-eyed priest or messiah or whatever he was, in a kaftan and beard, was standing in front of what was left of the Church of Scientific Achievement — a pile of smouldering, steaming ashes with a few beams and the remains of a chimney jutting forlornly up into the air. A microphone was shoved under his chin and he was telling a concerned TV journalist in a dark grey suit he couldn't understand why anyone would want to do something like this. Next were a couple of farmers with heads like Dorset Horn rams and talking as slow as they looked, half hinting to the same reporter that they'd been expecting something like this one day. The camera panned across to a bull-headed detective from the bomb squad standing beneath the row of pine trees holding the speaker leads. This was definitely the work of professional terrorists he said. Finally the camera shifted to Whittlesea, scanning up and down the dampened main street and across the war memorial and ending on the same TV journalist intoning:

'The octopus of international terrorism has now spread its evil tentacles from the Middle East and Europe, to sleepy Whittlesea in Victoria.'

Of course the station couldn't waste too much time on unimportant news like a bombing. It was straight on to the football. And what was the main story, from an even more worried looking reporter:

'Giant Essendon flanker Rick Bechara was badly injured in a brawl outside a city discoteque last night. Also badly hurt was Hawthorn full forward . . .'

That was enough for Norton. He almost stabbed his finger through the TV switching it off.

'Holy bloody shit,' he bellowed as he started pacing around the room. 'What have I done?'

Norton never intended to treat the church bombing as an insouciance. It just wasn't supposed to happen like that. He only meant to blow that pier away, that's all. And the fight

291

wasn't his fault either. Not really. Those two big bouncers shouldn't have chased him up the street. He was only defending himself. And how was he to know they were two local football heroes? The six words Norton was famous for were beginning to haunt him already: 'Yeah, but it wasn't my fault.' He could see himself saying that in a courtroom just before some judge gave him five years in Pentridge. Ahh bugger it anyway he cursed to himself. I'm not going to let my breakfast go cold. But Norton was doing a lot of deep thinking along with the chewing. And the main subject was Melbourne... and how to get out of the place.

He couldn't catch his plane. The airport would be the first place they'd be looking for him. The interstate train terminals would be watched too, so they were out. No good trying to hire a car. The people in the office would report him just on suspicion and you could bet it wouldn't be long before there'd be some kind of an identikit drawing of him on TV. And it wouldn't be selling St Kilda Kooler. Maybe it was a good thing he didn't get to see Pamela last night after all. Hitchhike? Out of the question. With cop cars everywhere on the road it would be more dangerous than catching his plane.

He chomped morosely into his breakfast. Things were looking as bleak as the weather over Port Phillip Bay, and he looked like being stuck in Melbourne. Melbourne a top town? Norton snorted to himself. Hah! Prick of a joint. They should have had the atomic bomb tests here instead of Maralinga. Then a thought struck him. What about the bus? Only brokies and backpackers doing it on the cheap ever catch the Uncle Gus. There'd be no metal detectors and not much chance of any cops being there either. He picked up his coffee and walked across to the phone.

The girl at Greyhound was very polite. Yes Mr Dudley, we can give you a seat on tonight's bus departing from Swanston Street at seven p.m. You have to pick up your ticket by four and be at the terminal with your bags by six forty-five. Thankyou Mr Dudley. No worries. Norton felt a little relieved after that. He rang the airport to cancel his flight and finished his breakfast.

It was raining outside now, and cool. Melbourne's freakish spring weather was back to normal. But the rain suited Les; he didn't want to be walking around in public anyway. It would be stay in the motel watching TV till three, then a cab into town and just keep out of sight till the bus left. And that was exactly what Norton did.

292

By one o'clock Les was sick to the teeth of Aussie Rules and commentators in $500 suits pontificating on every aspect of the game, almost to the size of the players' turds first thing in the morning, as if the fate of the free world hinged on the result. The news updates were rehashes of the church bombing and the assault on the two footballers; at least there were no identikit drawings of him yet. The player with the moustache that Norton had booted in the face declined to be interviewed. The taller one looked very sad and forlorn propped up in his hospital bed with a drip running into his nose between two beautiful black eyes. It all happened so quickly, he said, he didn't get much of a chance to identify his attackers. Attackers snorted Norton. The fuckin' big sheila. There wasn't even an old movie to watch. It was either Australian Rules or hockey on the ABC. Norton watched the hockey with the sound turned down and listened to the radio. Outside, the rain came down in buckets.

Two forty-five eventually rolled around and the rain eased off. Norton rang for a cab, picked up his bags and went down to the foyer. There was only one black-uniformed girl there. Maybe Mrs Perry had kept away to avoid another one of Les's smart remarks, and Mr Perry may have possibly smelled a bit of a rat so he kept away too. Whatever the reason, it suited Norton. He gave the girl his key, she smiled in return and tried her best not to make out she was staring at Norton's charred face. A toot on the horn outside told him his taxi was waiting so he made a smart exit.

He propped outside the door of the bus terminal for a while before going inside. He couldn't see any police cars around and when he walked in, full of trepidation, he didn't notice anyone who looked like a cop either. After a couple of years in his profession Norton could smell a cop five miles away through a six-inch lead shield. The bus terminal was quite crowded though, with people either lying and sitting around half asleep, or watching a TV built into the wall between some drink machines and the washrooms. They were what Norton expected too—backpackers and people travelling on the cheap. He paid for his ticket, checked in his travel bag and with his overnight bag slung across his shoulder walked down to the city to kill four hours.

Even though the sun was now peeking through, it was still quite cool. The wide, neat streets, with names like Bourke, Flinders, King, Queen, were fairly crowded with window shoppers. There were a number of uniformed police carrying walkie-talkies strolling around but Les just turned his back to them or blended in with the crowds. He was surprised to find a small hotel open near Chinatown and even more surprised to find the beer was pretty good and now on tap. He had six pots of Carlton Draught which gave him an appetite, so he had a feed of short soup and honeyed prawns in the restaurant next door. By then it was time to go.

No-one remotely resembling a cop was watching the queue boarding the double-decker bus and Norton, to his relief, boarded without incident. His seat was upstairs on the left, next to the window and one from the front. A young bloke in an old army jacket sat next to him; they nodded half a dozen words and Les settled back. Before long the bus started and they lurched off through the city, with the sun setting behind them, towards the outer suburbs. The skies suddenly blackened and it wasn't long before it was raining again.

Norton noticed there was no-one sitting on the front seat to his right, so he moved over there. This is all right he thought as he watched the rain spattering against the front window. The seats are comfortable and I've got two. There's no shortage of little pillows and blankets and rain always makes me sleep. There was a speaker tuned to some radio station above his head. And a bit of nice music on the trip too. Ripper.

If Norton thought the bus trip was going to be enjoyable, he was in for a rude shock. There was only one word to describe it. Ghastly. The top deck of the bus lurched from side to side like he was halfway up the mast of a windjammer going around Cape Horn. Every time the driver took a corner or hit the brakes he was flung against either the front or side window. By nine o'clock the radio had tuned to some country station and by eleven Norton was that sick of twanging guitars and cowboys singing through their noses and ads for water pumps and car yards he felt like ripping the speaker out of the roof. Mercifully, the driver switched it off at midnight. Still Les couldn't sleep. He couldn't get comfortable. He couldn't even stretch out. All he could do was rock from side to side and stare vacantly out the front window at the headlights of the oncoming traffic or the tail lights of the cars and trucks going past.

There was an old couple behind him who didn't seem to have any trouble getting to sleep, however. They snored blissfully on into the night, loud enough to wake the dead.

Every now and again one of them would drop a fart in their sleep that smelled like they'd been eating curried mongoose for the last two months. Norton could have quite cheerfully strangled both of them.

At twelve forty-five the driver woke anyone that was asleep to tell them they would soon be pulling into Albury for a thirty-minute meal break and to change drivers. Knowing he was getting off, the driver honked into the microphone like he was auctioning cars and let the passengers have about ten excrutiatingly corny one-liners. Most of the passengers stumbled out into the rain and cold to have a bit to eat and stretch their legs. The huge cafeteria was bright and modern and well staffed with neatly uniformed employees. The food, apart from the coffee, was atrocious. Almost inedible and a blatant rip-off. Two scrawny sausages, a couple of greasy fried eggs and a piece of tomato on a half-toasted slice of white bread was equivalent in price to a three-course meal in a top Sydney restaurant. They filed back onto the bus and Norton spent the next two hours trying to spit out the taste of his two bites off one sausage. They ground remorselessly into the black of the night.

Next stop Goulburn. Once again they shuffled out of the bus like zombies, into the cold. But not as many this time. Only those who, like Norton, were so numbed and uncomfortable they would have walked in front of a firing squad and dug their own graves just to stretch their legs and get a bit of fresh air. Les paid for a cup of coffee and stole two bottles of mineral water and that was it.

From then on it was bounce, bump and sway and try to get comfortable straight through to Sydney. About thirty kilometres west of Parramatta Norton was that tired he would have gone to sleep underneath a cow pissing. Out of sheer fatigue he slumped against the window and passed out. He'd blacked out for about half an hour when, like a burglar alarm going off, the speaker above his head roared into life tuned to 2WS. From then on it was Roy Orbison, Bobby Goldsboro and every schmaltzy record on the top forty that Norton despised all the way through the early morning crawl of traffic into Sydney. The weather had cleared and the sun was well and truly up, beating straight into the front window and making the bus like an oven. Les couldn't remember ever feeling so miserable in his life. He was dog tired but he couldn't sleep. His eyelids felt as if they were lined with coarse-grain sandpaper and his mouth, despite the two bottles of mineral water, still tasted like the floor of a bat cave from the sausage at Albury.

After what seemed like an eternity they finally reached the terminal at Taylor Square, only to find another bus stalled in the dock. So for another twenty minutes they all sat in the hot bus like a lot of battery hens. Eventually everyone filed out and stood around in the exhaust fumes till their luggage was unloaded. As soon as he spotted his travel bag Norton snatched it up and stormed up to Oxford Street to catch a taxi. He had a ten minute wait and the driver could hardly speak a word of English and drove like Jack Brabham. Norton gobbed sourly out of the window. It was great to be back in Sydney.

When they pulled up in Cox Avenue, Norton's semi hadn't looked so good since the time he got back from Long Bay. His old Ford was still out the front and still in one piece; the aerial hadn't even been broken off. After paying the driver Les fumbled the key into the lock and almost fell through the front door when he got it open. He dumped his bags in his bedroom, took off his leather jacket, then shuffled into the kitchen and stood there yawning and blinking wearily around him. Somehow he just couldn't seem to get his brain into gear. Maybe a cup of tea might help. After switching on the kettle, he pulled up a chair and nearly nodded off while it was boiling.

The tea made Les feel a little better. At least it took that rotten taste out of his mouth. Soon he began to relax as he realised he was home and everything was sweet. Before long he was grinning over some of the weekend's events. Halfway through cup of tea number two Norton began thinking about the old strongbox. Shit. I don't really feel like opening that right now he muttered to himself. But underneath his backside was burning to find out what was inside it. He finished his cup, yawned, then shuffled into his bedroom and sat on the edge of the bed dragging his travel bag over in front of him. It felt like it weighed a ton and when he got the strongbox out it seemed as if it was made out of lead. The lock looked like you'd need a blowtorch or gelignite to get it open. It was an ancient, cast-iron Yale as big as a Leon Uris novel. The lock's massive bar and the keyhole were jammed solid in a mass of greenish blue corrosion, as were the sides of the strongbox.

'Shit!' muttered Norton. 'How am I gonna get this bloody thing open?'

He stared at it a while longer, as though it was hypnotising him, and yawned again. Les would have kept on yawning and staring at it, but somehow his eyelids seemed to keep slamming shut. He yawned again, then toppled sideways onto the bed and crashed out.

A telephone ringing through a hundred thousand miles of blackness woke Norton around twelve-thirty. Like a robot, he rose from the bed, stumbled out into the lounge room and picked up the receiver.

'Ummmnh.'

'Is that Mr Norton the physiotherapist?' It was an elderly woman's voice at the other end.

'No. Yougodthewrongnumber,' mumbled Les.

'Oh. I'm terribly...'

Norton slammed down the phone and still puffy eyed and half asleep stumbled back into the bedroom and crashed face down on the bed again.

Another phone call woke him around six. Norton felt like a beaten man as once more he staggered out to the lounge room and picked up the receiver.

'Hullo,' he croaked.

'G'day Les. It's Warren. How are you goin'?' Warren's cheerful voice at the other end was a complete contrast to Norton's tired mumbling.

'Yeah. All right,' he replied thickly.

'You got home okay then?'

'Mmmhh.'

'Good trip was it?'

'Mmmhh.'

'You didn't have any trouble getting a cab?'

'Mmmhh.'

There was silence on Warren's end of the line for a moment. 'Are you okay Les?'

'Mmmhh.'

'You sound half asleep. You been in bed?'

'Mmmhh.'

'Sorry mate. I didn't mean to wake you.'

'Azorright.'

'Look, go back to bed and I'll see you when I get home tomorrow.'

Norton slumped back on the lounge and stared blankly at the phone for a few moments after he'd hung up. Outside the sun had almost set and the house was getting darker by the minute. It wasn't getting any warmer either. The whole day had been wasted lying around and Les still felt dismal and half asleep. He knew what was in front of him now. He wouldn't have the energy to do anything, yet he wouldn't be quite tired enough to go to sleep. If he didn't do something he'd sit around staring into space like a zombie till after midnight, then wake up after lunchtime tomorrow. Bugger that, he thought. I'll take the easy way out.

Due to the inhuman pressures of advertising, Warren kept a couple of bottles of 'mother's little helpers' in the bathroom. Serepax and Normison. Warren would drop a couple now and again if the strain got too much to bear and he couldn't sleep. Norton might bludge one on the odd occasion if he was a bit overtired from a late night at work. This was definitely one of those odd occasions.

The fuckin' things are in here somewhere. Norton noticed he was getting a little irritable as he switched on the bathroom light and began rummaging around in the cabinet beneath the basin. He found them behind a bottle of Mylanta and a large packet of Band-Aids. Two of each went down the hatch with a glass of water.

He went into the kitchen and made a toasted cheese sandwich and a mug of Ovaltine. By the time he'd made and eaten that, the tranquilizers were pumping through Norton's system and his craggy face began to look like a big, red smile-button. Happy as a lark, he switched off the kitchen light and floated back into the bedroom.

Les didn't have a worry in the world as he set his radio-alarm for six thirty and thirty minutes of music before he went to sleep. The bed felt like it was made out of marshmallow and Les felt like he was made out of jelly. He crawled in and pulled the blankets up under his chin. Ironically, the song playing on the radio was the Boomtown Rats singing 'I Don't Like Mondays.' I dunno about that Norton grinned to himself, I reckon they're beautiful. It was only a matter of seconds and once more he drifted off into the void. Completely this time.

The morning didn't get off to that good a start. Somehow, probably because he wasn't thinking straight from all the tranquilizers, Norton had made a slight mistake setting the radio-alarm. Instead of being woken up to a bit of nice cruising music on 2DAY-FM he'd tuned to 2JJJ and was pounded out of his sleep by the Cramps howling into 'What's Inside a Girl?' At six-thirty it sounded like the end of another ceasefire in Beirut.

'What the bloody hell's goin' on?' Norton blinked groggily at the radio-alarm for a second or two, then switched it off and buried his face back in the pillow. He could easily have gone straight back to sleep and he knew if he stayed there another couple of seconds he'd do just that. With a super-human effort he forced himself out of his nice warm bed into the bathroom.

He was still groggy from the pills and stiff from too much sleep. In the mirror his eyes were puffy and the burns on his face had coloured up some more along with his black eye. The missing eyebrow completed a picture of not the best looking man in Australia.

'G'day handsome,' he muttered.

A mug of coffee and a few stretches while listening to the radio had him feeling almost wide awake, but there was only one sure way to get the lethargy out of him. He got into his shorts and running shoes and headed for Centennial Park and a workout.

Norton chose Centennial Park in preference to Bondi Beach because he knew a lot of people who trained at Bondi and the first thing each one of them would say when they saw him would be 'G'day Les. What happened to your face?' There were quite a number of people running and walking in the park but Les had no trouble getting away on his own. He did two laps, then crisscrossed it several times. A couple of hundred push-ups and sit-ups had sweat running down his face and dripping off his nose and chin. It was a top day, sunny, mild, a light nor-wester ruffling the trees and hardly a cloud in the sky. Norton's mind, however, was somewhat removed from the weather. All he could think about was the old strongbox and what was in it. Keen to get back home, Les pushed himself faster and faster into his sprints and exercises. He was a lather of perspiration when he walked back to his car and rung his sweatband out.

After the work-out and a long hot shower, Norton felt like a million dollars sitting in the kitchen reading the morning paper. Although it was Tuesday, an interview with Easts' coach told Les the team had gone down to Balmain 15-0. The coach said they should never have had two tries disallowed, blah, blah, blah. But Easts would be back better than ever next year, blah, blah, blah.

Bugger it Norton cursed to himself. Losing the thousand

dollars wasn't all that bad, he had more than enough to cover it. But 15–0. That would be a slaughter to George Brennan and he'd bore it right up Les as soon as he got to work, on Wednesday night and probably every other night till the season ended. Christ! How am I gonna shut that fat turd up? thought Les. He's going to be unbearable. Oh well, probably serves me right. Still you'd think a team of cats'd do better than 15–0. Pricks. He finished his coffee, folded the paper and glanced at his watch. Time to do a bit of metalwork.

Norton's tool shed at the end of the backyard was one of those aluminium build-it-yourself jobs he'd bought off his builder mate Colin Jones, providing Jonesy got someone to put it up for him. It was about five metres by three with a workbench running along one wall, above which was a sheet of pegboard covered in all the tools and electric drills and other things you would expect to see. There'll be something here to open this with thought Les, as he switched on the light and dumped the old strongbox onto the workbench with a loud metallic thump.

He ran his hands over the strongbox, jangled the lock and had a good look at it for a while before he started. He would have to cut a whole section out of the lock and that wasn't going to be easy. Besides the bar being almost as thick as your finger, being attached to the strongbox made it too awkward to fit in the vice. Les picked up a pair of multigrips and a hacksaw. Before he started he gave the edges of the strongbox and the hinges on the back a good squirt of Penetrene then gave the hinges a few taps with a hammer. Okay. Here we go.

Gripping the old lock tightly with his left hand, Norton began rasping away with his right. Unable to grip the saw with both hands, and with the lock still moving around despite his solid grip, it was a slow, tedious process. After about ten minutes or so he was through. He opened and closed his right hand a few times to get the circulation back and started sawing again. Ten minutes more and the piece of lock rattled onto the workbench. Using a hammer and an old blunt chisel he prised around the edges of the box. After who knows how many years it didn't want to come open. But the Penetrene had done its work and with a bit of muscle the old strongbox reluctantly creaked open.

Whatever was inside was wrapped in ancient tar-paper which you rarely see now in the age of plastics. Norton's adrenalin was starting to pump and a huge grin had spread across his face as he peeled back the old brown paper. The next thing his eyes lit up like Tilly lamps. The strongbox contained just what he was hoping it would. Money. Heaps of it. Rows and rows of wads of bills, bound with old, perished, thick rubber bands. How much was there, Les couldn't estimate. But it had to be thousands.

'Mousey. You bloody little beauty,' he roared out loud. 'What a bloody ripper.' Norton could scarcely believe his luck.

Laughing fit to bust he picked up one of the wads of notes. Then the grin on Les's face faded to a crooked half-smile which completely disappeared as his jaw fell almost onto the workbench. 'Uhh?' he grunted.

There was stacks of money all right and absolutely nothing wrong with it. It wasn't mouldy, the borers hadn't been into it, and apart from the rubber bands holding the wads together it was in good shape considering how long it had been buried. The only trouble was all the money was in pounds sterling. Stacks and stacks of pound notes. Blue fivers and red tenners to be exact.

'What the fuck . . .'

Norton screwed up his face, picked a five pound note out of one of the wads and had a look at it. It was a dark blue, with the denominations in the corners surrounded by wriggly flowing lines. A drawing of George VI was on one end and a blank watermark on the other. Underneath this were two signatures. H. C. Coombs, Governor, Commonwealth Bank, and someone Watt, Secretary Treasurey. On the opposite side were more wriggly lines and a drawing of what looked like a team of wharfies unloading a ship. The ten pound notes were the same, only they were brown with a rural scene on the back of some farmers leading a draughthorse and carrying rakes and a woman holding a baby with a dog at her feet.

Norton could hardly believe his eyes. Pound bloody notes! Well how old are the bloody things? He shook his head and tried to do a bit of mental arithmetic. Australia didn't switch over to decimal currency until 1966. Les remembered because he was a kid at school at the time. Mousey had been in the can over twenty years and George VI died around 1952. So this money would have been printed around the late 1940s–early 50s. Probably around when Mousey had stolen it. Well how much is here, Norton wondered. He quickly counted one bundle of each denomination. They were in groups of one thousand pounds and a quick flick through said there were sixty. Sixty thousand pounds. When you consider the average wage was about five pounds a week then and you could buy a home for a few hundred pounds, sixty thousand would have been an absolute fortune back then. Probably equal to three-quarters of a million dollars today.

Norton kept staring at the pile of money and shaking his head. But despite his chagrin he found he couldn't help but laugh. This was what he'd almost blown himself up for and risked five years in gaol for if he'd been caught. An old metal strongbox full of pound notes that he couldn't spend. He may as well have dug up a box of Monopoly money. He shook his head and closed his eyes for a moment.

'Well Mousey,' he laughed out loud, 'I've got to give it to you mate. It wasn't a bad heist you pulled off. And thanks heaps for putting me in the whack. But what the fuck am I gonna do with it? You stupid little prick.'

Norton continued to gaze at the money when a thought occurred to him. He mightn't know what to do with all that old money, but there was one bloke in Sydney who would. He put all the money back in the box, placed it in a garbage bag, walked back into the lounge room and dialed a number in Vaucluse.

'Hello. Is that you Mrs Galese? It's Les.'

'Oh hello Les,' came a cheerful, well-spoken voice. 'How are you? How was your trip to Melbourne?'

'It wasn't too bad thanks Mrs Galese,' chuckled Norton. 'I had a bit of fun down there.'

'Price told me all about it. He said you're a regular movie star.'

'Ohh, I wouldn't bloody say that Mrs Galese,' laughed Norton. 'Far from it.'

Mrs Galese gave a bit of a laugh herself. 'Anyway, do you want to speak to Price do you?'

'Yeah. If I could please.'

'Hold on a sec love. I'll get him. He's just finished breakfast.'

The strongbox full of money was sitting on the coffee table in front of Norton, who smiled and gave it a nudge with his foot while he waited.

'Hullo movie star. How are you going?'

Norton couldn't mistake his boss's smiling voice on the phone. 'G'day Price,' he replied. 'How are you mate?'

'If I was any healthier it'd hurt. How was Melbourne?'

'Pretty good. Better than I thought actually.'

'I told you it wasn't all that bad. How many blokes did you have to belt down there?'

'Just a couple of Aussie Rules players. That's all.'

'Oh shit!'

Norton paused for a moment. 'Listen Price, I was wondering if I could come over and see you some time today?'

'Hello,' chuckled the silvery haired casino owner. 'You're in a bit of strife are you?'

'No. No trouble. But I would like to see you about something. It's a bloody good yarn. I can tell you that.'

'Yeah? Well I'll tell you what. Why don't you come over about two-thirty? I'll be by myself and we can have a couple of beers by the pool.'

'Righto Price. I'll see you then.'

Well thought Norton after he'd hung up, if Price can't sort out what to do with all those chops no-one can. Now what am I gonna do till two-thirty? He was staring absently at the strongbox and thinking on it when the phone rang.

It was Louise, wanting to know how he was and how the trip went. Norton replied that it was very quiet down there and he had two early nights. The ad went okay, but he had to stay there an extra day, which was why he didn't ring her earlier. Would he like to come over to her place for a baked chicken dinner that night? Is the Pope a catholic? Les told her he'd be there at seven with a couple of bottles of Taylor's. He'd no sooner hung up when Billy Dunne rang wanting to know how he was and did he want to go for a run later? Les said he'd already had one. What about tomorrow? Billy said he couldn't make it tomorrow. He was taking the family to Old Sydney Town. They chatted for a while till Les hung up saying he'd see him at work tomorrow night and tell him a bit more about what happened in Melbourne then.

Now where was I? thought Norton. Yeah. What to do till two o'clock. I know what I do have to do. Get a new bloody tracksuit. That one's full of bloody holes. I'll get one up Bondi Junction. Might have a few beers, a steak at the Pig's and a bit of a perv while I'm up there. He did exactly that.

Norton was in a good mood from the beers and feeling content in the stomach when he drove through the gates of Price's mansion later that afternoon. The front door was closed and it was still warm and sunny so Les figured Price would more than likely be sitting out by the pool. He picked up the strongbox, with the garbage bag still wrapped around it, and walked to the rear of the house.

Price was lying back on a recliner lounge by the edge of the pool with his hands behind his head. With his white shorts, sun-tanned good looks and neat, silvery hair, he looked exactly like what he was: a multimillionaire with not a worry in the world. As soon as he saw Norton approaching his face burst into a huge grin.

'Hello mate,' he called out. 'How's things?' Price screwed his face up slightly as Norton got closer. 'Christ! What happened to your face? And what have you got in the bag?'

Instead of replying straight away Norton started to laugh. He sat down next to Price and placed the strongbox on a wrought-iron table opposite them, next to an extension phone and a small esky.

'Well Price,' he grinned. 'It's not a bad story this one. You got an hour or so?'

'From the look of your moosh, it looks like I'm going to have to find one, don't it?' Price reached over and pushed a button on an answering service next to the phone.

Across the crystal-clear water sparkling in the pool Norton saw a figure wave from where he was pottering around amongst some shrubs in the immaculately landscaped grounds. It was Vince, the ex-Welsh Guards caretaker. It looked all nice and peaceful in the garden with Price on his own, but Les knew that in amongst Vince's rakes and hoes would be a fully loaded FN semi-automatic and the odd pistol or two. Vince was a lovely old bloke but he'd been decorated in Malaya and Korea and could shoot the name tag off a dog's collar on the run at 500 metres. If anyone had come in and tried anything they would have got a nice shock. Norton grinned and waved back.

'Righto Les.' Price nodded to the esky. 'There's some cool ones in there. Now what is it you want to tell me?'

Norton shook his head and smiled. 'I honestly don't know where to start,' he said. 'I suppose I'd better start in Lamrock Avenue Bondi last July.'

He took two bottles of Fourex from the esky, opened them and handed one to Price. Then after a quick 'cheers' he told his boss everything. How he got pinched in Bondi. Going to Long Bay. The fight with Chopper. His cellmate. Mousey. Mousey's map. Finding Goldschmidt's wallet. The casting. Arriving in Melbourne. Mrs Perry. Even by the time Les had got to Mrs Perry Price was laughing fit to burst. When he got to the home-made bomb and blowing up the church in Whittlesea, Price let out such a roar Vince dropped his rake and looked up to make sure everything was all right. Norton ended with the fight on the tram and the three girls back in his motel room and how he had to sneak out of Melbourne on the bus like a fugitive after what was in the papers and on TV. By this time Price was in a pitiful state. He was a jelly. His cheeks were scarlet, he was holding onto his ribs and tears were streaming down his well tanned face.

'Fair dinkum, Les,' he gasped when he managed to get his breath back. 'You're bloody unbelievable. You pull more strokes than a GPS Regatta.'

'I told you it wasn't a bad 'un, didn't I,' grinned Norton. 'But the best is yet to come.'

There were three bottles of Fourex left. Norton could see Price was nowhere near finished the one he was drinking so he took just one from the esky and opened it.

'Anyway,' he continued. 'I get up this morning still fumbling around the house like Winnie the Pooh from all those Serepax and I go for a run to try and liven meself up. All the time, though, I'm breaking my silly bloody neck to get back and open that fuckin' strongbox. I nearly break my wrist doing it. And when I do — guess what I find inside?' Norton unwrapped the garbage bag and opened the old strongbox. 'There you are. That's what I almost blew my silly bloody head off for. Can you believe it? And try and tell me I'm not the greatest fuckin' goose getting around on two legs.'

Price's reaction at his first sight of all the old pound notes was almost identical to what Norton's had been: stunned disbelief. Then he smiled and slowly his expression changed to one of nostalgia... almost to sadness.

'God strike me,' he breathed. 'Pound notes.'

'Yep,' nodded Norton. 'Sixty thousand of the bloody things to be exact.'

'Sixty thousand quid eh,' said Price slowly, still shaking his head. 'Christ! I haven't seen anything like this since... since I was more or less just a young bloke still kicking off.' The casino owner almost had tears in his eyes as he lovingly ran his hands over the old notes, pulling bundles out and flicking through them. 'Fivers and tenners eh. Lady Godivas and bricks we used to call them, Les. A quid was a fiddley did. Twenty-five quid was a pony. And fifty quid was a monkey. Jesus this brings back some memories, Les.'

'Yeah,' Norton nodded, smiling at the look in his boss's

eye. 'Little Mousey must've knocked this off from somewhere, buried it, then got life for something else. And I finished up with it. Funny ain't it.'

Price picked up a ten pound note and held it up to the light. 'I'd say these were printed in the late '40s Les. And did you say Mousey originally came from Melbourne?'

'Yeah. So big Bernie told me.'

'I'm just trying to think back. There was a big mail train robbery in 1950. Seventy thousand quid went missing. It was money going from a bank in Melbourne to pay the workers on the Snowy River Scheme. They never got the money. And they never got who did it. I reckon it was your mate Mousey that did the Snowy Mountains Job.'

Norton's face broke into a grin. 'Well I suppose we'd better do the right thing and hand it in eh, Price.'

'Ohh yeah,' snorted Price. 'Give it to Premier Atkins. He'd keep the lot and be cheeky enough to say he won it at the punt.' Price shook his head again and smiled up at Norton. 'So what are you going to do with it Les?'

Norton gave his shoulders a shrug. 'That's what I came to see you about Price. I can't actually walk into David Jones and buy myself half a dozen suits can I. What do you reckon I ought to do?'

Price drummed his fingers on the edge of the table for a few moments, then looked up at Les. 'I can do something with it for you.'

'Yeah?'

'Uh huh.' Price folded his arms and nodded his head at the stack of old money. 'I'll keep some myself, just for old time's sake. But I know a few blokes that deal in old coins and banknotes and other odds and ends. They'll take this off you. The only thing is the government still could have a note of the serial numbers. Even after thirty years or so they still wouldn't be able to move a big amount like this around openly. On the other hand some of these old banknotes could be worth fifty or sixty bucks each. Maybe more to a collector. So you've got an idea how these blokes work.' Norton nodded his head in agreement. 'Anyway, to save a lot of fart-arsing around I'll give you thirty grand for the lot. And you can throw in the strongbox too,' he added with a chuckle. 'That sound all right?'

Norton looked at the money for a moment and shrugged. 'Sounds pretty good to me.'

'Righto. Do you want cash or a cheque?'

'Make us out a cheque. To that bodgie account I got over at Randwick.'

'Okay. No worries.'

'Yeah,' chuckled Norton. 'No worries.'

Alone with their thoughts they both stared at the money while across the other side of the pool Vince continued to potter around in the garden and the afternoon sun mirrored off the sparkling blue water into their eyes. Then the hint of an odd smile formed on Norton's face. He took a suck on his beer and turned to his boss.

'I'll tell you what Price,' he said thoughtfully. 'I've got a better idea.'

'Yeah. What is it?'

'Make the cheque out for twenty-five grand.'

Price looked at Les curiously and shrugged. 'Okay. If that's what you want. What have you got in mind?'

'I'll keep a thousand pound for a souvenir myself.'

'Yeah.'

'And are you still sweet with that walloper that arranges all the transfers down in the city?'

'Yeah sure.'

'Well can you get that fat turd that pinched me in the first place transferred somewhere. His name's Kennewell. And he's stationed at Waverley.'

Price took a sip of beer and chuckled. 'You're not vindictive or spiteful, are you Les.'

'No,' replied Norton, innocently shaking his head. 'I just like to get even — that's all.'

'And where would you like officer Kennewell transferred to. The moon?'

'No.' Norton's face burst into a grin. 'How about Moree? It'd be just starting to get warm out there now. See how officer Kennewell handles twelve months of heat and flies and "the brudders and the cuddins" getting full of piss and rioting every weekend.'

'Okay.' Price smiled and gave his head a bit of a shake. 'That's as good as done. What else?'

'What about the Mouse? We must be able to do something for him?'

Price pursed his lips and drummed his fingers on the table for a moment. 'Well Les,' he replied slowly, 'if he's a lifer I doubt I could get him out of the nick straight away. But I could get him out to a farm or something. Say Berrima. Or maybe out to Silverwater.'

'That'll do. But just get him out of Long Bay.'

'Okay mate. I'll attend to that immediately. Well that's about your five grand gone, Les. Anything else you want?'

Norton drained his beer and once more that horrible grin returned to his face. 'Yeah,' he nodded. 'Just one more little thing...'

About six-thirty that evening Norton was sitting in his kitchen having a cup of tea and reading the paper before going around to Louise's for dinner. The front door opened and in came Warren. He threw his gear in his room and walked into the kitchen with a big grin spread over his face. He'd just had four sensational days at Palm Beach with the girl from *Cleo* and he was genuinely glad to see Les again, especially with the ad turning out as well as it did. The first thing he said when he saw Norton however was,

'Jesus Les. You sure did a job on your head, didn't you.'

'You noticed Warren,' Norton replied with a tight smile.

'Noticed. Christ, it looks like something you'd see after drinking metho for a week!'

'Thanks, arsehole.'

Warren continued to stare at Les as he moved over to the sink to make himself a cup of coffee. Then the grin came back on his face and he gave Norton a hefty slap on the back. 'Ahh you still look beautiful to me,' he said, and added a punch to Les's shoulder.

'Thanks Woz.'

'So,' said Warren as he fiddled around with his cup and spoon, 'Melbourne was all right eh. I told you the bosses are rapt in the ad. And I'll have your cheque for you on Friday.'

'Good,' grunted Norton. 'I'm a bit short at the moment.'

'Yeah. I'll bet. So what happened down there? What did you get up to, besides blowing yourself up at your uncle's.'

'Well to tell you the truth, I won myself a little heart down there.'

'Really?'

'And not a bad little sort either.'

Norton told Warren about his sexual romps with Mrs Perry and Dixie, without laying it on too thick about the young girl from Footscray. He told him about Mia and Penny going off on the lounge, but naturally he didn't mention blowing up the church or spitting in the girl's face at Richard's and belting the two bouncers on the tram. He added that he'd caught the plane back too; Warren wouldn't know the difference.

Even though Warren had only got about half the full story, he was still astonished and couldn't help staring at Norton while he sipped his coffee.

'You're amazing, Les,' he said. 'You pot the woman that runs the motel the first night you're in town. Then win yourself a grouse young babe as well.'

'And earned five grand into the bargain,' smiled Norton. 'But don't think there was any great skill in pantsing Mrs Perry. She was just a bloody case. She'd've jumped into the sack with Quasimodo to get a root. But little Dixie,' Norton winked. 'She was something else.'

'She sounds it.'

'In fact I've invited her up here for a weekend. I'm hoping she'll ring me.'

'Good on you.'

'Yeah. And thanks for tipping me into the ad Woz. I'd never been to Melbourne before.'

'That's okay.' Warren took another sip of coffee. 'So what are you doing tonight?'

'I'm going round to Louise's. What about yourself? You going out?'

Warren shook his head. 'No mate. Early to bed, early to rise. We've got another big campaign starting this week.'

'Ohh bloody hell,' groaned Norton. 'What is it this time?'

'Ripple coloured zinc cream,' grinned Warren. 'We've got to brainwash one million pimply-faced Australian teenagers into putting this shit on their rotten, acned little dials this summer. And we'll shit it in too, big Daddy,' he added with a wink.

Norton shook his head in disgust. 'Fair dinkum, Warren, you're kiddin' aren't you. That agency you work for has got about as much principle as a Japanese whaling company.'

'Now come on Les. We're not that fuckin' bad.'

'No. I guess you're right,' conceded Norton. 'Nothing's that low.'

'But we are pretty rotten,' grinned Warren. 'I've got to agree with you.'

'Anyway, I've got to go.' Norton got up and put his cup in the sink. 'I'll probably stay at Lou's tonight so I'll see you before I go to work tomorrow night.'

'Okay Les. I'll see you then.'

Norton went to the front door leaving Warren in the kitchen reflecting thoughtfully into his coffee.

Around seven-thirty the following morning Warren was sitting in the kitchen having a cup of coffee when Norton came through the front door, a very disgruntled look on his face as he walked into the kitchen.

'Hullo,' said Warren. 'Look what the cat's dragged in. You're home a bit early aren't you lover boy?'

'The rotten kiwi bitch kicked me out, didn't she,' Les replied. Despite the look on his face he was smiling a bit as he tossed the *Daily Telegraph* on the kitchen table.

'Kicked you out?'

'Yeah, the rotten moll. I was looking forward to a bit of a sleep in too.'

'Well you can't actually blame poor Louise for wanting to give you the heave out of bed early, can you? I mean, your head's not that crash-hot at the best of times, Les. But right now it'd frighten a bulldog out of a butcher's shop.'

'Listen mate. If you hadn't of sent me down to fuckin' Melbourne in the first place my melon wouldn't look like this. I ought to see Cameron and take a law suit out against your stinkin' agency. You skinny little prick.'

Norton switched on the electric kettle while Warren tried his best not to laugh too loud.

'So what happened? Did you have a blue with her?'

'No, just the opposite. The meal was the grouse. The two bottles of wine got Louise all fruity and we went for it hammer and tongs half the night. It was tops.'

'Well what happened?'

'Louise had to go to work early this morning — cleaning — and she didn't fancy leaving me alone with the new girl that's moved into her flat.'

'Why's that?'

'Ohh mate, you ought to see her. She's just come down from Surfers Paradise. She's the best sort I've ever seen in me life.'

'Fair dinkum.' Warren's eye lit up noticeably.

'She's twenty-two. Got a body that'd make a bishop kick a hole in a stained glass window.'

'Go on. You ah ... might be able to do a little something there for your old flatmate.'

'I might, but you keep insulting me all the time. And hurting my feelings.'

'Insult you?' Warren rose from the table and looked Norton straight in the eye. 'Les Norton,' he intoned. 'You are without a doubt one of the most ruggedly handsome individuals I've

310

ever seen. You are what advertising in Australia is all about. What it's crying out for. That classic Australian look. Les, with me guiding you, you . . .'

'Ohh look, piss off Warren. You wombat.'

'Yeah, you're right, Les. I never was much of a liar. Anyway I got to get cracking. I've got to take polaroids of about two hundred empty-headed surfies. And think up a slogan for Ripple Zinc.'

'Yeah? How about this?' suggested Norton sarcastically. 'Ripple Zinc, the little ripper for raving ratbags. Rip it up you and rip it into you.'

Warren paused at the kitchen door and pointed a finger at Norton. 'Hey. Didn't I always say you should be in advertising? I like it baby. It's got a certain ring to it.'

'Yeah. Just like your bathwater. Now fuck off Warren.'

'See you tomorrow Les.'

'Yeah hooray.'

Jesus I'm still tired he thought, and let out a cavernous yawn. Bloody Louise. I got plenty of bed last night, but she didn't let me get too much sleep. Crook head or no crook head. Oh well. I'm up now. I may as well do some training. He finished his coffee over the paper then got into his running gear and once again headed for Centennial Park.

It came over a bit cloudy by midday so that ruled the beach out in the afternoon. By the time Norton cooked himself a steak for lunch, put the cheque for $25,000 in his false account at Randwick, potted around the house and had a sleep in the afternoon, it was time to have a light tea, iron his shirt and go to work. Billy Dunne was already standing out the front of the Kelly Club when Norton came strolling down the street. Naturally the first thing he said when he saw him was,

'Jesus, Les. What happened to your Rocky Ned?'

'You should see it without all this Pinke-Zinke plastered on it,' Norton grinned. 'It's a good story. Anyway, I'll just go upstairs and let everyone know I'm here, then I'll tell you about it.'

Price hadn't arrived yet and George was busy with the croupiers. Les gave him a call from the top of the stairs, got waves and smiles all around in return then went back down to stand in front of the club.

For a Wednesday night they were a little busier than usual. The spring weather seemed to have brought more people out of their homes and somehow they seemd to be drawn towards Kings Cross like it was Mecca. There were no fights but Les and Billy had their work cut out turning away various off types and drunks who would be absolutely no use to anyone inside the club. The regular punters gave Norton's face a bit of a second look when they saw him standing underneath the pale blue light, but no one said anything. To the undesirables he just looked a little meaner than usual, and when he and Billy said no they quickly took it as 'no and don't bloody argue'.

Price and Eddie arrived around ten, gave the boys a big hello and went upstairs. Before long it was three-thirty, most of the staff had gone home, the money was in the safe and the boys were sitting in Price's office enjoying their customary after-work drink.

Les had given Billy part of the story earlier but George and Eddie hadn't been told anything, so Les gave them pretty much the same tale he'd told Warren, elaborating a little about Mrs Perry and the girls back in the motel room and tossing in gobbing in the girl's face at Richard's, belting the bouncers on the tram and how it was on TV Sunday morning. He didn't mention anything about Mousey's map or blowing up the church, however. He'd tell them about that another time. As for the burns, he gave them the same lie about his old uncle in South Melbourne's heater blowing up in his face.

When he'd finished George, Eddie and Billy were laughing like drains. Price, although he'd heard the whole story earlier, didn't let on and was chuckling away over his Scotch and soda; more at the dry way Les was telling it than anything else.

'And that was Melbourne fellas,' concluded Norton. 'Although I'd rather live in Sydney, it's not that bad down there. And nowhere near as crook as you two made out.'

There was silence in the plush office as they all stopped laughing and reflected into their drinks for a few moments.

Finally George Brennan spoke. All the time Les had been talking George had been acting a little fidgety, like he was dying for Les to finish so he could put his fat head in about something. Norton had half an idea what it was.

'So, movie star,' he said. 'Apart from almost ruining your good looks, it sounds like you had a pretty good time down there.'

'Yeah George,' nodded Norton. 'It was okay. And the lazy five grand falling in made it even better.'

'Five grand's not a bad earn for standing around in a pub drinking fizzy wine for a few hours,' said Price.

'No,' agreed Norton. 'And it'll come in very handy too.'

'Yes. It certainly will come in handy — won't it?' said George. He had this sardonic grin on his round face and he was looking hard at Norton. 'Have you had a chance to read the papers since you got back? The sports results?'

'Yes. I've read them,' replied Les slowly. 'Easts were a bit unlucky. They had four tries disallowed.'

'Unlucky?' snorted George Brennan. 'Unlucky my arse. And what paper said they had four tries disallowed? What have you been reading. The *Port Moresby Times*?'

'That's what it said,' shrugged Norton. 'Balmain played offside all day and the referee didn't know what he was doing.'

'Ohh arseholes. Listen bloodnut. I was there and it was a slaughter. Fifteen-nil. Easts were lucky it wasn't fifty-nil.'

'Yeah, Balmain won all right,' conceded Norton. 'But I still wouldn't say it was a slaughter.'

'Get out. The Tigers shat on them. Smacked their red, white and blue arses. It was beautiful to watch. And while we're on the subject of football. You haven't forgotten something have you Les?'

'What's that George?'

'Our little bet. One thousand dollars I think it was, you red-headed wombat.'

'Ohh yeah, that's right. We had a bet didn't we.'

'Yes. We did. And where's my money?'

Norton eased back a little in his chair and took a swig of Fourex. 'Well, George,' he drawled. 'I haven't had a chance to get to the bank yet and I don't get paid till Saturday. But you needn't worry. Here it is. Right here.'

Norton took a small white envelope from the inside pocket of his tuxedo and handed it to George. 'There you are mate. One thousand dollars. Good on you.'

George's eyes lit up almost in disbelief. He snatched the envelope from Norton's hand and waved it round the room at the others. 'Have a look at this,' he said excitedly. 'I got the big mug for a thousand dollars. How sweet it is.'

'No need to rub it in George,' said Les.

'Rub it in?' guffawed George, holding the envelope just under Norton's nose. 'You know what I'm going to do with this? I'm going to shout me and the missus to the best restaurant in Sydney. Champagne, caviar, the works. Then I'm going to buy myself a grouse pair of shoes which I'm going to wear everywhere. And when people ask me where I got such a grouse pair of shoes I'm going to say that big red-headed galah from Queensland bought them for me.' George was laughing and wheezing away almost fit to burst by now.

'Oh well,' said Norton, a little sadly. 'It's your money. Do what you want with it.'

'I will. And I reckon I'd better bloody count it too. Make sure it's all there.' George started tearing open the envelope. 'Boy am I going to have some fun with this. I might even shout myself...' Suddenly George's voice began to trail away as he pulled the money from the envelope. He screwed his face and looked at Norton for a second, looked over at Price, then looked back at Norton. 'What the fuckin' hell's this?' he howled.

'What the hell's what, George?' asked Norton.

'This!' George fanned the money out and held it up towards the others in the room. 'He's paid me in fuckin' pound notes.'

'What's wrong George?' asked Price, peering up from his glass.

'Have a go at this. The prick's paid me in pound bloody notes.' With his jaw almost sitting on his chest, George held the money out towards Price. There were 300 pounds in ten pound notes and 200 in five pound notes.

Price looked indifferently at it for a moment and shrugged his shoulders. 'So?' he said. And went back to his drink.

Eddie and Billy just sat there blinking.

'What are you blowing up about George?' said Norton. 'Your money's there isn't it? Five hundred quid. One thousand dollars. Same bloody thing isn't it?'

'Ohh you're fuckin' kiddin' aren't you.' George looked at the money, sniffed it then looked back at Norton. 'Where the bloody hell did you get this?'

'I told you George. I haven't been paid yet and I haven't had a chance to go to the bank. And rather than have you going around telling everyone I wouldn't settle I dug it up out of the backyard.'

'You dug it up out of the backyard?'

'Yeah. It's some money I brought down from Queensland with me.'

'You brought it down from Queensland with you. And what did you do? Bury it?'

'Yeah.'

'Ohh no. I don't bloody well believe this.' George moaned

and ran a hand over his face. 'You're the meanest man ever born, Les Norton. Ever.'

'What are you going on about George?' asked Price again.

'This!' George held the wad of old money up in the air like it was a time bomb. 'The bludger buries his money in the backyard.'

'Well what if he does?' said Price. 'You can't blame him for that. Remember what he said when he first came down from Queensland and he won all that money.'

George had to think for a moment. 'He said, something . . . something about how he didn't trust banks.'

'That's right.' Price made a bit of a gesture with his hands. 'So the answer's obvious, isn't it.'

'It is?'

'Of course it is.' Price finished his Scotch and dry, stood up and looked at Les for a second. 'He still doesn't — do you mate?'

Norton shook his head slowly and looked at George Brennan, completely without expression.

'Now,' said Price. 'If you've finished arguing about bloody money George, I might get myself another drink.' Price stepped behind the bar, picked up the Scotch bottle and looked over the top at the others. 'Anybody else want one while I'm up?'

Robert G. Barrett
The Godson

I wonder who that red-headed bloke is? He's come into town out of nowhere, flattened six of the best fighters in Yurriki plus the biggest man in the valley. Then he arrives at my dance in an army uniform drinking French champagne and imported beer like it's going out of style. And ups and leaves with the best young sort in the joint ... Don't know who he is. But he's not bloody bad.

Les thought they were going to be the easiest two weeks of his life. Playing minder for a young member of the Royal Family called Peregrine Normanhurst III sounded like a deadset snack. So what if he was a millionaire Hooray Henry and his godfather was the Attorney General of Australia? Les would keep Peregrine out of trouble ... So what if he was on the run from the IRA? They'd never follow him to Australia ...

The Godson moves at breakneck speed from the corridors of power in Canberra to the grimy tenements of Belfast, to climax in a nerve-shattering, blood-spattered shootout on a survivalist fortress in the Tweed Valley. *The Godson* features Les Norton at his hilarious best, whatever he's up against – giant inbreds, earth mothers, jealous husbands, Scandinavian au pair girls, violent thugs and vengeful terrorists.

If you thought Australia's favourite son could get up to some outrageous capers in his previous adventures, until you've read *The Godson*, you ain't read nothin' yet!

Robert G. Barrett
Davo's Little Something

All easy-going butcher Bob Davis wanted after his
divorce was to get on with his job, have a few beers
with his mates and be left alone. But this was Sydney
in the early eighties. The beginning of the AIDS
epidemic, street gangs, gay bashings, murders.

When a gang of skinheads bashed Davo's old school
friend to death simply because he was gay, and left
Davo almost dead in an intensive care unit, they
unleashed a crazed killer onto the city streets. Before
the summer had ended, over thirty corpses had
turned up in the morgue, leaving two bewildered
detectives to find out where they were coming from.

Robert G. Barrett's latest book is not for the
squeamish. Although written with lashings of black
humour the action is chillingly brutal – a story of a
serial killer bent on avenging himself on the street
tribes of Sydney.

Robert G. Barrett
Mele Kalikimaka Mr Walker

Les Norton's Hawaiian holiday should have been just
like in the tourist brochures. Balmy days, blue seas,
palm trees swaying in the moonlight. And it would
have been if Les had minded his own business. But
what are you supposed to do when a cop you know
and an old friend are in trouble? Especially at
Christmas?

The detective was okay. But Norton's old friend
turned out to be the biggest brothel owner in
America. Madam to the Stars. Through her, Les met
Mitzi Moonkiss; he also met the Japanese Yakuza,
lesbian geisha girls and every time he put his head
out the door some boofhead US marine was looking
for a fight. And these were all the nice people.
Somewhere in the middle a crazed serial killer was
on the loose with a bayonet. Aloha, Les.

Robert G. Barrett
The Day of the Gecko

When Les Norton moved into his old flame Side
Valve Susie's flat in Bondi for a few days while she
was out of town, everything should have been a
piece of cake – except Price and Eddie had other
ideas. Waverley Council were demolishing Bondi
baths and there were two bodies buried under the
handball court. The man to get them out? Major
Garrick Lewis, aka, The Gecko.

With Norton for company, The Gecko literally took
Bondi in his stride; and everything that went with it –
Mossad hit squads, the KGB, ASIO, yobbo builders
looking for trouble, loose women looking for action.
For once, Les was flat out keeping up.

Robert G. Barrett
Guns 'n' Rosé

Norton needed a holiday. *Anywhere*, as long as it
was out of Bondi. Price was only too willing to oblige.
Les could have his house at Terrigal. All he had to do
was look after George Brennan's nephew for a week
while he was there. Sounded okay to Norton, and it
was better than spending his own money.

Jimmy Rosewater was young, cool and the original
brown-eyed handsome man. He loved good wine,
going to restaurants, going linedancing and the
ladies loved him. This suited Les nicely. *But*, Jimmy
was also supposed to be in gaol. Before he knew it,
Norton was fighting off the usual yobbos looking for
trouble, sex-crazed feral aunties and getting shot at
by nutty bikies. That was during the quieter
moments. And all the time Les had a feeling Jimmy
was up to something. He *just* had a feeling ...